RL West grew up in Texas, though with separated parents, she also spent time in Colorado, and Missouri where she was born. She presently lives in Texas with her husband and two lively young daughters and their cat, Pumpkin. Growing up with a single mom, she had to put her dreams on hold as the youngest child. She grew up fast, always working and providing for her family. However, she has been writing stories since she was young, and after some encouragement from friends and family, she decided it was time to follow her dream of becoming an author. They say only the good die young, and I think it's to give the rest of us more time to become good. Wouldn't it be wonderful to know that some of the young we lost are not dead but reborn to become powerful guardians watching over others like them? That's a world RL West has created, and she can't wait to share it with her readers. Her series, *The Order of the Guardians*, follows Leyla Gray as she fights both good and evil to make her own way. Both Guardians and demonkinds are after her, and it won't be as easy as she thinks to avoid her destiny.

For V, thank you for reminding me that I'm only limited by my imagination. To my readers, never give up on your dreams, they are still waiting on you to catch them…

RL West

# THE ORDER OF THE GUARDIANS

## Book One - The Guard

AUSTIN MACAULEY PUBLISHERS™

LONDON * CAMBRIDGE * NEW YORK * SHARJAH

**Ordering Information**
Quantity sales: Special discounts are available on quantity purchases by corporations, associations, and others. For details, contact the publisher at the address below.

**Publisher's Cataloging-in-Publication data**
West, RL
The Order of the Guardians

ISBN 9781645759898 (Paperback)
ISBN 9781645759904 (Hardback)
ISBN 9781645759911 (ePub e-book)

Library of Congress Catalog Number: 2021900440

www.austinmacauley.com/us

First Published 2022
Austin Macauley Publishers LLC
40 Wall Street, 33rd Floor, Suite 3302
New York, NY 10005
USA

mail-usa@austinmacauley.com
+1 (646) 5125767

To my family and friends, thank you for believing in me and my story.

# Table of Contents

# Prologue

I feel more anxious with every passing second. My heart keeps skipping beats, and I'm trying to remind myself to breathe. This is the day I've yearned for. This is the day that has given a purpose to all the ones before, so trying to calm myself is proving difficult. I clasp my bracelet hanging on my right wrist. It's a habit. The cool touch of the metal is familiar and comforting. My fingers graze atop each dazzling stone along to the center where a large deep blue gem is set. It may look like just an exquisite piece of jewelry to most, but to me, it's everything this day represents. It's an heirloom that has been handed down to every daughter before me and the last owner, my mother, wore it on her wrist as I do today. Besides fleeting memories, this is all I have left of her. I sit with my chair facing away from my desk, looking out through my rectangular window. The thick glass spans the whole outside wall. I'm tempted to lean forward to look at the people down below scurrying around like ants, especially knowing that one of those people could be the reason for my current state of emotion. I hear a soft knock on my door, and it pulls my focus. Guessing at the person on the other side, I don't respond. Not taking a hint, I hear the door open to my dismay.

"Soto," I state flatly.

"My lady," he replies timidly, "please excuse the interruption." I hear him stop breathing for a moment in wait for my response. However, I don't respond, nor do I turn my chair to face him. "Forgive me, I know your schedule has been cleared for today, but I have someone on the line for you. He is," he pauses, thinking on his following words carefully, "persisting that you would want to hear from him. He sounds American." I finally turn around, my attention now required. I see him tense up as my body turns to him. His long onyx hair falls over his milky white face making only one dark narrow eye visible for me to see.

"Did he tell you what he wants to speak with me about?" I ask, giving him no indication in my tone that I am pleased about being interrupted.

"He asked me to say it's regarding the item you requested. He said it's most important you two speak," he answers, eager to explain his reason for interrupting me. I'm overcome again with anxiety.

"I'll take the call," I respond, not letting my worry come across in my tone or face.

"Yes, my lady," he replies, bowing his head slightly before closing the door on his way out. Just moments after he leaves the room, my phone lights up and I push the button to answer.

"I'm guessing this call isn't to let me know that you have arrived?" I ask sarcastically. I hear the man on the other side of the speaker begin to breathe heavily.

"Yes ma'am, I'm calling to tell you that we are unable to deliver the item you require," he replies and my temper flares, but I try to keep my composure. "The men we sent have not returned," he starts to elaborate. "We did send another, one who is *gifted*, but she returned empty-handed as well," he finishes, and I let out a small huff of air. My patience is spent and I'm nothing but disappointed at his news.

"Are you telling me that you failed to acquire something easier to pick than a flower? You've given up after just two attempts?" I add with a tone sounding as if I was getting on to a child. "Or did I mishear you?" my tone turns cold.

"You are correct, ma'am," he replies in such a soft hush. I almost thought I didn't hear it at all. I feel his nerves in his voice, and it annoys me.

"I'm afraid I require a better explanation," I spew letting out my anger. "Unless you want me to come and get it from you in person, now would be a good time," I suggest.

"That won't be necessary. I'm afraid what you require is being *guarded*," he replies cautiously. I catch the full meaning of his last word with the utmost clarity. This development is both welcomed and cumbersome news. On the one hand, it means my instincts were correct, but on the other, it's now going to make it difficult to expect someone else to handle it.

"Very well," I reply taciturnly. I hear masked sigh of relief in response. "Please prepare," I add, and I listen to him gulp.

"Prepare for what, ma'am?" he asks, even though he already knows what I mean.

I humor him. "My arrival," I explain and hang up the phone. I look down, catching my reflection looking back at me from the dark glass top covering my desk. My irises are glowing white. I clasp my bracelet once again, clenching it so tightly it could break. *I won't let anything get in my way, whatever that requires me to do. Until I fulfill my promise, I won't stop.*

# Chapter 1

## Interrupted Acquaintance

**Leyla Gray**

I watch as the sun slowly sinks in the sky through my open window. The clouds swirl together in soft pinks, purples, and orange color. Beneath the colorful sky are planted rows of gold and bright green corn stocks stretching out for miles onto the horizon. Each ways gently in the wind as if in a slow dance hypnotizing my eyes back and forth with each movement. The breeze coming in brings fresh smells of someone's clean laundry, no doubt just pulled out of our apartment's laundromat next door. I feel myself start to s sink down more comfortably into my couch. My eyelids keep blinking shut, and I have a hard time keeping them open. Suddenly, my phone rings, and I immediately recognize who is calling by the music playing. I grudgingly sit upright and move my papers and books off my lap. My hands search the cushions for my phone, but I can't seem to feel it. I turn my head around to see a flash of light blinking from inside my purse. I could have sworn I grabbed it out of there when I got home from the campus today. I rush over and grab it, sliding the button to answer at exactly the last ring.

"Hello Kat," I say breathing into the speaker a little heavy from rushing over. "I didn't expect to hear from you today," I remark thinking out loud. "Didn't you just get back?"

"Yes, we just landed, but I needed to call you," she answers. I pick up on the enthusiasm in her voice, and I can tell she is excited about something.

"Oh, is everything alright? Did you have a great time?" I ask.

"Yes, everything was perfect. I can't wait to tell you all about it. That's why I'm calling. Kent and I missed everyone, and we want to catch up with some of our close friends tonight," she informs me.

Kent, her boyfriend since she was a high school sophomore, had just swept my best friend away for a whole week. He surprised her with a trip to a luxury resort in Hawaii for their fifth anniversary. I'm a little envious, to say the least, but not of them. I'm jealous they are able to leave Iowa and see something other than fields of vegetables and herds of cattle. *Not that our sunsets weren't just as beautiful as the rest of the world*, I think, glancing back out my window. It's just Kat's always been fortunate enough to travel to amazing places, and I wish I could see one fantastic place, just once.

"That means you, you know," Kat states, and I snap back to our conversation.

"Sorry, what? You want me to come out tonight?" I ask, clarifying I heard her correctly.

"Yes, I would love for you to meet us at NightSky around nine or so," she replies.

I look down at my empty pages lying next to me on the couch. "I don't know Kat, I have an essay due this week," I hesitate. "Besides, aren't you jet-lagged? You did just get in from a several hours' trip," I point out.

"I'm a little tired, but as I said, I missed you and I don't want to wait to see you until class on Monday." Her tone is pitiful, and I can picture her frowning at me from the other side of the phone.

"I can come see you tomorrow," I deflect, "we can spend the whole day together. You know I'm not big about going to the bar, especially on Friday nights when all the frat boys are there for lady's night," I remind her.

I love Kat, but here lately when we go out, she uses me as bate thinking she can hook the cutest guy in the room for me. I'm not as bold and outgoing as she is. She could run circles around the energizer bunny. I want to see her too, but not in a crowded bar where I can barely hear what she has to say. Not to mention her friends aren't really mine, and I always feel a little left out of conversations. Not that she realizes it, she gets along with everyone so easily. She constantly nudges me to meet new people and to get out more. However, despite what she might think, having more friends means you just have to spend more time pleasing all of them. I barely have enough extra time for Kat, let alone anyone else. That may make me a little boring, but I'm happy with my uneventfulness.

"I promise I will see you tomorrow. You and Kent have fun tonight and get some rest. You may not think you're tired now, but you only have the weekend to acclimate yourself back on a schedule before having to get up at six am for class on Monday," I advise her caringly.

I hear her let out a little whine. "Are you sure there is nothing I can say to change your mind? I don't want to wait until tomorrow," she pouts.

"I'm sure," I insist.

"Alright," she lets out a disappointed sigh. "Well, you know where we will be if you change your mind. I want to see you there," she adds hopefully. I hear my phone's hang-up noise and I'm surprised she let it go that quickly. She's usually more stubborn and persistent.

I put my phone down and look back at my stack of blank pages, and my eyes roll in the back of my head. After an already eight-hour day in classes, the thought of more work doesn't sound appealing. I reluctantly pick up my advanced calculus book and flip to the last page we went over. Our professor seems to enjoy the class less than I do, and heaven forbid we ask him to repeat or explain anything. I loathe math, Mental Abuse to Humans, if you ask me. As much as I would love to put it off, I rather get it out of the way now and not have to worry about it this weekend. Knowing that my day will be spent hanging out with Kat tomorrow, that only leaves me Sunday to do the rest of my work. Luckily my history essay, I mentioned to Kat as an excuse technically wasn't due until Wednesday. I put the rest of my stuff aside and grab one piece of paper to practice with as I re-read. I try to concentrate on the numbers and words on the page, but I cannot focus. Maybe I should just bite the bullet and rest for a bit. Kat's not a morning person, so she won't expect me to come over first thing. I can stay up late and finish it tonight. I move my book and papers to the rest of my homework pile. I pull down the blanket lying array on the back of my couch and throw it over me. I curl up and close my eyes. It doesn't take me long to drift off.

My eyes open slowly, and my apartment is shadowed in darkness. There are only a few strands of soft moonlight coming in from my still open window, along with the frigid night air. I sit up slowly and turn on the lamp next to me. I pull my soft blanket around me like a cape as I walk over to shut my window. The temperature in the apartment is almost unbearably cold, and I contemplate turning on the heat for a while. I did love fall, but I forget that the warm days turn into chilly nights. My fingers rub my eyes trying to wake them up. I move back toward my couch and I spot my phone on the floor. It no doubt fell off me when I turned about in my sleep. I pick it up and I'm shocked to see that it's almost five in the morning. I hadn't meant to sleep that long. I must have been more tired than I realized. With finals just a month away, I've stayed up later to study and do homework than usual. I see I also missed many calls and texts from Kat. I scroll down and skim-read each one. I wonder if these are all meant for me or someone else? Between broken words and lines of emojis, if I didn't know any better, I would think she was a child discovering the keyboard for the first time. The only clear thing I see is a picture she sent of her, Kent, and a few of their close friends. She appears to be holding out the camera taking a selfie of all of them. She looks stunning as always. She's surprisingly tan after just one week on the beach. The sun has darkened her auburn hair making it appear more brown than red as it curls around her cheeks. The green in her hazel eyes stands out, as always, with her green eyeliner and eyeshadow she has on. Kent's standing to her right and the sun has done him more harm than good. He looks like someone has colored his skin red with a marker. Kat comes up to about his chest and her short arm couldn't fit all of him in the picture. I notice that his orange-red hair is cut off at the top. Kent's smile is so big that his freckles are all squishing together along his cheeks. His brown eyes are almost nonexistent since he is squinting, no doubt reacting to the camera's flash. *They look cheery.* I'm suddenly feeling a little guilty for not going out after all. Although my nap did turn into an almost full night's sleep. I doubt I would have been very energetic company. I make my way down the hall to my bedroom and crawl onto my bed. I send Kat a message back apologizing that I didn't respond and that I had fallen asleep. I'm sure she is fast asleep herself by now and probably won't read it. I know she will be upset with me since I didn't answer her calls or reply to her texts. However, I can make it up to her when we spend the day together later. As for my homework, it looks like I will be finishing it on Sunday after all.

I quickly get ready and down a few gulps of orange juice from the carton in my fridge before heading out the door. The upside to living alone is that you don't have to worry about sharing anything with anyone else. I even have my own parking spot with my apartment number on it. Before I jump in my vehicle, I notice two men across the street behind me carrying up furniture to a second-story apartment. *Strange*, I can't stop myself from staring. It's only October and someone is moving in? They usually don't have openings here until the endings of each semester. I remember putting my name on the list six months before I even started classes. I wonder if someone dropped out. *Stop being nosy, Leyla,* I scold myself. I inwardly shrug and climb up into my Jeep. I catch my reflection in the rear-view mirror. Maybe I should have brushed my hair better before I left? I run my fingers through my black less-than-straight mess. It doesn't do much good. I notice my skin is slightly darker from the summer sun, but it will soon turn pale again by the end of fall. My green eyes look more awake than the typical heaviness I'm used to seeing, and I have a slight pink color in my cheeks. I guess oversleeping was a good idea. I should do it more often. My hair can wait for now, I'll just borrow a brush from Kat when I get there.

Kat and Kent live minutes away from the campus. Both their parents help them afford an option so close to the school. On the other hand, my apartment is a cheap option that puts me about forty-five minutes away from the college. The drive seems quicker today though. When I pull up to their driveway, I notice Kent's truck is gone. I wonder if he is off at football practice. Kat's mini is parked under the carport, hopefully that means she's home. I'm now standing outside her door knocking, but there is no reply. I shoot her a text, no response. I call, but there is no answer. She must still be asleep. I dig into my black hole of a purse and find the extra key she had given me for emergencies, and I let myself in.

"Kat, are you here?" I shout out, my voice echoing.

I walk back to her and Kent's bedroom. The door is wide open, and I observe Kat sprawled out awkwardly on the bed. Her body is rolled in and out of the blankets, and one of her arms and legs is hanging off the edge of her mattress. One of her pillows is lying on the floor while the other is on top of her head. She is in a dead sleep, and I almost felt bad for what I was about to do. Almost.

I get a running start and jump onto the side of the bed that she is not occupying. I lose my balance for a second and almost fall off, but I manage to steady myself before I do. I watch her small figure fly up momentarily in the air, and she is immediately awake as she hits back down. She hurdles upright, and I catch a flash of panic and confusion on her face.

She looks over at me, and after the initial shock wears off, she furrows her brows and frowns angrily at me. She is less than pleased. I start to burst out in uncontrollable laughter. She doesn't find it funny, but anger leaves her face, and she rolls her eyes at me. It doesn't help that she looks like a hot mess. Her hair is wild and frizzy and her makeup is smeared and blotchy on her face. I finally calm down and start to say good morning, but she hastily puts her fingers up to my lips. Her skin smells like a mixture of perfume, cigarettes, and alcohol. I instinctively pull away. She moves her fingers from my direction and puts them up to her head and creases her forehead. She starts to wave her other hand towards the bedside table. I follow her gesture and realize what she is trying to communicate. There is a half-full glass of water and bottle of pills sitting on top of the table. I get up and grab each one and hand them to her. It was the least I could do after almost catapulting her off her bed. I play the image of her bolting up into the air again and I let out another giggle under my breath. Kat pushes what's left of the covers off her and gets up. She walks over to the adjourning bathroom and turns on the shower. She quickly turns back to grab a towel from hanging on the outside doorknob before shutting the door. I look around the room and it's more of a mess than usual. There are several suitcases around the floor from their trip, and I believe she didn't have time to tidy up before they left. He did kind of spring it on her if I remember correctly. I flip on her TV so I won't be bored while I wait.

Her shower doesn't last long. I didn't even get through one thirty-minute show before she stepped back out. She has one towel wrapped around her body and another around her hair. Her skin is bright red in spots from the heat of the water. She walks across the room to her walk-in closet and pulls some jeans out from one of her dresser drawers. She also grabs a burgundy top with white flowers off a hanger. She walks back into the bathroom, ignoring me, to get dressed. I frown at her, but she doesn't notice.

"Oh, Kat. I'm sorry I didn't come out last night. Believe it or not, I was tired, and I fell asleep. I texted you as soon as I woke up," I explain. Walking back out she gives a little nod of understanding in my direction, but she still doesn't speak to me. I watch her pull her hair into a tight bun with one of her hair ties. She sits down at her vanity facing the mirror. "I've come to hang out and take you to lunch. I missed you, bestie," I whine a little, hoping it helps adjust her mood.

She lets out a little defeated sigh. "I missed you too," she finally speaks, "and I am hungry." I watch a small smile creep over her face in the mirror. She picks up her phone and I notice her skimming through her messages. I wonder if she is looking at her texts to me from last night. I keep from saying anything, not wanting to ruin the now good mood she is in. "You would have thought that at least one of these calls or texts would have woken you up," she complains playfully as she starts to apply her makeup.

"You would have thought," I agree. "I wasn't kidding about being tired. I was completely out cold, apparently," I laugh at myself.

She starts to apply her eyeliner, and my eyes catch something on her finger that hasn't been there before. It's shining a small amount of light around the room. I let out a little gasp. She instantly turns around and looks at me with worry.

"What, did I mess up?" she asks with a look of confusion.

"You're engaged!" I announce and run up to her. I grab and tightly squeeze her petite frame, almost knocking her off the stool. She hugs me back and lets out a little squeal of excitement. I let her go, her face is beaming with joy.

"I was wondering how long it would take you to notice," she teases wearing a triumphant smile.

"Is this why you wanted me to come out so bad last night?" I ask realizing it myself. She nods still smiling, and I feel guilty all over again that I didn't go out after all.

"I told Kent not to say anything. I wanted to tell you first," she reveals, and I give her another quick hug. I loved her for wanting to tell me first. She would be the first person I told as well if it happened to me.

"I'm so happy for you two!" I shriek excitedly. I pull her hand up to my eyes so I can inspect the ring. It's gorgeous. "My best friend is getting married!"

Kat takes us in her car to the restaurant. I felt my stomach's emptiness the whole way, I was starving by the time we pull up, and I'm sure Kat's feeling hung-over hungry. We head into our favorite off-the-wall spot, the Golden Cow. It's a small authentic Chinese place that makes ramen. They have the best noodles for miles around, hands down. We both order our usuals and chow down. In-between bites, Kat shows me pictures from their trip. Everything looks romantic and the views are breathtaking.

"He got down on his knee on our last night and completely surprised me. He even called my dad before we left and got his blessing. It was so amazing! I couldn't wait to get home and tell you," she announces a little too loudly, but no one seems to notice. I smile with excitement as I swallow my last bite. "It was nice being out of school, no homework, or boring lectures, and most of all no alarm clocks," she admits letting out a small sigh. "I hate that we have school Monday. I wish he would have waited closer to the holiday, but then again, I guess I would have missed home," she confesses, and I nod in understanding. I start to think about the appending end of the semester myself. I too couldn't wait for the break to start so I could be back home for a while.

"Speaking of school," I mention with a grave realization, "I completely forgot to go by and get some books for my essay after school yesterday." Kat begins to frown at me from the other side of the booth. She knows where I'm going with this.

"No way, Leyla Gray," she starts shaking her head. "You are not asking me to go to the school on a Saturday," she protests.

"Please, I'll be quick, I promise," I plead holding my hands together like I'm praying. "I need to get started on it tonight. I can't wait until Monday," I add. History is my best subject, as well as my major. However, this essay must be at least six pages long, and it counts as one-third of my grade. Also, my professor is old school and insists we use actual books to reference from, instead of the readily available internet. I had to go. "Please," I repeat batting my eyelashes at her.

I watch her lips press together in annoyance, and she crosses her arms. "Fine, but after ten minutes, I'm leaving with or without you," she agrees stating her terms.

"Ten minutes," I repeat and smile at her graciously.

She takes me to the campus and as we pull in, I'm a little stunned by how many cars are here. I know there are classes on Saturday, but I didn't expect the parking lot to be this packed. Kat finally picks a spot and we head towards the campus. As we enter, Kat is stopped by a few of her classmates from her nursing class. I recognized them, but I don't remember their names. She's all too happy to stop and show them her ring. Now that I know about their engagement, she can start telling everyone else. This is good timing. Hopefully, her chat will take longer than ten minutes, buying me some more time. She waives me on ahead and I leave her to socialize.

I make it up the third flight of stairs to the library. It takes up the entire third floor. The doors are open, and several students walk out as I make my way inside. It appears a class just let out by the looks of it. To my left are rooms for classes and groups to request for projects. To my right are several long tables that students use to study and computers for research. In the middle of the room sits an oval desk where the librarians check-in or out books. There is also a half story on the top left for offices for the staff. Scattered around most of the room are rows after rows of bookshelves. I wait at the desk for a while, but all the librarians are busy. I look over to the computers, but they are all taken. I decide to try and find the books the old fashion way.

So far, I'm not having any luck. After wandering around for at least five minutes, I spot a young man reading. He is seated against a tall skinny window with a small bench pushed underneath it. His blond strands shine atop his head from the light coming in through the glass behind him. He seems to be enthralled in whatever he is reading to notice me. I don't know why, but I have a sudden urge to go up to him. Maybe he knows his way around and could help me find the section I need. It's worth a shot. I walk a little closer hoping he will hear me, but he continues reading. I get about four feet away from him when I decide to let out a quiet cough. This seems to grab his attention, and he slowly raises his head to look at me.

For less than a second, a look of utter shock cross over his face, as if he thought himself invisible from anyone around him. The look of confusion is quickly replaced instead with a piercing stare. His eyes, deep and blue like the sea, are sharply taking me in. I don't know what to say. I'm being pulled in like waves, unable to break free from his steady gaze. I know I should look away by now, but I can't. He lays his book down and gets up slowly. I stand still. He is a head or two taller than me, and his posture is stiff. He wasn't quite as tall as Kent, but he was close. He takes a step closer and I hold in my breath for a moment. I finally pull my eyes away from his and start to stammer.

"Ss, sorry to disturb you. I was looking for some help to find a certain section," I manage to get out. "Excuse me," I add. I take a step back, allowing him to pass.

He takes it without saying a word. As he walks by me, his arm grazes mine. As soon as we touch, my head begins to throb. My eyes close instantly, and I wrinkle my forehead in response. Blurry images start to flash in my mind. I can't make out any one of them, and everything appears fuzzy. The throbbing turns into sharp intense pain. I've never felt a headache like this before. I start to stumble down into the seat that blue eyes just unoccupied. The images are spinning so fast behind my eyelids like a machine you would find at a casino. I cringe at the agony, and I let out a muffled cry. Rapidly they disappear, and so does the pain. I open my eyes and turn to see blue ones looking over me blankly. I can't make out what he is thinking. Maybe he thinks I'm ill and I need help, and perhaps I do? I'm still confused by what just happened. This time when I look at him, I sense something. It's a nagging feeling, one that makes me think I know him from somewhere.

"Have we met before?" I ask instantly biting down on my bottom lip. I can't believe I let that slip out. We could have met. It's a big campus, and I'm sure I've seen him subconsciously walking to class. I feel stupid all of a sudden. He doesn't answer. His face is straight, and it wasn't giving anything away. I thought he would walk off again, but instead he comes over and reaches out his hand to mine. With what happened last time we touched. I pause for a moment. I give in to my better judgment and let him pull me up off the bench. His skin feels clammy. When I'm standing again, he quickly releases his hand from mine. He takes a few steps back to get a better look at him this time. He is dressed more professional than a normal college student. He is wearing black slacks with a loosely fitted button-up dress shirt. It's the color of a dark blue sapphire complementing his eyes stand out even more.

"Thank you," I mummer.

"Are you alright?" he whispers and his voice is quiet but firm. I nod and start to fidget with the ends of my dark hair.

"I think so. I just got an instant headache all of a sudden. Sorry again to have bothered you. I'll leave. You don't need to move on my account," I insist looking around the shelves to each book to avoid eye contact.

"You mentioned you are looking for a certain section. What is it that you're looking for?" He asks softly, and his question throws me off. I wasn't expecting that, he was about to leave after all, wasn't he?

"I'm looking for books on George Washington. I have an essay due and we had to choose from the presidents," I explain, still avoiding looking directly at him. Maybe he is one of the librarians or a professor. He looks young, but he seems to carry himself more maturely than most of the college boys I've encountered. I catch him nod, and then he turns and takes off down the row of books. I stand there watching him leave. He stops at the end of the row and turns only his head back to me.

"Are you coming?" he asks flexing his jawline. I'm reading that as a sign that he is annoyed.

If he is, why help me? I find my feet and start to head off after him. He leads me to almost the end of the rows of books and proceeds to point at several different novels. I look each one over briefly as I pull them off the shelf. They all appear to be what I need. We didn't exchange looks or words the whole time. His whole demeanor is tense, and it's making me feel the same. I'm having a hard time letting go of my breaths. Once he stops pointing, I look down to see myself holding six or so books. He just saved me a lot of time. I stagger a little as I start to turn the corner to head for the checkout desk. Unexpectedly, his hand briefly touches the small of my back. I lean into it for support, and I might have lingered a moment too long. I steady myself as he walks around to the front of me. I catch him flex his jaw again as he takes each of the books from me. I didn't object. Even though they weren't heavy, I was just clumsy. He follows behind me. As we reach the desk, he sets each book silently down. None of the librarians take notice of us yet. He starts to walk off again.

"Wait," I call out a little too loudly. He pauses turning back around towards me hesitantly.

"Yes," his tone is short. I tuck my long hair behind my ear nervously and look away from him.

"I'm Leyla. Thank you again. I appreciate your help," I whisper introducing myself. I look back over at him and make the mistake of looking directly into his eyes. I get hit with that nagging sensation again. "I know I asked earlier, but have we met?" Something inside me is pushing for an answer. He starts to part his lips to reply, but then stops. I watch his eyes move through me. I can't resist the urge to follow his gaze. I turn around to see Kat standing right behind me.

"There you are!" she exclaims annoyed. "I've been texting you. It's been almost thirty minutes," she enlightens me. I feel many eyes turn towards us, and in response my cheeks start to turn red. I didn't mean to make her go around looking for me, but this wasn't the place to be shouting.

"I'm sorry. I have the books. I'm waiting to get checked out," I reply in a hushed tone trying to avoid looking around the room again to the people starting over at us. I wave my hand to hint at the books on the counter next to me. Her rage dies out as she looks around realizing she might have been a little too loud earlier. She turns and storms off. Sometimes she can let her red-headed temper get the better of her. I turn back around to apologize, but to my surprise, there is no one there to apologize to.

# Chapter 2
## Useless Information

I have been insistent to Kat that someone was beside me when she yelled at me in the library over two weeks ago. She swears she only saw me, and did admit she could have overlooked him. I know I shouldn't care as much as I do, but that nagging sense that I knew him never went away. If anything, it's getting worse. I even stupidly returned to the library asking the staff if anyone working there might meet his description. It got me nowhere.

Bridget, one of the students that volunteer at the library, was especially kind to me. I think she took pity on me after explaining that he had helped me, and I only wanted to thank him. At least that was my guess. She pointed out all the volunteers to me, and even pulled the log from that day to see who worked, but that was a dead end as well. I'm beginning to believe I might have dreamed the whole thing up. There are hundreds of teachers and thousands of students that are here on campus. I'm probably never going to be able to find him again, except by dumb luck. I did want to thank him. He got me an almost perfect score on my essay thanks to those books. Coincidentally, I'm on my way back to the library now to check back in the books I got with him that day. I spot Bridget behind the large oval desk. She immediately waves in my direction.

"Hey, Ley," she uses my nickname, one she gave me after we first met. Since she helped me, I didn't feel like correcting her. "Back again to search for your mystery man?" she guesses.

I give her a quick smile. "No, just returning these," I reply and set the books on the counter. "I think I've given up on that quest," I inform her. I watch a brief frown form on her lips.

"That's too bad. I feel like you were Prince Charming trying to find the maiden that left her glass slipper," she replies. "Only in this case, you're a girl searching for the boy, and there is no slipper," she clarifies.

"I guess," I agree politely, though I'm not quite following her logic. "Well, I'm giving up on Cinderella," I humor her, and I can tell she appreciates me playing along.

She picks up the books and scans them one by one. I notice a small tattoo on her inner left wrist that I hadn't realized was there before. It's three same-sized circles overlapping each other in a row. She catches me staring at it and moves her arm up to push her short caramel brown hair behind her ear. Her wavy strands don't stay in place long, and each of them starts to slip back out almost instantly. Her hair compliments her hazelnut skin tone. She has appealing big chocolate-colored eyes with flecks of gold. Long black eyelashes outline them. She notices me staring, but she doesn't say anything. She just keeps a smile on her face as she continues to check in my books.

"You're all good," she informs me as she places the last book on the cart behind her to be put back on the shelf.

"Thanks, and I want you to know I really do appreciate all your help," I relay sincerely. Bridget smiles again, this time showing off her teeth. "I'll see you around." I end our conversation there, not wanting to keep her from her work.

"Ley, wait," Bridget tries to warn me as I turn away from her, but it's too late. I walk straight into a stocky and immovable figure. I'm knocked instantly to the ground and I hear a familiar chuckle coming from up above me. A hand appears before my eyes and I reach my hand up to take it. It pulls me up effortlessly and I rub my face where I collided with the person in front of me.

"Ow," I let out a delayed reaction. I decided against looking around the room, trying to save myself from looks making me more embarrassed.

"Are you okay?" the voice asks, still snickering? He isn't doing a very good job of making me feel better. Kent has on a mile-wide smile, and I can't help but to want to smile back. "You know you really should be more careful," he advises me patronizingly.

"Thanks Kent, I'll keep that in mind," I reply. "Why do you have to be so buff? Seriously, eat some potato chips like the rest of us," I comment. I hear Bridget let out a little laugh behind me. Kent is our school's star lineman, so he probably didn't feel anything but a tickle when I collided with him. His dad is an alumnus and played ball here too, back in his day. Kent smirks down at me. His hair in this light is the color of a copper penny. He's wearing jeans and a loose t-shirt and has his letterman on over his shirt. "What are you doing here anyway?" I ask, genuinely curious. "I didn't think you knew where the library was," I joke. He smiles slyly at me and all of his freckles bunch up on his face.

"I can see Kat's sarcasm has finally rubbed off on you," he answers amused. "I was looking for you. I've heard from Kat that you've been looking for someone," he tells me. My interest is peaked. "She described him to me, and I think I have found someone that matches his description. He is…"

"Are you sure?" I interrupt him. "Where?" I ask with excitement. He sighs looking a little put off he didn't get to finish his sentence.

"I think he is on the track team. I've noticed him after football practice running laps," he reveals. I didn't exactly peg him as the jock type, but I didn't know anything about him to rule it out either.

"Well, let's go," I state in a matter-of-a-fact way. I start to head for the exit.

"Good luck," Bridget shouts after me. I turn back and give her a thankful smile.

"Slow down, Leyla," Kent starts after me, but I ignore his request. I know my way to the field by heart.

When we arrive, I follow Kent up to the bleachers and sit down. I glance over and shoot him a nervous look. He ignores it and pulls out his phone to pass the time while we wait. I turn my attention to the sky and watch the clouds slowly roll by. The sun is setting, and it will be dark in an hour or two. I hate that it gets dark so early. It smells like hotdogs and popcorn, and the smell makes me think of every football game I've attended. I've been going since I was seven, since Kat decided she wanted to become a cheerleader. She doesn't cheer now, but we both come and watch Kent play.

"What are you planning on saying when you see him?" Kent asks, and I look over at him dumbfounded.

"What are you talking about?" He raises one of his eyebrows at me. "I'm not going to talk to him. At least I hadn't planned on it," I inform him. "I mean, I want to thank him, but I'm not sure the words will be there to do so. Today I just came to see if he is real," I confess. I get a sudden chill as the wind picks up and I shiver. Noticing, Kent politely takes off his jacket and leans over to wrap it around my shoulders. "Thank you," I say gratefully.

"I will never understand you girls," he declares shaking his head. "What's the point in being out here if you're not going to talk to him?" he asks rhetorically and crosses his arms, flexing his muscles in the process.

"I told you, I just want to make sure he is real for one thing. Also, what am I supposed to say," I retort, and he blinks at me. "Hey, I know you left the other day, but I want you to know that I'm thankful. I've been searching for you ever since that day and asking around campus about you. I just wanted to know if you were a real person or not," I pause again, and he just stares at me. "Ya, that's what I thought. It sounds crazy," I finish hopefully making my point.

"Right. Well, they are coming out now, so I guess here is your chance to not talk to him," he makes sure to gesture his hands in quotations.

I roll my eyes at him before moving my focus to the field. I didn't see anyone that resembled my mysterious helper. I glance over at Kent with disappointment. He points, and I follow the direction he is pointing towards. I observe a young man with dirty blonde hair. He is wearing glasses, and I had to admit that he appears more nerdy than knightly. I look back at Kent with a look of, *Are you serious*?

"That's not him," I sigh displeased.

"Kat told me that he had blonde hair, was tall, and skinny. He seems in shape and this is the first time he's had those glasses on," he waves his hands at me defensively. "I asked about him and he is the captain, and he doesn't have a girlfr..." He stops mid-word when he sees the panic cross my face.

"You asked about him?" I repeat his words back to him hoping I heard wrong. "What did you say about me?" I fear what he is going to say in response.

"I stopped some of the track guys yesterday and told them my friend was looking for a guy that met his description, and they told me who he was. They told me he would be out again today, and I let them know I would bring you," he explains.

My heart stops dead in my chest then starts again at an unnatural pace. My face starts to heat up and my head is about to pop. I peek over to the guys on the field and I notice some staring and pointing towards our direction. I completely lose it. I jump up from my seat and Kent moves back a little in response. I'm livid and I want to punch him.

"So does this mean you don't want to stay and meet him?" he questions trying to make light of this situation. It succeeds in making me more upset.

"Have you completely lost it? You told them you were bringing me? You didn't even know if this was the right guy. Why would you do that?" I fume. My body starts to shake from my anger. "If you weren't so ripped, I would punch you right in the gut." I throw back the jacket he gave me earlier, aiming for his face, and I begin to leave.

"Whoa, wait. Leyla, where are you going? Why are you so mad? I just wanted to help," he calls after me. I didn't look back, but I did stop for a moment to answer him.

"You weren't wrong when you said you *don't* understand girls," I scold him. I start off again and I can't get away fast enough. I just want to go home and forget this ever happened.

I thought about stopping for food on the way home, but I have lost my appetite. I step out of my Jeep and instantly get goosebumps, but it wasn't from the temperature. It is getting dark, but none of the outside lights have come on. I look around but no one is near me. I can't hear any voices. However, I sense someone is watching me. After a few still moments, I shake it off as my mind playing tricks and walk up to my door. I walk in and turn on the lights locking both locks on the door behind me. My phone blew up the whole time I drove home. I pull it out and see it's all been from Kat. She sent me several apologies on Kent's behalf. I assume he must have filled her in. She didn't need to apologize though. I know he didn't mean any harm by it. I should be the one apologizing to him for getting so worked up about it. I do feel bad for going off on him like that. I decide not to text back. I don't feel like going over it again at the moment. I had made up my mind on the way home to give up on the blue-eyed man and anyone who may look like him. For now, I will just wallow in disappointment. I flop down onto my couch and grab my head phones laying on the coffee table. I plug them into my phone and shuffle one of my many playlists. Music always makes me feel better.

The next day I answered Kat back, and she offered to take me shopping. Her way of cheering me up after yesterday's fiasco. I accepted her offer and we are now both in her car headed to one of the strip malls not far from her house. Truthfully, I don't feel like going anywhere today, but I needed an outfit for her engagement party coming up. She's throwing it on Halloween, so naturally it's a costume party. She informs me it's more of an engagement announcement, and no one needed to bring gifts or anything. It's the only reason I gave in, and I'm not still sulking at home.

"I just feel awful about what happened," Kat apologizes shooting me a guilty look. She should be looking at the road. I turn and stare out the window and don't respond. She has already agreed about twenty minutes ago to stop bringing it up, she wasn't doing a very good job. I told her earlier to stop apologizing. I wasn't mad about it anymore. I told her I just wanted to forget about it and pretend it never happened and move on. "I know," she lets out a sigh, "I'm not supposed to bring it up. I'm done, I promise." As we pull into the parking lot, I can see that we are not the only ones looking for a costume today. There are hordes of people walking in and out of the shops.

"Today is going to be fun," Kat announces stepping out of the car. I get out myself and walk around to meet her. "I think we should get our costumes first and then head to the other stores. I need some more clothes for the upcoming winter weather," she informs me and wraps one of her arms around mine. Her tone is full of excitement. I don't know another person who enjoys shopping more than she does. Following her suggestion, we walk into the costume shop first. With all the people walking out, I hope we will find something that fits or like. Halloween is only a week away, so we've waited until the last minute.

Despite the crowd, we each find an outfit pretty quickly. Once we check out, we walk over to the next store full of regular clothing. I look through the racks, and so far, nothing has caught my eye. I notice Kat already has a handful of hangers in her hand. She worked at a small boutique in our town for a while before deciding to work for her Dad. He owns a small pediatrician practice in the city, and it does very well. She catches me staring and flashes me a pleased smile.

"Do you want to give me a hand?" I ask from across the rack. She stops in her tracks and gives me an odd look. I know she won't be able to resist, and besides, it's probably time I start taking some of her fashion advice.

"Seriously, you want me to help pick out your clothes?" she asks with that silly look still on her face. I nod. "I'd love to," she replies giddily. She rushes over, almost as if she thinks I'm going to change my mind.

I follow her from store to store. I think she might have gone a little overboard, but I kind of expected that. I'm happy to indulge her since she was keeping my mind off of everything. We both walk back to her car with way too many bags. She pops her trunk and we both throw them in. As I start to step up to the door my skin starts to crawl. I look up and have the same feeling as last night, like someone is watching me. There are many people around us, but I don't see anyone in particular staring directly at me. However, I couldn't shake the feeling away as easily as I did last night. I keep looking towards the back of the parking lot, the part where no one ever parks, I thought I caught a glimpse of someone.

"Leyla," I turn to Kat, "what are you staring at?" She looks at me with concern. I turn back, but no one is there now that I can see.

"I'm not sure. I feel like someone was watching me. Did you notice anyone staring at us as we walked out?" I ask in return.

"No," she says and looks around herself. "I'm sure it's nothing, are you ready to go?" I look around one more time before getting in. As soon as I clip my seatbelt, she put the car in drive and speeds off. "Everything alright, you seem a little freaked out?" she pries.

"Ya, I'm fine. Like you said, it was probably nothing," I agree with Kat, even though my gut is telling me otherwise.

I avoid admitting that I keep seeing people that I can't prove were there in the first place. I put my hand up to my head and rub it. Something is wrong with me, but I don't know what. First, I thought I knew someone that I didn't. Then I tried to track him down, just because I hoped I did. On top of that, within the past two days I've gotten paranoid about being watched. Whatever is going on with me, hopefully it ends soon.

The next week goes by in a flash. I'm already out of my classes for the day and heading towards Kat's house. I let her keep my costume last week in order to not forget it at my apartment. Kat has one less class than me so she was already home. I told her I would help with the decorating before everyone arrives. The party starts at seven, It's currently only half past four, so we have plenty of time. When walk up to her house the door is already open so I walk right in.

"Kat," I call out.

"Back here," she answers.

She sticks just her arm out into the hall and waves me back to her room. As I walk down towards her, I notice most of the decorations are already up. I glance to my right and see through the glass screen doors leading outside, and I notice Kent has lights hanging up attached from the roof and tied up to the trees on the other side of the yard. There are also some glow sticks inside balloons floating in the pool. I walk into their bedroom and Kat is in the middle of putting on her costume.

"Yours is on the bed. I've already pulled it out of the package," she informs me and nods toward it.

"I see you've already gotten the décor done. I could have helped. Why are we getting dressed so early?"

"There is going to be plenty of food and free beer, and if I know Kent's friends, they aren't going to wait until seven. I'm afraid they don't understand the meaning of fashionable late," she explains half laughing.

I see her point. I change out of my clothes and pick up the outfit and slip in on. It fits snuggly and it's a little shorter than I'm comfortable with. I decided to go as Batgirl. The costume I picked has a dark grey leather-type skirt and a black corset top. There is a purple bat symbol, of course, across the chest area. It comes with a cape and a mask, but I just throw on the cape. Mostly to conceal my bare shoulders, the top defiantly emphasized more of me than I would have preferred. I notice Kat has laid out some high-heeled black boots for me to wear with my outfit. I pull them on and they come up to my mid-thigh.

"Maybe I should have picked up a large instead of a medium," I tell Kat as I walk over to her floor-length mirror.

"Nonsense, you're just being self-conscience. You look great," she compliments me.

I turn around as Kat comes out of the bathroom completely dressed in her outfit as well. She picked Poison Ivy, and it looks like she just stepped out of a comic book. Her dress is dark green, tightly fitted around her figure, with golden leaves as a belt around the waist. On her head lays a golden crown that matches the design on the belt. She has on dark green stilettos to complete her look. She walks over to her vanity and picks up her curling iron, already heated, and starts to curl her hair even tighter than normal. After she's done with that, she moves on to her makeup finishing with a nice dark red lipstick.

"Wow, that's perfect. You look like the real thing," I gawk.

"Thank you, and soon so will you," she states and comes over taking my arm in hers. She leads me to her vanity and makes me sit down. She takes my hair in sections and starts to curl it loosely. She starts to apply her make-up on me as well. "Do you want to try my lipstick?" she offers.

"Maybe not that shade," I reply truthfully. My best friend shrugs and pulls out one of her vanity drawers to dig out a softer shade of pink to apply to my lips.

"Finished, you look gorgeous," she informs me, and I stare at myself. I almost didn't recognize the girl looking back. I had to admit; I look pretty good.

My skin looks smooth and my pink cheeks match the pink shade of lipstick she used. Her favorite green eyeliner emphasizes my already green eyes. They're practically shining like emeralds back at me in the mirror. My eyeshadow has a smoky effect with a touch of purple but mostly greys and blacks. My black lashes match my hair perfectly. They are so long they almost look fake. My dark hair is shiny and smooth until the curls at just the ends reaching down past my shoulders.

"What do you think?" I can tell she is dying to know my response.

"I think it's great, thanks Kat," I reply quickly, not making her wait. She lets out a happy squeal, and it makes me smile.

"I'm back. I'll be outside, ladies," I hear Kent yelling from the front of the house. I can hear other voices as well, which means Kat was right about his friends arriving early. I couldn't have been here more than thirty minutes at this point.

"Go on, I'll be out in a second," Kat commands, and I obey. I didn't exactly want to go out to everyone without her, but she wasn't leaving me much choice. I walk outside towards Kent and his friends, mostly his teammates from what I can tell under their costumes. Kent spots me from over the lid of his grill and waives me over.

"Leyla. I think you know most of my guys," Kent states and nods over his shoulder to his friends sitting on a fold-out table behind him. His costume is Superman and his stalky build fits the costume to a T. "John, Eli, Luke, and Tim, you all remember Leyla, right?" he asks and they all nod or wave hello in my direction. I've known Tim since high school. The others I've met here and there, after games, or at parties Kat has dragged me to.

"It's nice to see you all again, and good to see you, Tim. How's your brother?" I ask nervously.

"He's great, thanks for asking. He just enrolled this year. He is staying with me, but he couldn't make it tonight," Tim replies with a sweet appreciative smile.

"Kent, careful not to catch your cape on fire. We don't want another incident," I warn him and a couple of the guys start to laugh, which makes me feel a little less nervous.

"Whoa, what do you mean incident?" John asks curiously. He and Eli are twins and are both dressed up as gangsters. They even had fake MK 47s. Each of them had short blonde hair, brown eyes, the same build, and height. I could never tell them apart until Kat pointed out that Eli has freckles and John doesn't. Besides that, they are identical.

"No need to fill him in, and that was a long time ago," Kent brushes it off quickly looking up at me with a stern face.

"Oh, come on, Kent, this sounds like a great story," Luke retorts, and I hear Eli and John agree. Luke's the shortest of the bunch. Even I'm taller than him. He has come as an axe murder, I think. His white shirt is lined with rips, and there is fake blood everywhere. He's holding a dull ax, with layers of fake blood on it as well.

"It is a great story," Tim agrees with a smirk.

I forgot for a moment he was there too, but it did happen our freshman year in high school. Thinking back, Tim hasn't changed much since then. He's almost as tall as Kent, although his skin color is about three times darker, and his hair is long and brown. He's dressed up as a werewolf.

"We just won our way into state and Kent had a big bar-b-que at his parents' house. He had invited half the school too, and they all showed up. Kent fires up the grill and goes in the house for some more meat, and when he comes back there is at least ten feet of smoke and a huge blaze coming from the grill. Everyone is running in the house and grabbing water bottles to throw at this thing. Some people are even jumping in the pool, even though it wasn't exactly warm. It was crazy. Turns out genius here threw his apron on the side of the grill a little too close to the flames," he fills everyone in. We all start to laugh, well, all of us except Kent. His face turns beat red and he glares at me.

"What did I miss?" Kat comes out, looking confused. "Wait, let me guess. Judging by the look on Kent's face it was probably the apron story," she guesses correctly and we all start to laugh again.

The rest of the night went smoothly. I'm normally very shy around other people, guys especially, but tonight wasn't bad. I had a great time. wound up crashing in the guest room and driving home. I only had a couple of drinks, but I didn't want to drive home regardless. Plus the party didn't end until about two or so. At least that was when I headed to bed. I had woken up before everyone else. I used the guest bathroom to get in a quick shower and wash off my makeup. I changed back into the jeans and T-shirt I wore here last night before putting on my costume. I notice some of the guys have crashed in the living room as I head out the door. As I'm about to get in my Jeep, I get a familiar unsettling feeling, the one that's telling me I'm being watched. I'm probably just being paranoid again. *Just get in the car*, I tell myself, but the urge otherwise is too overwhelming. I slam the door to my Jeep and walk around to the sidewalk.

"Is someone there?" I say aloud and I hear my voice echo down the road.

*"Leyla,"* the wind carries my name back to me and I freeze in place.

"Who's there?" I ask softly my voice shaking. My eyes keep searching, but I can't see anyone. A sudden head rush comes over me and I throw my head back and close my eyes tightly. I start to see blurred images. They are passing too quickly for me to make out clearly. My head feels like it's going to explode. Why is this happening? "It hurts," I plea out loud to whoever is flipping this switch in my brain. "Stop!" I demand, and to my relief, they stop. I'm left only with a slight headache. I look up to see someone standing across the street from me. I freeze in place with shock. I widen my eyes trying not to blink. I can't believe this.

# Chapter 3

## Familiar Faces and Worn Out Places

I finally blink, and he is still standing there. I see his jawline clench and his fist ball up. How is he here? Is he following me, or was this my dumb luck showing up? He pulls his gaze away from mine and starts to walk off. *Where did he think he was going*? I don't hesitate. I just start after him. I'm not going to let him get away from me this time. I pick up my pace, and luckily I'm in sneakers. I don't think he realizes yet that I'm following him, or he doesn't care. I cross the street when he crosses and turn in the directions he turns. I want to shout out stop, but I don't want to spook him. I don't think I could catch him if he decides to run.

Shortly, he comes up to a crosswalk, and the intersection is busy with cars whizzing by forcing him to stop. Out of breath, I reach out and tug on his shirt. He turns around, and his expression is hard as stone. He stands stoically in front of me, and his blue eyes are staring into mine harshly, but I'm not going to leave. Not until I can figure out if he is following me, or if this is just a coincidence.

"Sorry to follow you, but I've wanted to say thank you for your help the other day. I didn't think I would get another chance to do so," I explain still catching my breath. I give him the benefit of the doubt. He remains silent and takes a step back away from me. "Wait, do you live around here, or were you just following me?" I come out and ask, realizing I may not get another chance to do so.

"No," he answers sternly.

"No, what? You don't live around here, or no you weren't following me?" I try to clarify. The wind blows briefly between us and his hair and mine begin to whip around our faces. Mine more than his. The cool breeze feels good after I had just jogged after him. I push my hair behind my ears and try to remain in eye contact. He remains silent, and I'm beginning to feel annoyed. "Were you following me or not?" I ask again impatiently. He still doesn't reply; he just looks at me with a blank expression. He begins to back away from me once more and, without thinking, I reach out and grab his arm. He flinches at my touch and I catch a brief moment of pain come over his face. There is no way my grip is that strong. Why did he look like that? "Why do you keep running away from me?" I ask, no plead. My impatience is replaced instead with frustration. "Do you know me, do I know you, do you know what's going on with me?" I ask in a panic, though I doubt those are questions he will or can answer.

I'm overwhelmed. I breathe out deeply and slowly let him go. As I look up at his vacant expression, I'm instantly filled with embarrassment. I slowly take a few steps back. *I'm crazy*. I'm a crazy lady who just grabbed someone she barely met after following after him for several blocks. He's probably headed to school and not following me at all. It is Saturday, after all. Unexpectedly, he moves his arm out and opens his hand towards me for a fleeting minute. The pain in his face comes back briefly, but he says nothing. He quickly moves his arm back down to his side and clenches both his fists.

His stance stiffens and he turns his head slightly away from mine. "I don't know who you are, and besides the other day, we've never met," his voice is quiet, but each word is convincing. I nod and feel crazy all over again.

"I'm sorry," I declare. *What's wrong with you, Leyla*? "I'll never bother you again," I promise, and I turn away as he starts to look back at me. I didn't want him to look at me, or more so. I couldn't face him after acting this way. I couldn't stay here and feel this way anymore, so I practically sprint back the way I came.

I never looked back to see if he watched me leave. I can honestly say any desire to see him again has vanished. I don't want to remember how I made such a fool of myself. I'm still embarrassed and have been sulking it, but I can't stop playing the scene over and over in my head. He has to think I'm crazy. I know I do. My phone starts to buzz from the end of the bed, where I had thrown it earlier. I roll my torso upright and grab it. I had a voicemail from a call I didn't hear. *Aunt Alice*? I press the message to play and tap the speaker button.

"Leyla, it's me. I need you to call me back as soon as you can please. Call me, love you, bye dear," her voice sounds sweet but anxious. It reminds me of mom's. Both her and my aunt sound the same on the phone. It is nice to hear her voice. I better call her right back. It could be important. It rings once and she answers immediately.

"Hello, sorry I missed your call," I start.

"I know you're busy dear. I'm sorry to call so out of the blue. How is school going?"

"It's great. What did you want to get with me on? Is everything alright?" I ask in return, curious to know what she is going to say.

"Well, I've got some unpleasant news I'm afraid," she begins, and I can't help but feel a little worry rise in my chest. "Your uncle Scott has a very important business trip coming up, and you know how they are. He's normally gone for days. I've been going with him when I can since you've been at school, as you know. We were supposed to take this trip together after the holiday, but they bumped it up its next week," she ends. I slowly soak in what her revelation means for me.

"I see. Well then, I can just come for Christmas," I suggest.

"No dear, I'm afraid this trip will last over a month. I'm not sure we will be back in time, only because it's so hard to book flights around that time," she explains. My heart sinks. I wouldn't have anyone to go home to for the holidays. "Don't worry though. I told your uncle I would call you first. I wanted to stay home with you, just us two girls, but he informed me that his company bumped us up to first-class which means the tickets are non-refundable," she adds genuinely sounding disappointed. "I'm so sorry dear," she apologizes.

"It's fine. It's not your fault. Thank you for letting me know. It's just one holiday, I'll be fine," I assure my aunt, though I wasn't doing a great job of convincing myself.

I hear a sigh of relief, and I can tell this was weighing on her. I appreciated that. My uncle on the other hand, I'm sure he didn't care one bit. He married my aunt just a few years before my mother passed. One of the reasons he liked my aunt was that she didn't have, or plan on having, any children. You can imagine his surprise when she got me. My aunt told me one day that he didn't want children because he traveled so much, and he didn't have the time needed to spend with them. The notion sounds reasonable, but deep down, I feel like he just didn't want to have to choose them over his work. However, for me I was glad he was gone so much. He never treated me badly or anything, but he made it clear that I would never be more to him than aunt Alice's niece from day one.

"Thank you, sweetheart, and again I'm sorry. I want you to know I'm going to miss you and hopefully, when we get back, you can visit one weekend," she states.

"Yes, that sounds nice," I reply trying to keep my voice from sounding sad.

"Okay, dear, I'll let you get back to whatever. Love you, bye," she ends.

"Love you," I mimic as I hang up.

The next few weeks drag on as I now have nothing to look forward to. I'm glad finals are over, but other than that, I didn't like dwelling on the fact that I would be alone for the holidays. Kat was just as disappointed when I told her I wouldn't be seeing her over the break. She even had some not-so-nice things to say about my uncle under her breath that I conveniently ignored. I never mention to her that I had run-down blue eyes from the library. As much as I wanted to tell her he is a real person, I didn't feel like speaking about our second and last encounter. I'm sure he never wants to see me again, and I'm happy to oblige. The desire to seek him out is still non-existent, but the nagging feeling that I somehow know him keeps persisting within my mind. As I head back out to my Jeep to leave for the break, I notice a slim, short Kat leaning up against it. Her hair is straight today the strands blow every which way in the wind. She's wearing a sweater and some skinny jeans, and tall boots. I can smell her go-to vanilla lotion from four cars down. She notices me, and I watch as a satisfying smile forms on her lips.

"What are you so happy about, and what are you still doing here? Didn't your finals end an hour ago? Why aren't you headed home?" My questions spill out. She continues to smile, and I can tell she enjoys holding something in that she knows, and I don't.

"I'm here to ride with you to your apartment and help you pack," she divulges. "I'm not going home without you, and I'm not leaving my best friend here to spend the holiday alone. You're coming home with me and that's final," she states, her tone serious, but her smile is playful. I'm surprised, but I don't argue. I unlock my Jeep and we both jump inside. "Kent will pick us up and drive us to my parents' house," she looks over at me from the passenger seat, "they know you're coming. They're happy to have you stay," she explains answering a question I didn't ask. I'm relieved to hear they were involved with this decision, not that they would have turned me away if I had come unannounced.

Kat helped me pack in no time. We have been driving non-stop since Kent picked us both up. I begin to feel little butterflies in my stomach knowing we are so close to home. Something about returning lifts my spirits and makes me forget about all my troubles. It's like I'm going back in time and escaping from my present. As we pull into the long driveway infront of Kat's home. I spot Kat's mom, Margret Archer, coming out of the front door. We come to the circle part of the drive with a small fountain with a little garden in the center. Their home is one of the biggest I've seen in Ashton. With Mr. Archer's practice and Mrs. Archer being the realtor queen of our town, they needed for nothing. Kat jumps out of the truck and Margret is quick to run up for a hug. I can tell they missed each other. I get out and she extends her hug to me as well.

"We are thrilled to have you back, girls. Come on in. I've got dinner on the table," she states, and we follow her inside. Margret and Kat favored each other to the extreme. Kat's a hair shorter, and a little less filled out in some places, but there is no denying they are related. The main difference between them is their personalities. Margret, though sweet, is a bit of a peacock and doesn't mind the attention. Kat, on the other hand, though attention comes to her, doesn't seek it out. She gets her easy-going people skills from her dad.

"They have arrived," I hear a familiar light-hearted voice come down the entry hall. Mr. Aaron Archer, Kat's dad, comes straight up to Kat and me. He hugs us for what feels like forever. I notice a mustache barely growing around his mouth, an odd but not horrible look for him. His brown hair looks recently cut, and he smells like he just smoked a cigar.

"Will you help our future son-in-law with the girl's bags, please?" Margret asks. I had forgotten that they knew about the engagement for a moment.

"Of course, darling," he smiles and walks past us out the door.

"You are staying for dinner, aren't you?" Margret turns back and looks at Kent.

"Yes, ma'am," he answers hesitantly. I get the feeling he planned on getting home to see his parents, but he smiles and doesn't let it show on his face.

"Mom, you changed the room again," Kat calls out from the dining room as more of a statement than a question. "What was wrong with the way it looked before?" Kat asks with a displeasing look. Her mother changes décor every few years. I'm not sure why Kat is surprised. This year she went from rustic to a more modern look. Everything is white with touches of gold and deep blue accents. *That blue*, reminds me of someone I'm trying to forget.

"You know your mother kitty Kat, always trying to make things look better," Mr. Archer speaks up taking the bags up the stairs with Kent right behind him.

"Ya, kitty Kat," Kent winks at Kat. I see a flash of annoyance in Kat's eyes. She scrounges her forehead and her cheeks turn pink for a moment. She doesn't allow anyone but her father to call her by her pet name, and Kent knew it. I never understood why. I've always thought it was cute.

During our meal the bulk of the conversation is revolving around the wedding. Kat and her mother politely disagreed back and forth about different details. Kat's dad is staying silent, letting them talk, knowing it's better not to butt in. In many ways, he is just as much my dad as he is Kat's. I never met my father, he ran off before I was born, and Aaron has always treated me as his daughter. He built Kat and me a treehouse when we were in middle school. He taught us both how to drive in high school. He packed and drove Kat and me to college, and if I ever get married, he will probably walk me down the aisle. My thoughts keep drifting back to a few weeks ago, to the man I ran after and away from. The scenes between us play in a loop in my mind. The part that stood out the most was when he had reached out to me briefly. I couldn't help but wonder if he wanted to say something to me but couldn't find the words to do so. I know it was silly, but it bothers me that he never said his name. *You don't introduce yourself to someone you don't plan on meeting again*, I realize.

Kent excused himself as soon as he was finished eating, eager to get home as I had guessed. Kat and I help clean up by clearing the table and putting the dishes in the dishwasher. Her parents retire to their rooms and we do so after we finish. I don't know about Kat, but I'm tired from a morning of finals and an afternoon of driving. As we make our way up to her room, it is nice to see that it is the same as I remember. It's the one room in the house her mother never changes. The room is as big as the main area in my apartment, maybe even a little bigger. It has an adjourning private bathroom to my left. A soft fluffy round pink rug lays right in the center, and her bed was on the wall beside the bathroom door. My favorite feature of her room is the tall window on the back wall with a built-in bench underneath. It has the best view in the whole house, looking out on their many acres filled with plush grass and old tall trees. I remember watching TV until after midnight, sneaking in snacks and drinks, painting our nails or Kat trying to give me makeovers in here. This room is full of shared secrets, tears, and many laughs.

"Get some sleep. I've got a full day planned tomorrow," Kat chimes cheerfully and jumps into her spot on the bed.

"Big how?" I ask with a suspicious look and cross my arms over my chest.

"That's for me know and you to find out," she replies giving nothing away but a quick smile. She rolls into the covers and turns off the lamp next to her. I roll my eyes, but she didn't see it. When my head hits the pillow on the other side of her, I realize how just how tired I am. I stayed up late last night studying for my test this morning. I close my eyes and sleep comes easily.

*I'm alone. That's all I know for sure. I look around to empty darkness and I feel isolated. My heart starts to beat more quickly. Street lamps start to light up one by one out of the blackness. I blink, and a road begins to form in front of me as well. It's a regular street that seems to be getting longer by the second. Along either side of the road are house, familiar-looking, though I can't put my finger on exactly where I've seen them before. It's silent and still, and I don't understand what I'm doing here or how I got here in the first place.*

*"Leyla," I hear a voice whisper my name. I'm overcome with panic. This isn't the first time I've heard that voice. I start to follow the road ahead of me. My footsteps softly hit the pavement. It's neither day nor night, and I don't see any signs of life besides my own. Suddenly the darkness lifts, and the sky is covered with ominous dark grey rain clouds. The change startles me and I stop in my tracks. What is going on?*

*As a response lightning strikes far in the distance. Rolls of drumming thunder quickly follow its flash. I feel warm drops of water random places on my exposed skin as it begins to sprinkle. The lightning strikes again, and I'm pulled towards it. I have a sense the lightning is marking a destination for me. It's only striking in one place. I ignore the soft fall of the rain as I push ahead. I realize that I'm no longer walking, but I've managed to start running, somehow. I'm going faster than I ever have in my entire life. I seem to be in a hurry, but I don't know what I'm rushing to or why. As I get closer to the lightning, I hear a glass-shattering shriek. I'm no longer alone, and there is someone else out there. Is that why I'm running? Does someone need my help?*

*I'm almost there. The lightning can't be but a street or two away now. The scream is getting louder as well, though I didn't think it was possible to reach such a high sound volume. Finally, I reach it, and there is a tree that the lightning has been striking continuously. My eyes look over the tree and stop at the limp figure curled up at the base. Whoever is lying there is sprawled out in an unnatural position. I look on in horror. Am I too late? What happened? I start to feel sick, and my stomach turns in knots. The rain starts to pour, and now every inch of me is drenched. The water runs from the tree over the grass and down to my feet. I let out a scream! The water it's… red!*

"Leyla, Leyla, wake up!" I feel someone's hands shaking me. "Leyla!" the voice pleads, and I bolt up. I hear a sigh of relief and look up to see Kat looking over me with worry. She's halfway off the bed. I realize somehow I ended up on the ground.

"What happened?" I ask still coming to.

"You were tossing and turning," she frowns, "then you screamed and rolled off the bed." Her eyes search over me with concern.

"Just a dream. Sorry to wake you," I reply. "I'm okay now, go back to sleep," I lie. I'm far from okay. I push myself up and walk towards the bedroom door.

"Wait, where are you going?" she asks with alarm.

"I'm thirsty, going to grab some water. I'll be back," I explain walking out into the hall before she can say anything otherwise. I follow the hall down the stairs and into the kitchen. There is bright moonlight coming in from the two large windows above the sink. I grab a water bottle out of the fridge. The cool liquid is welcomed as it runs down my throat. I'm burning up, and I wipe away some sweat from my forehead. I exhale a long breath and try to calm myself. That wasn't like any other dream I've ever had. It felt real, so real that my skin and clothes still feel wet from the rain. *It was just a dream Leyla.* A dream that I never want to have again.

I slept in later than normal. I couldn't help it I was up until after four. I couldn't go back to sleep. I was scared, scared to have that dream again. I didn't want to chance it. When I finally did give in, thankfully, I slept without dreams. I wanted to stay in bed, but I forced myself up anyway. I had taken a hot shower and it didn't help me feel any more awake. It just made me want to go back to sleep. I unzip one of my suitcases and pull out an outfit. As I get dressed, I notice Kat has already gone downstairs. I walk down to join her, and she looks over at me with an odd look.

"How are you feeling?"

"I'm fine. What have you got planned for today?" I try to detour her from bringing up last night's event. She pauses for a moment, then shifts her eyes from me to over her shoulder.

"Kent's here to pick us up, and don't worry, you'll find out soon," she replies. I nod, and I'm grateful she's not insisting on talking about it. I follow her out the front door. The cold temperature causes goosebumps to form on my arms as soon as I take a step outside. I look up and notice the cloudy sky above. I wonder if it's going to snow today.

"So, Kent, where are we going?" I ask before Kat gets in, hoping he would slip up and spill the beans.

"No clue," he responds naively with a big grin.

"Ha, ha, very funny," I scoff back. I guess he is in on this too. Wherever we were going, I hope it has caffeine, I need something to wake me up.

"Don't worry, it's not far," Kat chimes in. She seems happy, but I'm not sure if it's because of where we are going, or because I don't know what she has planned.

As we leave her house and make our way towards the center of the town everything around me feel nostalgic. Ashton, our hometown, is named after a grove of white ash trees near the edge of town. If I had to guess, I would say there are only about five hundred people living here, and everyone knows everyone here in Ashton. We turn down the main street, and I see Sweet Treats ice cream and candy store. Even in the cold there is a long line out the door, and it puts a grin on my face. Next, we pass our small library, and I wonder if Miss Griffin is still trying to stay awake behind the counter inside. We used to joke that she's been here since this town's existence in the late eighteen hundreds. Then I see the closed-down Movie Palace. I was sad when it went under, but I wasn't surprised. They only ran movies after they had already been released on DVD, so after Netflix exploded there wasn't any reason for people to go anymore. I prefer seeing it on the big screen myself, not to mention the popcorn. It's always better at the theater than from the microwave at home. As we turn off the main road I see the high school coming up on our right.

"Why are we going this way?" I question. Neither replies, and I can hear them both try and conceal giggles from the front seats. I just roll my eyes and look back out the window. There isn't anything past the high school, so why would we be going this way? It doesn't make any sense. "No way!" I exclaim after I finally see where it is we are going. Kat leans around her seat smiling from ear to ear. "I don't understand. I thought it was gone?" I shake my head in amazement.

"It was," she agrees still smiling. "They rebuilt it!" she squeals.

"How?" I ask looking ahead in a stupor at the sunshine coming off a metal 50's retro diner. Queen's Diner, to be exact, only the best food in all of Iowa.

"My mom told me Mr. Queen sold the land to the town after the fire. The current mayor vowed if he won, he would rebuild it," she pauses and smiles. "The town still owns the land, but Mr. Queen's family rebuilt the diner and they still run it. Ah, the look on your face was so worth it," she admits, and I can't say I disagree. I'm so excited. Queen's was the center point of our town. Celebrities even came through here just to eat there.

I practically jump out of the door before Kent has the truck in park. I walk up with Kat and Kent not far behind. I couldn't believe how much it resembles the original. The shine was a little brighter and there were a few new neon signs, but it looks the same from the outside. We walk in and the only difference I see, besides the newness, is they added a few more booths and a dessert case. The original Mr. Queen was really into card games. I heard he even won this place from someone in a game of poker, but as far as I know that's just a rumor. The décor mirrored his hobby, and his last name was just a coincidence. The glass tabletops all have a large picture of a face card from a playing deck underneath. The booths are green and red, like the color you would find on a poker table. As we are seated in one of the booths, I'm pleased to see a deck of Queen's diner playing cards on the table. Every table has one, so you can play with your family or friends while waiting for your food. They even have them to buy at the counter when you check out. I have several stored away somewhere that mom had bought me over the years. This place reminds me of her. It was also a place of memories for Kat, Kent, and I as well. As you could guess, with it being just down the street from the high school, it was a popular Friday and Saturday night hang out for the students. I look over the menu. I'm pleased to see they still have all the same choices as the original menu.

"Are you guys ready to order, or do you need a few more minutes," our waitress walks up with a typical line.

"I'll have a King's triple cheeseburger with fries and a sweet tea," Kent replies and hands her his menu.

"I would like the Queen's bar-b-que chicken salad with ranch dressing and a root beer," Kat states, and also hands the menu to the young girl. "Thank you," she adds.

"And for you?" The waitress turns to me after writing down their orders.

"The Joker BLT with curly fries and a coke, please," I decide. She nods and walks away to put in our order.

Ten minutes later, she places our food in front of us, the drinks she had brought earlier. We stop talking and begin to shove food in our mouths as soon as the plates hit the table. I bite into mine and the savory bacon, mixed with the crisp lettuce and fresh tomatoes melts into a heavenly trio in my mouth.

"Is it possible it's even better than before?" I ask. Kat nods at me and smiles.

"I'm definitely going to have another one," Kent declares. Kat and I exchange a glance before looking over at Kent.

"You might want to finish your first one babe before ordering another," Kat suggests holding back a laugh. I don't know where he puts it all. That guy can eat for ten. He glances over at her disapprovingly.

"Are you kidding," his voice is completely serious, "I've got to catch up." I let out a laugh, and Kat just shakes her head and rolls her eyes.

"Remind me why I'm with him again?" she points at him and turns to ask me sarcastically.

"I believe it was the offer of free food that won you over, plus I'm pretty irresistible," Kent answers smiling and then proceeds to gulp down his tea.

"Oh right, your first date was here," I speak up remembering. The waitress comes over and refills our drinks. Kent asks her for another burger. She doesn't take him seriously at first, and Kat and I both laugh as she walks away looking appalled at the fact that he could even eat a second one.

"I can't believe you forgot, Leyla, you were here too," Kat manages to get out after she stops laughing, "with Chris, remember?" I stop laughing and choke slightly on a drink I just took.

"I blocked that night out on purpose, so no wonder it slipped my mind," I inform her. I take another drink of my Coke and it burns as it goes down. Kat had conveniently forgotten to tell me that she had a date that night, and if that wasn't bad enough, it turned into a double date when Chris arrived. Kent hadn't exactly told him the plan either, and neither one of us was thrilled about it. I spent the whole night silently wishing I could leave.

"Oh, it wasn't that bad," she pouts, surprised to hear me still upset about it. "Kent and I thought that you and Chris would make a good couple. You know best friends dating best friends," she reminds me. I just shrug in her direction. It would have been a good idea if Kent's best friend didn't happen to be a self-absorbed jerk. He was so full of himself and he had a new conquest every month. I wasn't lining up to be one of them. I can't say I was sad to see him and Kent drift apart after high school. "Well speaking of old friends," Kat starts to change the subject, "we are going to a party tonight." She stares over at me innocently waiting for me to protest.

"I know better than to argue, where's party, and which one of *your* friends is throwing it?" I ask. I hear Kent let out a little laugh, and Kat quickly shoots him a scary look. He instantly looks away, avoiding her glare.

"Why can't it be our friend?" she retorts leaning back in her seat crossing her arms.

"Because Kat," I look towards her and then to Kent, "both my friends are right here." I answer, and she pouts her face.

"The party is at Cherry's house, well her parent's to be exact. She invited anyone from our class that would be home for the holidays. Since we didn't have any other plans, I thought it would be nice to see everyone again," she answers. I cringe a little on the inside. Cherry, I wasn't a fan. In fact, I think I might dislike her even more than I do Chris.

"There has to be someone you wouldn't mind seeing again?" Kent speaks up agreeing with Kat. She smiles over in his direction, appreciative of the backup.

I let out a sigh. "I already said I wasn't going to argue with you. Although I feel like I should point out that I didn't get an invite, and I won't pretend it wasn't on purpose," I inform smiling to my best friend.

# Chapter 4

## A Red Dress and a Charming Smile

I start to dig through my suitcase for something to wear to tonight's party. After all, it would be the first time I've seen anyone from my class, that didn't go to college in Ames after graduation. The only dress I brought was the one Kat had picked out for me when we went shopping together. I had planned to wear it to the annual Christmas fundraiser Mr. Archer always sponsors. It's to raise money for gifts to give to the children who wouldn't get any otherwise, or who are sick and in the hospital. It's a great cause, and always a little boring, at least it was when I was younger.

"Definitely that one," Kat states from over her shoulder, and I turn to see her give me an approving nod.

I change out of my more comfortable attire, and slip on the crimson dress over my head and walk over to the mirror in her bathroom. The hem stopped just below my knee and it shows off my hourglass figure nicely. The color complimented my fair skin, a color I got from the dad I've never met. The sleeves fall loosely off my shoulders. The top scoops down in a heart shape showing off my neckline, collar bone, and a small amount of my chest. The material didn't stretch well, and I felt a little stiff. "My bestie is all grown up and going to parties," Kat fake cries from behind me. I try not to humor her and avoid commenting back.

"You'll need these. They go perfectly." I turn around and she hands me a pair of matching heels. I'm not a fan of trying to walk in them, but she is right. It did match perfectly, so I take them. "Come sit on the end of the bed and I'll do your makeup and hair," she beckons.

" Are you sure it's necessary to dress up? This seems a little over board?" I ask her unsure about wearing this.

"Yes, it's an adult party, we're all adults now, we get to dress like them," she retorts half-joking half-serious. She picks up the bottom ends of my hair and begins to curl it around the hot iron. Her dress matches my crow black-colored hair, As she leans around me, it blends together. Her tan had worn away, so now her skin looks paler against her dress than normal. Her hair, however, still stands out like a dark red flame. She had already curled it and done her makeup. She reminds me of a perfect doll you would find at the store. Petite, with big eyes, and a flawless complexion, she doesn't even need the makeup she's wearing. "What are you staring at," she notices, "do I have something on my face?"

"You look gorgeous, as always," I respond.

"So do you, Leyla," she flatters me back. I fidget with my hands avoiding eye contact. "You are, and I want to point out that we aren't in high school anymore. You're in college now. You may or may not see any of these people again after tonight." I look up at her. I'm curious to see where she is going with this. "What I'm trying to say is that you don't have to worry what they think about you anymore. You're amazing, smart, and beautiful, and I'm not just saying this because I'm your best friend." She puts the curler down and sits next to me wrapping her arm around my shoulder. "You just need to start believing it yourself and you'll be fine," she finishes. I reach over and give her a long tight hug.

"You're the best, Kat," I notify her. She was right. I'm not in high school anymore, and she can't always be around to push me out of my shell. I have to do it on my own.

After she finishes my make-up, I follow her downstairs and out the back door. We walk across the driveway to the detached garage. She lets us in through the side door and flips on the lights. She grabs the key to her mom's Bentley and the headlights flash as she unlocks it.

"We are taking mom's car," she reveals, and my mouth instantly gaps open in shock. Margret never lets Kat borrow her car, ever. "Okay, my dad said I could, and we aren't telling my mom," she admits the truth.

Kat is careful and parks on the opposite side of the road from Cherry's house. One because she doesn't want to get blocked in, and two she doesn't want to chance anyone hitting it. I'm glad she is cautious, but it's a cold walk across the street and up the drive to the house. The entry door is wood with decretive glass you can see through to the inside. The door swings open right before we walk up. It's nice and warm inside. I can feel myself thawing as I walk in. The home is expensively furnished and decorated for the holidays. There are pumpkins, gourds, and wreaths with fall leaves placed around the rooms I can see. It even smells like fall. If I had to guess, I would say a mixture of cranberries and cinnamon. Cherry is standing at the end of the entryway hall with Wesley, who probably opened the door for us. Cherry is your everyday blonde beauty queen with a heart of stone and a head full of hot air. She purposely pulls Wesley closer to her as we reach them. I remember her chasing him throughout high school, but I also remember he always had a thing for Kat. I felt a little bad for him, he was one of the good ones, but Kat and Kent are meant to be. Too bad he had to settle for her. I always thought he was cute, with his long dark hair and soft blue eyes. I guess she wants everyone to know they are a couple now. It's no secret she was constantly jealous of Kat. I asked Kat once why they were friends, and she gave me the line of "keeping your enemies closer." Cherry hugs Kat. She smiles over at me briefly. I do the same and then quickly look away. Wesley just waves hello, and I notice his focus is on Kat.

"So glad you both could make it. Kent's already here, out in the back." Cherry points behind her past the living area and through the glass doors leading to the backyard.

*Why would he be out there in the cold?* I want to ask but don't. I take that as my queue to leave, and I did. As Kat lingers a moment with them, I look around the room to see if I could spot anyone I wouldn't mind seeing again. I didn't see anyone so far.

"Kat, Leyla, come out here!" I hear my name called out and I follow its sound as my face starts to turn red.

I find Kent poking his head through the sliding glass doors. *Why*, Kent, just why would you announce us to the whole party? Kat comes over and gets me and we follow Kent outside. I look over at Kat who shrugs, like we've just got to accept he has no graces. Kent leads us to a large group, of mostly guys, huddled outside. There are a few fold-out tables where everyone is sitting down. I look around realizing they are all mostly his old teammates and their current girlfriends. I'm happy to see there is a fire pit with plenty of burning wood going. It would seem Kat was right, and most of them are dressed up. Even Kent was wearing slacks, and I'm guessing a button-up shirt under his heavy coat. Everyone exchanges hellos and congratulations to Kent and Kat on their engagement.

"Thank you, guys. It's great to see everyone," Kat states.

"I can't believe you're still holding on to him, Kat," I hear a guy's voice shout from the other end of the yard.

We all turn to see Chris walking over towards the group. *Great, he's here too*. I suddenly want to leave. When they all see who it is the group laughs, well everyone but me. Kent and Chris exchange a handshake and a quick bro hug. Kat leans over and nudges me with her elbow. If she thinks I'm interested in him being here, she's insane. She hits me again and I turn in annoyance.

"There is a guy over there who keeps looking at you," she whispers in my ear.

I follow her gaze slowly, trying not to be obvious, over to my right. There is a guy who is talking with another girl just inside the house. He has messy walnut brown hair and thick matching color eyebrows. His skin is the color of sand and his face is strong with high cheekbones and a straight jawline. He glances over in our direction, and before I look away, I notice his eyes. They are bright green like grass in springtime after ample rain. One look and I forget to breathe for a moment. *I don't remember him being in our class*.

"I don't think he's looking at me. I'm sure he is just wanting to know where all the noise is coming from," I disagree hinting to Kent and his friends. She rolls her eyes. I start to back away from the group, no longer interested in the conversation. I take another peek at him. He is talking to a different girl this time. I couldn't pull my eyes away. I move around to get a better view.

"Hey!" I look over at Kat, unsure if she was talking to me, to see a look of panic on her face.

"What?" I ask aloud. I instinctively take another step back.

"Leyla!" Kent yells my name and, before I know it, I feel his hand pull mine forward. I freeze in place and turn my head to see myself inches away from falling into the deep end of Cherry's pool. "That was close," he signs with relief and pulls me further away.

"Thanks Kent," I utter and look around to realize all eyes are on me.

"Hey, Leyla, do you want to grab some food?" Kat asks, and I nod. Anything to escape this moment and everyone's eyes.

"Get me something too babe, please?" Kent shoots Kat a puppy dog look.

"Dude, you just ate two hamburgers when you got here," one of his friends announces.

"That's Kent, some things never change," Chris states and the group laughs. Kat and I head back into the house and into the kitchen. I see people hanging around the food like flies at a picnic. They make room for us as we walk by. We both pick up a plate. Kat starts grabbing handfuls of whatever is closest, for Kent I'm assuming. I look up and see Cherry and Westley heading our way, and suddenly my appetite dies.

"Are you both having a good time? Doesn't this bring back great memories?" Cherry asks with enthusiasm.

"Tons, thanks for asking," I relay as nicely as I can, but I think it still came off a bit too sarcastic.

"Great party, as always," Kat abruptly utters trying to make up for my comment. Her tone is sincerer than mine.

"Wonderful, and I just wanted to say happy engagement. I saw the good news on Facebook," she comments. "Leyla, I noticed your close call earlier. You alright?" Of course, she witnessed that. Her tone is laced with malintent, and I believe I was being led into a trap if I answered, so I didn't. "What luck that dress didn't get ruined," she continues. She is always like this. She's a cat that plays with everyone else as if they were a ball of yarn. She toys with you until you don't know where you start and where you end. You're caught in her claws until she's done with you, and when she is done all that's left is little pieces. She looks between Kat and me. and I don't appreciate the look on her face. "That was awful nice of Kent to come to your rescue. I'm glad to see you two are still," she pauses, and I squeeze the plate in my hand, "close." She smiles, and I read between the lines of her suggestion.

"Well, that's what friends do, they look out for each other. If you had any you would know," the words slip out like someone else is talking for me. Kat chokes on something next to me. Cherry's face turns the color of her name and she lets out a little huff. Wesley's mouth is gaped open. Cherry grabs his shirt as they storm off. I turn back to Kat, who is still trying to catch her breath. She grabs a nearby water bottle and gulps half of it down.

"Where did that come from?" she asks with a serious tone, but she was smiling. "I think you might have taken that confident speech and ran with it a little too much," she jokes, but I can tell deep down she is impressed. "I'm going to take this food to Kent. Play nice," she warns and heads off with a full plate. As she leaves, I sense another presence next to mine. I turn to see a pair of green eyes shining at me.

"Hello," his voice is smooth, and I thought I caught a bit of an accent underneath.

"Hi," I reply a little out of breath. He surprised me. He smiles at me and it's the epitome of charm. It makes my knees bend for a moment. He stands a few inches taller than me and he is closer to me than I'm comfortable with. I take in his smell. It's enticing and familiar. I couldn't say anything else, but I can only stare back at him.

He smiles with amusement. "Sorry if I startled you. I'm Drake. It's nice to meet you," he introduces himself. I blink a few times. *Come on, say something.* I'm trying to form words, but they wouldn't leave my brain. "Are you not hungry?" he asks looking down at my empty plate. I shake my head no. "I didn't mean to eavesdrop, I apologize, but I'm glad you're okay." He looks back over his shoulder towards Cherry, standing on the opposite side of the living room glaring at me. "She was right about that dress. It would be a shame if it had gotten wet." I feel heat rush up through my veins and I can only imagine what my face looks like right now. I'm positive it's redder than my dress. He smiles again, and I feel my head start to hurt. I know this feeling. *No, not here, not right now.* I can't stop it. I drop my plate and place both my hands instantly on my temples. My head starts to throb and I close my eyes tightly. The images, they're back, and faster than ever. I wish it would stop. I want to cry out, but I just shut my eyes tighter and pray it's over soon. I feel a gentle touch on both my hands, and unexpectedly, the images dissipate. I open my eyes and see two green one staring back at me with distress. "Are you okay?" his voice is calm and quiet.

"Yes, I think. I've been getting these headaches randomly…" I stop, realizing that I was talking to him. My brain has finally caught up with my mouth. *Why is it so hard for me to speak to him?* I clear my throat as he drops his hands from mine. *Am I going to get headaches every time I meet an attractive guy?* I certainly hope not.

"Can I get you anything?" he offers. I shake my head no. "Well, I'm sorry to bother you," he apologizes and hesitantly turns to leave. My heart sinks low in my chest.

"Leyla," I manage to get out. Automatically, he turns back around. "My name is Leyla," I repeat, not wanting him to leave without telling him my name in return. I know how it feels not to know someone's name. His charming smile forms curling his lips up to his right cheek. My skin starts to heat up again. I wish he wouldn't smile at me like that.

"Very nice to meet you, Leyla," my name leaves his lips and I wouldn't mind him saying it again. "Are you enjoying your break?" he asks starting a conversation.

"Yes, I am," I reply and manage a shy smile.

"I bet getting to be back home and getting to spend time with family is nice," he states, and he seems almost sadden by his statement.

"I am glad to be home, but I'm staying with my friend, although she is practically family," I confess. He gives me an odd look. "My dad hasn't been in the picture since I was born and my mom passed away a few years ago," I explain.

"I'm sorry, I didn't mean to pry. I lost my mom too when I was young. I miss her every day," he admits with a look of understanding. "I'll leave you to get your food. Sorry again for disturbing you." He turns and walks off. As he does, I feel my limbs untense. I let out a long breath I didn't realize I was holding in.

I walk back out to Kat and she walks up to me with a knowing smile. "I noticed you bumped into someone. I told you he was looking at you," she says in a matter-of-a-fact way. "In case you were wondering, he's not from around here. According to Cassie, who bumped into him earlier today. She invited him to the party," she informs me. I already knew he wasn't from here. I would have remembered someone like him. I look back and see Drake heading out the front door. *Remember*, that word lingers on my thoughts, is there something about him I'm supposed to remember?

We leave the party and make the cold walk back to Margert's car. We had to get back to the house before Kat's parent's date was over and her mother realized her car was gone. Kat walks around the car with her phone's flashlight, ensuring there aren't any dings or scratches. When she is satisfied, we get in and head back to her house. I was ready for sleep. It had been a long day, and last night wasn't exactly restful. My thoughts turn to Drake as we drive back. I wonder if I would ever see him again. I wonder what had brought him to our small town.

Kat parks the car and we rush in, just in time. We both notice the lights of Mr. Archer's car pulling in at the start of the driveway. We bolt inside hurrying up to her room. We quickly change out of our dresses and into our pajamas. "Tonight wasn't so bad, was it?" Kat asks me getting into her bed.

"No, it wasn't too bad," I agree. "Do we have another exciting day planned tomorrow?" I ask her.

"Not particularly. Kent will be here to takes us to Queen's again for lunch and then to his house so that I can catch up with his parents," she informs me.

That doesn't sound too bad. I was okay with an easy-going day. I turn out the light and start to head for the bed when I notice something out of the corner of my eye. I walk over to her window instead. I see small flakes dancing in the wind falling gracefully to the ground below. *Snow*. The first snow of winter, it's later than normal.

"Are you coming to bed, or are you going to stare at the snow all night?" Kat asks. I thought about the latter for a moment, but ultimately I crawled in the bed next to her. I hope I will get some rest tonight.

I bolt up, waking to reality. I'm trying to catch my breath as sweat is rolling down my arms and neck. I feel as if I was just running instead of lying in bed this whole time. I push the covers off of me and rush into Kat's bathroom. I wash cool water over my face and start to still my breathing. I study myself in the mirror seeing my makeup begin to run everywhere it shouldn't. My hair is matted to the sides of my face and neck from the sweat. My green eyes are glazed over and bloodshot. That dream, why would I dream about the same thing, just the night after? I walk back out to the room where Kat is still sound asleep. I'm glad to see I didn't wake her up with a scream like last night. I look out her window to see it's still snowing. My throat feels dry, so I decide to go downstairs for another late drink. I close her door behind me quietly as possible as I leave the room.

"Can't sleep?" I jump back several feet and put my hand over my chest. I look over to see Mr. Archer at the end of the hall smiling at me.

"You scared me half to death," I accuse, but judging by his snickers, I think he is already aware of that.

"Sorry about that. Are you going down?" he asks waiving his hand back behind him towards the stairs. I nod yes and follow him to the kitchen. "You hungry?" he asks turning on the soft lights above the sink? I nod yes again. I never ate anything at the party. I watch him pull out a large box of Pagio's Pizza from the fridge. I should have known, it is his favorite. "Can I grab you a slice?" he offers, and I shake my head no to decline. I wasn't a fan of cold pizza, never have been. "You don't know what you're missing," he shrugs.

"How about some cereal?" I suggest. He waves a finger in the air and then turns around several times until he finds the right cabinet hiding the cereal.

"I'm not even going to mention the boring ones," he looks back at me and winks. "Let's see we have Cocoa Puffs or Lucky Charms?"

"Cocoa Puffs, I would just pick out all the marshmallows from the Lucky Charms, and it would be a waste," I answer. He grabs everything I need, and I pour the cereal and milk into my bowl. I take a big spoon full into my mouth and I hear the satisfying crunch sound as I bite down.

"So, why are you up so late?" he questions with one of his eyebrows raised. I notice that there are some strands of grey mixed with his brown hair.

*When did that happen*? I even spot some new wrinkles around his hazel eyes and small lips. I guess I'm getting older, so why wouldn't he?

"No reason," I reply, dismissing the question. I get a look that tells me he wasn't buying it.

"Okay, I get it," he pouts, "don't tell the old guy anything. What could he know? It's not like he's been around for a while," he jokes.

"I had a bad dream," I reply giving in.

"Ah, I see. Well, you know those aren't really my field of expertise. I'm not a psychic," he plays, and it makes me smile, "but I can tell you that our brain dreams for several different reasons." I perk up suddenly interested. "Sometimes dreams can come from us being stressed or dreading over something. Or, sometimes if we are looking forward to, or excited about something we will have them. Most are typically nonsense, but sometimes they can be our minds' way of warning us about something." I think I can guess which one mine was. I also think he is more of an expert on the matter than he let on. "The best dreams, of course, are the ones where we get to play out our deepest desires. Your brain can fantasize them for you, like learning how to fly and saving the world, or having a voice like an opera singer," he adds with a smile grabbing another slice from the box before putting it back in the fridge. "So which one did you have?" he inquires, turning back around to face me.

"I'm not sure. I don't really remember much of it once I woke up," I lie, only because I didn't feel like reliving it out loud.

"I see. Well if you can't remember, then it's probably not important," he concludes. My heart sinks. I hope it wasn't. "Did you and kitty Kat have fun at the party?" he asks, changing the subject.

"Yes, we did," I tell him happy to move on to something different.

"I vaguely recall my college days, but I do believe my breaks were used to take lots of naps and eat lots of food," he says fondly as he seems to be thinking back to those years. "Of course, the naps were to make up for staying up all night, and the food was to help absorb all the alcohol, but it was good times," he further explains, and I can't help but laugh. "Well, I'd love to stay, but I better get back in bed before Margret wakes up to an empty spot next to her. She insists that these midnight snacks are going to catch up with me." I very much doubt that, he's never been over weight in his life. He chuckles as if he read my mind and walks out. For the moment our talk took away the feeling of dread I had. It wasn't until he left that I realized I would have to return to bed. Would I dream again?

# Chapter 5
## A Surprising Introduction

I did dream. I dreamt that same dream non-stop all night. I decide to get out of bed before anyone else had woken up. I didn't see the point in trying to fall back asleep when I knew what awaited me if I did. I have already showered and dressed. I head towards the barn. It's freezing outside, but I didn't care, I just pull my coat I have on closer together. There is at least two or three inches of snow on the ground, but it's no longer falling at the moment. The coolness feels good, sobering. I open the door to the barn to hear the horses stir as I enter. Knowing Kent would be here later to take us to lunch, I decided to go for a ride first and clear my head. I walk up to Midnight's stall. She's unofficially mine, since no one else rides her but me. I felt bad that I hadn't already come out here to see her before today. She lets out a happy neigh and walks towards me letting her head hang slightly over the stall. I pick up one of the brushes and begin to brush her. She nuzzles her nose into my side.

"I missed you too girl," I coo. Her mane is black as coal, except for a single gray strip between Midnights eyes and the tips of her ears. There is something about horses. Being around them always calms me.

"Majestic creatures," a familiar but surprising voice states.

I turn my whole body to face this uninvited guest. I drop my brush to the ground and I freeze in place. *This is a dream.* I start to blink, but every time I open my eyes again, he is still there. He can't be here. The horses didn't even stir, so how could he be standing there right now? The light shines through the open door behind him, like the day at the library. It illuminated his figure and his hair. His eyes, still blue and still pulling me in.

"Please don't be frightened," he instructs, and I want to laugh at the fact that he would even suggest that. Don't be frightened, how was I supposed to act? I realize I didn't have my phone on me, and I doubt anyone from the house could hear me scream from here. I couldn't exactly run away either, not unless I wanted to run right through him. Reading my panic, he moves to the side. "I won't stop you if you wish to leave," he assures me. Is he serious? Can I trust that? Can I trust that I was even awake right now and having this conversation?

"Is this a dream?" I ask aloud. He looks back at me with confusion.

"No," he answers as if my question was out of the ordinary, but it seemed like a reasonable one to me.

"I don't understand what's going on right now. Why are you here?" I ask. He takes a step closer to me, and I react by pushing my body against the stall as close as humanly possible. "Please don't come closer," I warn still trying to process all of this logically, but I'm failing miserably.

"I'm sorry, I can see this wasn't a good idea, it's just." he pauses, and I see him clench his fist.

"It's just, what?" I couldn't help myself. He takes a long time to respond as if he is trying to think of the best way to explain.

"You can see me," he finally answers.

"Am I not supposed to?" I ask confused, and my head starts to spin. He shakes his head no, unwilling to give me any other explanation. Exhausted and feeling trapped, I decide I'm done with whatever this was. "Look either explain to me what's going on or disappear!" I announce loudly, and I hear the horses stir.

I didn't mean to frighten them. His eyes turn sad, and to my surprise, he disappears. I let out a shocked gasp. I run over to where he stood inspecting the spot. I look out the door of the barn towards the house. He is gone. *What just happened?* I walk back to the stall and slide down the door. I feel midnight's warm breath on my neck as I sit there. I needed to go back to sleep I'm starting to hallucinate things.

I manage to pull myself together though. I never went back to sleep. I just stayed downstairs and waited for Kat to come down. She gave me an odd look when she realized I was already awake, but she didn't say anything about it. Kent arrived at eleven to take us to Queens. The drive there wasn't as exciting today as it was previously. I'm very distracted by the earlier events. I've kept quiet, letting them do most of the talking. I try to bury the thoughts away from my earlier encounter and focus on eating. We walk in and sit in the same seat as yesterday, though we had a different waitress today. I stare off out the window and don't even bother looking over the menu. I feel a slight tap on my shoulder and I turn my head quickly around.

"Hello again." I look up to familiar green eyes looking down at me. Drake.

"Hello," Kat replies for me. "I'm Kat, and this is Kent, and I think you've already met Leyla. Won't you join us?" she offers and looks over to me.

"If you want," I add, not looking directly at him. I scoot over so he can sit down next to me.

"Alright, thanks. It's nice to meet you. I'm Drake," he introduces himself back. He's too close. I couldn't help but to tense. I catch his smell again, and it smells just as good as before.

"What brings you to Ashton?" Kent asks.

"I was just passing through on my way to the college to get settled in for this upcoming semester," he replies, and I think I might scream. He is going to be in the same school as me? *Calm down. It's not like you are going to have the same classes.*

"Well, since you're new in town we could show you around today. We don't have to be at your parents' until this evening. Right Kent?" I catch Kat give him a small nudge with her elbow.

"Right," Kent speaks up looking over at me with an apologetic look.

"That's very nice of you, but I would hate to impose on your day," Drake declines politely. "It was nice to meet you," he adds. I feel like he is about to get up to leave, but I didn't want him to go. I bravely put my hand lightly on top of his arm.

"Wait, if you were going to eat," I look over at him directly, "you can at least stay and eat with us before you go." I release him, and I feel a little awkward for touching him in the first place. I don't know him. His eyes search mine for a moment mulling over my request.

"I'd love to," he agrees cheerfully, and I watch his fingers move his hair away from his forehead. I turn back away. How can one guy ooze that much charisma? I dare a look over at Kat who is radiating with satisfaction. *It's just food, Kat.* She is way too happy about this. We all hide momentarily behind our menus, even though I think three out of the four of us already know what we want. I think Kat is using hers as an excuse to whisper to Kent. My eyes dart over to my side to see Drake studying his.

"Everything is good here," I suggest looking over at him, trying to be helpful.

"Oh," he flashes me a grin and glances over at me, "that doesn't make my choice very easy then, does it?" He half laughs.

"I guess not, sorry," I reply quickly looking back down at my menu. The waitress walks over and her eyes stop on Drake. I see her blush a little, and I want to tell her I know exactly how she feels.

"What would you like?" she asks, still staring. Kent, Kat, and I all repeat our orders from yesterday.

"I think I'll have the same burger as my new friend over here, but I would prefer a root beer float instead of a tea." Drake decides and hands the waitress his menu.

"Good choice," Kent approves. The waitress stays for a moment too long, and when she notices me looking at her, she realizes it herself and rushes off.

"What are you majoring in?" Kat asks. It takes Drake a moment to respond, as if he didn't realize he was the one being asked the question.

"I haven't decided yet," he answers vaguely. I wish Kat wouldn't pry. The waitress comes back over with our drinks. Drake takes one gulp and he can't stop. I see his eyes go wide as he slurps down the entire float in a matter of minutes. When he realizes we are all staring at him, he starts to chuckle. His laugh is so genuine and humble. I can't help but smile. "Sorry, it's just been a long time since I've had one of these," he admits, and we all laugh with him.

It felt like we talked for hours, and well, we might have. I think our waitress had ended her shift and left before we did. Drake got along great with Kat and Kent. They both offered to let him tag along with us for the rest of the holiday, but he insisted he needed to get to the campus before the break ended. He did tell us that he planned on tracking us down once school started. I was happy and nervous about his plans, but I tried not to put too much stock in it. After all, he could change his mind later or simply forget us. Either way, I wouldn't be seeing him again any time soon. I couldn't say the same about blue eyes. He is all I've been able to think about after our lunch. Even while we were at Kent's house, it was the main thing consuming my mind. I keep expecting him to pop up at random places. I'm to the point of paranoia. Once Kent drops Kat and me back at her parents' house, my focus turns to my dream instead of him. Would I have it again? Would I be able to sleep without waking up in a panic? I almost didn't want to lay down to find out.

Much to my disappointment, I did have the nightmare, continuously all night. I'm no longer calling it a dream. Dreams are mostly happy and random, but this is cruel and relentless. I always wake up at the end, in terror, because it feels so real. The most patronizing thing about it is I can never seem to reach the body in time. My feet always seem glued to the road. I can never save them, no matter how hard or fast I run. I look over at my phone to see it's almost six a.m. I don't know how much more of these restless nights I can take. I just want to go to sleep once without having this dream.

Five weeks, the holidays have now come and gone, but my nightmare never stops. Gratefully, the only thing that's changed is I only have it once per night instead of several times. I woke up early this morning, our last morning here, before heading back to go for a ride. I've been trying to push myself to come out here since my encounter with blue eyes. I didn't let my anxiety about possibly seeing him again stop me. I needed this. As I lead Midnight out of the barn I'm stopped by a sleepy Kat. I can tell in her eyes she isn't ready to be awake yet, but here she is anyway. Her clothes wrinkled under her coat, which I think might be inside out, and her hair is lazily pulled back into a ponytail. She has on her riding boots, and I can guess what she is here to do.

"Going somewhere?" she asks me, already knowing the answer.

"Yes, are you?" I grin, but she doesn't smile back. She crosses her arms and looks me all over with a suspicious look.

"Is everything okay with you?" she pauses. "You haven't been sleeping," she calls me out and I feel my grin disappear. I didn't think she knew. I didn't know me waking up was disturbing her sleep too. What can I say? I can't tell her I've had the same dream every night. I know how crazy that sounds.

"I'm fine, sorry if I've been restless. I guess I'm just not used to sleeping with someone," I reply. "Are you coming along?" I ask trying to bypass this conversation.

"I wouldn't be up this early if I weren't," she retorts storming off to saddle her horse.

Moments later, she comes out riding atop Herman, her prize barrel racing horse. He's quick, but Midnight beats his stamina hands down. I speak from experience. She trots off in the lead and so I give Midnight a swift soft kick to hurry. I catch up with Kat, and she smiles over at me. I can see she is enjoying this just as much as I am. Herman starts to gallop and Midnight follows along. The snow is flying all around the bottom of their hoofs. Luckily, the snow isn't too deep for us to be riding in. The wind is icy but at the moment I don't mind. As the wind stings my skin, I forget about my dream and just focus on the rush of adrenaline. Riding is the closest thing to flying I've ever felt. I glance over at Kat to see she has the reins gripped tightly. She is always in control, concentrating on the ground in front of her. I, on the other hand, let Midnight guide me. My hands are loosely gripping her reigns and my focus is scattered. We start to slow the horses after going around once in a large square in the fenced-off pasture. Kat jumps off and I do the same.

"Are you sure you are alright?" she asks again looking forward.

"Yes, I'm fine," I try to assure her. Even if I told her the truth, there wasn't anything she could do for me. "Really, everything is…" I stop my sentence, I stop my horse, and I stop walking.

"Leyla, are you okay? Why did you stop," Kat asks stopping her horse as well? She follows my gaze to the barn and then back to me. "Leyla, your face is white, are you too cold," she rephrases? I couldn't say anything. She looks over towards the barn again. "Is something there? I don't see anything," her voice is low and full of worry.

"Sorry, it's nothing," I reply calmly. "Could you do me a favor and make us some hot chocolate? It's really cold and I could use something to warm me up. I'll put Herman up for you," I offer. She looks over at me quizzically.

"Sure, I'll make you some hot cocoa, but I'm having coffee. See you inside," Kat grins, handing me Herman's reigns. She heads off towards the house as I hurry into the barn. I let the horses in and quickly close the door behind me.

"I know you're in here. What do you want?" I shout. My eyes search around the stalls. "Why are you still here?" I yell louder and with frustration. He finally appears out of thin air only a couple feet away from me. I can't help but take a few steps back. "Why are you here, why are you watching me, and how the hell do you keep appearing out of nowhere?" I demand.

"I don't think you're ready for all the answers Leyla," he says my name and it sounds too familiar on his lips. I don't like it.

"Oh, is that right? Well, since you have no problem saying my name, I'd be ever so grateful if you would finally tell me yours," I command. He doesn't respond. "I'm done playing this game," I add. There is an unsettling and long silence between us. Every moment passing adds to my unrest. "It's the least you can do," I complain almost begging. He stands there still and somber. Can he not see how I am feeling right now? Can he not give me this one straight answer?

"Darrius," he answers cautiously, and I almost feel it's too good to be true. *Darrius*, that's his name. Well, at least now we are getting somewhere. I don't want to push it, but now that he is talking, I don't want to waste this chance either.

"Darrius," he cringes slightly when I say his name, "are you going to tell me why you are here?" I ask shyly, hoping to catch the fly with honey. Though, inside me right now I'm choking down vinegar.

"Protection," he replies flatly.

"Protection?" I parrot. *Is he serious*? He looks serious, and I don't think I'm going to get another word out of him about it. "Mine or yours, and from what exactly?" I try to find a way to get him to elaborate.

"Yours, and I don't know," he replies, this time at least with more than one word, but it wasn't any more useful. I rub my thumb and pointer finger along my brows. I'm trying to stay calm, but I'm having a hard time.

"Can you explain to me why I can see you and no one else can, and how you can disappear into thin air?" I ask. I'm not getting my hopes up for any reasonable answer.

"I can, but I don't think I should," he taunts.

"What kind of answer," I pause and breathe. "Please, for my sanity's sake, can you tell me anyway," I beg.

"If I do, will you promise to stop asking me any more questions?" he asks, and I'm taken back by his statement.

"I most certainly will not," I sternly shout crossing my arms defiantly.

"Magic," he answers, surprisingly. *That is the answer?* I literally laugh out loud. He doesn't smile. In fact, he seems put off at my response.

"I'm sorry, did you actually think I would believe that?" I laugh again. "You're crazy, or I'm crazy, one of us is definitely crazy," I announce and he presses his lips together. I can tell he doesn't appreciate my comment. I no longer care. I just don't care anymore. "You know what, I honestly don't know how to handle this, I don't know what you want from me, and I can't help the feeling you're not telling me anything truthful."

"I cannot lie," he retorts. His voice is sharp. For the first time since I met him, I was frightened of him. He's real, he's here, and this conversation is really happening. "I'm sorry," he apologizes realizing the repercussions of his tone. "I know this is difficult, but—" it was my turn to cut him off.

"Difficult? I think that's understating it. You show up in a place you shouldn't be, you give me one-word answers that make even less sense than you somehow being here, and you have the nerve to get angry at me about not understanding," I shake my head. "Darrius, however it is you do it, disappear. Disappear from this barn, disappear from this town, disappear from this state, and disappear from my life!" I finally see a shred of emotion in his face. He now looks just as uncomfortable as I feel. "I never want to see you again, now leave me alone!" I walk past him and out of the barn. I didn't look back. I'm done. I'm finished with him. I'm done with random flashing visions. I'm over feeling paranoid, and I'm defiantly over my nightmare. I am ready to be home.

# Chapter 6

## Friends and Enemies

I didn't care much for the country music Kent played on the radio all the way back to my apartment. I have my headphones on listening to my music instead. Not that I hated every song, I just didn't care much for him trying to sing along with every single one of them. I don't see how Kat can stand it. She and I said our goodbyes to her parents earlier. I was going to miss them and my hometown, but I was hoping to get back to some kind of normal. After all, I didn't start having my nightmare until the first night here. It was just this morning I told blue eyes to leave me alone forever. I knew his name now, but I couldn't bring myself to use it for some reason. As we pull into my apartment complex, I take my headphones off and shove them in my purse.

"We will see you tomorrow night for new year's, won't we?" Kat pokes her head around the front see to ask. It was more of a reminder than a question, I think.

"I'll be there, I'm not going to bale on you this time," I assure her, and she gives me a nod. Kent helps me out with my bags after I let him. I follow him back out to see Kat has jumped out of the truck. She comes over to hug me.

"Thanks for kidnaping me," I tell her as I hug her back.

"Any time. See you tomorrow," Kat says, and I hug Kent goodbye as well.

"See you tomorrow," I repeat.

I linger outside to watch them drive off. I look up at the sky noticing it's already dark. Everything around me seems quiet, peaceful. I drop my head back down seeing a number of empty parking spots. People must still be gone for the holiday. The lights of the apartments and parking lot start to turn on one by one. As I turn back to head into my apartment, I see two men head my way. They are walking very closely together, one is much taller than the other, and they are wearing long black coats.

"Excuse me, miss?" The taller one grabs my attention as they reach me. "Sorry to bother you this evening, but would you happen to live in number 205?" He points up to my apartment. *What could they want with me?*

"I'm sorry, but if you're selling something, unless it's cookies, I'm not interested," I tell him, thinking that could be the only logical explanation. He lets out a small laugh as the other man stands silently beside him as if he is waiting for something.

"No miss, we aren't selling anything," he replies and smiles widely. His tone is somewhat foreboding, and I didn't like the way he is eyeing me. The shorter one hasn't taken his eyes off me since they walked up either, making me feel uncomfortable. They both exchange a glance and then look back at me. I swallow.

"Then what do you want?" I ask slowly backing away. I wonder if I can make it to my door, something about this whole scene is unsettling.

"We want you," the shorter man reveals, speaking for the first time.

At that, I make a run for the door. The shorter man cuts me off from my front door. The taller man is fast behind me and grabs my arm so hard. I almost fall backward as he yanks me. I turn to look at him and start to let out a scream. He quickly takes his other hand and tries to couple it over my mouth. Less than an inch from my lips his hand suddenly slows. It's barely inching forward. I look around stunned to see that's not the only thing that has. It's as if someone has hit a pause button on the world around me. I didn't question it too much; it wasn't the first thing out of the ordinary I've encountered. I pull my arm away from his and shove my way past him and the other one. I make it into the street before whoever hit pause decides to hit play instead. Both men turn to look at me. Their faces are a mixture of shock and confusion.

"How did she get over there?" the shorter one asks in disbelief. "I thought she was normal," the man states, and I didn't follow his meaning. I see the light on in an apartment nearby. The keys to my Jeep are currently in my purse inside my apartment. The only way to get to them was to go through them, and I didn't see that happening. If I could just get to someone's door quick enough, I could get help.

"Don't bother running, we don't want to take you in injured," the taller man commands forming a serious face.

He taps the side of his coat with his fingers, and from watching plenty of old movies, I know what he is trying to say. He has a gun, and if I try to run, he will shoot me. I think that would draw attention to him, but he could probably get me into a car and drive off before anyone knew what was going on. Besides, if I heard a gunshot, my reaction would be to stay inside and call the police. No one was coming to save me, so why did I still want to run and resist?

"I suggest you move away from the lady, or I'll be forced to end both of you where you stand!" *Drake?*

I turn around stunned to see him standing a few feet away. He looks different. He has on some kind of armor that covers everything but his neck, head, and hands. It's dark brown, like his hair, and it's fitted to him like a glove. If I had to guess, I would say it was made out of thick leather, he also has on matching colored boots. The armor has a symbol on the chest area, but I couldn't make it out, shadows darken it from my view. His normally loose hair are gelled back. Every strand is pulled back from forehead. His green eyes are the only bright thing on him, catching the light from one of the lamps around us. His expression is grim, and if that wasn't enough, he is holding something alarming in both his hands. I'm seeing two short sharp-edged swords. I can't think of any rational reason why he would be carrying weapons like that around with him.

"Drake," I say his name as if I'm unsure he's really there, "they have guns," I reveal. I watch a smile, one of a boy about to get into mischief, cross his face. He wasn't taking me seriously. His eyes turn from me to the men standing on the other side. His eyes narrow in on them like a bird from the sky eyeing its prey. I didn't know what to make of it.

"Listen to the girl," the shorter man suggests, and both men pull out their guns. "This is no time to play hero," he warns.

"Get back home, leave. This is none of your concern," the other man follows suit. Drake doesn't back down. He starts walking past me. He places himself in-between me and the two men without a second thought.

"I'm afraid anything to do with this lady is my concern." He looks back at me and smiles. Then gives a look that says, don't worry, I got this. "I suggest you leave. I've told you once I will cut you down where you stand," he reminds them. His stance implies that he is ready to back up his statement. The way they are all talking to each other, you would think I wasn't here at all.

"Look, either you leave now, or we will shoot you, and then if she tries to run, we will shoot her," he looks past Drake to me. "We will be taking her with us either way. So go now." The taller man takes a step closer shifting the safety on his weapon off in the process. He pulls the spring back and loads a bullet in the chamber. He aims the gun straight for Drake's head.

"Drake, run!" I shout. "I'll go with you. Please just put away your guns," I plead. All three of them continue to ignore me and keep staring each other down instead. "Drake, just run!" I shout again even louder, somehow thinking it could make a difference.

"Listen, whoever you are, this is your last warning. Leave now or die," the taller one instructs calmly.

I'm abruptly overtaken by the cold. It's like I'm standing in front of a freezer and someone just opened the door. I watch the shivers of air go out as I breathe. It's gotten colder. As proof of my suspicion, I watch a single snowflake fall in front of me. As it hits the ground, I see another and another. Soon, too many are falling at once that I can barely make out three men standing in front of me. Drake is unaffected by the iciness of the wind or the cold, wet snow. However, I notice the other two men's arms start to shake slightly.

"Who am I? If you really want to find out, threaten the lady again," he taunts. Is he completely insane? They have guns, and all he has is a sword. The men laugh and the shorter of the two loads his weapon as well. Drake doesn't move. "I can never lie. I can never die. I come for you with vengeance. I come for you with justice. I am balance. I am death." What kind of game is he playing with them, and was he just reciting a poem?

"Enough, on the count of three we shoot," the taller man announces annoyed. "One…two…" the man's next count was cut short as Drake finally makes his move.

He is over there so fast all I see is a couple of swings of his sword. He was nothing but a blur holding it. The taller man is down, and before the shorter one can even process what happened, he is cut down as well. In a matter of seconds, both of them are lying on the ground in front of me, dead. Like blades of grass, he mowed them both down like it was nothing. I let out a scream in horror. Drake ignores me. I know I should run, but I'm frozen in shock. Drake bends over the bodies. He moves his hand slowly over each limb. Both men quickly turn into ash and blow away with the wind. The blood that started pooling on the snow is covered by even more snow falling on top of it. Unless I had just witnessed it, I would have never even known they were there in the first place. Drake takes both his swords to the ground letting the wet snow clean off the blood that dripped down the steel. I get a sick feeling watching him. I don't think this is the first time he's done this. He stands and looks back at me. *Am I next?* The thought briefly crosses my mind.

"Leyla, please come with me. I know you're in shock and scared, but we need to move," he advises, his tone gentle. He stretches out his arm and extends me his left hand. I stay still like a deer in headlights. How can this charming man I shared a meal with at Queen's diner become a harbinger of death? "There may be more. We must get out of this storm. The temperature is well below freezing. If you keep standing out here, you'll freeze to death," he pleads taking a step closer to me. I finally reach for his hand hesitantly.

I'm not sure if I'm more scared of the thought of more people after me or what he would do to me if I didn't go with him. He leads me across the street and up one flight of stairs to a second-story apartment. He opens the door for us to walk in. The warmth hits me, and I feel like I can't breathe. I look around and realize something.

"Wait, I saw someone move in here months ago. Was that you? Have you been here this whole time?" I ask looking straight into his eyes. He slowly nods his head yes. I think I might throw up.

"Please sit. I'll explain everything," he offers, his voice still gentle. How can he be so calm after murdering two strangers? I panic. I don't want to stay here. I turn back towards the front door, and in a flash, he is now standing in front of me blocking the way out.

*How is he moving so fast?*

"It's snowing pretty heavily. It's hard to see. I don't think you should go back to your apartment," he points out in a hushed tone. He avoids eye contact with me and moves his head away from my face. "They know where you live," he reminds me. I walk slowly backward.

"So, you're planning on keeping me here against my will?" I accuse.

"No, but where are you going to go? You can't drive in this storm. Your closest friend is almost an hour away, and you can't go back to your apartment," he declares, and I didn't like that he knew where Kat lived. He has been avoiding my gaze this whole time, and it was a smart decision on his part. I'm sure my looks would tear him to pieces right now.

"So, I'm stuck here," I imply.

"Not forever. You can take my room," Darke points to a door behind me, "I'll stay out here," he adds as if to make me feel safe. I know what he said makes sense. I will be unable to safely drive far in this storm, and I didn't want to go back to my apartment if it wasn't safe. He is my only option, but I don't like it.

"I will stay until the storm is gone and the roads are safe enough to leave," I start to agree. "But I need my phone and my charger," I demand. If he is serious about letting me leave, he won't mind if I have my phone. He doesn't bother to respond. He zooms out the door, and within seconds, he is back with my charger and phone. He tries to hand them to me, but I refuse to take them. He set's them on the kitchen bar to my left and slowly backs away from me.

"I'm sorry," he apologizes running his fingers through his hair, "I couldn't let them take you. I didn't want to kill them, but they left me no choice. I didn't plan on us meeting again like this," he admits and there is nothing but remorse in his voice. His eyes finally lock onto mine, and they hold my gaze.

"I don't care," I comment harshly. Drake twitches his lips in agony at my response. "Sorry or not, you just murdered two men," I tell him honestly.

"Only to save you," he whispers. That doesn't make me feel better about it. Yes, without him, they would have taken me, and who knows what for, but that didn't mean I approved of murder.

"Did you have to kill them?" I ask wanting to know. "I saw how fast you moved. If you really wanted to, you could have taken their guns and simply knocked them out," I voice my opinion.

"Yes, you're right," he agrees, and I'm taken aback. "However, tomorrow they would have returned, and it wouldn't have been a headfirst approach like today." He takes a few steps closer to me. "They would have broken into your apartment and taken you. Or they would have sent someone else you didn't recognize to grab you at school. Whoever wants you is still out there, and next time they will send someone with more intelligence, or someone much more dangerous," he says in his defense. I get it. In his mind it was the only option that permanently guaranteed my safety. "Leyla, do you have any idea why they wanted to take you?" he asks seriously.

"No, I don't," I answer truthfully. "However, you're not the only one stalking me," I reveal.

"What are you talking about?" he asks puzzled. "Are you saying someone has been following you? Who?"

"Why does it matter?" I snap back.

"If someone else is following you, it could be the person responsible for sending those men. Who is it?" his tone is elevated, but with worry, not with anger.

"I don't think he did. He told me he was following me to protect me," I reply.

"What is his name, Leyla?" he asks again with urgency.

"Darrius," I reply, not liking that I had to say blue eyes' name aloud. To my surprise Drake looks even more displeased than me. I watch his face turn a few shades lighter and his eyes widen. He lightly wraps his fingers around the upper part of my arm. He looks me straight in the eyes. He is so close I can feel his breath on my skin. I notice for the first time that inside his green irises he has slight black slits, almost like a reptile. My heart stops, not because I'm scared of him, but because he is so close. This is the first time I've ever let a guy this close to me, ever.

"Darrius, you've met Darrius?" he asks softly, his face growing paler by the moment. I nod yes, and he slowly lets go of my arm.

Now I'm the confused one. We both hear a knock on the door. I freeze in place as my heart sinks into my chest. Drake puts one of his fingers up to my lips. I nod, understanding what he is asking. He shifts his eyes to his room, and I follow his gaze. I back away into his room and close the door, pressing my ear up to it to listen. I hear Drake answer his door and there is an exchange of greetings. I can tell the other voice is a man's but other than that, nothing. It gets quiet, and for a while I start to feel nervous. I can't help myself. I slowly open the door. I'm not prepared for what I see on the other side.

"Darrius!" I exclaim in complete shock.

I march out in a hurry, and I see him. He and Drake break apart and turn their focus to me. I think I might have interrupted a heated discussion they were having. He didn't say anything at first, which gave me time to soak up what I was seeing. Like Drake, he is wearing similar leather armor, and his hair on the top part is slicked back in place. The sides aren't long enough to need gel. He has one long sword attached to the sides of his armor. Why are they both dressed in similar outfits, and why are they both carrying weapons like it's perfectly normal?

"I know seeing me must be unwanted," he chooses his words carefully, "but I'm here because of what I told you before. I'm here for your protection," he explains.

"Well, I think you're a little late," Drake chimes in sarcastically crossing his arms together. He doesn't look happy about Darrius being here.

*Wait…*

"You two know each other, don't you?" The unsettling thought finally hits me. I don't know what took me so long to put it together. Neither one of them disagrees with me, which is all the confirmation I need. I can't believe this. "You've both been in on this from the start, stocking me, watching me," I feel betrayed, sick, and humiliated all at the same time.

"Leyla, we didn't know about one another. It wasn't until I saw Drake tonight come to your aid that I even knew he was here. We do know each other, but we didn't plot together against you. I can assure you we both have our reasons for watching out for you," Darrius speaks up sternly. He acts appalled that I would even imply such a thing.

"Well, whatever is going on here, it is going to stop. I'm not in the mood to hear any explanations. I've had enough craziness for one night," I announce firmly. "I'm going to go back into this room, and as soon as the snow stops, I'm leaving!" I inform him a little too loudly. "As for the future, I'm serious when I say I don't want to see either of you again." I look mostly at Darrius since this is the second time I've had to tell him this. Darrius looks over at Drake with disapproval.

"We can't make her stay. I've already told her that she could leave once the roads are safe," Drake fills him in, sounding put out that he had to in the first place. Darrius furrows his brows.

Before anything else can be said, I grab my phone and its charger, walk back into the room and close the door. I stop and lock the door behind me. I know it won't do any good against them. I know they could both break down this door if they wanted to. However, something about it makes me feel better all the same.

I flip on a lamp and look around. This barely qualifies as a bedroom. There is only a bed, a nightstand, and a lamp. It looks lonely and sad. There is nothing personal about this room, and somehow I doubt this is even where Drake lives. I look down at my phone, and it's after ten. I feel my adrenaline wearing off, and in its place, exhaustion is setting in. I look out his window and the snow still falls just as hard as when it first started. I didn't see any signs of it stopping anytime soon. I curl up in a ball on Drake's bed as tears begin to fall down my cheek. I start to sob silently in Drake's pillow. I couldn't help it.

My emotions came bursting out. I didn't want them to hear me, so I try to cry as quietly as possible. Why would someone want to take me? Where would they have taken me if they had gotten me? Who is behind all this? What was so important about me that two strange boys would be following me around to protect me? *If that's what they were doing*, I thought. The scene of death haunts me. Even though it happened in a flash, I won't ever be able to forget it. The only comfort I feel right now is coming from the smell of Drake's cologne in his pillow. It's somewhat calming. I try to think of anything other than those two men, the ones who died, and those outside the door right now. It's no use though, the tears keep coming. I cry myself to sleep.

### Darrius Stone

"She is scared of us," I say aloud after hearing Leyla lock the door to Drake's bedroom.

"Can you blame her?" Drake ask rhetorically. "We've both been following her, and she doesn't know why. Someone just tried to grab her, and she doesn't know why. Although, I think you and I could probably guess. Not to mention I did just kill two people in front of her. She's had a lot happen to her in a matter of thirty minutes," he states, not telling me anything I didn't already know. "I offered to explain everything to her," he adds.

"Don't you think that's a bad idea?" I interject looking at him crossly.

"No, I think withholding the truth from her is just making it worse. I think she deserves the truth, especially after tonight, and we are the only two that can give it to her," Drake disagrees. I'm not sure I'm for telling her something that could make things worse. However, I did agree that we were the only two that could offer her some type of explanation.

"Well, it seems you have earned her trust better than I. I'm sure she will talk to you in the morning," I guess. Drake shakes his head no at me.

"Whatever trust I had was lost when I got her to agree to come up here with me and to stay until morning," he argues. "I'm afraid we are in the same place with her now," he informs me letting out a sigh. It's been years since I've seen him, and yet he hasn't changed a bit. The thought of us being in the same

.

room together is a fact I would have never believed, but here we are. Not only that, but we were both drawn to her, and we didn't even know it.

"Do you think she will leave in the morning?" I ask though I feel like I might already know the answer. It would just be nice to hear it confirmed.

"Yes, I think so," he replies. If Leyla does leave, I will follow. I look over at Drake and wonder if he will do the same. Silence falls between us and neither of us knows what to say next it would seem. "Did you run here?" he guesses breaking the awkwardness.

"I did," I confirm.

"You're welcome to rest on the couch," he offers walking over to the window looking outside. "I'll keep watch. I'll let you know if anything comes up," he promises. Part of me wants to refuse, but I need to rest and recoup my energy. I walk over to his couch and lay down. Hopefully, I won't sleep too long.

I had barely drifted off when I felt someone's hand on my shoulder. I rise to see Drake staring down at me. I rub my hand over my face and look up at him. "What's wrong?" I ask getting straight to the point.

"It's Leyla," he answers and I'm instantly standing. I follow him to the door where she is sleeping. "Listen," he instructs. I close my eyes and concentrate, blocking out every other noise around me but her. I hear her tossing and turning and the bed squeaking from it. She is breathing inconsistently, and her heartbeat is racing. I look up at Drake annoyed. I didn't see what was so important about her dreaming. "Just keep listening," he insists. I'm not sure what I'm supposed to be hearing. Moments pass, and then, I hear her cry out. She whispers one word, one name. I take a few steps back from the door and look up at Drake. "You heard it too then?" I nod my head yes. "Do you think she knows?"

"No, I think it's just a dream, one she probably won't remember in the morning. I think she would have recognized us if she knew anything," I reply thinking logically.

"Right, but this can't be a coincidence," he retorts, and I couldn't completely disagree. "Darrius if it is somehow *her*, what are we supposed to do?" he states thinking aloud.

"It's not *her*," I reply angrily clenching my fists. We both stare at each other. We both want to say something to each other, but neither of us wants to go first.

"If that's what you think, then why are you here?" he questions me. I'm not too fond of having to think about that answer. "If there weren't just an ounce of hope, you would leave her alone as she asked, but we're both still here, aren't we?" he continues raising one of his eyebrows. I break eye contact.

"It can't be her," I pause, not wanting to say the rest, "she's gone." I walk away from the door hearing him follow behind me. "There is something else going on. I want an explanation, and that is the only reason I'm still here," I admit.

"I trust you will still be here when she wakes up?" he asks but I'm not sure why. "Will you stay here with her if I leave?" I look at him with surprise.

"You're leaving?" I reply unsure where he would go or why he would leave after what just happened.

"Briefly, I want answers just like you. I would also like to prove you wrong as well, but that's not important," my old friend adds grinning.

"Just where do you think you are going to find these answers," I demand to know? He just looks back at me letting me realize the answer for myself. "No, you can't. If you go start poking around, someone might be curious and follow you back here. You are going to bring more unwanted attention. This isn't a good idea," I object.

"It's not your choice. I'm going to head for the closest Order. I'm just going to do a bit of reading. No one will think anything of me being there. You may be able to hide your feelings from yourself, but I can still see right through you after all this time. You want to know just as much or more as I do about what's going on. We both felt something pulling us here. We both felt the pull to her. Tonight proves our instincts were right. We are no longer the only ones that know about her. I give you my word no one will know what I'm up to. No one will find her," he tries to assure me.

Before I can object, he disappears, and I don't bother to go after him. I look over to the room where Leyla is asleep. Nothing is more important than her safety, so he better be right about this.

# Chapter 7
## New Year, Old Feelings

**Leyla Gray**

I wake up to a sunlit room. I panic for a moment forgetting where I am. *You're in Drake's room*, I remind myself calming down. I look over at the door to my left. It wasn't a dream, last night happened. Speaking of dreams, I had one about both of them last night. I was in an outrageous and outdated ball gown. I was dancing with one and then the other being past back and forth vigorously between them. I couldn't make out the room or any of the faces dancing near us, just them. *Why did I have to dream about them*? Like I wasn't seeing them enough already. At least it was a better dream than my normal one. I didn't have that one, thankfully. Despite the cold outside, I slept warmly last night.

I push the covers off me and roll out of bed. I walk over to the adjourning bathroom. I see myself in the mirror and look like how I feel, tired and stressed. I rub my fingers over the circles under my eyes. My green eyes look cloudy and dull. I wash some water over my face hoping to wake myself up. I pull my unruly hair over to one side in a low ponytail. I happened to have a hair tie with me. I walk over to the door, but my hand stops at the handle. I asked them both to leave last night, but something tells me they're both still out there. Could I keep my cool if they were? I would be lying to myself if I didn't say I had questions I wanted to ask. Questions I might even consider sticking around to hear answered. *Are you going to leave, Leyla*, a little voice asks? I want to tell it to shut up.

I turn the knob and walk out into the hall. Delicious smells of bacon and syrup fill my nose. My tummy grumbles in response. I can see the dining table full of food. There is a bowl of scrambled eggs, a plate of bacon, and a platter of pancakes. It looks so good. I walk straight up to the table before realizing I'm not the only one in the room.

"I hope you're hungry?" Darrius blurts our standing behind me, grabbing the orange juice from the fridge.

"Did you make all this?" I ask in astonishment. He nods yes. I start to pull out my chair to sit and he is there behind me in an instant pushing it in for me. I guess Drake's not the only one with super speed. Speaking of. "Where is Drake?" I ask looking around to an otherwise empty room.

"He left in search of answers," he replies vaguely avoiding my gaze. "I'm sure he will be back soon," he adds as an afterthought.

"You don't approve?" I assume. He looks over at me from across the table, now seated. His face is unreadable. His hair isn't as flat as last night, but he is still in his armor. He looks stiff, and I can't help but to wonder if he ever relaxes.

"Drake does as he wishes," he humors me. "We should eat before it gets cold," he suggests trying to steer me away from asking another question.

I wonder what answers Drake left to find. Did he know something I don't? They knew each other. That much was clear, but did I know them? I already had a sense about Darrius. Since the first moment we met, something was telling me that we knew each other. Drake, well there are plenty of things about him that seems familiar to me. So maybe I did know both of them, but how? I certainly wasn't going to get any answers from my present company. My stomach growls again. I decide to push my questions for later, and focus on making my plate. I take one bite of the pancake and I'm on cloud nine. Everything is delicious. It sure beats the weeks of cereal I've been eating. Who would have thought a statue could cook? I scarf down one bite after the other, and between me and him, there wasn't much food left. I hear my phone go off from Drake's room. Darrius looks over at me to see what I'm going to do. I get up from the table and grab it from the charger. It was Kat.

Kat: Hey. We are planning on going to NightSky around nine. You are still coming, aren't you???

Me: I had kind of a rough night, not sure.

Kat: Oh? Well too bad, you're coming! I have a dress for you. Do you want to come over early and get ready?

Me: I have a dress. I'll come, see you later.

I put my phone down and walk back into the kitchen. Darrius is putting up the food and running water over the dishes. There was something so ordinary about the act. It doesn't seem to fit him at all. He glances at me.

"Something wrong?"

"Drake promised I could go. You're not going to stop me from leaving, are you?" I question.

"No, I will not stop you," he replies with a short-tempered tone.

"You're not happy about my decision?" I surmise.

"No, and I cannot promise I won't follow you," he admits, and I can't help but smile at his candor. I didn't want him looming in the shadows all night watching me. I wouldn't be able to stop thinking about him being out there. So, I believe I have another idea that will satisfy both of us.

"I have a proposal for you," I state. Darrius turns off the water to give me his full attention. "Tonight is New Year's. I plan on meeting my friends at a bar near the campus to celebrate. I've given up on the idea of you leaving me be, so if you're going to tag along, why don't you come with me," I suggest. He looks at me unsure what to say. "You don't agree?"

"I don't think you should be going out. It doesn't seem like a wise choice, given last night's events," he disapproves. "I believe you would be better off here, at least until we know what's going on," he suggests. "There is no doubt someone out there is still looking for you," he adds ominously. I'm not surprised by his objections.

"I hate to disappoint you, but I'm not going to stay caged up when we don't know what's going on. I won't spend my whole life hiding while you try and figure it out. I'm trying to meet you halfway. Honestly, I don't want you around at all, but I've decided to give you a chance. So no more disappearing, no more hiding in the shadows, no more avoiding my questions, and no more secrets. My way, your *choice*," I end throwing his word back at him. He stays silent for a few moments, hopefully thinking over my offer.

"Very well, I will escort you tonight," he finally answers, his voice is calm, and his face is still unreadable. He walks over into my personal space making me feel uneasy by how close he is. His eyes are intense as they stare into mine. They hold me in place, and I couldn't move away even if I wanted to. "However, if there is any sign of danger, I will take you as far away from it as I possibly can," he warns.

"Alright, I understand." How could I say no to that?

We make our way back to my apartment. Darrius is at my back with both his sword held high. I pray no one sees us, and if they do, I can only imagine what they must think. Hopefully, that he is just really into cosplay. I saw him grab some of Drake's clothes to change into for later tonight before we left.

"Couldn't you have changed?" I suggest.

"No one can see me but you," he replies.

I didn't stop for an explanation as I hurry to my door through the thick snow. The door is already unlocked. I never had a chance to come back inside and lock it. The lights are still on as well. I pull my luggage from the front door into my room. I start to unpack without a word to him. I fought the urge to stay in my room until it was time to leave, but I felt it would be rude.

After I finished unpacking, I walk out to see Darrius in the middle of changing into regular clothes. He had on Drake's jeans, but he was in the process of buttoning up his shirt. I quickly avert my eyes, but the image is still there. His pale pink skin is perfectly smooth, no scratches or scars, just muscles. I make a noise to clear my throat, announcing my presence.

"Leyla, pardon my appearance. I didn't see you come out," he tells me quickly finishing the last button. I should be the one apologizing, I did walk in on him, not the other way around. "Did those men happen to tell you why they were after you?" he asks bringing up an unwanted subject.

"No," I frown but answer, "but do you?" I ask back. "You seem to know I needed protection. You said you didn't know why at the time, but I feel like maybe you know more than me at this point," I accuse.

"I don't know exactly why, and I don't want to put any false ideas in your head. I won't bring it up again, but if you do think of anything, please let me know." His eyes look me over me, and I wish I knew what he is thinking. "I'm sure you have questions yourself. I told you I couldn't lie, so please ask me anything you like," he directs the conversation back to me.

I'm surprised by his offer, but I don't hesitate. "Out there," I look over to the door leading outside, "you said no one could see you, but I could. You also commented in the barn that I could see you like I shouldn't be able to. Explain."

"I have a magical aura or cloaking around me at all times. It only works on mortals. Unless, I let it down they can't see me. The day in the library I was fully cloaked, but you came right up to me anyway," he divulges.

"So, are you saying I'm not human?" I question.

"No, you are, at least I believe so," he answers, and I feel somewhat relieved.

"Are you saying there are people out there that aren't?" I go on, a little worried about the answer I will get back.

"Yes, there are other people out there that have magic. If their magic is strong enough, they can see through mine," he explains. "Would you like to know anything else?"

"Yes, I have a lot more questions," I reply, but I pause. "However, I'm not completely sure I'm ready to hear them," I reveal. "Something tells me you're not going anywhere. I'll have plenty of time to find out. I want one last normal night," I request. One more normal day to spend with my best friends before he turns my world as I know it upside down more than he already has.

"As you wish," he agrees. His eyes look into mine with understanding, as if he knows what I'm thinking. I look over at my clock on the microwave. We still have hours until we need to leave. I decide to sit on the couch and turn on the TV to pass the time. I look over at him and give him a look that it's okay to sit down as well.

"Do you have a favorite show?" I turn to ask him. He looks blankly back at me.

He comes over and sits down next to me. "I don't watch television," he informs me. Why am I not surprised? I wonder what he does do in his spare time. I flip through and decide on the cooking channel. It's always my go-to when I can't decide anything else. "What is this?" he asks seeming interested. He leans forward his eyes fixed on the screen. I didn't reply, as it's pretty self-explanatory. I just let him watch so he can answer his own question.

I had unknowingly dozed off. To my surprise, when I woke, I had a blanket wrapped around me. Aslo, the top of my head was ever so slightly leaning on Darrius' shoulder. I look up at him intime to notice he is still glued to the TV. When I stir, he looks down at me.

"Did you have a good rest?" he asks softly.

"Yes, actually," I reply. I had slept, actually slept. No dreams. "What time is it?" I lean away from him, trying not to make it a big deal that I had fallen asleep on him. I let out a little yawn.

"It's past seven," he answers.

"Oh, no! I need hurry. We are supposed to be at the bar by nine, and it's going to take at least an hour to get there after this snow." I jump up and head straight for my shower. Kat is going to kill me if I'm late.

After my shower I dig through my closet and find a specific dress. I was never brave enough to wear it, and it has been hiding among my clothes since I bought it. The dress is a neutral color with a gold sequence shining all around it. It has long slit sleeves that fall evenly around my knees. The zipper ran up my back, and I'm only able to get it halfway up. Curse it, too many trips to Queen's. It's a little snug. I give my hand a rest and move on to my hair. I blow dry it and straighten it. It lays long around my shoulders dropping below my chest. I apply my makeup as best as I can remember Kat doing it. It comes out as natural-looking when I'm done, which I'm happy with. I get up and try the zipper again, but it won't budge. I'm already running late, and I didn't have any other dress to wear.

"Darrius," I cry out defeated. I hear him walking down the hall. I turn around to see him stop at my doorway, his eyes looking anywhere but to me. As much as I appreciated his chivalry, now wasn't the time. "Come on, I need your help," I inform him. He doesn't move. "It's alright, really, please I can't get this dang zipper to come up anymore," I explain. He slowly walks over to me. I move my hair pulling it to the front of my body. I feel one of his hands touch my shoulder gently as his other hand slides the zipper easily up. "Thank you," I tell him.

As I turn back around, he nods his head and then leaves the room. I wasn't sure, but he almost looked a little nervous. I take a look at myself in the mirror. My dress is gleaming. I walk out into the living room as Darrius is pulling on his jacket. The jacket and his slacks fit a little short due to him being slightly taller than Drake. The shirt is nice and tight, and its light blue color goes well with his pale skin.

"You look very dashing," I state.

"You look lovely as well," he compliments me back, and I feel my face warm up. I walk up to him and he lets me straighten his collar. He stiffens straight as a board on my contact, but he doesn't stop me. "Do you have a coat?" He asks, his eyes avoiding mine. "It's cold outside," he informs me looking down at my exposed legs briefly.

"Yes, I'll grab it and we can go," I reply. I think that was the most normal conversation we've ever had.

I had decided to let him drive. It was almost comical watching him adjust the seat and the mirrors trying to get comfortable. I sent Kat a text that we were on our way. I don't want her blowing up my phone when we don't make it at exactly nine. We made good time and park at a nearby parking garage; after I explained to him that the bar parking lot would already be full at this point. Darrius comes over to let me out, like a gentleman. I take his hand and as I step out one of my heels slips out from under me on the slick running board. I fall forward, right into his chest. His arms catch me, and I throw mine around his lower back for support. I feel his grip tighten around my hips as he steadies me. I raise my head and our noses are almost touching. I'm now about the same height as him since he is holding me up. My head starts to spin, and I know what's coming next. I close my eyes seeing flashing images, but I can make them out this time. They are reels of what looks like Darrius and me. We are eating or reading. Other times we are holding hands. I see Drake as well in some of them. We appear to be fighting. My head starts to throb.

"Stop!" I cry out. It's too much, too much at once. I can't process it.

"Leyla, what's wrong," Darrius' voice sounds concerned? "Am I hurting you?" The images stop as I feel my feet hit the ground. I slowly open my eyes to see a worried look in Darrius' eyes.

"No, you didn't. I just had a head rush," I tell him, and I let him go. He does the same. "Thank you for catching me," I express. *What did I just see*? Why could I see the images this time? Were they always of Darrius and Drake, and me? It couldn't be me. I decide to keep it to myself for now. "Let's go. My friends are waiting," I nudge him and start walking.

We hurry to the bar and there is a bit of line. As we wait, I start to feel colder and colder. The snow begins to fall again, but it's soft and slow, unlike last night. I start to shiver. Darrius pulls me into his chest, and I can hear his heartbeat, it's starting to beat fast. His warmth is welcome, so allow him to hold me. Once we reach the end of the line he lets go, and I can't get into the building fast enough. We stand in the entrance and the heat starts to warm my frozen limbs. I take my coat off to give to the young-looking guy at the coat check. Darrius keeps his. I wasn't sure why since it's very warm in here. I notice his eyes canvassing the room. I'm not sure what he is looking for. I doubt I'm in any danger here.

"Ley, is that you?" a female voice calls out, and I know by the nickname who the voice belongs to. I'm shocked to see her behind the counter of the bar.

"Bridget, what are you doing here?" I ask in return. I walk up closer to her, so we don't have to keep yelling over everyone.

"I work here," she replies, and I look down to see her black work apron. There are a few pens, straws, and a small notebook sticking out of it. "I need all the money I can get to feed my coffee addiction," she jokes flashing me a quick smile. She is wearing makeup making her appear older than she is. She is wearing a tightly fitted black T-shirt with the NightSky logo, which is an aura of lights. She looks past me, and her face tightens when she's who is with me. "This wouldn't happen to be Cinderella, would it?" Before I could respond, I see a long arm reach around me with an open handheld out to Bridget.

"Darrius, it's nice to meet you," they exchange a handshake. I look up at Darrius, who is giving me a weird look for being called Cinderella. I didn't want to go into that explanation.

"No wonder you didn't want to give up looking for him," Bridget winks at me. I look past her to the mirror wall shelved with a never-ending variety of alcohol, and my face is beat red. "I can take you two back to my section if you want," she offers picking up two menus.

"Sounds good. Lead the way," I tell her. I'll just have to grab Kat and Kent to come over once I found them.

We follow her towards the back and walk along the long black bar that stretches down almost the whole wall to our left. There are several bar tables to our right, and in the far corner is a small dance floor and modern jukebox. My favorite thing about this place is the ceiling. It's painted to look like the night sky, hence the name, and there are small lights the size of dimes that lit up like stars. The music is blaring and many conversations are going on around us at once. I look around noticing everyone is dressed up. I'm not the only one. All the TVs are set to the channel showing the count down to the ball drop in New York. Bridget seats us at the very back next to the door that leads to an outside gated patio. There are lights strung up everywhere making it nice and bright, but no one is out there because of the cold.

"I'll be right back," Bridget says setting the menus down on the top of the table.

The tabletop is black marble, with flecks of silver, matching the bar. It feels cool to the touch, even though my long sleeves. I recoil my arms and shiver. Darrius silently takes off his coat and places it around my shoulders. I look up and give him an appreciative glance. I turn and start to search the bar for Kent. I wasn't going to waste my time on Kat being as short as she is. Sure enough, I see his copper-top hair bobbing in and out of the crowd. He notices me and begins to pull Kat over. She looks confused for a moment until she catches sight of me as well. She runs through the crowd to hug me, almost knocking me out of the chair.

"Did you think I wouldn't come?" I ask between breaths because she was squeezing me so hard.

"Maybe, you look amazing!" She observes, finally letting me go, her eyes giving me a once over. She looks great as well with her silver smooth drees. The sleeves are black lace as well as the hem at the bottom of her dress. She has her hair pulled back away from her face in a bun. "Whose coat?" she inquires. I look behind me to see Darrius not there. *I thought I told him no disappearing.* I find him through the glass sitting outside in the cold. What is he doing out there?

"I have a date," I confess, turning back to see a look of surprise on her face at my answer.

"Is Drake here?" she guesses pleasingly.

"No, not Drake," I shake my head and turn to point outside. "That is Darrius. He's the guy, the one from the day at the library," I explain gladly proving I wasn't seeing things.

"Leyla, he's cute!" she exclaims impressed.

"Hey, I'm standing right here," Kent chimes in. I guess he doesn't appreciate his fiancé ogling another man. I let out a little laugh. Kat just turns back and gives him a weak slap on the shoulder. They both sit down across from me as Bridget walks back up.

"Hey sorry about that. I grabbed these for you," she informs us and sets down a tray of chili cheese fries. "They're on the house," she winks at me, and something tells me they weren't meant for our table. "I'll have someone come get your drink orders. I had to clock out. It was great to see you. I didn't mean to interrupt," she states glancing over at Kat and Kent.

"Oh, thank you. You didn't have to stay for me. What are you doing now?" I ask.

"I don't have any plans exactly," she confesses and shrugs.

"Why don't you hang with us?" I offer. I wouldn't mind getting to know her a little better. Kat and Kent didn't object. She looks unsure and proceeds to push back some of her corkscrew brown hair behind her ears.

"Okay, if you insist," she agrees and sets down, pulling another chair out from someone else behind her in the process. She flashes a sweet smile at the guy, and he didn't seem to mind so much that she just stole his seat. She wasn't shy.

The other waitress comes up and we all order drinks. Well, I get water for now, and the others order something with alcohol. I almost forgot about Darrius for a moment. I make a quick introduction of Bridget to Kat and Kent and vice versa. I leave them to get better acquainted and slip out of my seat to check on my bodyguard. As my feet touch the floor, I feel something hit my thigh. I reach down into his jacket and realize why he didn't want to give it to the coat check guy. His sword is conveniently hidden inside his coat pocket. I push my way outside. Once the frigid air hits me I'm instantly cold all over. Darrius notices my presence and I can see him tense a little. I walk around and sit down next to him.

"I thought we said no hiding," I remind him.

"I can see more clearly out here. If anyone makes a move, I'll know," blue-eyes explains.

"Maybe, but this is supposed to be my last night of normal. You hanging back in the shadows watching everyone isn't exactly what I meant," I flash him a frown. "Plus, was bringing your sword along really necessary?" I question revealing the handle to him.

"I brought it as a precaution. You'll understand once you're ready for me to explain everything to you," Darrius says defensively. I pick up on a slight accent I hadn't heard before.

"Where are you from Darrius?" I blurt out, and he wasn't expecting my question.

"I was born in England, but that was a very long time ago," his eyes fade away from me as if he is thinking back on it. I notice an unsettling look on his face. Since he is sitting in the shadows his eyes look dark, almost black. His hair, normally gleaming, looks more like strands of hay, thick and dull. The tip of his nose and his cheeks are nice a rosy from sitting out here in the cold. I can't see how he can stand to be out here without his coat on. "I did promise to escort you, and I can't lie," he groans shifting and pulling himself up.

Something has changed in me within this past day, I feel drawn to him. *Was it because of my visions and my dream of us dancing?*

"Right. Well, we better head back inside. I want to introduce you to someone," I smile. I wasn't scared of him anymore. In fact, I'm looking forward to talking with him later and asking him more questions. I hold out my hand, and to my surprise, he takes it. His hand is cold, and it sends a shiver up my arm.

Hours fly by and I'm stunned that Darrius makes for good company. He carried on conversations with the others without shying away. Either he is the best actor I know, or he just doesn't like talking to me. I notice Bridget eyeing him throughout the night. Not in a he's cute way but in more of a watchful one. It's like she knows something about him I don't. Her, Kat, and Kent, however, are getting along swimmingly. Kent has dared Bridget to kiss the first guy she sees at midnight, and she has enthusiastically accepted. As it reaches midnight, the bar counting down in unison from twenty. All eyes around the room are glued to the TV screens. "Five, four, three, two, one..."

# Chapter 8

## Truth and Nothing but the Truth

"Happy New Year!" all of our voices ring out harmoniously as confetti starts to fly around everywhere like snow.

People race from one to another, kissing and hugging each other. Some are toasting and gulping down their drinks. I look over catching Kent lean down to kiss Kat sweetly. As promised, Bridget grabs one of the waiters walking by and surprises him with a big kiss on the mouth. Kent and Kat start to laugh almost out of their seats, and I can't help but let out a chuckle myself.

I turn to look at Darrius, and much to my astonishment, he is smiling too. A big and full smile comes over his face while he's watching Bridget. I can't believe what I'm seeing right now. This isn't the solemn, uptight Darrius I've come to know. The happiness in his face makes him look even more handsome than he normally does. I close my eyes, and suddenly flashes of him come to me. My head doesn't hurt this time, maybe because I'm not trying to fight them back. I see him smiling happily in each one of them. He looks carefree and attractive. The visions quickly pass, and I'm filled with a new emotion for him. It almost feels as if someone has taken possession of me and I'm no longer in control.

I stand up on the top of my toes and rest my hands around his shoulders. His smile vanishes at my touch as his eyes look into mine. He seems unsure of what is going on. He didn't move though, and I have his undivided attention. I close my eyes and lean up and press my lips against his. Something inside me is satisfied as if I had been subconsciously waiting to do this since the moment I laid eyes on him. Satisfaction turns into longing, and longing turns to something else I couldn't admit to myself. I wasn't sure how he felt until his arms wrapped around my waist and my dress gathers against my lower back. He pulls me in and kisses me back. Our kiss is deep and slow. My body starts to heat up. His lips are soft, and his body feels warm pressed up against mine. He tightens his grip. His hand begins to move up my back to my neck pulling me in even deeper to him. Our connection becomes too intense. I open my eyes and whatever feeling I felt pushing me to do this slowly fades away. It's like I woke up from a daydream. He looks at me for answers that I can't give him. *What did you just do, Leyla*? He lets go of me, and I take off his coat and swing it over my seat. It's too warm. I'm too warm. I can't look into his eyes anymore. I make my way through the sea of people. I can't breathe in here. I need out.

I push open the door and inhale more air than I need. The music and voices go quiet as the door closes behind me. There is a bus bench a block down the road. I walk to it and sit down. Something had taken over me. Something consumed my thoughts and my actions. I'm scared of whatever it was. I wasn't in control of my own body. What's even more frightening are these feelings for Darrius. I just met him. I don't even know if I like him. So why did it feel like I have an intimate relationship with him? Why did it feel like I've known him all my life? Maybe it's time to go home and ask all those questions I've been putting off.

After I calm myself down, I could face him again. I take a long breath and tilt my head up towards the sky. I see a small crescent moon floating in and out of the clouds rolling by. My warmth starts to fade, and I feel how frosty it is out here. I look back down to see a womanly figure crossing the street towards me. She walks right up to me.

"Are you feeling alright?" she asks, her voice high-pitched.

She acts concerned, but her tone doesn't sound it. She is very abrupt and stands with her arm on her hip leaning her head to the side looking over me. She's wearing tall black boots and a short fitted black dress. She also had on a long white leather coat. Her skin is barely darker than the jacket. Her hair is long, thin, and blonde hanging in a low ponytail over her shoulder.

"I'm fine, thank you," I reply feeling a little uncomfortable. The stranger smiles at me wickedly and I'm not sure how to take it. Whatever she came up to me for, it wasn't to check on my health.

"You don't seem like the kind of girl that's going to come quietly," she observes as a statement making me tense up with fear.

What is she talking about? I look around at the empty streets all around us. There is no one around to hear me scream. I'm so stupid. Why didn't I listen to Darrius? Why did I run outside by myself? I make a run for the bar. I look back over my shoulder to see her laughing at me. Her mouth moves, but I didn't hear the words she said. I feel something hit me from behind. Whatever the feeling, it resonates throughout my body. It's the strangest sensation I've ever felt. I can't fight what's happening to me. My limbs start to get heavier and heavier forcing me to stop. I wind up lying face down on the cold pavement. I hear the heels of her boots hit the ground as she walks closer to me. She bends down to gloat and smiles at me again cruelly. Her eyes are glowing white around where her eye color should be. She mouths a word and touches me on the forehead. My eyes start closing, unwillingly. I hear her laughing at me as I fall into darkness.

### Darrius Stone

I watch Leyla run out, and I can't bring myself to stop her. I'm not sure what came over her or me. I push past my emotions about the kiss, leaving me with an uneasy feeling. She's been gone too long. I abruptly excuse myself from the group and grab my coat. Leyla's friends don't seem to question me going after her. As I step outside and she's nowhere to be found. Something's wrong. *She wouldn't just leave*, I tell myself. Doubting for a moment, I speed off to the Jeep, it's still there. I speed back to the bar after running the block in a flash, and there is no sign of her. My stomach turns in knots as I start to worry she didn't leave here out of her own desire. I curse myself for not running after her sooner. I'm supposed to be here to protect her. How could I let her go off by herself? I start to pace back and forth, trying to think of what to do. All that kept popping up in my head was our kiss. *Why, Leyla, why did you have to kiss me*? I held her at bay, but I don't know how much resolve I have left. I close my eyes and try to connect with her mind, I know it's a long shot, but it's my only option at this point. There is nothing but blackness, so much for that.

"Hey, Ley forgot her purse," I turn around to see Bridget walk out with Leyla's purse in her hand. She looks at me and then looks around. "Where's Ley?" she asks, sounding concerned. I stay silent because I don't have the answer. "You don't know, do you?" she guesses. I glare at her, that comment was not helping. "Aren't you Guardians supposed to be able to locate your charges? Are you new to this or something?" she mocks.

"Who are you?" I ask harshly. I haven't used any magic in front of her, so how does she know what I am? I pull out one of my swords and point it towards her. I'm not going to take any chances. "Did you have something to do with this? Do you know where Leyla is? I warn you I don't play games."

"Whoa, calm down Cinderella. I come in peace," she protests throwing up her arms.

"My name is Darrius," I correct her. "Leyla was almost kidnaped yesterday, and it's not by chance she is gone now. If you're her friend, explain to me how you know what I am and prove you had nothing to do with this," I demand taking a step closer.

"Don't get mad at me because you lost her," she hisses, and I see her eyes light up for a brief moment.

"You're a Caster," I announce. *I didn't see that coming.* "Explain yourself," I insist.

"Oh please, I saw you that day in the library when you were cloaked. Leyla wasn't the only one that saw past your magic," she informs me, though she isn't happy about it.

"Very well," I accept her explanation lowering my sword. "If you're not part of this, then I guess we have nothing further to discuss," I state and hide my sword back in my coat.

"I'm not a part of this, but Ley is my friend. I'll help you find her, but not because I like you," she announces. I didn't care one way or the other. "I can just use a simple tracking spell. Luckily, I have something personal of hers, so it will make the connection more accurate," she gestures towards Leyla's purse.

"No," I pause, forgetting my manors, "thank you but I can't," I notify her.

"Well, I'm not asking, and I already told you, I'm not doing it to help you," she reminds me. I didn't say anything else. I can't stop her. Technically, she's not breaking any rules. She held on tightly to the purse. The Caster's eyes glow white as she begins to cast the spell. Tt's been a long time since I've been around her kind of magic.

"Now watch this fairy godmother in action," she speaks up no longer casting. I didn't feel like explaining to her that I've already seen how this spell works many times. "Follow me," she barks. A steady stream of fog starts to appear in front of her. Like a path, it forms only inches in front of us at a time and dissipates after we walk through it. She clutches the purse, silently walking to one road after the next. "Why couldn't you connect with her," she questions as we walk along. I debate whether or not to answer her. She is being helpful, at the moment, so I humor her.

"Leyla isn't my charge," I admit. "So I can't track her," I add. She didn't say anything else after that. I won't elaborate anymore. About ten minutes later she slows down, and the fog turns translucent. She comes to a stop, and we both look around the area to see if we can spot Leyla anywhere. I wondered for a moment if the spell has worked. I notice movement in one of the buildings at the end of the street. It looks to be abandoned, so there shouldn't be anyone there.

"I saw someone move behind one of those windows," I whisper over to Bridget. She nods as we both duck behind a white van parked not far down from the building. "I'm going to try and concentrate on what I can hear," I inform her, and she remains silent. I close my eyes and clear my thoughts. I focus on the building, I can hear a soft heartbeat, and steady breathing. Leyla seems to be asleep. There is another presence. They are speaking softly the same words over and over. I open my eyes and look over at Bridget with alarm.

"What is it, what did you hear?" She wrinkles her forehead. She looks concerned, and she should be.

"There is another Caster," I try to judge her reaction, but she doesn't flinch. "I think she is keeping Leyla asleep," I reveal.

"Did you hear anyone else, are you sure there is only one?" she confirms.

"Yes, I'm sure," I reply sternly. I don't like being questioned, especially from someone like her. "Are you sure you don't know what's going on?" I retort.

She rolls her eyes at me. "Just because I'm a Caster doesn't mean I know every other one in the area. Believe it or not, we try and keep to ourselves," she huffs defensively. I don't respond. "Look, if there is only one, I can help. I can create a distraction so you can slip in and grab Ley," she affirms. I look over at her feeling unsure. I'm not allowed to take help from her kind. Plus, just because she got me here doesn't mean I completely trust her. "Stop looking at me like that," she lets out a frustrated sigh, "stop wasting time worrying about me. I'll get you in, you get her out. Got it," she commands me crossing her arms.

"What gift do you have? How can you get me in?" I question not sure of her ability to promise such a thing. One wrong move and she could get me killed. If the Caster stops focusing on Leyla and decides to cast her spell on me instead, no one would be left to protect Leyla. I can't take any unnecessary chances.

"Don't worry, it's something useful, unlike your skills apparently," she retorts. Her eyes turn white again, and she smiles from ear to ear. I don't know whether to be impressed or worried.

## Leyla Gray

I hear a scream, a shrill, terrified scream. My eyes are allowed to open, and I feel fidget from the cold air around me. I'm lying on my back. That's all I know right now. I don't recognize where I am or how I got here. My eyes are heavy, and I'm having trouble keeping them open for more than a few moments at a time. My body aches and my limbs feel weighed down. I can't manage to move any faster than a sloth. I inch myself up little by little until I'm sitting upright. I look around, but I still can't comprehend where I am. It's dark, wherever this is. I see a small amount of light coming through underneath a door on the opposite side of the room. I'm guessing I'm inside some old dirty building. There is dust everywhere and cobwebs in every corner. How did I get here? I still can't remember. I feel lightheaded, and my head starts to sink towards the floor like a rock in the water. Before I hit the ground, I hear the door burst open, and someone's hand catch my head. Someone lifts me, and I feel their warmth against my cool skin. We start moving quickly. I look up, and through the slit in my eyes I make out two blue ones looking down at me. *Darrius, he came for me*. I don't have the strength to speak. I lean my head into his chest, and I blackout.

"Leyla," I hear a voice call out my name. "Leyla, you need to wake up," the voice states urgently. "Wake up," it pleads. I force my eyes open. I look around using my eyes, not turning my head. I recognize what I can see. I'm home. My eyes start to close again. "Don't go back to sleep. You need to wake up," the voice instructs. I reluctantly do as I'm told. I manage to turn my head to see Darrius sitting on the coffee table watching me. "You're home now," he confirms, and it feels good to hear the words aloud.

"What happened?" I ask. Everything is fuzzy. He looks over at me with concern. There is a gentleness in his eyes. "Can you help me sit up?" I ask knowing I won't be able to do it by myself. He leans over and pulls me up by my shoulders. My back settles into the couch. "You look worried; do I look that bad?" I joke, trying to lighten the mood.

"You look a little worse for wear but, you'll be fine once the effect wears completely off. Everyone's first time is a little different," he informs me. I give him a puzzled look. "You were exposed to magic. The person who took you was a Caster. She was using her power to keep you asleep. Once the magic is fully gone, you'll feel much better," he assures me.

"It doesn't sound as cool when he explains it," I hear a familiar voice. I turn surprised to see Bridget. She's standing in my hallway leaning against the wall. I look back at Darrius, waiting on one of them to explain what's going on.

"I thought you were resting?" Darrius asks his voice sounding annoyed. He looks back at me. I'm still waiting on an explanation. "Bridget helped me rescue you. She is a Caster, like the woman who took you," he enlightens me. I wasn't sure how to process this news. Out of everything I've learned about him and Drake, learning Bridget is a Caster is the most shocking revelation I've had yet.

"So Caster?" I look over at Bridget, and she nods. "Like a witch?" I try to understand. I see a frown cross her face.

"Most of them don't like that term. They normally prefer the latter," Darrius clarifies. "Bridget I'm grateful for your help, but I need to speak with Leyla privately," he tries to dismiss her politely. She rolls her eyes.

"Sure, thanks for the help, but now you better run away and hide so you can't hear what I say about you behind your back," she scoffs and walks into my bedroom slamming the door behind her. I look back at Darrius.

"Is it true? Are you planning on talking about her behind her back?" I just come out and ask.

"No, it's not like that. There are some things I'm going to tell you that she can't hear." I give him a look of disapproval. "I'm going to tell you what I am," he elaborates.

"I'm listening," I reply.

"Keep in mind everything I'm telling you isn't something you should know. It's also nothing you should tell anyone else." I nod in understanding. *Who am I going to tell anyway?* "Magic is something that comes from above," he chooses his last word carefully. I already can't wait to see where he is going with this. "The magical creatures you've heard about in fairy tales and lore, some of them are true, some of those creatures are real. Some still exist today. Many died off long ago, others are in hiding. We don't know if they're still around or not. We refer to them as demonkind, or magicalkind. Ages ago, mortals would make deals with demons, only the most powerful. They would sell their souls to have whatever kind of magic the demon could provide. Those who took the deal unknowingly passed on their magic to anyone that shared the same blood as them," he discloses. I look appalled. How could someone even think about doing that?

"So you're saying that someone, like Bridget, inherited her magic from a relative that sold their soul? Do they not still get powers from demons themselves now?" I ask.

"A new magicalkind hasn't been created in centuries, that we know of. So yes, Bridget got her magic through one of her ancestors. Drake and I on the other hand we were granted our magic from an angel. Our magical gifts cannot be passed down as we are technically not alive," he pauses and with good reason. I shake my head and lean forward a little.

"Wait, are you saying that you and Drake, you're both dead?" I can't believe that.

"Not dead, but we all did die tragic and early deaths. As far as the world is concerned, we no longer exist. We belong to the Order of the Guardians. Our magic was bestowed upon us to help people. Have you ever heard the term grim reaper or guardian angel?" he asks, and I shake my head yes. "We are both. As a Guardian we can cloak ourselves from mortals, as you know. However, we also have perfect agility, enhanced speed, self-healing abilities, and we stop aging. We aid the Angel of Death. The angel is the one who picks us. When chosen, we are bestowed these abilities and give our lives to the purpose we were saved for. We are charged to protect those who are going to meet a similar fate as we did, people who die before their time, and we get to decide," he stops there.

"What is that you get to decide?" I ask trying to keep up.

"We chose whether or not to be the guardian or the reaper, to put it simply. Sometimes we decide to save our charge and give them a second chance at life. If someone is going to be hit by a drunk driver, for example, we might choose to save them. You would hear of a story of someone who miraculously survived a fatal car crash. However, other times we may decide to let the crash happen and that it's better not to change fate. As much as we would love to save everyone, there has to be some kind of balance." *I am balance. I am death.* I remembered the words that Drake spoke to those two men that night in the snow. It now makes sense. "The people who die of natural causes, like old age, illness, or sickness or circumstances they put themselves into, the Angel of Death comes for them. We don't intervene in those instances. Also, we do not, for any reason, save any of the demonkind. It is forbidden," he adds sternly. I wasn't sure why, and I don't feel like asking for an explanation right now.

"How could anyone choose to be someone with that much responsibility. Life and death, that's too much for one person to decide?" I'm seriously appalled at the thought. He doesn't answer, so I move on to a different point. "I think I somewhat grasp most of this. However, there is one thing that still doesn't fit," I conclude, and he gives me a blank look. "Me?" He sits back now following my train of thought. "I'm not a Guardian, I'm not Caster, and I don't have any other magical abilities that I know of." I look up at him. My heart stops as the obvious answer crosses my mind. I almost couldn't say the words out loud. "Darrius, are you here to choose whether I live or die?" I shudder at the thought.

"No Leyla, if I were, we would have never met," he answers softly, but I don't feel relieved. "You don't look so good. Maybe we should take a break for right now," he suggests. I disagree. I feel like I'm getting close to something he doesn't want to explain right now.

"I'd be better if I had something to wake me up," I state honestly feeling drained.

"I think I can help with that," I hear Bridget's voice again. Darrius shifts and I can tell he doesn't like her being here. "Why don't you give the girl some breathing room. She just got hit with magic for the first time. She needs some time to process," she winks at me. "Why don't we go grab a cup of coffee? That will wake you right up," she offers, but Darrius doesn't look too thrilled at the idea.

"No way, she's not leaving," he grumbles and looks back at me with a foreboding look. He's worried if I leave again something will happen.

"Look, my car is still at the bar. I'm not going to walk back from here. Besides, I did help rescue her. She'll be safe with me," she reminds him. Darrius starts to object again but I put my hand gently on his.

"I'll be fine. It's just coffee. I'll come right back, I promise. I know you' are worried, but if she helped me, then I trust her." He doesn't say anything, though I can tell he doesn't approve.

"Great, I'll drive," Bridget states and walks out the front door. I get up from the couch and walk over and grab my purse off the dining table. I head for the door only to find it blocked.

"Don't go Leyla. I know you trust her, but I don't," he gives me his opinion.

"Darrius, I told you once before I'm not going to stop living because someone is after me," he clenches his fists and doesn't move. "I realize I have to be more careful. I won't do anything so reckless this time. What is it about her that you don't like?" I ask, trying to understand.

"It's not her, it's them. The demonkind are dangerous and unpredictable. I told you our magic comes from good and we use it only for good. Their magic came from evil and was meant to unleash that evil and bring chaos into this world," he implies agitated. He stares at me with those eyes trying to change my mind, but I stand my ground. "I can see I won't win this one, but I think you should stay away from her after today," he warns and clenches his jaw.

"I'm afraid that's not your decision. Until she proves otherwise, Bridget is my friend, and I would appreciate it if you wouldn't treat her as if she is inherently evil," I argue. At that, I push myself past him, open the door, and head towards my Jeep.

# Chapter 9

## Dreams or Memories

Darrius is upset. That much is clear, but he doesn't get to run into my life and dictate who I'm and who I'm not friends with. Bridget has only ever helped me. I don't know what makes him distrust the magicalkind, and I don't feel like staying there to find out.

"I'm sorry about this. It must be a lot for you to digest," Bridget comments pulling onto the main road.

I shrug. There is a lot I'm starting to get used to. "Where are we going for coffee?" I ask wanting to change the subject.

"Prairie Rose Café, where else," she replies, as if there are no other options. Although, I probably should have guessed. It is the most popular and crowded, café among the campus students. It helps that it's practically across the street.

"I've never been in," I admit. The lines are always too long.

"What, you're joking?" she asks appalled. "Aren't you just full of surprises," she laughs. I could say the same about her.

We pull into a spot right up front. I guess with it still being the holiday not everyone is back yet. As we walk in, I'm immediately surprised by how big it is in here. It appears smaller from the outside. The wall to my left is nothing but windows, although the shades are pulled down for today. The back wall is lined with booths and small chandeliers hang down over each one. There are perfectly spaced pictures of different colored roses framed over each table. The open room is mostly full of tables and in the back-left corner sits a small raised stage with one lonely stool and a microphone. According to the sign hanging on the wall, its poetry reading night. Back to my right I see the registers and walk up to order.

Their entire menu is written on three large chalkboards behind the short brunette barista. A take a moment to order and the Barista is patient with me.

I finally decide on a mocha cappuccino and a turkey avocado panini. I only ate those fries last night, and my stomach is sick with hunger. Before I go, she asks me if I'm going to sign up for the poetry reading, but I quickly decline. I spot Bridget seated at a table in the middle of the building. I walk up and join her.

"You're not going to order?" I ask. No sooner did the words leave my lips, does a short young man walk up to us with two cups of hot brown liquid. He sets both cups in front of us with a shy smile. "Thanks," I tell him.

He doesn't answer, and I notice him staring down at Bridget. He doesn't appear to be tall, and his skin is as dark as a coffee bean. His head is completely shaved, making his dark brown eyes look bigger on his face. His physical features are strong and broad. He most defiantly works out. I can see his muscles bulging from both his arms. His left arm is also covered in tattoos. It's some kind of design, but I can't quite make it out from this angle.

"Thanks Mark," Bridget says blowing down into her cup. She misses the most adoring smile he gives her in return. He rushes off as quickly as he appeared.

"I think he likes you," I inform her. She pulls her eyes from her cup and looks at me. She tucks some of her short and crinkled hair behind her ears. Her eyes look tired, and I think she might need this coffee more than I do.

"You're probably right," she smiles sadly. She acts like him liking her is a bad thing. I look down at my cup to see a beautiful rose floating on top created out of foam. I almost don't want to mess it up by drinking it. As I take my first sip, Mark comes back over and sets my food down. The warm liquid feels good going down.

"Wow, that looks incredible. I'll have one too, please." Bridget asks, and he is happy to oblige nodding his head yes. I take another sip and it taste like heaven. I understand why people line up out the door for this stuff. "It's good right," Bridget states seeing my reaction.

"It's so good," I agree licking some foam off my lips. "I shouldn't have come. Now I won't be able to stop," I admit and half-laugh.

She grins looking pleased. "You're welcome," she states, in a very matter of a fact way.

I took one bite and I don't stop until my sandwich is devoured. I'm starving. I've never felt this hungry before. You would have thought I hadn't eaten in days. I look up at Bridget catching her grinning at me with amusement.

"The power of magic," she alludes. I shoot her a curious look. "Being hit with magic is almost like getting drunk and when it wears off, well, it's like being hungover," she explains. "When you first get introduced, depending on the spell, you can feel happy, tired, touchy-feely, or angry. It reacts to everyone slightly different. Some true mortals are very reactive to it, and it can become an addiction. Otherscan take a while for them to feel the effects, and sometimes they are even immune. Unless you are dealing with a very old and very practice Caster, there isn't anyone who can resist if that happens. Regardless, once the effects start to wear off, you can feel sick, drained, hungry, dehydrated, dizzy, or in most cases your memory becomes fuzzy. Again, it depends on the person and how long they were exposed to the magic. Those who have it happen over and over, may or may not have any side effects after a while," she finishes, and I try to soak up as much as I can. Mark comes over with her food this time, but he doesn't linger for a thank you. "Sorry," she shoves a fry in her mouth, "I know we didn't come here to talk about that. I can't help you take your mind off of magic if I keep bringing it up," she shrugs apologetically.

"It's okay. I don't mind, at least I know why I feel so famished," I giggle. "Honestly, I wanted to ask you some questions about," I pause to look around making sure no one is earshot, "the Guardians." She smiles as if she knew I would bring it up.

"I don't know a lot, and what I do know are mostly rumors. We don't normally interact with each other. Honestly, meeting one is pretty rare," she laughs to herself and takes another bite.

"You said something about true mortals earlier. What did you mean?" I interject off-topic.

"Ah, that's what you are. You're truly mortal. No magic runs through your veins," she explains, and I get it.

"So magicalkinds and the Guardians, you two don't exactly get along?" I say without trying to act like I know too much about it, because I don't.

"They hate us," she clarifies, and I'm surprised on how casually she says it. "In their eyes we have magic, and we shouldn't. Most of them think we have no souls either. There is a lot of history between us. Back when most magicalkinds were created they did more bad than good. I can't completely blame the Guardians for their actions against us, but time has gone on. We're not like that anymore. In fact, I doubt there is even that many of us even left. We are the ancestors, ancestors, and we didn't exactly ask for this power. But to the Guardians, we are just the same as those who came before us. The Guardians believe we will never change from our evil ways," she tries to put on a cheerful smile, but she isn't fooling me. She acts like it's okay, but I don't think it is.

"You said there aren't many of you left? Do you not know any other Casters?" I inquire.

"There are other Casters, but we keep to ourselves or our family line. We do our best not to draw attention to ourselves. When we have tried to reveal ourselves in the past, we found that true mortals always find a way to take advantage of our abilities. We want so badly to fit in that we try and do whatever we can to please them. Most of you aren't that great with the real idea of knowing we are around. Although having our own schools to practice magic at would be epic, unfortunately, it doesn't work like that," she enlightens me, sounding truly disappointed. "Also, we can't cast just any kind of magic we want on a whim either. We have basic spells, sure, but our strongest magic comes from our individual ability that we are gifted with. Magic takes a lot to cast, especially since we inherited our powers. The strongest Casters are the ones who have been around the longest. As more Casters are born to your family line the more weak their abilities become. The idea that one person can cast an unlimited amount of magic and not have any consequences for doing so is just unrealistic. Using too much magic at once or trying to perform spells that you aren't exactly your ability can be deadly," she pauses for effect. "There are other magicalkinds, but I don't know much about them. Your new friend would be able to tell you more about that than me," she adds.

I decide to start asking her about her life and not some much the magical side of it. We order more coffee and sit and talk for at least another hour. Bridget didn't grow up here. She moved from Nebraska, where her family lives to go to school here. It's the first time she's been away from them. She also informs me that her mother, and her brother are Caster's. She didn't say much about her dad, just that he passed when she was little. I told her about my mom, and I gave her a quick re-cap of Kat's, Kent's, and my relationship to each other. I learn she is studying to become a linguist. She wants to travel the world to translate for people. I can see how that would suit her. I'm surprised to learn that she already knows over six languages, and she briefly demonstrated each one of them. Mark brings up our check. I notice he left off a couple of drinks, which was a sweet gesture. I wonder if Bridget noticed as well. I know he did it for her and not me.

I take Bridget back to her car, and I'm sad we have to part ways. I've taken up her a full night and almost an entire day, so I'm sure she is ready to get back home. Before she gets out, she grabs my phone and types in her number.

"Call me any time," she offers and hands my phone back to me. "It's nice to have someone to talk to about the other side of me," she confesses. I feel a little sad for her. I can't imagine how hard it is to hide such a big part of who you are from everyone.

"By the way, I didn't get to say a proper thank you for saving me. I'll have to make it up to you with coffee on me next time," I propose. "Also, I was going to ask what exactly is your gift?" I inquire hoping I'm not overstepping.

"Illusion," she grins with pride. "After I tracked you down, Darrius needed a distraction to get you out of there. I might have flooded the building with imaginary snakes. It worked rather well," she recalls satisfyingly with a smirk.

"Wow. I guess that Caster didn't stop to question if they were real or not," I respond, trying not to picture all those snakes myself.

"True, but luckily for me, my illusions appear real to the person I'm casting it on. If I want you to, I can make you feel, see, taste, smell, and hear anything I want. I have the illusion of the senses," she explains further. I'm impressed.

"Bridget, I think this goes without saying, but if you ever flood my apartment with snakes, I don't think we could be friends anymore," I joke, and we both laugh.

When I make it home Darrius is nowhere to be found. I don't think too much about it. My brain is full of all the information I had gotten throughout the day to worry about where he ran off to. I've learned much in a short amount of time. I'm doing my best to sort through it. Magic, Casters, Guardians, abilities, demons, and angels. There is a whole other hidden world wrapped up in the normal one around me, and nothing is what it seems. I suddenly feel beat. I leave the lamp on in my living room for when Darrius returns, I have no doubt he would be back. I head straight for my bed and flop ungracefully down atop my comforter, face first. As soon as I hit the bed my eyes close, and I'm out like a light.

*I'm walking down a long elegantly designed hall that leads into an enormous ballroom. I've never seen anything like it before. I look down and*

*I'm wearing a full-length round-shaped burgundy ball gown. I have on small red heels that perfectly match the color of my dress. I reach out my arms to find them covered with long gold satin gloves reaching up past my elbows. My skin appears olive-colored, but I don't put too much stock in it at the moment. I feel my hair pinned up. Not one stand is touching my neck or face. I hear a beautiful melody start to play, and in one of the corners of the room, a small orchestra appears out of thin air. I step into the middle of the room when I realize I'm not the one who is moving. I feel everything I'm doing, but I'm not in control of it. I'm stuck watching from the inside of myself while someone else pulls my strings. I take a moment to turn around the room, taking it all in. Behind the orchestra is a tall wall of windows. A large ornate door leads outside to the gardens stretching for miles. It's dark out, but it doesn't reach in here. An enormous crystal chandelier hanging down illuminating the whole room. It must have at least one hundred candles flickering. It hangs down on a long rod attached to the pointed top of a dome ceiling. Besides where it attaches, most of the dome is made of glass, I see stars in the night sky above. The other three walls have different scenic paintings, the kind you can get lost in for hours. The first is a garden of red rose bushes, the next is a field full of tall golden sunflowers, and the last is rolling hills of lavender. In front of each wall sits golden chairs covered in plush forest green cushions.*

*"I hope you didn't run here in that dress," a voice sounds from behind me with a strong British accent. I feel myself smile, still not in control, and I turn to greet the person behind me. I see Darrius. His hair is closely and evenly shaved around his head. His eyes, ever blue as normal, and he is smiling shyly at me. Since when does Darrius joke? He is wearing an all-black suit hugged tightly to his figure. It looks old-fashion, nothing you would see nowadays. "May I have the first dance with you?" he asks reaching out his hand. I take it without pause.*

*"You may," I reply, but it's not my voice. This voice is sultry and thick with an accent I couldn't quite put my finger on. I'm in my body, but I'm not me. Darrius pulls me into him, and we start to move gracefully around the floor. Couples start to appear around the room dancing as if they had always been there. Darrius never takes his eyes off me as we continue to glide around the room. His touch, I barely feel through the back of my thick dress. "Is this room not the loveliest view you have ever seen?" I ask taking the room in one more time.*

"It comes second compared to yourself tonight. You look breathtaking," he reveals looking deeper into my eyes than before. I feel my skin prickle and heat comes to my face. He's never looked this way before. Darrius seems to be happiest man on earth dancing around this room with whomever I am.

"Excuse me, may I cut in?" I look over to see Drake. I look back at Darrius who doesn't seem to tense up at his arrival.

"Of course," he nods, extending my hand over to Drake's and letting me go. What is going on in this twilight zone? Darrius is happy and him and Drake are acting as if they like each other. What did I miss? Drake takes the lead and we start to move to the music. He is dressed in a similar all-black suit and his is tailored as well to fit him snuggly. He appears just as eager to dance with me as Darrius had been. His hair is even more wild and curly than I've seen before, and his eyes in this light are the color of evergreen leaves.

"Sorry for cutting in, but you said you would have your answer for me tonight," he reveals quietly leaning down to whisper in my ear. He looks suddenly nervous. I had no idea what he was referring to.

"Drake, I'm afraid I cannot return your affections. Your revelations come too late, I'm afraid," I answer. Well she answered. He doesn't look angry. He simply twirls me around and then keeps moving around the dance floor.

"Are you saying that you might have returned them had I asked sooner?" he asks keeping his voice low.

"I cannot lie, and I never would about my feelings when asked. So, I cannot say that I don't have feelings for you. However, those feelings are of friendship. I'm afraid I'm not in love with you because I'm in love with someone else," she finishes, and my heart sinks as I feel his hand squeeze mine tightly for a brief moment. I watch as sorrow fills his eyes and pain covers his sun-kissed face, but he says nothing. I know she is being honest with him, but I just felt his heartbreak into a million pieces. The music slows then comes to a stop. Everyone stops to clap, everyone but Drake and me. We are stuck in a moment, neither of us is taking our eyes off the other. He finally breaks his focus and brings my hand to his face. His lips gently leave a kiss on my hand as he bows down for a moment.

"Thank you for being honest. I respect your decision. I'm sorry if I've caused you any trouble over this," he lets go of my hand and leaves the dance floor. If I was myself, I think I might have followed after him.

*"Is everything alright? Where did Drake go in such a hurry?" Darrius'*
*voice graces my ears as I turn to look at him. He looks back at me with*
*confusion. He takes one of his fingers and wipes away a tear from my cheek. I*
*hadn't realized one had fallen from my eye. "Alexandra, why are you crying,"*
*he questions compassionately. Who is Alexandra?*

*I'm forcefully pulled out of the ballroom, and in a flash, Darrius, the dance*
*floor, and the music fade into blackness. I'm standing in the dark. I hear a loud*
*crack from above. Thunder? As I think it, lightning strikes in the distance, and*
*the darkness lifts. I'm now staring up at a dark, ominous sky. I feel raindrops*
*hit my skin as I look ahead to a familiar scene. A long road full of streetlamps*
*and houses of all different colors and sizes forms into my view. My endless*
*nightmare haunts me once again. After just two days of relief, it persists. The*
*lightning strikes once more, and the thunder follows as if it's mocking me. How*
*dare you think you could escape. It seems to tell me. "I refuse!" I shout out to*
*nothing and no one. I refuse to play this out. I'm done. The road beneath me*
*starts to move like a treadmill. My dream is going to play out whether I will it*
*to or not. Damn this dream. I guess I'm doomed to repeat it until I die!*

I sit straight up full of terror. The nightmare has ended, and I'm left in a
pool of sweat. I wish more than anything it would just leave me be. I roll over
and reach out for my lamp switch in the pitch black of my room. I grip the
knob and twist it on. The light is too bright at first, and I have to blink several
times before my eyes adjusted. I need water. As I roll off the bed, I notice
someone sitting in the corner watching me.

"Darrius, for heaven's sake, you're going to give me a heart attack!" I
exclaim out of breath. "Just what do you think you are doing in my bedroom
staring at me in the dark?" *What the hell is wrong with him?* He doesn't answer
me, and it would appear he has gone back to his normal silent self. There is a
serious stressed-out look on his face. "What's wrong? Why are you looking at
me like that?" I ask curtly.

"Tell me what is causing you so much pain?" *What is he talking about?* It
is my turn to be silent. "Your dreams, what are you dreaming about?" he
clarifies.

"I don't understand," I reply my heart still pounding.

"You were screaming in your sleep," he reveals, and now I comprehend.
He gets up from the floor and walks over to me. Blue-eyes is standing right in

front of me, and I feel very intimidated by his gaze. "So, tell me what is going on, what are you dreaming about?" he asks again impatiently.

I can't believe this is the same Darrius that was in my dream earlier. It's as if someone turned on a switch in my head. I had almost forgotten the first dream after the nightmare took over. *Was it a dream though, or was it something else?* I guess there is only one way to find out.

"I will tell you, but I have my own question first," I retort. He doesn't look pleased, but doesn't object. "Who is Alexandra?"

# Chapter 10

## Be Careful What You Wish For

Besides the day we first met, I've never seen Darrius surprised, that is until this moment. He takes a few steps back from me, but he never breaks eye contact. I was about to ask again, but I'm rudely interrupted by a knock on my front door. I look over to my clock to see it's almost four in the morning. Maybe I was just hearing things. There is another knock, this time louder. I make my way past Darrius and head towards the door. *Why would someone be here this early?* I see a blur of a figure speed past me cutting me off.

"What do you think you are doing?" Darrius questions firmly.

"I'm answering my door," I reply unshaken by his tone.

"You've learned nothing from being kidnaped, have you?" he asks sarcastically agitated. "I'll get it," he insists.

"I can get my own door!" I almost yell. I'm angry that my answer about Alexandra got interrupted, and I'm taking it out on him, not meaning to. He grabs the handle and turns it before I can reach it myself. I see the last person I expect tumble in. "Drake!" I gasp.

He falls into Darrius' arms as he helps Drake over to the couch. I walk over and shut the door. Drake's breathing is heavy, and his skin is pale. He is dressed in his armor like the last time I saw him.

"What's going on? Are you okay?" I ask excitedly walking quickly over to the couch to examine him. Darrius doesn't say anything. He just looks Drake over with a slightly concerned glare.

"I'm fine. I just ran here and spent a little too much energy. I'll be okay once I rest," Drake answers and looks up at me with a soft smile. His eyes are heavy and don't shine as brightly as normal. I see him clutch his left arm with his right hand. When he pulls the hand away, it's dripping with blood.

"You are not okay. You're bleeding," I announce, and he gives me another small smile. He was about to rebut but is stopped as we all turn our focus to the door. Someone else has knocked.

"It's okay. She's with me," Drake speaks up. Darrius cautiously walks over and opens *my* door once again. A new face is standing on the other side, and she walks in hesitantly. Darrius quickly shuts the door behind her, and his face is so still and somber. My first impression of her is one of intimidation.

"Forgive me, I'm Helen," she remembers her manors and introduces herself. Her voice is as soft and pretty as a flower.

Her face is flawless and glowing. Her soft arctic blue eyes look to each one of us, and I'm not sure if her cheeks are naturally flushed or if she had been just running. She has her light-blonde hair tied up in a single long braid hanging over her right shoulder. She is striking in her armor fitted to her full figure, only hers' is a lighter brown color than Drake's. She also has a full belt of small daggers, blade down, all around her waist. What could she be doing here, and how does Drake know her?

"Helen, thank you for accompanying me back. It wasn't necessary. This is Darrius, and this is Leyla," he politely introduces Darrius and I in return.

"Hello," I greet her, my voice a little shaky. I wonder if she knows I'm not a Guardian. She certainly has to be.

"Hello, sorry to come so late. Drake refused to see a healer back at the Order and wait for the morning to journey here. I was simply making sure he got here safely," she explains.

"Thank you. Since he didn't go see a healer," I say trying to act like I know what she is talking about, "I'll go grab some bandages and be right back, excuse me." I leave the room. I grab my phone off the charger and call Kat. It takes her a few calls before she finally picks up. "Hey Kat, sorry to wake you. I got up for a midnight snack and I cut my finger. What do I do?" It sounds like a good story to cover up the real reason I called. "No, it's still attached, there is just a lot of blood," I explain. "Okay, yes, I have all that in my kit," I tell her. "Yes, if it doesn't stop bleeding, I'll call back," I assure her and hang up the phone.

Her instructions are simple, and I feel like I could have figured it out on my own, but I wanted to be sure. I grab my first-aid kit from under my sink and walk back out to catching the end of an awkward conversation. I hang back in the hall, not wanting to interrupt.

"I'll see you soon," Helen states as she walks back through my front door.

She glances over at me before leaving. She glares at me with a look that runs shivers down my spine. She shuts the door and is gone. What did she mean? Is she coming back?

"This is exactly what I told you would happen if you went off looking for answers!" Darrius voice raises, and this is the first time I've ever seen him truly angry. At the moment I'm too confused to know what I should be feeling.

"This was going to happen whether I went or not," Drake retorts in his defense, crossing his arms together.

"Let's keep it civil you two. I do have neighbors," I remind them trying to break up the tension. I walk over to Drake with my kit and take out the alcohol swabs and start to apply them to his arm. He doesn't even flinch. "What happened?" I ask. Once I wipe away the blood, I see four deep wounds that ripped right through his armor. "Are these claw marks?" I question with doubt. I grab the bandages and start to wrap them around his upper arm and shoulder.

"Thank you, but this really isn't necessary," he tells me kindly. I give him a look that says otherwise, and he looks away. He seems to ignore my questions.

"Are you going to tell me what happened or not? Is Helen a Guardian too, like you and Darrius?" I throw in, and he looks back at me with surprise. His jaw straightens and his green eyes open wide as he looks over between Darrius and me. "Yes, he told me some things while you were gone," I fill him in. "I remember someone telling me that they would tell me anything I wanted to know before he left, or has that offer been rescinded?" I remind him, and he lets out a small sigh.

"No, of course not. I'm just surprised, that's all," he replies. "Helen is a Guardian," he answers. "I was helping her Order track down some magicalkind. Their leader was captured, and her followers are now gone, as of a few hours ago. I was injured by one of them," he explains. "A Theiran managed to get one of his claws into me before he met his end," he continues, and I give him a confused look. "Theirans are a type of magicalkind that can change into certain types of animals," he enlightens me. *Interesting.*

"Darrius said you left to find answers?" I confirm. "Were you looking for a reason why I look like Alexandra?" I ask bluntly, and his face turns almost translucent as I utter her name. I catch Darrius shift in his seat out of the corner of my eye. Drake looks over at Darrius, and they exchange a look before he says anything back. "He didn't tell me about her," I confirm answering his unasked question. Drake stiffens.

"Leyla, if Darrius didn't tell you, then how do you know about Alexandra?" he asks looking at me dumbfoundedly.

"I had a dream. Actually I should say dreams. I've been seeing you and Drake in them, not to mention all the feelings I have around both of you as if we know each other. Last night in one of them I realized that I was having a dream of someone, who wasn't me," I pause, and his eyes widen and his mouth slightly parts open in awe at my revelation. I look over at Darrius, "You called her Alexandra," I go on. I look back over at Drake. "Are you two following me because of her?" I ask, not wanting the answer.

"It started that way, yes," Drake replies, and I feel my stomach do a flip.

"I see," I whisper turning away from both their gazes. I should have known better to think there was any other reason. "Wait," I start to realize something, "do I look like her?" I glance at Drake who he nods.

"You have subtle differences, your skin is a little paler, your voice is softer, but everything else is a perfect replica. It's uncanny," Drake reveals.

"We've had a theory," Darrius speaks up, and I pull my attention towards him. "We believe that whoever is after you believes you're Alexandra," he divulges. "A theory that was confirmed tonight," he pauses and looks over at Drake, and I do the same.

"The reason we were hunting the magicalkind is because they attacked the Order earlier tonight. They managed to get inside the Order, which you wouldn't know, but that shouldn't have been possible. We hunted them down, and the one responsible for the attack is a Caster," he pauses.

"A Caster? Like the girl who kidnaped me?" I ask, and he looks taken aback.

"On New Year's, Leyla was captured by a Caster," Darrius fills Drake in. "I think she's working for the one Drake captured," he concludes.

"Why do you think that?" I wasn't following.

"When we brought the Caster in for questioning, she swore she would only speak to one Guardian. That Guardian being Alexandra," Drake replies filling in the missing piece.

"Why don't we get Alexandra. She can explain that I'm not her, and then people will stop trying to kidnap me," I relay thinking of the simplest solution.

They both fall silent and exchange some more looks. It's like there talking to each other without actually using any words.

"I'm afraid that won't work. You see, Alexandra is, she is…" Drake's words fade, and he looks away from me.

"Alexandra is dead," Darrius finishes for him coldly.

I feel so stupid. They can't help but see her in me, and they aren't the only ones. I dare not ask why this Caster would be after Alexandra or why she is no longer alive. I don't want to drudge up any more things from their past than I already had.

"I'm sorry," I comment sadly. Both of them look to me, then themselves. "Is there something else?" I guess hating the looks they were exchanging.

"The Order has requested we bring you to this Caster. They are hoping you can fool her into thinking that you actually are Alexandra, so she will reveal why and how she got into the Order," Drake answers. I take a moment to process. I feel my eyes blink one too many times.

"So you want me to go see a Caster that has been after me and not explain that I'm not Alexandra, but try and convince her that I am instead?" I ask in amazement. They both just look at each other again. "Let me guess. I don't have a choice?" I presume my tone irritated.

"I didn't want to get you involved, Leyla, really I didn't. However, I couldn't explain why I needed to come back here without telling them about you. I think it was just a matter of time until the Order found out about you, and at least this way we are bringing you to them on our terms instead of them coming to get you," Drake states his point. "It's not something I want to ask you to do, but if you don't go, then the Order might suspect something," he adds, and I'm not sure how to take that.

"Let me think about it," I request. I look over at Darrius, I wonder how he feels about this.

"If you decide yes, we'll need to leave tomorrow. I think the sooner we go, the sooner we can put this behind us." I turn back to Drake. He wasn't leaving me much time to think it over. I look at his arm where he has the cuts, and the blood seems to have stopped gushing out.

"I almost forgot. Kat said to keep applying pressure and to change the bandages as needed," I remember.

"I appreciate that, but it won't be necessary," he smiles and removes the bandage. The rips in the leather are still there, but the scratch marks are completely gone. "We heal quickly," he explains. I do recall Darrius mentioning that is one of their abilities. I feel silly I got so worked up over it.

"We should let you get some rest. We'll come for your answer tomorrow," Drake suggests and gets up from the couch. He looks over at Darrius, and after a moment of hesitation, he gets up as well. "Whatever you decide, we'll still be here," Drake says softly turning the knob on my door to leave.

I lay awake all night. So many things ran through my mind making it impossible to even think about sleeping. I have been requested to go to an Order even though I'm not a Guardian, and I have to convince this Caster that I'm someone I'm not. I disliked that last part the most. However, if this Caster is the one after me, I should be safe now that she is locked up, right? Honestly, all I wanted to prove to her, and everyone, is that I'm not Alexandra. Am I going to volunteer to go into a world I know nothing about? *I don't think you have a choice, Leyla.*

Just before noon Darrius and Drake are outside my door waiting for my answer as promised. I've been ready for them, and I reply by opening the door with my bags in hand. "I guess this means you've decided to go," Drake observes with an amused smile. I shake my head yes. Darrius' is impassive as ever. I lock the door behind me before heading out to Drake's car. I didn't think of Guardian's having such things, but I'm glad that we don't have to take my Jeep.

"So where is this Order? How long do you think we will be gone?"

"St. Louis, it's one of the biggest Order's in the states," Drake informs me, "as for how long I'm hoping no more than a couple of days," he adds. I hope his guess is correct. School starts in a few days, and I would like to be back when the semester begins. I do look like Alexandra. If these two think so, why wouldn't this Caster?

# Chapter 11

## A Whole New World

*For a moment I'm engulfed in darkness, then the sky is lit above me with a full moon and thousands of stars. I look around at my surrounding. I'm standing outside in a vast garden with rows of precise and evenly cut shrubbery. Looking straight ahead, I spot Darrius dressed in leather armor similar to what I've seen him in before. I look down at myself to see I'm dressed in armor as I walk quickly towards him. Why do I keep having dreams like this? Are they even real? Darrius looks at me and smiles. He is leaning against a grand stone arch. The stone is soft white and its pillars are wrapped in ivy from top to bottom. Small lilac flowers sprout out here and there from the vines. It's beautiful.*

*"Pray tell, what brings you out this night?" he asks as I get within a couple of feet of him. His tone is playful. I must have given him a serious look because the smile on his face quickly disappears. "What was it you wanted to discuss?" he asks more seriously. You, meaning Alexandra?*

*"There is something I want to say that I wish no one else to hear," she replies, and her voice affirms my hunch. I feel myself shaking, and I wonder if she is nervous about something? He doesn't say anything else, waiting for me to speak. "Please believe me when I say this wasn't something I went searching for, but something that I feel in my heart that I need to do," she starts. He looks confused, and I feel the same. "I want to stop hunting the demonkind." Her words sink in, and I watch Darrius take a step back from her in a stupor. His blue eyes widen, and they search hers as if he heard her words wrong. "I want to help them, Darrius. I think, or yet I feel, as if there needs to be something in place. A system to judge them fairly before we just rush in and kill them all," she elaborates. Kill? I couldn't believe what I was hearing. I'm just as shocked as Darrius, but for different reasons.*

*"Why?" he asks, his voice soft.*

*"I don't think we, Guardians, were meant for this reason. We are meant for good so it feels wrong. Not all their kind are evil. I know you've seen that too. If we do have to rid the world of them, should we not make sure first that they all deserve this fate?" she insists. I can feel how much she needs him to understand, her palms are sweaty, and her body is still shaking. This isn't something she is easily able to speak of.*

*"That may be true, but it's not up to us, Alexandra. What you talk about, it's forbidden. We can't help the demonkind. We must stop them. They may not be all evil, but that doesn't mean that they won't become such. Again, it's not up to us," he reminds her firmly.*

*"Not all of them had a choice, Darrius. They can't help that they were born or cursed with their magic. Why should we punish every generation for something their relative decided?" she retorts.*

*"Their relative damned them when they made their choice, Alexandra. It's the consequences they have to live with for having magic. We are supposed to protect mortals from facing their demise before their time. Anyone who has magic can alter or harm mortals. They have done horrible things. They can't be controlled or reasoned with. You need to let this go!" he shouts, and his voice booms in the night. I feel her heart shrivel in her chest and her frustration. She's disappointed he doesn't understand.*

*"You don't think they deserve our compassion. Do you not think they deserve mercy?" she asks coolly, trying to keep her hurt bottled inside.*

*"No, Alexandra, I do not," he doesn't shout this time, but his voice is unyielding of any sympathy. After a few moments of silence, his posture relaxes, and he lets out a sigh. He walks over towards her and pulls Alexandra into his arms. "You have a big heart, but I don't want to think about what the Order would do to you if they heard such nonsense. I think we should not talk about this matter any longer," he suggests, his voice gentle. "I love you…"*

"Leyla, wake up. We've arrived," I pop up too fast giving me an instead head rush. I look around to see it's dark outside, but there are multitudes of lights from surrounding buildings and streetlamps all around. I look behind me to catch a glimp of the arch standing tall in the distance. It's incredible. "I'm afraid you've slept the whole way. You must have been pretty tired." I realize the voice that has been talking to me belongs to Drake. He parks the car across from one of the longest buildings I've ever seen.

"I didn't sleep much last night," I reveal. "Is that the Order?" I ask in amazement.

"Yes, this is the City Hall building, but most of it belongs to the Order," Darrius answers. I look over at him and I'm reminded of my dream. He and Alexandra, were they together? I look back at Drake. Were they both in love with Alexandra? If these dreams were meant to be her memories, Drake had already made his feelings clear. Did she fall for Darrius? This is crazy. "Are you feeling okay, you look a little pale?" Darrius observes as his eyes look over me.

"I'm fine," I reply. Right now, I'm going to push this aside. Besides, it was a dream. It's not real. "Did I sleep the whole way?" I ask as a distraction.

"Like a baby," Drake replies with a quick grin. I get out of the car, and I see Darius grab our bags. I notice they have changed into their armor somewhere along the way. "I'm going to have to carry you inside," Drake says holding out his arms waiting for permission. I nod letting him pick me up. I didn't think it was necessary until he started to run. Everything becomes hazy. My vision doesn't become clear until we get inside the building. Drake lets go letting my feet slide to the floor. "Sorry I had to get you in past the night guards. This was the easiest way," he explains.

"Does that mean we are inside the Order?" I guess looking toward a dead-end hallway.

"Not quite," he winks. "It's just through there," he points to the dead end.

*That can't be right.* "Through the wall, is there like a secret door that opens or something?" I ask sarcastically.

"No," he laughs, "we are going to faze through it. That's the only way to enter a Guardian Order, which is how we keep mortals and magicalkinds out. Only Guardians should be able to enter," he explains. "Don't worry, I'll take you through. As long as we are touching, I can faze you through as well," he adds. I look at him skeptically waiting for the punch line. "Trust me," he says holding out his hand. I take it and we walk to the end of the hall. "See this," he points to a chiseled-out symbol in the crown molding halfway up the wall. I shake my head yes. "This is the Guardian symbol. There are three types of Guardians, the Guard, the Sword, and the Light. The Guard is portrayed here as the shield, clearly, the crossed swords represent the Sword, and lastly the sun on the shield represents the Light. I wanted to explain that before we got inside. I wish I could tell you more, but we haven't got the time. I'm sure they are already waiting for us on the other side. Just try to keep silent and let Darrius or I do the talking. I'm pretty sure you're the first mortal ever to be let into the Order, at least that I know of," his words resonate making me feel nervous. I nod my head in understanding, and he squeezes my hand in his.

"So you're going to faze me through this wall. How does it work?" I can't help but to be curious. I've never walked through a wall before.

"I'll explain later, just whatever you do, don't let go of my hand, understand," he instructs seriously.

"Alright, I'm ready, let's do it," I tell him, and he smiles at me proudly.

For a moment nothing happens, but then I watch him disappear from my view. I look down, and I start to as well. Beginning from where my hand is touching his. We are standing in the same place as before, but now everything is in black and white. I can't hear a sound, and I can no longer feel his hand on mine. I panic for a moment. I look down noticing I haven't let got. I just can't feel it. I look back up at Drake who nods his head at me as if this is normal. The complete silence around us is serial. I try not to imagine what it would be like being stuck in this state for too long. Drake begins to walk forward, and I follow. He does it so casually. Everything starts to take color again, I hear myself breathe, and I can feel that we are no longer holding hands. That is one of the strangest things I've ever experienced.

I look over to my right to see Darrius already standing on the other side of the wall with our luggage. The ceiling is much taller on this side than the other. We all stand in a long corridor with doors on either side all the way down. Little lamps hang by each doorway, lighting up the hall. The Guardian symbol is etched every few feet on the floor. The doors open followed by a small group of Guardians come walking towards us.

"Stay silent," Darrius whispers in my ear before they reach us.

He wasn't the only one to offer me that advice. My stomach twist in knots. I don't think I could speak a word anyway, even if I wanted to. I instantly recognize Helen, who is leading a group of four male Guardians behind her. They are all dressed in armor and have some kind of weapon on their persons. She looks more intimidating now that when we first met. I'm the only one not dressed in armor making me wonder if that was an obvious giveaway that I'm mortal. However, I've seen both Darrius and Drake in normal clothes before, so maybe not. I still feel out of place regardless. They finally reach us after what feels like minutes of agony. I can't help but hold my breath.

"Thank you for coming so quickly," Helen speaks first. "Our Order owes you a debt Drake for your service in helping us track down those magicalkinds that dared to attack us." Drake gives her a little nod and flashes her one of his charming smiles. She looks him over with a straight face, and I have to say she is the only girl I've met so far that he seems to have no effect over. "The Master is waiting for you all. Please follow me," she informs us and starts to move back the way she came. We all follow.

The other Guardians she brought with her stay at our flank. I remind myself to keep breathing in and out as I keep my eyes ahead of me. We walk through the double doors and enter into an enormous oval-shaped room. At the center of the room sits a round table where several young-looking men and woman are seated. There is only one empty seat next to one of the most striking men I've ever seen.

The man is seated in what would be the middle directly across from where we are all standing. My eyes meet his and I can't draw them away. His most prominent feature is his thick white hair. It makes him appear older than those around him. Could this be the Master Helen spoke of? His hair falls long outlining his pale face, His bangs hang low over his eyes. I watch his hand move them over to one side revealing his eyes that are the color of amber. Hanging low above the round table is a chandelier. It reminds me of the one from my dream of Alexandra at the ball. The light is catching his eyes and they mimic a flickering flame. His armor is just as different from the other Guardians as his features. It's still leather, but it's as black as a crow's feather.

I finally pull my eyes away and notice that the seat next to him is no longer empty. Helen takes a seat next to him, and the three Guardians who had accompanied her vanished from the room. The fourth stands a ways away from the table and us. I look around the room itself and there is a staircase to my left leading up to the second story. Six tall pearl-colored marble pillars hold up the room. To my right is a large window that has the glass-covered up by floor-to-ceiling curtains.

"Good evening," the striking man speaks, and it pulls my full attention to him. "Please come closer," his deep voice commands. Darrius, Drake, and I walk slowly closer to the table. "Welcome, I am the Master of this Order. I would like to make it clear that these are very untoward circumstances. and

Only the people at this table know *what* you are," he states disapprovingly looking directly at me. The light in his eyes still dance like flames. "I'm holding you two personally responsible for keeping it that way, am I understood?" he asks. He takes his eyes off me and looking from Darrius to Drake with a frightening glare. They both answer yes sir. "Leyla," he turns back to me relaxing his face, "I appreciate your cooperation, and I want to assure you that you are in no danger here." He leans over to Helen and whispers something in her ear. She doesn't say anything, just nods. "Helen will be responsible for your day-to-day here," he informs us. I don't have a great feeling about that. I can't help thinking she doesn't like me very much. "I'm sorry to have to cut these pleasantries short. I have much I would like to discuss, but it will have to wait until a decent hour. Helen will show you to your quarters. Please get some rest," he stands up abruptly.

The others around the table stand when he does, and they don't leave until he has walked through the doors behind him leading down another long hallway. Helen stays behind. The Guardian who was standing in the room, walks over to Helen's side. He is taller than average with broad shoulders, and a long neck. His light brown hair is cut very short. His eyes are a doe-brown color to match.

"This is Xander. He will be assisting me in your protection while you are here," Helen extends her hands gesturing to him. "Xander, please take their bags to their rooms." Xander instantly obeys her command, picks up our bags with ease, and speeds off up the stairs with all of them in hand. "Please follow me," she instructs.

As we reach the third floor, Helen leads us down a long dimly lit corridor. There are no windows, only small lights hanging from the ceiling. It's a bit drafty and cool. It reminds me of the entry we came through with doorways on either side of the walkway. However, between each of these doors are antique wooden tables. On top of each one sits an expensive-looking vase filled with different kinds of fresh flowers. There are also paintings, as well as, some tapestries hanging along the walls. We reach the end of the long hallway to a pair of double doors. Beside each door are glass cases full of different types of weaponry. I didn't get a good look inside as Xander opens the doors as we reach them, blocking both cases from view. As the doors open, I see a sitting area in the middle of the revealed room with tall bookcases on either side of a roaring fireplace on the back wall. The room is more brightly lit than the hall we just walked down. It's nice and warm thanks to the fire. On either side of the walls are two doors each.

"This floor houses the heads of the Order, so you won't be disbursed by any of the other Guardians here," Helen enlightens us. "If you need anything Xander will be out here in the hallway. These will be your quarters while you visit. Please make yourselves comfortable. Drake and Darrius, your rooms are on the right, and Leyla, you may take the far one on the left," she states reaching out towards the corresponding doors as she spoke. "I will be here at eight sharp to escort you to breakfast," she informs us taking her leave without so much as a goodbye. Xander follows her out closing the doors behind him.

"We are on their time now," Darrius speaks out unhappily. He opens the first door on the right side of the room and walks in shutting the door forcefully. Drake walks over to me and places his hand on one of my shoulders sympathetically. "You did great Leyla, don't mind Darrius. He's just grumpy and needs some rest. You should get some as well. I expect it will be a long day for us tomorrow," he remarks and removes both hands from my shoulders. He starts to walk off towards his door but stops suddenly and turns back around. "By the way, I almost forgot. I promised to explain how we got through the wall. Fazing is a specific gift only Guardians have. It allows us to walk through anything. However, as you might have noticed it's not a pleasant state to be in for long periods. Think of it as a type of mirrored world to the one we are in right now." I had forgotten about that at this point, but I'm glad he explained it to me. I suddenly realize something.

"Drake you said Guardians are the only ones who can faze, so how did the Caster get into the Order?" I ask confused.

"That is a question we all are asking. There are only two disturbing possibilities, I'm afraid. One a Guardian here at this Order has conspired with the Caster and let her in that night. Or somehow this Caster can faze," he replies. Both of his answers are unsettling.

"But is that even possible?"

"That's why the Master has allowed you to come. He hopes that the Caster will reveal what happened when he brings you to her. You see, if we already knew the answer this Caster would not still live, and you would not be here," he explains. I shiver at the thought of death, no matter what the reason. "You must rest now, goodnight Leyla," he says leaving me alone in the room.

I walk into my assigned room and notice that my bags are already laid on top of my bed. The room is almost as big as my apartment. It has a small reading nook, a glass door that leads to a tiny balcony, and bathroom. I set my bags next to my bed only grabbing my charger and phone. I search for a plug, and there is one behind my nightstand. I unplugged the lamp and switched it out for my charger cord. I set my alarm to seven. I'm glad I slept on the way here because it was already two in the morning. I lay down on the bed and start to sink. It's so comfortable, and I'm not sure if I will be able to convince myself to get out of it in the morning. I look up at the ceiling and think back to the Master's warning to Drake and Darrius earlier. I hope for their sake I don't mess up and reveal what I truly am. I couldn't bear it if something bad happened to them because of me. Although, I'm pretty sure that somehow I'm here in the first place because of them.

# Chapter 12
## Questions Without Answers

I wake up before my alarm ever goes off. Thanks to all that sleep on the car ride here, I didn't need much this morning. I step out of the shower to a whole bathroom is engulfed in steam. I pull open each of the drawers to find a plethora of bath products for men and women. There was already shampoo and bodywash in the shower itself, as well as sponges, and clean cloths. They even had fresh towels under the sink. I also found plenty of clips and bands for your hair, as well as a hair dryer, straightener, and curling iron. I feel a little silly for packing all of my own stuff. I walk back into my room to notice something lying on my bed that wasn't there before. I walk over to get a better look. Laying nicely folded on the edge of my bed is a light brown leather armor suit. I look around, feeling a little uneasy, wondering who just walked freely into my room. *Maybe they knocked Leyla, but you were in the shower*, I tell myself. As I pick up the suit a small white card falls out slowly. I pick it up and open the envelope to see a handwritten note inside. It read...

*In order to fit in, you must look the part.*

It wasn't signed, but I believe I know who wrote it. I dry off, slip into the armor, and whoever picked it out guessed my size perfectly. It fit like a glove, and it's surprisingly flexible. It's more comfortable than it looked, and it had almost no weight to it at all. I walk over to the body length mirror and stare at myself. It makes me look different, more serious. I walk back into the bathroom and blow dry my hair. I decide to put it up into a tall ponytail on top of my head. I would have to leave my phone here in the room. This thing apparently didn't come designed with pockets. I place my charger back into my purse and plug back in the lamp. I hide my phone in the drawer of the nightstand and turn it off. I didn't want anyone to hear it go off and pry through it, not that I had anything to hide.

It's almost eight, according to the time on my phone before I turned it off. I walk to my door, and before I tun the handle, I inhale a deep breath and then let it gradually out. As I walk out into the sitting area, I observe Drake and Darrius talking face to face by the door leading to the hallway. They are whispering back and forth to each other. They don't notice me come out until I walk up pretty close to them. Drake spots me first. He gawks at me, his look says it all. Darrius realizes Drake is no longer talking or listening to him, and he turns his head in my direction. His face turns flat like he's trying hard to hide his stunned expression, unlike Drake.

"Wow, you look…" Drake fails to finish his sentence.

"Like Alexandra," I finish it for him.

"Good morning, I hope you all slept well," Helen's voice breaks their attention away from me. We all look over to see her walking up the corridor.

Xander pops up out of nowhere, making me wonder if he was the one who left the armor on my bed. Helen has arrived exactly at eight like she said she would, and I'm glad I was ready. I'm also glad this new situation has broken up the awkward moment between Darrius, Drake, and I. Xander starts to walk off, and Darrius and Drake begin to follow him. Helen stays back and walks closer to me as if she has something to say.

"Leyla, I'm sorry to ask, but while you're here, the Master would prefer that you go by Alexandra," she informs me, but her tone doesn't sound apologetic. It's more direct and commanding.

"Oh, alright," I reply, not thrilled about the idea, but what choice did I have.

"Thank you, Xander has instructed Darrius and Drake to do the same. However, you are more than welcome to use your name in your quarters," she tries a smile, but it's not very convincing. I wonder if all Guardians are this serious or if it's just her. She starts to walk off, and I follow.

The aroma of the food is the first thing that hits you before you even step in. We are led into a large square open dining hall. It's full of tables. The round ones are for sitting at. The long rectangles ones are lined with food on top. The food is set out buffet style. There are eggs made every way you could imagine, pancakes, waffles, several types of meat, and even some dishes I don't recognize. Everything is sitting on real silver platters, bowls, or trays. The fruits and vegetables are precisely stacked in layers by color like a rainbow. Atop the seating tables are off-white table clothes already set with nice china plates and silverware. There is an empty glass flute in front of each dish, and cloth napkins folded in triangles centered on top of the plates. It's simply astonishing. I've never seen food prepared or presented in such lavish.

"Try not to look so impressed, after all, this is something you should already be accustomed to," Darrius bends down and whispers in my ear. He's not wrong, but what did he expect. I am seeing this for the first time. It's hard not to be in awe of it. He grabs a plate off one of the tables, and the others follow suit, so I do the same.

There are too many choices. It's a little overwhelming. I finally decide on some mixed fruit, some bacon, and a couple of poached eggs. As we sit down, I get a better look around the room. I see the same marble columns in all four corners as the room had when we entered last night. There is a large painting of a vineyard hanging on one of the walls. There is also some scattered floral and greenery in grand vases sitting on the marble floor. I notice beautifully sculpted fruits spilling out of bowls placed on top of small stands. Behind the food tables are small windows from one side of the wall to the other, letting in all the light in the room. I notice that some of the Guardians around us aren't dressed in armor but normal clothes. It makes me question why I'm not?

Every one of them appears so young and dazzling. I know Darrius said that they don't age, but I didn't exactly picture this. Each person here could be a model or a doll. Their features are flawless and healthy. All of them have rosy completions, perfectly groomed eyebrows, beards, and nails as if they all just stepped out of a salon. I catch a few glancing in our direction in between their bites. I try to ignore them and eat my food.

Drake sits down next to me. His plate is piled with as much food as he could fit on it. Helen comes over next and makes a point to move Xander over to on the other side of Drake. She has a couple pieces of dry toast on her plate. *Her meal is as boring as her personality.* Darrius has a few pieces of sausage, two eggs, and a biscuit. He spreads them all apart evenly making sure one doesn't touch the other. Xander is staring down at an empty plate. He looks rather displeased about it too. If he was a couple inches taller, had red hair and freckles, I swear he could be Kent's twin. Although, the real Kent wouldn't be able to keep silent about not eating as he is. Speaking of Kent, I wish I could talk with Kat about all this, but I can't exactly tell her what's going on. I'm afraid I'll have to keep all this to myself for the moment.

It doesn't take us long to finish eating, We are currently following Helen and Xander to the Mater's quarters. We were previously informed that the whole fourth floor belongs to him. My heart is beating so fast, and I feel my palms start to get sweaty. I'm nervous about meeting the Master again. He wasn't like anyone I've ever seen. He is both beautiful and terrifying. I notice Helen walking closely to Drake. Earlier she made Xander switch spots with her so she could sit by him at breakfast. Now she is walking so close to him that I'm surprised they aren't bumping into each other. Perhaps I was wrong about her. Maybe she is drawn to Drake after all. She might just be better at hiding it. Not that it bothers me, I don't know why I'm so worried about it. I glance over at Darrius, who keeps glancing over at me, with possible concern on his face. He has been more tense than usual since arriving, which is saying a lot. I realize he is probably just as nervous as I am, or maybe more so. I don't believe he wanted me to come here, nor do I guess he wants to be here either.

We are led into a rectangle-size study. I see the Master sitting behind a sturdy wooden desk. He doesn't seem to notice we've all walked in. The desk takes up an enormous space in the middle of the room. Below the desk is a circular ruby-red rug with the Guardian symbol in the center. Directly behind him hangs a grand painting of an angel. The frame stretches from just off the floor to almost touching the ceiling. The angel is wearing golden armor and has a long sword in his hand as if ready for battle. There are clouds and light in the background, and I wonder if this is a picture of the Angel of Death? Around the room are the same decorative pillars, one in each corner.

Something moves out of the corner of my eye making me jump a little on the inside. I turn my head to the right to see a good-size dog lying comfortably on a large pillow. Its hair is medium length and golden brown, I'm guessing a retriever. It looks back at me slightly moving its tail from one side to the other. It doesn't see any of us as a threat.

I turn my attention to the many book shelves around the room filled with volumes of books. Some appear to be ancient. Mixed in the décor are small artifacts or weapon fragments in glass cases like you would see at a museum. To the left of the desk is a big bay window that outlooks a small garden down below. I didn't look out my window this morning, but I wonder if I could see it from my view as well. It looks lovely from up here, a small touch of nature amid the modern city. I hear the Master writing vigorously. He still hasn't acknowledged us. I realize he is wearing yet a different color armor today. It's white, like the color of his hair, with golden ornamental shoulder pads. There is a chain that starts at the shoulder and connects to each side of his collar. He folds what appears to be his last piece of paper and seals it in an envelope with a wax seal. The seal is a picture of the Guardian symbol. His desk is neat and orderly like the rest of his study.

"Sorry to keep you all waiting," he finally addresses us. "I needed to finish these letters to the other Orders. They need to be aware of this attack in case we aren't the only ones," he informs us. "Xander, please take these to Alia. She will know what to do with them," he instructs. Xander walks over the letters off the Master's desk. He walks past the retriever and then fades from view. *Did he just faze and walk through the wall?* I guess that would be faster. Why use the stairs when you can walk through walls? "Drake, Darrius if you wouldn't mind, I would like to speak with miss Grey alone." The Master looks over at both Drake and Darrius, and his expression makes me think he is waiting for one of them to object. However, neither of them do.

I glance over to see Darrius clenching both his fist. Drake straightens and flexes his jawline. Neither one of them is pleased about his request. "Helen, please close the door and wait outside as well," he commands. I look back at her, and she looks stunned.

However, she doesn't say anything, she waits for both guys to walk back into the hallway. She slowly starts to close both doors, and I look past her to Drake and Darrius with a look of unrest. Darrius locks eyes with me, and I can see him walking back in. However, Drake quickly grabs his arm to stop him. I slowly shake my head no making him stop fighting to get free from Drake's grip. He starts to walk off down the hall. I turn back around, and I see the Master's eyes looking me over. Once the doors are completely shut the Master gets up from his desk and walks around. He is about as tall as Darrius, but he is body is stockier. He moves over to one of the empty cushion chairs seated by the window.

"Please Leyla, come sit," he asks politely. I do as he wishes. At least the view from here is pleasant. I glance out the window. "I have to say that armor suits you," he says, sitting down across from me, I instinctively blush. He lets out a little whistle and his retriever walks over and sits down beside him loyally. "This is Oscar. I rescued him when he was a puppy. He's seven years old now," he introduces me, patting the top of Oscars' head with his right hand. "You know golden retrievers are very smart, and if properly trained, they are great hunting dogs. I've spent years with Oscar training him to be a great hunter. He's one of a kind you know. He is the only dog in the world that can pick up the scent of the magicalkinds," he reveals bragging on himself and Oscar.

"That is very unique," I respond.

"Indeed, between Drake's assistance, and Oscar's nose, we were able to track down and capture those responsible for the attempted invasion," he smiles at me making me feel anxious. His skin is so fair, and I realize he has his white hair fixed back away from his face. His eyes seem to be studying me. I can't help but feel like I'm on trial. Even though I have nothing to hide, nor am I guilty of anything, it still doesn't stop it from being intimidating. "I've been the Master of this Order for just over seventy years now, and this is the first time we've ever been attacked. This is also the first time a mortal has been let in," he divulges. The Master leans forward, hands pressed tightly together, before continuing. "I thank you for your continued discretion while here and for having to go by a name other than yours. It's rather an unfortunate circumstance you are currently in," he states, and he isn't telling me anything I don't already know. "How much do you know about Alexandra or Drake and Darrius for that matter?" He finally takes his eyes off me, and I feel like I can breathe again. He leans back in his chair and looks out the window, silently waiting for me to reply.

"I honestly don't know very much at all about any of them," I answer. "This is all very overwhelming for me," I add in, and his focus turns back to me with a smirk.

"Now that statement, I believe," he tells me looking amused at my reply. "I never met Alexandra. I wasn't a Guardian until after her death," he discloses. "However, based on the information I've recently acquired, you're a stunning replica," he adds looking me over again. I stir uncomfortably in my seat. I wish people would stop comparing me to her.

"Well, it's because of her that I'm here, why I've agreed to all of this. I want everyone to know I'm not Alexandra. I don't know what she did, and frankly, I don't care. I know I can't exactly go back to the way things were, but at least I can start putting this behind me. I don't want to be scared to walk out my door because someone might be there to kidnap me. I don't want to have to worry about if Drake and Darrius are invisibly guarding me wherever I go. I just want this to be over," I say in frustration.

I finally let go of every word and emotion I've been bottling up. He wanted to hear the truth, so I gave it to him. Oscar leaves the Master's side and comes over to me, reacting to my outburst. The dog leans his head down on my knees and I start to pet his forehead. I look down, a little embarrassed at letting my emotions fly, and as I look into his sympathetic brown eyes, I start to feel better. I regain my composure and look back up at the Master, who doesn't seem to mind my reaction one bit.

"I'm sorry," I apologize.

"It's quite alright. Anyone who has this type of situation thrust upon them and doesn't act a little irritated, now that's someone I would worry about," he reveals looking pleased. I'm glad me losing my temper was so amusing to him. "I think it's time to let the others back in. We have someone who's been dying to see you," he declares and stands up abruptly, one of his habits, it would seem. Oscar and I follow him as he goes to the door and opens it. Drake and Darrius look relieved to see me, while Helen still looks upset that she had to wait outside. "Thank you for waiting, if you will all follow me," he instructs and we all follow.

The Master leads us all down to what appears to be the basement. It's silent and frigid down here, and I start to shiver as soon as we enter. I see two Guardians standing outside a large sealed door. When they see the Master walking towards them, one hits a button and the door opens. It makes a loud and unpleasant noise, and I wouldn't be surprised if the whole Order heard it opening.

"Alexandra will come with me, the rest of you, please wait here," the Master commands, and I follow him inside the door.

The door starts to close behind me, and I fight the urge to look back at Drake and Darrius. There are rows of cells on each side of us with thick metal bars. It's even colder in here than it was out there. We walk past more Guardians on the way to the end of the room. I stay silent and I wonder if anyone can hear my heartbeats. It's racing so fast I think it's going to burst out of my chest.

"Don't be afraid," the Master says silently, looking back briefly at me as we continue to walk. Maybe he did hear it, or perhaps he just assumed I would be nervous. "Please give us the room," he orders, and I notice the Guardians start to disappear one after the other. They have all fazed. Why would he have them leave us? "They are still here, and see us. They just can't hear us," he explains. I remember back to when Drake fazed me into the Order, and I understand now. "Let us see if she will be more loosed-lipped today," he states, though I think it was more to himself. "Caster, I've brought you what you have requested," he announces.

I see her, the Caster, and she isn't what I expected. She perks up her sunken down head making me freeze in place. Even through her scars, and bruises, she is still a beauty. Her skin is as silky and smooth as a pure white pearl. Her long jet-black hair hangs down, touching to the ground, outlining her tiny frame. She is sitting down, legs crossed, and I wonder if she was asleep. She slowly raises herself off the ground. I notice some of her limbs are limp. She is wearing a deep blue dress pinned up on one side of her body. It's smooth like satin still giving off a shine in certain places. However, most of her dress is ripped or splatted with dirt and spots of red. She's clearly been tortured or beaten, but still she stands up tall. Her eyes focus on the Master with fury. They are russet brown with flecks of dark green.

It feels as if I'm invisible. She has yet to look over at me. I, on the other hand, can't stop staring at her. The more I look the more cuts and bruises I observe on her exposed arms, legs, neck, and face. I can't help but to feel empathy for her. She smiles and wraps both her hands around the bars. I notice a silver bracelet on her wrist with a large dark blue gem at the center, surrounded by small diamonds on each side. It's unique.

She starts to speak, but I can't understand a word of it. "What did she say?" I ask aloud, unintentionally.

"She speaks in riddles," the Master replies, his back turned to me. "She said there are many paths to the top of the mountain, but the view is always the same." I'm not sure what to say. I don't get the meaning, but I am finding it a bit humorous. I push back a smile.

"I will only speak with Alexandra," she says, this time in English, throwing me off guard. Her voice is alluring, but there is an undertone of demand.

"I have brought Alexandra, now speak," he demands impatiently. "How did you get in the Order?" his voice booms, echoing around the room. I can't help but feel a little frighten. She replies in the same foreign language as before, leaving me in the dark. His tone didn't seem to trouble her one bit. I had to admire her for that. The Master is not someone that you can easily dismiss.

"Pearls don't lie on the seashore. If you want one, you must dive for it," he translates, without me having to ask. "Your game is over, and I will no longer play. Either speak now, or it will be the end of you," his tone is calm, but it sends shivers down my spine, nonetheless. I knew he meant every word, after all, Guardians don't lie. Silence falls around us as they continue to stare at each other, neither one of them budging. The Master raises his hand and all the Guardians come back into view. "No food until she comes to her senses and decides to speak. We will return, and for your sake, I hope you have more than riddles to say," he warns her and starts to walk off. I can tell he is still furious.

The Caster finally looks over at me after he turns away. She whispers two words to me, and I go into shock. I'm able to read the words clearly. The door to the dungeon starts to open. I use everything in my power not to walk up to her. I turn away slowly and head for the door looking back at her every step of the way. She keeps a knowing smile on her face the whole time.

"Are you alright?" Drake's voice breaks my focus from the Caster.

Now that the door is fully open, I see him and the others waiting on us. I look over at him and nod my head yes, even though I'm nowhere near okay. I realize Oscar had followed us down here, and he is sitting patiently at the stairs waiting for his master to return. Helen has her arms crossed, still brooding at the fact that she keeps getting left out, no doubt. Darrius' face is unemotional, but something tells me he is burning up on the inside. Another familiar face is standing next to Helen. Xander has rejoined the group from his earlier task.

"I'm sorry things didn't go well," the Master tells me sounding upset. "We will try again tomorrow," he states and starts to head for the stairs. "Helen, please accommodate our guest for the rest of the afternoon," he commands as he leaves the room. Oscar follows happily after him wagging his tail.

With Helen accompanying us all day, I won't get a chance to speak with Drake or Darrius until this evening. I'm sure they will have plenty of questions for me. I had to tell them what the Caster had mouthed to me. It's going to change everything. Everyone starts to leave, and I take one last look back at the metal door behind me. I wish more than anything I could go back in. I assumed this visit would bring me answers, instead, all it's done is leave me with more questions.

# Chapter 13

## Do I Stay or Do I Go?

We've been here for three days, and each morning the Caster still refuses to divulge any information. I've learned that the language she sometimes speaks is Mandarin. The riddles she likes to tell are different Chinese proverbs. As amusing as they are, they're anything but helpful. Every day she puts on an act and tries to look strong. However, her body keeps getting weaker. I could tell she was holding onto the bars just to keep from falling. She had fresh bruises and more cuts than I've seen before. She wasn't doing well at all, and she was getting worse at hiding it. The Master added no water to her already getting no food today, and I'm not sure how much longer she can hold out. As far as the Master goes, his temper just gets worse every day. I dare not tell him that our continued visits are in vain. I don't see how that benefit her or me.

I haven't been able to speak with Darrius or Drake about our visits. Being able to have a private conversation with them has been proving difficult. Helen is attached to Drake's hip at all times, and every day she becomes more and more comfortable around him. Her feelings for him are anything but obvious at this point, and I can't believe he is completely oblivious to it, that or he just doesn't mind the attention. On a good note, Drake and Darrius have become closer. They spend most of their day at the training grounds, meant for new Guardians to train in combat and arms. They spar for hours. Xander, Helen, and I just watch most of the time. Though Xander sometimes joins in. He goes wherever Darrius goes. He even stands outside our rooms in the sitting area every night, hence my difficulty to speak with Drake and Darrius alone.

If I'm not watching Drake and Darrius fight, I'm either down in the garden or the library. I try to learn as much about the Guardians while I'm here since I've got nothing better to do. I'm starting to get worried though. I don't know how long I will be expected to stay. School starts in just two days, and I'm beginning to think I'm going to miss it. Luckily thanks to my new guard, Helen and Xander have left me be. Oscar and I are currently headed to the outside garden. He's taken a liking to me after our first encounter, and he now follows me everywhere I go. He has even been sleeping in my room. The Master doesn't seem to mind. He appears too preoccupied with other matters. Letters come daily to him from other Orders about the recent attack. He's always stuck in his study addressing them. The garden has become my place to escape all the odd stares from the other Guardians, as well as, a place to think. Me accompanying the Master every morning hasn't gone unnoticed. It's nice and sunny out today, though the air is cold. I sit down on one of the benches, and Oscar jumps up to sit beside me, laying his head on my lap. His warmth is welcome.

"School starts in two days, and we are no closer to answers then we were three days ago. I don't want to leave without them, but staying here is driving me crazy," I say aloud and let out a short sigh. I can see a small puff of air leave my lips. "This is hopeless," I add in despair.

"I'm sorry we've stayed here so long. If I had known the Caster wasn't going to talk, I would have refused to let you come," Darrius apologizes and pops up out of nowhere. I jump up a little, and Oscar perks up as well. I see him walking towards me, I wonder how he lost his escort. "Drake is keeping Xander busy sparring, and Helen is content to watch. She didn't bother to follow after me. We don't have long, but Drake and I agreed it was time to speak with you. I'm sorry it wasn't sooner," he fills me in.

"I'm glad you had a chance to get away. I've been meaning to speak with you guys as well," I admit. "It's not your fault I decided to come. Besides, I know the reason why the Caster won't talk to me," I reveal.

"What do you mean Leyla?" he questions.

"She isn't going to reveal anything to me because she knows I'm not Alexandra," I explain. He peers down at me unconvinced.

"Leyla, that's not possible," he retorts.

"I'm afraid it is," I insist. "I've been trying to tell you both this since the first time I met the Caster. I know it's hard to believe. Trust me, I've been stirring about it these past few days. On that first day I met her as the Master turned to leave, she whispered two words to me," I tell him. "She said dark beauty." He looks at me like I expected him to. "Dark beauty, it's what my mom used to call me when she was doting on me or trying to make me feel better. My name, Leyla, means dark beauty. Unless you can tell me that Alexandra had that same nickname, I don't see how it can be a coincidence. She knows who I am, and she knows I'm not Alexandra," I clarify and wait for him to mull it over.

"That makes no sense. Why would she tell us to get you if she knew you weren't really Alexandra?" He's confused, creasing his forehead.

"I don't know, but I do know that she will never tell me unless the Master isn't around to hear it. I think we both know the chances of that happening. I'm going in circles trying to figure out the answer to that question. I don't know what to do about it, I feel so stuck here," I relay frustrated. I start to stand, and Darrius walks over to me and brings my body into his. I'm completely taken off guard by his embrace.

"Don't worry Leyla, you have Drake and I. We may not get the answers we seek desperately, but we will get you out of here. You're more important than anything that Caster has to say," he whispers tenderly in my ear. I know in my gut he meant every word he said. I wrap my arms around him in return. I let him comfort me. I don't know where this sudden softness was coming from, but I treasured the moment for as long as possible. "I have to be getting back. I'm sure it won't take Drake long to defeat Xander. He's not exactly good at holding back. I'll make sure and fill him in on what you've told me." He lets me go, much to my regret and speeds off back the way he came. As I watch him go, I feel a change in me, and I can't help but want my cake and eat it too. I didn't come all this way to leave empty-handed. I just need to figure out a way to talk with the Caster alone.

I've been running different scenarios through my mind all day, and most of them end pretty badly. I skip dinner and head up to my room early. I lay back on my bed, and Oscar jumps up and lays beside me. If only I had someone else to talk to about it. I can't call Kat, and the guys would just talk me out of it. Well, I do know someone that doesn't seem opposed to a little mischief. I pull out my phone and call her.

"Hello?" Bridget answers right away so I think she must be at the bar. It's very noisy in the background.

"I'm sorry to bother you while you're at work. I can call back later," I tell her.

"No, it's fine, I'm on break," she tells me, and I hear her shout out to someone that she's going on break. The noise starts to get quieter and quieter; she must have walked outside or something. "What's up?"

"Well, it's a long story, but I think I might have found who is after me. Or at least someone who may know who is," I inform her. "I'm at the Guardian Order in St. Louis," I add.

"What, you're at an Order?" she repeats in shock. "How in the world, why would they let in a true mortal?" she sounds flustered.

"Like I said, it's kind of a long story. I need a favor, or rather I need to know if there is a spell that can make me look like someone else?"

"Well, ya sure, but it takes a while to cast, and I have to be nearby you the whole time I cast it. Normally we don't cast that type of spell on true mortals, only ourselves. Luckily I know the spell, but it would take almost all my energy to cast it on you. Are you in some kind of danger?" she concluded sounding slightly concerned.

"No, not me exactly. I guess my idea won't work. I can't exactly have you walking around in the Order," I tell her my hopes suddenly dashed. "You see, there is Caster held prisoner here. She attacked the Order. I think she is behind the attacks on me or knows who is. She knows me, but she won't reveal anything with any of the Guardians around. I'm afraid the Guardian in charge here is going to lose interest in her any day now. If he does, it will be the end of her and the end of any chance I have to understand what is going on with me," I explain.

"Oh, gotcha," she replies. "Well, just for example, if I could be there to cast a spell on you, what was your plan exactly?" she sounds intrigued, so I humor her and fill her in. She asks a few questions along the way, but she seems to understand.

"Wow, that's good in theory if you don't get caught," she remarks, and she's not wrong. My idea would have to go perfectly for it to work. There are no room for any errors. "This Caster, how dangerous is she? Do you know what her ability is?"

"Not one hundred percent on this, but the theory is she might be able to faze," I reply.

"What!" she exclaims in complete disbelief. "That's crazy, I didn't even know that was possible. I guess if you really think about it, it is a magical gift, but up till now it's only an ability a Guardian can possess," she pauses, and I can hear her let out a little sigh. "I'm probably going to regret this, but I can't resist. I need to know if one of us can possess such an ability. I'm going to come, and I'm going to help," she proclaims, and I'm stunned.

"Really, but you won't be safe here," I caution. I don't want my new friend to end up in a cell next to the other Caster. I couldn't bear it if something happened to her because of my crazy idea. This is why I was hoping she could just help me from afar and cast a spell from where she was. "I don't know Bridget."

"It's fine. Besides, I think with a little modification to your plan, we could not only talk to this Caster, but break her out," she informs me, and I don't know what to say. "Trust me Leyla, if she can do what you say, it's worth it," she assures me.

Before she hangs up, she fills me in on her idea, and I have to say it's a good improvement. So good in fact, I think we may have a chance to get the Caster out of the Order. It will require Drake and Darrius now though, and I wasn't sure how they would feel about it. I only have until tomorrow to convince them. Hopefully, I can catch them tonight before they head for their rooms. Maybe I'll get lucky and Xander won't' be right outside our doors tonight. I head out to the sitting room and grab one of the books I borrowed from the library to read while waiting for them to arrive. It shouldn't be long now. Dinner started about an hour ago. It's precisely at six every evening.

I finally hear them talking loudly coming down the corridor. I try not to look too obvious and avert looking towards their direction. I continue to read by the fire as Oscar nuzzles my left leg sitting beside me on this oversized chair. I'm trying to pretend I'm not on edge.

"Leyla, there you are. Were you not hungry?" Darrius asks sitting directly across from me in a matching chair. Drake and Xander walk over and sit on the couch to my right. I need to think of a way to get Xander out of the room for a bit.

"No, not particularly. However, I think Oscar is," I hint looking over at Xander. "Xander, I don't suppose you mind taking him to get some food?" I ask as politely as I can muster. I even bat my eyelashes. He seems to hesitate at first but then rises from the couch.

"Come on Oscar, let's go," he says. Oscar perks up and follows him out. Good thing Oscar is hungry, or that would have never worked. I wait a few minutes before speaking again since I've learned Guardians can hear for miles away, if they wish.

"Do you think it's safe to talk now?" I whisper looking over and at both Darrius and Drake. They both nod.

"That was quick thinking." Drake sounds impressed and gives me a big grin.

"Thank you," I tell him hoping he stays in good spirits. The plan is to convince him first and get him to persuade Darrius for me. It seems like my best option. "I have a crazy idea, and I'm hoping that I can count on you to help me carry it out. Please hear me out before you say anything," I request looking over at Darrius. "I called Bridget earlier. You see I've decided that I didn't come all this way and go through everything I have to leave empty-handed. I think I've got a way to get our answers."

"Oh, do tell?" Drake states sounding interested, for the moment.

I fill them in on Bridget's and my plan to help the Caster escape. I try to talk as fast as possible and stick to the main points since I knew Xander could be back at any moment. They both listen and don't interrupt. They do, however, look back and forth to each other a lot, with worried looks. It doesn't make me feel very sure about their decisions.

"I know it's insane and stupid, and if one thing goes wrong, we all could end up down in a cell, but..." I didn't get a chance to finish.

"But we have to do it," Drake interrupts, and his response surprises me. I didn't think it was going to be that easy to convince him. "Don't look so surprised," he starts reading my thoughts, "you and Bridget's idea is pretty good. Darrius found time to fill me in on your earlier conversation, and I completely understand why you want to go through with this. Something tells me you're going to try with or without our help, and I'd rather help," he adds. I look over at Darrius, who has yet to say anything thus far.

"I have my objects, of course, but I agree with Drake. I can see your mind is made up, and I would never forgive myself if something bad happened because I refused to help. Leyla, I feel this Caster doesn't deserve to be set free, and I don't like that we are going to help her. As much as I want answers, I feel like this may not work out like you think it will," he cautions me.

"You're right Darrius, this could wind up backfiring, and it could just make things worse. However, I can't live with myself if I don't at least try. I think this is the right thing to do. I know this Caster did something unspeakable, but

I have to know what she knows. I have to believe that this will work out," I tell him.

"Very well," Darrius replies and stands up abruptly. He looks directly at me with those blue eyes of his, instantly swept into his waves. "Leyla, I agree to help you, but if this Caster becomes difficult to control, or she threatens your life in any way," he pauses and his face turns cold, "I will end her life myself." His voice is void of any emotion.

"Xander is coming back," Drake announces. "Goodnight Leyla, we will see you in the morning," Drake softly smiles in my direction, and both him, and Darrius step into their rooms. Xander enters almost immediately after with Oscar not far behind.

"Where did everyone go?" he asks me looking around the room disappointedly.

"They went to their rooms. Thank you for feeding Oscar for me. I'm going to bed now as well. Goodnight," I tell him, and he nods briefly as to say, goodnight back. I head into my room with Oscar at my heels. Darrius' words still haunt me, I do not wish to see any more death. I'm already haunted enough by those two men. I pray this will not be the outcome of my decision.

The next morning, I follow the Master into the dungeon once again. As we reach the cell, the Caster doesn't even bother standing at our arrival. *I wonder if she will have enough strength for what is to come.*

"Today is your last here if you do not comply. Tell us who you are and why you attacked our Order?" the Master demands. She says nothing in return, or even look up at him. "Perhaps you are too weak to speak **witch**," he says disgustedly.

Her head raises only to glare at him with rage. He used that word on purpose to get a rise out of her. Why else say it? On a certain level I understand why he is doing this. Her gift, if it is what I believe, could indeed threaten all the Orders. Not to mention he feels justified to take her life in exchange for the Guardian's life's she took when she attacked. However, I couldn't let things end this way. I just couldn't.

"Perhaps all your questions will be revealed to you in a dream," she mocks. "Or perhaps you will never know. I cannot grant what you wish. You know what I ask. I am prepared to die for it," she promises harshly, holding nothing back. She still has some strength left in her yet.

"Bold words, however, they are wasted on me. I will return one last time tonight. Be warned, if you do not have anything useful to give me your life will end tomorrow morning," he assures her. He waives his hands and the Guardians come back into view.

"Please, please don't you have anything to say," I beg in desperation, speaking to her directly for the first time since I've been down here.

She looks at me as if she pities me instead of the other way around. She smiles sweetly, but she does not respond. I can feel the Master's eyes piercing me, though I'm not looking at him. I know he might be angry at me for speaking, but I couldn't stay silent any longer. I hear the Master walk off as the door begins to open.

I keep my eyes on her and whisper. "Hold on, just hold on." I turn and walk out before I can see her reaction.

Not long after breakfast, I go upstairs to check my phone. Bridget has already left Iowa and will be here in a few hours. It's up to Darrius and Drake to find an alternate way to get her in the building so she can fulfill her part in our plan. I hope they figure it out soon, preferably before she arrives. I hear a quiet knock on my door, and I walk over to answer it. Drake is on the other side. He quickly comes in and shuts the door behind him.

"I only have a moment. I wanted to let you know I've found a way in for Bridget. There is a secret exit in the Master's office. If one of us can access it we can let Bridget inside," he tells me.

"How will you get Bridget up to the fourth floor?" I ask him, not sure if he has thought this through.

"Don't you worry about that," he says and winks at me. "Leyla, listen, if things don't go as planned, I need you to promise me something." His tone turns serious. "Darrius and I have agreed that if something doesn't go according to plan, we will both take responsibility so you can go home," he reveals.

"I can't let you both do that for me," I strongly object. Drake smiles at me as if he knew I was going to say that.

"I'm afraid it's already decided. You have to promise me that you will play along and act like you had no idea what was going on, do you understand," he pleads.

"I can't promise that Drake, I won't," I insist.

"Leyla, before Darrius and I showed up, you had a life, a dream. We aren't going to take that away from you. Go back to school, go hang out with your friends, live the normal life you were supposed to have before we came in and ruined it," he declares.

"Please don't ask me to do this. You haven't ruined anything. I'm learning to live with a little chaos. I don't want you and Darrius to be punished because of my idea, how could I live with myself?" I disagree desperately. He smiles at me tenderly making my heart skip a beat. He's never looked at me that way before, with such feelings in his eyes. I can't believe he and Darrius would do this for me. How could I mean that much to them? They don't even really know me.

"Don't put that on yourself, Leyla. We agreed to help you, remember. We want to do this for you, and we want you to promise this to us in return." I fight back the tears and try to be strong. What kind of person would I be if I let them do this for me? "Please Leyla, you must promise. We, I, couldn't bear it if anything happened to you." I look into his snake charming eyes making me want to agree. His voice is full of pain, and I want to take that pain away.

"I promise." I give in, no longer able to resist his request, though I wanted to.

"Thank you," he states relieved, and walks over slowly and stops inches from me. He gently kisses the top of my forehead, as he does, it sends shocks of electricity from where his lips touched me down to my toes. "I have to go now. I'll see you soon," he promises and leaves my room.

Hours drag on as I hide in my room, waiting for everything to be set in motion. I received a text from Bridget a few minutes ago letting me know she has arrived and is nearby. We only have the dinner time for our plan to work, which is about thirty minutes or so. Thirty minutes for everything to happen without a hitch or to go horribly wrong. Bridget, Darrius, and Drake could all wind up at the Master's wrath if this doesn't work. I remember my promise to Drake, and I cringe. I don't want to watch any one of them being dragged down to the dungeon and tortured. This is defiantly the craziest thing I've ever done or ask anyone to do. I pull on my armor and walk down to the dining hall. When I enter, I'm relieved to see the Master seated in his usual spot. Someone brings him a plate and he glances up at me. I notice Oscar isn't with him, speaking of, I haven't seen that dog since breakfast. The Master nods in my direction and I give him a quick smile in return. Now that he's seen me, and I him, I would have an alibi. I pick a plate off a nearby table and make my way to the line of food. As I grab a spoon full of mashed potatoes, I feel someone standing next to me. I look over to see Darrius hovering.

"Bridget is in. I gave her some advice on how to proceed. I hope this works, Leyla," he whispers sounding unsure.

"It will," I declare, trying to convince him and myself. *It has to work!*

# Chapter 14

## Risky Business

**Drake Aljera**

I see Darrius coming down the corridor as I head to my room. He looks as if everything is normal. I can only guess that means phase one is complete. He couldn't stop and chat since Helen is right beside me. From what Darrius told me, Bridget's magic seems to be adequate for this task. If she is as good as he says with her ability, we should pull this next part off without a hiccup. Helen waits outside while I change into a new armor suit. I walk out so she can accompany me down to dinner, though I know that's not where we will wind up.

"Thank you for waiting. You didn't need to," I tell her.

"No problem, are you ready to join the others?"

I realize she has her hair down today, and it's no longer in her normal braid. It's loose and long falling in waves around her shoulders and arms. It is much more flattering this way. Her light blue eyes are holding mine as if she has something she wants to say. She pulls them suddenly away from me in alarm as someone walks up the hallway towards us. I turn to see Xander hurrying toward our direction.

"Darrius has already gone down to dinner. I see you lost track of him yet again," she grumbles in Xander's direction with disappointment.

"I'm sorry, I'm here on orders," he explains, and I see Helen's figure straighten. "The Master would like us three to meet him down below to accompany him to visit the Caster," he informs us. *Perfect*, things are moving along. Helen glares at Xander for a moment as if she is about to question his statement.

"Very well," she finally answers. Xander speeds off ahead of us, but we walk down the stairs at a normal pace. Before we reach the bottom floor, Helen stops and turns to face me. "Drake," she starts, and her voice sounds nervous. Her eyes are avoiding mine, "We will be hosting the Creation Ball here in about a month. I was wondering if you would accompany me?" She's still looking anywhere but directly at me. She clasps her hands together behind her back while awaiting my answer.

"Oh, is that here already? I didn't realize," I reply thinking aloud. "I'm afraid I don't attend that event," I tell her truthfully. Her eyebrows crinkle as she gives me a confused look. "However, if I do come, I promise to escort you. It would be my pleasure," I add. I didn't have the heart to refuse her entirely, but I meant it when I said I don't attend.

"Oh. Well, if you do decide to attend, please let me know so I can be prepared to expect you," she requests. Her face goes back to her normal stern look of indifference.

I can tell she wasn't expecting a lukewarm response, but she handled it very well. As we reach the basement, we both see the Master standing outside the open metal doorway. Xander is already there. He looks between me and Helen with an odd look, as if he realizes what happened between us.

"Good, you've arrived. I need you three to escort the prisoner and me to my study," the Master instructs. I see Helen presses her lips together. I knew she would be suspicious.

"Master, you want us to remove the Caster from her cell. There are no wards outside the prison, she will have nothing blocking her magic once we lead her out of this room!" Helen sounds appalled.

The Master, who had started walking to the cell, turns on his heels and stares back at Helen. "Are you questioning my decision?" he accuses.

Xander and I can't help but look between the two of them. I'm all but holding my breath. The guards in the cell peek over at them as well, and we are all waiting to hear her response. She is quiet for a moment, and I can tell she is carefully thinking over her next words.

"No Master, forgive me," she apologizes through clenched teeth. Xander, Helen, and I both walk in behind the Master.

I can feel the anger emanating off Helen as she walks beside me. She may be silent now, but she isn't happy about this. As we reach the cell, I lay eyes on the Caster for the first time. I've seen many in my years. She looks close to death, and I'm starting to doubt she will be able to get up, let alone walk. This may be a bad sign, but there is nothing I can do about it now. She barely raises her head to greet us. I can see in her eyes she is ready for death. It appears that her spirit and her fight have dissolved. Her lips are chapped, and her eyes have dark rings around them. Her dress is nothing more than rags falling loosely around her already thin figure. There isn't a place on her skin that I can't see a bruise or scar of some kind. I didn't approve of the Master's methods, especially when they have no obvious effect.

"Open the cell, get her to her feet," the Master commands.

The guards closest open the cell and raise her off the ground. Xander goes in and takes her. I watch as her feet drag on the floor. I walk over to the other side and balance her. She weighs nothing. The Master starts to walk out, and we follow along with Helen and few guards from the prison. I don't think this Caster could use any of her magic even if she wanted to. She has lasted this long, so that means she's been strong up to this point. I hope she can last a little longer.

We reach the Master's study a few minutes later. The guards from the prison stay in the hallway as Xander and I walk the Caster inside. They gently sit her down in one of the chairs. Helen is glaring over at the Caster as if she is waiting for her to strike. She is still furious.

"Please wait outside. I believe the Caster and I have some things to discuss." The Master has his back turned to us and waved his hand for us to leave.

I look over at Helen. Her face is turning three shades of red. I hear a growl all of a sudden, and I pull my focus to the other side of the room. Oscar has gotten up from his bed to staring at all of us. That dog, I completely forgot about him. He could blow this whole thing, and we are so close. I try to stay calm.

"I think Oscar looks hungry. I'm sure the presence of the magicalkind isn't too good for his instincts. I better take him down to eat, if that's alright with you?" I ask, starting to walk over to put myself between the dog and the Master.

"Please do. Helen, do I need to repeat myself?" he states rhetorically, his back still turned away from us. "Wait outside."

I grab Oscar's collar, who now is in a full growl baring his teeth. I take him unwilling out of the room. I look back at Helen to see both fists clenched at her sides. She turns around in a huff, and I know she is fighting with every bit of her might not to say something back. She closes the door and starts to pace back and forth on the other side. I can feel Oscar fighting me to get back inside.

"Xander, can you take him down to eat please?" I beg. "He doesn't know me as well," I add.

Xander looks annoyed at my request, but he comes over and takes him from me. Luckily, he has a better time getting him to follow. I let go of my breath. That was too close. I look back at Helen who is still pacing and now mumbling to herself under her breath. I dare not say anything. I just let her stew. She catches me staring and she glares at me.

"Don't you think something about this is off?" she asks me infuriated.

"You know the Master better than I. Besides, that Caster can't even walk. I doubt she can cast any spells. She is no threat to him in her current condition," I try and assure her, but it doesn't work. I try to be indirect since I can't lie to her and tell her she is right. Seconds later the doors open, and Helen rushes in.

"Take the prisoner back to her cell," the Master commands. The guards from the prison obey and come in to drag the Caster out of the room. "Helen, Drake, speak of this to no one for now, understand?" He pauses and we both nod silently. "You may go," he instructs.

Helen lingers for only a moment and then storms off past me down the hall. I look back at the Master. *He* gives me a wink. His eyes glow white for a brief moment, and then he quickly closes the doors again. *I can't believe we just pulled that off!* I turn around and speed up to catch Helen who is already halfway down to the second level.

"Helen, are you going to be okay?" She stops and turns to look at me. She looks ten times scary than Darrius ever has at this moment, which is not an easy feat.

"I'm not sure what just happened, but something was off about that whole thing!" she practically shouts. I don't press her any further. As we reach the entry of the banquet hall Helen stops suddenly in front of me. "Drake, can you honestly tell me you didn't feel something off about that whole charade. What could have been so important to take the Caster out of her cell?" She turns to ask me, her eyes peering into mine with anger and confusion.

"Your instincts are obviously telling you there is," I reply trying to avoid directly answering her question. "Would you like to return to the Master to speak with him about this? If he is going to tell anyone, it would be you," I point out. She stares at me for a few more moments before letting out a small sigh. She turns her face away from mine and looks down at the floor.

"If the Master wanted to tell me, he would have already shared it with me before this," she concludes. "Let's go eat," she starts to walk in, and I follow her inside. I spot Xander walking in on the opposite side of the room with Oscar. He heads over to where Darrius and Leyla are already sitting. We might have succeeded in getting the Caster out of her cell, but now the real trick is going to be able to get away with it. Plus, Darrius still has to get the Caster and Bridget out of the Order. I head to the table to grab a plate. I walk over to the buffet, pile it with food, and head back to the table.

"Are you not hungry?" Leyla turns to Helen who is sitting in front of an empty plate.

"I'm afraid I've lost my appetite," she replies sounding disgruntled. Darrius seems to be done eating and he gets up abruptly. I want to say good luck to him, but I dare not.

"If you will excuse me for a moment," Darrius says dryly. Xander starts to get up as well. "I do not need an escort to the bathroom," Darrius states annoyed to Xander. Xander's checks turn a little red, and he quickly sits back down.

*Good thinking my friend.* It won't buy him a lot of time, but it should be just enough.

"Alexandra," the Master's voice sounds out. I turn to see him walking over toward our table as Darrius is leaving. "If you've finished eating, would please come with me to visit our friend," he asks referring to the caster.

"I've finished," Leyla answers. The Master reaches out his hand to Leyla, who takes it. He pulls her up from the chair with a brief smile. Something in me flares when they touch.

## Leyla Gray

As I take the Master's hand, I notice all eyes in the room fall on me, and it makes me feel uneasy. I thought he didn't want any attention on me, if so, this was an odd way to go about it. He doesn't seem bothered by it one bit. Oscar follows closely behind us. I notice he seems to be on edge and very alert. I wish I could have stayed and asked Drake how it went, but I'm assuming it went well. Now Darrius just has to do his part before everything escalates. As we make our way to the stairs, several blurs come up to meet us. They stop inches in front of us. I recognize each one of them at once. They are some of the Guardians who have been guarding the Caster. They all have a look of panic on their faces, which can only mean good things for me.

"What is the meaning of this? Why are you not at your post?" the Master asks annoyed, letting go of my hand.

"It's the Caster, sir. She's vanished," one of them answer with a softly shaking voice. I let out a gasp trying to play along.

"That's impossible," he replies. "Explain!" he demands with an unforgiving tone.

"We don't know what happened," another one speaks up, "she just vanished right in front of us," he replies in shock. "What do you want us to do?"

"You've done enough, alert every Guardian. I want everyone searching every inch of this Order and the surrounding area. She couldn't have gone far in her condition. Bring her back, now!" he snaps. I'm suddenly feeling afraid, and can't help but move slowly away from him. He turns to look at me freezing me in place from his glare. His amber eyes are sparking. "If you would be so kind as to give Darrius and Drake a message. Tell them to meet me in my office immediately," he says coldly and calmly, his eyes still ablaze.

I can't muster any words. I nod my head and turn to deliver his message. I see Drake, Helen, and Xander still sitting at the table. Darrius must not have returned.

"Alexandra, what are you doing? Why aren't you with the Master?" Helen looks concerned.

"The Master would like to see you, Drake, and Darrius in his office right now," I state urgently. Helen rises from the table, and Drake does the same.

"Xander, go get Darrius and meet us up there," Helen instructs. Xander gets up from the table and does as she commands. Helen and Drake start speed off as my heart sinks a little in my chest. *Good luck.*

### Darrius Stone

I've finished my errand, and I'm currently speeding back down to the dining hall before Xander starts looking for me. As I turn the corner, I spot him headed up the hall. I quickly turn around and head towards the closest bathroom before he notices me. Things must have already progressed. I hear him getting closer so I walk out of the bathroom.

"Darrius, you must come with me at once. The Master is requesting to see you and Drake in his study," he informs me.

"Alright, any idea what the rush is?" I inquire.

"No, but we better hurry. Helen and Drake will have already arrived there by now," he answers.

I follow behind him and we both speed off. Just as I thought, the Master believes we are involved, as I knew he would. I don't think he's trusted us one minute since we've arrived. If he did, he wouldn't have assigned Helen and Xander to follow us around all day and night. There is only two outcomes we face now. One, we get away with this, and we can finally leave this place. The second. and more ominous, we get caught and suffer the consequences. As we reach the Master's study, I see Drake, Helen, and the other heads of the Order, inside and waiting on me. Xander and I both slow down. I walk in, but he stops just before the door.

"Go on in. I'll be waiting out here," he states.

He isn't one of the heads, so he isn't permitted any further. He pulls the doors shut behind me as I walk over to stand by Drake. All eyes are on us, and I wish nothing more but to get this over with. The Master stands in the middle of the room, everyone else is on either side of him. Helen walks over and stands beside us. Why, I don't know.

"Master what is the meaning of this? Did something happen?" Helen speaks her voice is full of confusion. The Master doesn't seem to hear her. He instead glares at Drake and I intently.

"I would like to give you two a chance to come forward now with any information you might have," the Master announces, and everyone stands still and quiet. Neither I, nor Drake, say anything. "Very well, your chance to win my favor has expired," he gripes angrily. "Head of the Order of the Caster has escaped, or should I say has been liberated. I don't think for one moment she didn't have help. I want to know what you two know about this," the Master demands pointing his finger at Drake and me. Everyone in the room gasp and murmurs to each other in astonishment.

"You think they had something to do with it, Master?" Helen questions.

"This is the first time I'm hearing she's escaped," I state defensively.

"Me as well," Drake speaks up. "Maybe we should be pointing fingers at one of the guards who escorted her back to her cell," Drake suggests. The murmurs start again, and the Master looks around confused.

"What do you speak of? The Caster hasn't been in her cell," he argues outraged.

"Master you asked Drake, Xander, and I to meet you at the prison during dinner. You asked us not to speak of it, so I will say no more," Helen replies, and the others start to whisper again among themselves.

"I did no such thing! Explain the meaning of this," the Master demands.

"We escorted the prisoner here to this very room. The guards took her back to her cell, as me, and Helen went down to dinner as instructed," Drake enlightens everyone.

"Is this true, Helen?" One of the Order heads asks. Helen nods her head yes.

"I was at dinner. I saw the Master there the whole time. Something isn't adding up," I speak up in the Master's defense. Everyone starts to speak among themselves, trying to figure out what a reasonable explanation could be.

"Master, fellow Guardians, if I may. Could it be possible that the attack was a distraction? I fought the Caster and her followers, and Casters weren't the only demonkinds among the group. We fought Theirans as well. What if the Caster also had Mimic with her," Helen suggests.

"A Mimic? Do be serious. They died long ago. No one has seen or heard of one in years," another one of Order Heads speaks up with disapproval.

"That doesn't mean they aren't still alive. If the Caster had Theirans following her because of her gift, demonkind she could have other demonkind at her disposal. Helen has a point. However, if it wasn't a Mimic, it could very well have been a Caster with an ability to change their appearance," Drake comments, agreeing with Helen. As I look around the room, I see that his theory started to catch like fire.

"Being able to change yourself into someone else is a special gift indeed, at least for that long of time," a man to my right speaks up. "If this is true, once they made their move the prisoner could have very easily fazed them both out of here. No one would be the wiser," he concludes.

"If you want to know the truth, I thought it was too easy that she got caught, but if she knew she had a way out the whole time, then that would explain why she stayed so silent," Helen reveals. "She wanted to speak with Alexandra, but what if we didn't agree to her terms? She would need some way to escape," she adds. I stay silent and let things play out. I never imagined it would go this well. However, I look over to the Master who is the only one in the room not buying it. How far will he go to pin this on us, I wonder.

"Master, with all due respect, I believe this makes more sense than these two orchestrating this all by themselves," a woman to my left states.

"Drake was with me the whole time. As per your instructions, I've personally kept close to him throughout his stay. I doubt he had anything to do with this. Also, Darrius just said that he saw you during dinner, which means you must have seen him as well. I don't see how he could have done this. Master, please, we have all been tricked by this wicked witch. She attacked us to divert us from noticing she placed one of her underlings here. She will pay. I will hunt her down myself!" Helen announces and bends down on one knee and puts her clenched right hand over her chest.

"I didn't come up with a plan to help her escape, and I will gladly assist in hunting her back down if that is what you command," Drake speaks up.

The Master looks around the room and then turns his attention back to us. No doubt he realizes he will never convince the others that we had anything to do with the Caster's disappearance. At least not without any hard proof.

"Very well, you are free to leave us," the Master says unwillingly.

"Master, and other leaders of the Order. Now that the Caster is gone, we wish to remove Leyla and leave the Order," I boldly state.

"No!" The Master gives me a look that could kill. He realizes everyone is watching him and relaxes. "With the Caster on the loose, I think you all should stay here," he adds to back up his decision.

"Leyla is a mortal, not a Guardian. She came as you wished because the Caster requested her. Should she not be able to leave now that we are no longer holding the prisoner?" I point out. He didn't scare me. He has no power over Leyla now. The fact that he's even been allowed around her these past few days have been enough. Leyla doesn't belong here.

"The mortal has already stayed here longer than she probably should have. We don't want to run the risk of anyone outside this group learning what she really is," the man from my right speaks up again. The Master doesn't look over at him, but it's setting in on his face that he doesn't have a good enough reason to keep us here.

"I believe she has proven that she is willing to corporate with us. When we catch the Caster, we can call on her again, if necessary. Drake and Darrius have proven they can guard her, and they have earned her trust. I believe they should stay with this mortal," the woman from earlier suggests. I hear the Order Heads start to agree. It would seem the Master has once again been overruled.

"Leave and take Leyla home. Watch over her, and if you find this Caster, you are to report back to us immediately," he commands, and we both nod in agreeance. "Helen and Xander will see you out, and we will be checking in," he warns.

We take our leave and follow Helen out of the room. I'm glad to be leaving this place. I've wanted to leave before we ever even arrived. Drake and I hurry off to our rooms. I'm happy to see Helen and Xander stay behind. As we open the doors to our suite, Leyla is pacing back and forth in front of the roaring fire.

"Darrius, Drake, what's going on? Are you both alright?" Leyla asks desperately walking over to greet us.

She didn't put her hair up today, and her midnight waves move ever so slightly around her porcelain skin as she steps towards us. I wonder if she knows how hard it's been for me to hold back around her since our brief moment on New Year's. She's worried about us. I can see it in her jeweled green eyes. I want to go over and embrace her and tell her everything is okay, but I resist.

"We are fine Leyla," Drake answers her. "We have good news," he says changing the subject. She looks at both of us with an uncertain look.

"We are taking you home," I tell her.

# Chapter 15

## Past, Present, and Future

**Leyla Gray**

Though our plan worked, the fallout was still far from over. Darrius and Drake both inform me that the Order would be watching us and that once we arrived home, it would be wise not to mention anything about the event. I understand, of course, and I'm just glad to be leaving that place. I send Bridget a message. I don't want to risk texting her while still in the Order. She had stayed behind to get some rest. She used a lot of her magic in order to disguise herself as the Master. Not to mention projecting that the Caster went back to her cell when in reality, she was hiding under the desk until Darrius could come up and let them out. Bridget promised she would take the Caster somewhere safe until her recovery. Apparently, she was as close to death as she appeared. I ask Bridget not to tell me where so I won't accidentally reveal it to Darrius or Drake. Since they can't lie, it's best if they don't know for now. I'm grateful to Bridget, she risked her life to help us, and didn't seem to mind one bit. Thank goodness for her bold personality, or should I say reckless. The only thing Bridget was able to get out of the Caster so far is her name, Liling Mei. Bridget informed me that in China, the first name is last, and the last name is first. So I guess we would call her Mei. Neither Bridget, Darrius, nor Drake has heard of her, so we still don't know much at this point. I lay down in the back of Drake's car and try to stop my mind from racing, but it's hard. I have so many questions, and I'm worried about keeping up appearances. Plus, I have school tomorrow, the new semester will start, and I need to try and get some rest. I close my eyes and try to relax.

*Lightning, it strikes the tree repeatedly in front of me. My nightmare has skipped forward, starting me where I'm standing a few feet from the body. The* only good thing about being at the Order these past few days is that my nightmare hadn't seemed to haunt my dreams, but now it's back. However, it seems rushed. The thunders rolls in the sky above, and the clouds begin to let free the rain. I look forward to study the limp figure in front of me. I dare and take a step up on the grass, and I'm able to. I've never gotten past the sidewalk. Why is this time any different? Lightning strikes again making me almost jump back.

Keep calm Leyla, just keep calm. I move slowly forward. I feel the wet soggy grass underneath my shoes. The ground below feels like it's going to sink in any moment. I get a tad closer and reach out my hand to touch the body. I think I think it's a girl. My hand gets closer. I'm inches away from rolling the body over to see a face. As I lay a finger on their skin, my whole body lowers into the wet ground and I'm falling into darkness. I hold my breath, and I'm scared. This has never happened before. I don't understand what's going on. I was so close, so close.

I land down on a hard surface, but I'm not hurt. I no longer feel wet or hear thunder. I'm crouching down and move my eyes up to see a dark sky with scattered starlight. I stand up and look down at myself. I'm wearing armor, like a Guardian. I look around noticing I'm on the roof of a building. I don't recognize anything around me. In the distance I see tall peaks of mountains and fields separated in squares. Where am I, and why am I dressed like this?

I start to move so quickly it feels as though I'm flying, yet my eyes can focus clearly. I feel myself leaping and I'm jumping from one rooftop to the next. It feels effortless, like a deer jumping over a tall fence like its short grass. When I land I barely feel any resistance at all, gravity seems to be almost nonexistent. I realize something is slightly moving against my back, and I hear it catching the wind as I move. Whatever it is, I don't seem burdened by it. I start to slow down as I leap off the roof and down to the ground. Again, I barely feel a thing when my feet touch the street as if I jumped down onto a soft mattress. Could I be in Alexandra's body again? She was a Guardian after all. Why else would I be dressed like this?

I make my way to a dark and long alley that dead ends. My eyes search the wall, but I can't make out anything. This place is enveloped in shadows making it hard to see. I start to raise my right arm and I turn my palm face up. My skin starts to get warm as if it's up against a heater. All of a sudden, a small globe of soft white light appears. It forms into a flame floating atop my palm. The *light is warm, but it's not burning me. I have no idea how I'm able to produce such a thing. I start to move my hand and the light, back and forth against the stone wall. I pause when I notice a single white lotus flower recently painted on the stone. It seems to be the sign I'm looking for and I suddenly close my palm and put out the light. The warmth goes away instantly as if it was never there. Then, I walk right through the wall in front of me. This person has to be Alexandra. Only a Guardian can faze.*

*Once on the other side I see an unexpected sight. I'm in a hallway with one door at the end of it. By the door is a man dressed in heavy armor colored white. His armor is partly leather, and the painted part appears to be made of metal. The man's ink-black hair is pulled back into a small bun. He carries a large sword, and he is built like a giant. He is so tall and so muscular; he must be at least three times my size. However, I don't feel intimidated by him in the slightest. He is alarmed by my entry and starts towards me immediately with his sword drawn. He begins speaking to me forcefully in a different language. Still, I don't feel frightened, and whomever I'm in seems to understand his orders for me. I slowly grab for the thing secured to my back to bring it forward. It's a weapon, a double-sided scythe, to be exact. The blades themselves are mirrored on both ends. They are the color of emeralds. It looks like they might be made out of glass-like material. The handle has a black leather grip right in the center. The metal staff is chiseled with a design of vines sprouted with leaves.*

*I lay it gently on the ground in front of me. I step back from it and turn in a small circle. The guard gives the door three knocks. After the third, the door opens and a man wearing the same type of armor steps out. He sees me and raises his sword to me and speaks to the other one in the same foreign language. The only word I understood was Guardian. I grab something hanging around my neck and pull it off. I hold it up towards the two of them. It's a necklace, and it has a beautiful lotus pendant hanging on it. At my revelation the first man starts auguring with the other, and I wish I knew what they were saying.*

*Finally, the one who recently walked out steps closer to grab the necklace from my hand forcefully. The new guard picks up my weapon from off the ground and waves me forward to follow him. The other one opens the door for us, and I'm led through it. I can hear voices as soon as we walk down a hallway leading into a big open room. It's packed with people sitting around tables.*

*There is a stairway in the back right that leads up to the top floor. There is also a bar along the right wall. This room is completely enclosed, and I didn't notice any other entrances or exits besides what I was just led through. This is odd. How can there be no outside doors to this place? Once we enter the voices fall dead silent, and all eyes turn to me and the guard escorting me. I notice someone at the head of the room start to walk closer towards us. She is a beautiful woman wearing a long silk purple dress. There is a lighter purple sash hanging from over her shoulder that continues wrapping around her waist. Her hair is so long, even braided, it hangs down to her hips.*

*"What is the meaning of this," she demands? Her lips clearly moved in a different language, but it would seem that my brain is finally translating for me. She looks remarkably like Liling Mei. Her voice is a tad off, and her build a bit curvier, but they could be sisters. The guard holds up the pendant he took from me and hands it to her. "Where did you get this?" she asks holding it out to me, and I can understand her plain as day.*

*"I borrowed it from the rightful owner. I came here to meet with the Lotus," I announce. Now that I hear my voice, there is no mistake, this is Alexandra. Everyone around her starts to shout out in an uproar. I've said something I shouldn't.*

*"My name is Liling Lien. Who are you, Guardian, and why have you come to this place?" she asks in return, her eyes glaring at me. Her voice is strong, but I notice worry in her dark eyes.*

*"My name and purpose I will only give to the one called Lotus," I answer. "I mean you no harm, and I come alone," I add. Liling Lien, that's the same last name as Mei. This can't be a coincidence.*

*"Very well, I will grant your request. You are standing in the presence of the Lotus," she reveals and bows her head slightly towards me. I return the gesture, and I can start to hear whispers around us in the crowd. "I will speak with you in a moment. Hai, take the Guardian upstairs to my room," she instructs. The guard waves me forward, and I don't hesitate to follow. As he does the crowd around me starts to get louder, seeming to object to Liling's decision. "Silence!" she shouts, and I look back to see her eyes begin to glow white. The same color of white as the small flame I held in my hand earlier. She's a Caster. The crowd falls silent. They all seem to fear her more than they are intimidated by the presence of a Guardian. As I head up the stairs my view starts to go blurry until I see nothing but blackness.*

I awake suddenly and forget where I am for a moment. I look around and realize we are still in Drake's car headed back to Iowa.

"We're almost home," I hear Drake's voice from the front seat. I turn my attention towards him. I look over at Darrius, who is fast asleep in the passenger seat. "Were you dreaming again?" he asks a little concerned.

"Yes," I reply. "Drake, does the name Lotus mean anything to you?" If I'm seeing Alexandra's memories, I needed to know. I've been pushing off the idea that we could be connected. I didn't want to admit to myself that we were. However, after that last dream, I don't think I can deny it any longer.

"The Lotus, how do you know that name?" he asks reflecting the question back at me.

"Who is she?" I ask again, refusing to answer his question before he answers mine.

"She was a powerful Caster. Why do you ask, Leyla," he answers.

"I just had a dream about her, well as Alexandra. She was looking for the Lotus, and she found her. She told Alexandra her name was Liling Ling, that's the same last name as the Caster we just help get out of the Order. Drake, I think Alexandra is trying to tell me they are connected." Drake looks a little hesitant to believe me. However, he slows the car down and pulls over to the side of the road. He reaches over and starts shaking Darrius.

"Hey, wake up," Drake says stilling shaking him. Darrius raises his head and looks over at Drake, a little annoyed to be awoken. "Leyla just had a dream of Alexandra meeting the Lotus. She says her real name is Liling Lien. Which happens to be the same last name as the Caster we just freed," he catches him up to our conversation. Darrius takes a moment to process the information then looks back at me.

"Leyla, are you sure about this?" Darrius looks at me, not convinced. "We never found the Lotus, and it may be a common last name. It doesn't mean they are related," he suggests.

"Then why else would I have the dream if it wasn't connected somehow?"

"Leyla, are you saying that you think you and Alexandra have a connection?" Drake chimes in.

"Maybe, I can no longer deny that there are other things besides our looks that we have in common, and these dreams I've been having seem to be her memories. It's bizarre, but I don't know what else would make sense," I admit and look at both of them.

They look at each other. They seem to be talking to themselves with their eyes again, and I wish I could learn this voiceless language they keep speaking. It's getting very old.

"I can tell you don't believe me, but I know it has to be related. Alexandra did meet this Lotus person, and she is somehow connected. I just know it," I tell them and cross my arms and turn my focus instead to the cars whizzing by us on the road.

"It's not that we don't believe you. It's just I think Alexandra would have told me if she had," Darrius replies.

I think back to the dream I had of them in the garden. There were things Alexandra kept from Darrius, and maybe I stumbled onto one of them. Or perhaps she would have told him, but was too afraid of how he might have reacted. I roll my eyes and decide to let it go for now. I can tell this conversation is going nowhere fast. None of us speak to each other for the rest of the ride home.

I missed my alarm, and I'm running very late for school. I rush to get ready and when I walk outside, it's cold and still dark. When I arrive at the campus the only parking spots available are ones furthest away from the buildings. Luckily the snow has been shoveled or plowed to the sides. I can't wait for springtime. I'm so over this cold weather.

I walk into my first classroom about twenty minutes after it started, but no one seems to pay me any mind. As soon as I get settled, another late arrival enters, and I definitely notice him. He sits down right beside me. It's none other than Darrius. *Why is he in my class?* Maybe I'm still asleep, and this is a weird dream. I pinch myself. Nope, I'm most certainly awake. *Ow!* That was a stupid idea. Darrius doesn't make eye contact with me and I'm not happy about this. How am I supposed to focus if he is here? I feel a soft tap on my shoulder, and I turn around to see the girl behind me smiling at me.

"Staring at him isn't going to get you his number. You might want to look away for a bit," she suggests. She winks at me and sits back in her chair. I heed her advice and turn my attention back to the professor, even though that wasn't the reason I was staring at him. I would just have to wait until the end of class to talk with him, I guess.

The hour dragged on making it feel like five by the time the class was over. As people start vacating the room, I turn to stare at Darrius again. He starts to get up to leave, and I quickly reach up and pull on his arm. He stops and stares down at me.

"Shouldn't we be getting to your history class now Leyla?" he asks puzzled as to why I stopped him. I'm going to ignore for the moment that he knows what my next class is.

"What are you doing here?" I ask back impatiently.

"I'm your protection," he answers as if I just asked a stupid question.

"Just what exactly do I need protection from?" My voice heightens with anger. He looks around the room waiting for the last student to leave before he responds.

"The recently escaped Caster, Drake and I were given an order to watch over you. It's my duty to be here," he finishes and slightly nods his head at me.

I understand now. He is here to keep face just in case we are being watched. I guess I didn't realize he would take it this far. I should probably be more grateful, but I'm still angry with him and Drake from last night. They weren't taking me seriously, and it annoyed me that they didn't trust or believe me.

"I see, well, that doesn't explain how you managed to get into my classes?" I retort. I wonder how he managed that.

"Drake and I had already enrolled in your classes during your break, as a precaution," he explains. *Why would they do that*?

I let our conversation end there and grab my books shoving them into my bag. Blue-eyes follows me to my next class, and he sits right beside me. I sigh and roll my eyes and get up. I walk one row down and to the left picking a new seat. He doesn't follow, so I guess he got the hint. Just because he has to be here doesn't mean he has to sit right next to me.

"Leyla!" Kat exclaims and hurries over to sit next to me. I forgot she was in this class with me. I'm so happy to see her. "Oh, Darrius, hello," she says seeing him and waives in his direction. "Leyla, why aren't you sitting next to Darrius?" she questions me looking from me to Darrius with a confused expression on her face.

"We don't want to be a distraction to each other," I reply, and it seems like a good enough excuse.

"Oh really, Leyla, I think you're being silly. Darrius," she looks over at him and he looks over at us, "why don't you come sit next to us," she beckons.

"Thank you, but Leyla is right. We will be less distracted this way," he replies, backing me up much to my surprise. I shoot him a thankful look, but he just turns away from me.

Maybe I've upset him. I was acting a little childish, I guess. As I look at him, I see he is wearing a normal shirt and some jeans. He seems relaxed, and I think he is happier about being out of the Order than I am. I wonder how boring this day will be to him. After all, I'm sure there isn't anything he hasn't already learned. I mean, he's lived through history, so he doesn't exactly need to be taught it. I wonder what kind of things he's seen or who he could have met or saved. I never really got to ask him or Drake any questions about their past while at the Order. Now that I think about it, I wonder how old they are. *Would it be rude to ask?* He glances over at me making me look away quickly. I guess I was telling Kat the truth after all. He does seem to be distracting me.

After history, Kat leaves for biology while Darrius and I head to my government class. As we walk there, I glance over at him. He is quiet and stoic as usual. "Hey," I speak out softly and he looks over towards me, "I'm sorry I was upset earlier. I'm just tired, and I wasn't expecting to see you here," I apologize.

"We should have told you last night. I caught you off guard, and should be the one apologizing. You've been through so much lately," he says solemnly.

"No, don't. You're following through on what you said you would do, and I can't fault you for it. Not after everything you and Drake sacrificed to do for me. I'm so grateful that you were both willing to help. It couldn't have been easy. I should have said thank you sooner," I tell him graciously.

"It wasn't a hard choice," he replies. We both stop, and I look up at him. "It was the right thing to do Leyla," he affirms and my heart flutters as my name leaves his lips. We silently stare at each other and he seems to soften his face a little. *Was he finally letting his guard down around me?* "This will be the last class I have with you," he informs me, and we start to walk down the hall again. "Drake will be attending your afternoon classes. I will be waiting for both of you when your classes are finished. I promise you won't have to be bothered by us for long. Attending your classes is only temporary until we feel you are no longer being watched," he admits.

"You're not a bother Darrius," I disagree.

I hope he knew how much I mean it. I might have been upset to see him earlier, but I don't know if I want to go back to a life without him or Drake, if

I'm being honest. Having them around completes me. They are two missing pieces of me that I didn't know were lost until they found me. I just have to remind myself not to get carried away by them and the world they belong to.

After government, Darrius leaves me at my next class without waiting for Drake to arrive. I walk into my advanced Spanish class and take a seat. There doesn't seem to be too many students in here yet.

"Leyla," I hear Drake's voice call my name from behind me. He seems to be in a good mood. He comes over and sits in front of me turning around to talk. "I'm guessing Darrius filled you in. I'm sorry to spring this on you. You seemed a little upset last night, so we agreed it wasn't the best time to bring it up," he reveals.

"I understand," but I wish they still would have told me anyway.

I feel my phone vibrate and quickly pull it out. It was Bridget. I read over the words several times before letting myself believe them. She says Mei wants to talk to me after school. *What do I do?* Is it too soon to go? We did just break her out yesterday. My eagerness gets the better of me, and I ask her when and where she wants to meet.

"Everything all right? That was a pretty serious look you just had on your face," Drake ask jokingly.

"Bridget just text me. Liling wants to meet me after school."

His face goes from laid back to completely serious. He doesn't look thrilled at the thought, and I understand why. However, I'm finally going to get closer to the truth about what's happening to me. I know Mei knows something and I'm finally going to ask her everything I wanted to back at the Order. This day suddenly couldn't end fast enough.

Of course, Darrius and Drake followed me to the bar. Bridget wanted to meet at her work, which made sense. It's public and we can eat there so if anyone is watching us, they wouldn't think anything of it. Though I wasn't sure how we would see Mei without her being out in the open. I hope Bridget has a plan for that. I get out of my Jeep to see Darrius walking up towards me with a serious look on his face.

"Leyla before we go in, I have something to say," he states. I nod and let him go on. "If Mei is related to the Lotus as you say, I want you to be cautious. The Lotus was a powerful Caster. She was said to only be the third or fourth down in her line from the original Caster who asked for the magical gift. Depending on how long down the line Mei is in her generation, she could be just as powerful. Casters aren't just special because of their magical gifts, and they also know how to use their words to influence people into getting what they want. Please remember Mei isn't innocent. She attacked one of our Orders killing some of my fellow Guardians. Don't forget she sacrificed her own followers in the process as well to get to this point," he warns, and his point is valid.

"I will be careful," I assure him. I appreciate his concern. I know what he says is the truth. I don't know anything about her, or her true motives for attacking the Order were, only guesses. I would have to keep my guard up.

As we walk in NightSky I look around, but I don't see Bridget or the Caster anywhere. I text Bridget that we have arrived, but she doesn't respond. We all three take a seat and I notice the bartender walking over to our table. I believe his name is Nick. I've seen him here plenty of times. He has his dirty blonde hair pulled up into a man bun. His skin is tan, even for winter. I think I've seen him around campus too. I catch myself staring and turn away to see Darrius and Drake looking at me.

"Someone you know?" Drake inquires.

"No, not particularly," I reply dodging his eye contact. I hear my phone go off and Bridget has finally responded. She asks me to walk to the bathroom. I'm not sure why, but I do as she asks. "Excuse me for a moment," I get up from the table feeling their eyes on me as I walk off. The bathrooms were down a long hallway on the left at the end of the bar. I start to push the door open to the ladies room when I hear someone trying to get my attention.

"Psst, over here." I follow the voice to find Bridget at the end of the hallway standing in a doorway. "Follow me," she instructs. I follow her through the door and up a flight of stairs and to a room above the bar. "This loft is the owners. She lets the employees crash here if they have a late night or if someone has one too many on their day off. I told the owner my roommate had the flu and asked if I could crash here for a few days. It's the perfect place to hide Liling. No one will bother her up here," Bridget explains.

"If she is here, I should probably go down and grab Darrius and Drake," I tell her and start to turn back.

"No Leyla, she just wants to talk to you. I told her she should rest more but she insists on seeing you," Bridget informs me sounding insistent. "I'll be here to translate if you need me to, but she speaks English fluently," she adds, and I turn back. "I used a basic healing spell, but Mei was deprived food for almost a week. So she can't feel the pain, but her body still needs rest," she reveals shutting the door quietly behind her as we walk in.

I find Mei, and I watch as she rises from the bed on the opposite side of the loft. She is in fresh clothes and her hair is brushed and looks recently washed. Her cuts and bruises are still clearly visible against her pale skin.

"Leyla, we finally get a chance to talk," Mei croaks, her voice breaking. She manages a quick smile as she walks over.

Bridget and I sit down at the small table in the kitchen area. Before Mei sits down, she puts her hands slightly together and bows her head quickly towards my direction.

"I would like to thank you for saving my life. I want you to know I will not forget what you did for me," she promises sounding sincerely grateful. "I would love to know how you pulled it off," she adds, "but I think that can wait for a different visit. I know there are things you are dying to ask me, so please, what would you like to know?" She finally takes a seat across from me at the table.

"How did you know I wasn't Alexandra?" I ask the first and most important question.

"Because Alexandra is dead," she answers calmly, her voice hoarse.

"If you already knew that, then why did you ask for her?" I question trying to keep my nerves under control. I had to remind myself that she isn't my friend. She is just a means to an end.

"I've been trying to meet you for weeks now. When I realized you were under Guardianship, I knew I couldn't get to you unless you were brought to me. I made my move and went to the Order for you, but I didn't want them to know I knew who you were," she answers.

"What do you mean when you couldn't get to me? We are talking now aren't we? You could have just come up to me anytime," I suggest. She smiles sweetly at me, but I feel like it's more making fun of me.

"I wasn't exactly in the country Leyla. I sent men and a Caster to acquire you and bring you to me. I would have explained everything once we met, but you were impossible to get, apparently," she reveals. So she sent those men and that Caster after me. *Why?* "However, I think it's good we met this way. I believe you have a better understanding of the world that's been hiding in your own and the things that go around you that are unseen to most. I think it's easier now for you to understand me," she finishes. I don't fully follow her, but she seems sure of herself. I don't think she regrets how things played out one bit.

"Now I'm here. Tell me why you want me?" I ask, getting straight to the point. She replies in Mandarin. I look over at Bridget who has just dropped her phone out of her hands onto the table, her mouth gaping open.

"I don't suppose you could translate that?" I look over at Bridget annoyed.

"Sorry," Bridget snaps out of her shock and looks over at me with a serious face, "she said Spirit Link," she translates, but I still don't follow. "It's a dangerous and very advanced spell. Only a very old and very powerful Caster could even think about casting it," she elaborates somewhat. She has a grim look on her face making me feel nervous. Bridget never looks serious, so this must not be a good thing.

"What to does this Spirit Link spell do, and what does it have to do with me?"

"If the spell is done properly, the Caster's spirit is reborn in their future self. The link comes into play so your future self can have all your knowledge, as well as your magic of your previous life. If everything works the way it should, your old self merges with your new self, becoming one," Mei explains. "Most Casters who have tried the spell have failed, hurting themselves in the process. Also, even if you can cast the spell, it doesn't guarantee a perfect result. For instance, sometimes the past self can overwhelm your future self. Another possibility is you could reject your old self entirely. It's not always a happy outcome."

"I still don't understand. I'm not a Caster, so why would this spell apply to me in any way?" I state the obvious. I look over at Bridget and I think she is thinking the same thing.

"True, you are not, and neither was Alexandra. However, she did have magic. The spell worked on her, and now you are connected by this spell. You are the only non-Caster this spell has ever worked on," her words make my head spin. Why would Alexandra let this spell be cast on her? Why would she want to become one with her future self? I look over at Mei and notice her coloring doesn't look so good. It's taking everything she has to sit here and talk to me. Bridget looks at her as well looking concerned.

"Leyla, I know this is important, but I think you should be getting back. Mei you need your rest. You should not have even gotten out of bed in the first place," Bridget scolds.

161

"Okay, I'm going. I will wait for more answers once you recover," I tell them both, though I didn't want to leave. However, I don't know how long Mei can last before she passes out on the table. Before I go though, something in the back of my mind pops up. "Mei, do you know someone by the name of Liling Lien?" She looks up at me and smiles. She nods her head.

"Yes, of course," she says her voice is softer than a whisper. She's talked too much already, and her words are barely coming out as sound. "She is the Caster who cast the Spirit Link spell on Alexandra," she answers, and my eyes go wide.

"She cast the Spirit Link spell?" I ask for confirmation I hear her correctly. She nods her head again and starts to lean over out of her chair. Bridget catchers her and looks up at me.

"She needs to lay down. I'll let you know when it's time to come back," Bridget instructs.

"Thanks for watching out for her," I reply and leave the room.

# Chapter 16
## Revelations

"Leyla, where have you been?" Darrius asks frantically as I get back to my seat.

"I'm sorry, I ran into Bridget and we got to talking. I lost track of time," I inform them. "She's gone now," I lie. I couldn't risk talking about anything else, not if someone else happens to be listening. "I think we should get some food to go and head home," I suggest.

"Leyla, what do you mean Bridget left?" Drake questions. "Why do you want to leave? What is going on?" I want to put my hand on my head and shake it. He just wasn't getting it. I give him a quick kick under the table. He doesn't look phased by it.

"Leyla, do I need to move over to give you more room?" Darrius asks annoyed. *Oh no.* I kicked Darrius instead of Drake.

"Ugh, no, sorry. I just really want to go home. I've had a long day," I tell them. They both just look at me with blank faces. "Okay, you know what, I'm going to go and I'll see you guys later." I decide to no longer beat around the bush. I get up to leave and they hurry off after me. I get to my Jeep and start it up and wait for the windows to defrost.

As soon as I pull up to my apartment, I see Darrius and Drake speed by me, and are waiting on my steps before I can even kill the Jeep. Talk about impatience. I let them and myself in and quickly lock the door behind me.

"Seriously, Leyla, why did you just run off like that?" Drake asks.

"I'm sorry, but I didn't want to tell you anything at the restaurant, and I could no longer think of how else to get you both out of there. I did meet Bridget who took me to see Liling Mei. I didn't exactly want to announce that to the whole restaurant," I explain annoyed.

"Seems like she is taking this seriously, which is more than I can say for you," Darrius accused looking over at Drake. "I do wish you could avoid physical ques next time though." Darrius looks back at me, hinting at my kick.

"I said I was sorry, and if it makes you feel any better, it was for Drake not you," I state in my defense. I see Darrius almost smile and Drake crosses his arms. "Mei is still in pretty bad shape, so I didn't get much out of her. However, I did learn that she is the one who sent those two men and that Caster to kidnap me. She also confirmed that Alexandra and I are connected, though she never really answered why she wanted me," I inform them both.

"How are you and Alexandra connected?" Drake doesn't sound convinced.

"You remember the Caster I had a dream about. She is the one who casts a spell on Alexandra. It's called Spirit Link," I reveal.

"How would Mei know about this?" Darrius sounds slightly angry.

"I don't know, we didn't get that far, she was about to pass out, so I left," I answer.

"What did you say that spell was again?" Drake asks.

"Spirit Link, it's supposed to merge a Casters' former spirit with their future self. According to Mei, Liling Lien casted the spell on Alexandra, and I'm her future self. We are now one," I reply. They both fall silent. I don't want to ask this next question, but I couldn't hold it back. "Do either of you know why Alexandra would want that spell cast on her? Do you think she knew she was going to die?" Drake looks appalled at my question, and Darrius clenches his fists and furors his brows. I look away from them, not wanting to see the looks on their faces anymore.

"Leyla, you've had a long day, with not much sleep last night. This information is a lot to process. We should all sleep on it. Mei will recover sooner or later. We should just wait for more of an explanation. We'll let you get some rest. See you tomorrow," Drake states his voice sounds tired.

I dare raise my head to him. I must have hit a nerve. It's the first time I've ever seen him act uncomfortable. I glance at Darrius. He avoids my gaze. They both walkout, ending our conversation before I can say anything else. *Way to go Leyla.*

I've been stuck in the same routine now for the past few weeks. I wake up and then attend my morning classes with Darrius. Afterward, I attend my afternoon classes with Drake. I anxiously await a text from Bridget hopeful she will message me to meet her and Mei, but nothing. Bridget says she is still recovering, and she isn't up for talking right now. I've had my nightmare every night since I got back, but I haven't had any other memory or dream about Alexandra. Besides class, I don't see much of Darrius and Drake after school. They haven't been the same since I revealed what Mei told me. I don't think they are mad at me, just at what I said. Knowing that Alexandra kept from them that she sought out a powerful Caster to perform a highly complicated spell to save her spirit, It couldn't be easy for them to handle. I can see why they would be upset, but I wish they wouldn't be so reclusive around me. I wish they would share their feelings with me, but I guess that's too much to hope for. After all, I'm not Alexandra. I'm just her vessel. The more I think about it, the more I'm mad at her too for making me a part of it. I didn't choose this.

"What's wrong?" I look over at Kat who is studying me intently as we wait for our professor to show up for history class. "You look tired. Are you having dreams again?" she asks, not tip-toeing around the question.

"I'm fine. I just didn't sleep well last night," I reply brushing it off.

"If you want to copy my notes later and sleep through class, you can, I don't mind," she offers.

"Thank you, but I'm okay. How's the wedding planning going?" I ask changing the subject.

"Great, although my mother and I have different ideas about how it should go. I just want a small wedding with only our closest family and friends, but if she had her way, she would invite the whole town," she states and we both laugh. I can picture that.

"Well, let me know if you need help. I'm pretty sure the maid of honor is supposed to help the bride," I remind her.

" Are you sure," she jokes and tilts her head to one side. "Well, I do need to go pick out a dress soon, and it wouldn't be right without you there," she suggests.

"You better not go without me!" I tell her sternly waiving my pen at her.

"Never," she crosses her heart with her fingers and laughs. She always knows how to cheer me up.

I look over at Darrius who is in his own little world staring at nothing. As much as I've gotten accustomed to having him and Drake around, maybe I need to wake up to the reality that they may not be around forever. Whatever connection I have with Alexandra, it doesn't mean that they will get to stay by my side because of it. They have one job as a Guardian, and it's to protect every mortal, not just me. I look over at Kat and smile at her warmly. I'll always have my best friends at least. I can lean on her if they do leave me. She will always be around to cheer me up. My phone buzzes in my pocket so I pull it out to see who is texting me. It's Bridget, and she has good news. She says Mei has recovered and wants me to visit. It's about time.

After class is over, I let Darrius know that I'm going to skip the rest of the day. I was too anxious to wait until classes ended. He didn't exactly approve, but he didn't stop me. He told me he would let Drake know and they would meet me at NightSky. I get to the bar first. I walk in and one of the waitresses sits me at an empty table towards the back. I don't want to leave until I know Darrius and Drake have arrived. It's the least I could do since I know they couldn't go up with me. If we all left the table to go to the bathroom all at once that would look odd. They arrive minutes later, and they both sit down, but they don't say anything to me. I feel disheartened. They are still shutting me out. Both of them look tired, like they haven't slept in days. They are here, but they aren't present. Getting Mei out of the Order has caused them more harm than good. I was just thinking of myself when I ask them to get her out, and now I wish, I wish things wouldn't have turned out like this. I can't stand how they ignore me. I want to fix it, but I don't know how. I'm not Alexandra, we might be connected, but I'm not her.

"I'll be right back," I get up to leave, not able to stand the looks on their faces any longer.

I walk past the bathroom and up the stairs to the loft. I knock gently on the door and wait for Bridget to answer. I hope she is here. I did arrive earlier than she probably had expected. A few moments pass before I knock again. I hear movement, this time on the other side of the door, and then it opens.

"Leyla," Bridget says surprised, "you're early." She grins, and I guess that means she doesn't mind. She lets me in, and I sit down at the small table again without being prompted to do so this time.

"Leyla, so good to see you again," Mei speaks up and comes over to join me. I wish I could say the same. I'm happy to get more answers, but she is the cause of the wedge between Darrius, Drake, and me. She looks much better than our previous meetings. Her bruises are mostly gone, and I didn't see any scars. I wonder if she used magic to get rid of them. Her cheeks are nice and rosy, and her eyes are alert. "Would you like some tea?" she offers.

"No thank you, I don't think I'll have time to finish it," I reply. I couldn't stay up here for very long. Mei nods in understanding. Bridget set's a cup of hot tea in front of her before sitting down next to us. Mei pushes her shiny black hair away from the front of her body to behind her shoulder then picks the cup up to take a sip.

"Last time I was here, you told me that Liling Lien was the one who cast the Spirit Link spell on Alexandra. Can you tell me why?" I ask getting straight to it.

She swallows and then answers me. "Alexandra wanted to help the magicalkinds, so she sought out my mother's help. They formed a bond, a friendship. Right before Alexandra's death she cast the spell, she did so to ensure that Alexandra could fight for us once again so the goal they shared would not be lost. Right after Lien casted the spell she died as well," she reveals.

"Are you serious? A Guardian actually wanted to help us?" Bridget spoke first in shock. Mei simply nods yes.

"If they both died, how do you know all this?" I question.

"I know because Liling Lien is my mother, and I've been living all this time to make sure that she didn't give her life away for nothing," she picks up her teacup and takes another sip. I stare at her completely dumbfounded. I wasn't expecting this. "Leyla you are the future self-Alexandra chose. It would seem she wants you to fulfill what she started all those years ago," she finishes setting the cup down again. "I want to bring peace between the magicalkinds and the Guardians. We are not the same as we were back then. Not all of us are evil," she adds.

"If you want peace, why did you attack the Order? Why did you kill those Guardians?" I ask bluntly. She lets out a laugh and it surprises me.

"Is that what the Master told you?" Her tone is dark, and her eyes jolt up and capture mine as I watch them start to glow soft white. "He told you *I* attacked the Order and that *I* killed the Guardians?" I nod my head yes. She takes a deep breath turning her eyes back to their normal dark brown color, with just a speck or two of dark green. "I went to that Order to request an audience with the Master. I was hoping when he heard what I had to say, he would request Darrius and Drake to come to the Order. However, once I stepped through the wall, the Guardians on the other side were shocked when it wasn't another one of them that came through. I stayed at the entrance never going any further. They came at me in their confusion. Instead of being taken in, I fled. I did have others with me, but they were all instructed to wait outside," she starts to explain. "You see magicalkinds like myself aren't supposed to be killed on sight anymore. We are allowed to request an audience with a Master if we are reporting on other magicalkinds who are causing trouble. If the Master accepts an audience, we are to be escorted to him or her. However, if they reject the audience, then we are supposed to be released without harm unless we provoke it first," she continues. "I knew that the Master upon hearing what I had to say, would be curious enough to request Darrius and Drake to come to the Order, which would have left you unprotected. Which would have allowed me to seek you out unguarded by them," she smiles taking a break to sip her tea again. "However, when the Master heard what I could do, he thought that I meant to attack. Which then gave him cause to go after me. He is not the first one to fear my gift. After all, if a *demonkind* can have an ability of a Guardian, then how are we so different from them? Also, if Guardians did die, it was only because they hunted us down for no reason. We were only defending ourselves," she finishes.

"Look Mei, I understand there are two sides to every story, but I can honestly say I don't know what to believe. I mean, you did send people to try and kidnap me," I remind her.

"Yes, I see now that wasn't such a good idea. Believe me or not, it's your choice. I've said my part," Mei calmly replies, shrugging her shoulders. I don't think she is completely lying. I can defiantly see the Master over reacting, but I feel like something about her story is a little off. "It worked out, and that's all that matters for now," she adds. I disagree. I'm still unsure I did the right thing by freeing her, but there wasn't much I could do about it now.

"Ley, it's been a while. You should probably head back down," Bridget suggest. I didn't want to leave yet, but that wasn't new.

"Don't worry, I'm better now. You can come back tomorrow and visit me again," Mei assures me, picking up on my hesitation.

I hurry down the stairs, back to Darrius and Drake, no doubt eagerly awaiting my return. As I walk out into the bar, I spot an unexpected guest sitting at our table. My heart starts to race, and my palms become clammy. Helen, what is she doing here? I sit down at the table with all of them, and I'm shocked to see Helen in normal clothes. To all around her, she would appear to be a normal college student. Her blonde locks fall wavily around her face, her icy-blue eyes are outlined with mascara, and her cheeks are soft pink with blush. She is wearing jeans and a pale pink sweater. I can't help but to wonder if she has that belt of knives underneath her shirt.

"So nice of you to join us. What kept you?" Helen ask suspiciously.

"I was talking with my friend. Her shift is about to start," I lie. "I'm sorry. If I knew you were waiting, I would have come out sooner," I relay, hoping it will appease her. She seems to not have feelings either way about my response. She pulls out three envelopes, each with our name spelled out in black ink, and hands them to each of us.

"I'm here on orders to invite you all to our creation ball. We have the honor to host it this year. The Master requests all of you to attend," she clarifies sweetly, but it's implied as an order and not a request. I turn towards Darrius, and he looks furious. I wonder what has him so worked up? They aren't here to bust us, so why does he look so mad? Drake seems to be a little uneasy as well. What I'm missing?

"A ball? Wow! I've never been to one. Do those things still happen?" I ask rhetorically, trying to lighten the mood. "When is it?"

"February fourteenth, otherwise known as Valentine's day. However, to us, it's the anniversary of the Orders creation," she explains. "All of the northern and some of the central states will be attending. The Master requests that you all arrive a few days early so you may still keep your old rooms since we will be expecting so many guests." I try to imagine how many people there would have to be to fill that place up. She looks at Drake, but he doesn't respond. He instead turns to Darrius.

"Is that all?" Darrius asks, reading in between the lines.

"The Master also requests that you relay any information you may have found out about the escaped Caster. He would also like to know if she has tried any attempt to capture Leyla?" she answers with a question. "If you have nothing to report to me now, he asks that you do so when you arrive," she adds.

"What if there is no information to offer?" Darrius replies harshly. He leans forward, and his eyes cut into her. I don't see how she can stand it. It's making me shrink into a shell, and he's not even looking at me.

"If the Master would like to ask us questions, we need not wait until the ball. We can go now. We have not seen her, and she has not attempted to capture Leyla," Drake finally speaks obscuring the truth.

"This is just an attempt to accuse us. I'm sorry to disappoint the Master, but we won't be attending. You may keep your invitations," Darrius hands his back to Helen, and his tone is cruel.

Helen does not accept it. I can tell she is starting to get impatient and upset. I can see her left hand under the table next to me, it's sitting on her leg. I watch her knuckles turn white from how hard she is clenching down on them.

"I'm afraid this is a mandatory request," Helen informs us, though I think that was already obvious. Her tone is unyielding, and she glares right back into Darrius' eyes. It's nothing but intense to watch. Neither one of them are willing to budge. "The Master has given you an order, and it must be obeyed. You don't have a choice," she states a little smug.

"You're wrong," Darrius answers angrily. He also smiles slightly, but it's not a happy one. This is the most upset I've ever seen him. I swear with that firefly anger in his eyes, I'm surprised Helen hasn't caught fire. She doesn't like his answer. I can see sparks start to light up in her eyes. It's like watching two wolves growling about to fight to become alpha of the pack. "You still have much to learn. Your Master is not our Master. While on the premises of his Order we must yield to his commands. However, he has no right to command us to do anything out here. His last request to us while we were still obligated to comply was to protect Leyla. If you think I'm going to escort her right back into the Order where a dangerous Caster attacked and then escaped from, you would be mistaken. Unless we have anything to report regarding the Caster, we have no other reason to return. As the future leader of your Order, you may want to brush up on what you can and cannot request from Guardians not assigned to you," he finishes with both fists clenched on the table. His accent came out a little as he became angrier.

Each one of his words cut deeper and deeper into Helen. In her eyes I can see that she is now backed up into a corner, and what Darrius speaks of is the truth. She just got knocked down a few pegs, which I believe is the first time in her life. She looks like she is going to be sick. As much as I appreciate Darrius knocking her down, I feel like it may have been a little too much. After all, she is just carrying out her orders. Also, this rejection won't sit well with the Master. From what the guys told me, he was not eager to let us go. If we anger him, he will be breathing down our necks, and that is the last thing I want.

I make a rash decision. "I greatly accept. I will go to the ball," everyone looks over at me. Their looks make it seem as if I had just arrived and hadn't been sitting here this whole time.

"Leyla, what are you saying? You actually want to go back to that place?" Drake asks with skepticism.

"I told you I've never been to a ball. I doubt the Caster would try anything with you both there to protect me, not to mention all the other Guardians that will be in attendance," I smile innocently, even though I know exactly what I'm doing. I glance over at Helen, and I see the light go on in her head.

"If Leyla is attending, then as her Guardians, you must protect her. You have to accompany her," Helen points out. "I am pleased, and I will return immediately and let the Master know. Please excuse my interruption," she says and gets up abruptly, almost knocking her chair down behind her. "Don't forget, please arrive a few days ahead of time so we may accommodate your arrival," she reminds us.

As she walks towards the exit, several other people get up around the room and follow after her. She didn't come alone. It was like watching an old western where everyone in the saloon follows the bad guy out after threatening the good guy. Helen stops at the door and looks back at me. Our eyes lock onto each other as she gives me a little nod and then quickly walks out. Does that mean she knows I only agreed to come to save Darrius and Drake? Was that her way of thanking me? Surely I'm just seeing things.

Things are quite tense between the three of us after Helen, and the other Guardians, leave NightSky. When we leave, Darrius surprises me and climbs in my Jeep instead of riding with Drake. I guess he has something he wants to say to me. Once my Jeep warms up, I start up the engine, and drive towards home.

I keep peeking over at Darrius who is gazing out onto the road ahead of us. If he wasn't going to say anything, then why ride with me? I just keep driving and waiting. Suddenly he reaches down for my radio and turns it off. I glance over at him. His skin looks like the white snow on the ground behind him outside the car window. There is no color in his cheeks, and his blue irises appear to be swirling in a never-ending whirlpool. He is drowning me in his hurt and sorrow. This was a new look for Darrius, he's vulnerable. What could I have done to make him look at me this way? What was so horrible about me accepting an invitation to a ball? Nothing I can do lately is right. Ever since we left the Order I just keep hurting him and Drake, and I don't know how to stop. I just want to help them. I just want to keep them safe.

"Ugh, I can't take it anymore!" I almost scream. "Please tell me, tell me what I did. Please!" I beg.

"Leyla," Darrius speaks my name softly making my heart sink low in my chest. His tone is somber. "Whatever your reason for accepting, I can't go with you," he informs me. His head turns around to avoid my gaze. I hear a click, and I see that his hand has moved to the handle on the door.

"Darrius, what are you doing? Stop that. What are you thinking?" I shout at him in alarm. He ignores me. Is he trying to scare me because if so, it's working?

"I'm sorry, but this is the one thing I cannot do. So please, Leyla, don't ask me to go," he starts to open the door, and I slam on the brakes. My car slides quite a ways before coming to a stop.

He doesn't wait for the car to slow before jumping out, and disappearing into the night. Luckily, there is no one behind me when I suddenly stop. I pull over and jump out of my seat. It's dark. I can't see anything but streetlights and the road. What would possess him to do such a thing? I go around to close the door he jumped out. I know that Guardians are supposed to be indestructible, but that was just stupid. I look down at my hands, and I realize I'm shaking. I don't know if I can drive myself the rest of the way at this point. I take a deep breath and calm myself down. I can't stay out here on the side of the road in the snow.

I walk back around my Jeep and get back in. I pull slowly back onto the road and continue home. As I drive, I start to feel wet teardrops roll down my cheeks. I've started to cry. Something inside of me was tearing itself apart making my emotions are jumping all over the place. I keep playing that look he gave me over and over in my head and the words he spoke. It's like I committed the most unforgivable act of betrayal when I accepted that stupid invitation. I did something so unspeakable that he just left me. Darrius left me. Am I crying because he left, or am I crying because I fear he isn't coming back?

I pull up to my parking spot to see Drake sitting on my steps waiting for me to arrive. He looks alarmed when he notices the empty seat next to me. As I get out, I wipe my tears away as quickly as I can. I didn't want him to see me upset like this. He stands up and walks over to me. His green eyes flash brightly at me. Even in the dark they stand out. He doesn't have a smile on his face for me though, just a look of worry.

"Leyla, where is Darrius?" he asks, his tone just as concerned as the look he's wearing. I think of the answer and I can't help it. Tears start flowing down my face again. I can stop it, I want to, but I can't.

"What did I do Drake, what is so horrible about a ball? I just don't understand," I tell him wiping away my tears.

His look turns from worry to something else, and suddenly he pulls me into him. I can smell traces of his cologne in his coat. He holds me tightly and hiding my tears, I bury my head into his chest. I try to stop them, and I make no noise, but I am shaking. I feel him lay his cheek on the top of my head.

"You've done nothing wrong. Please stop crying. We should have told you, but I don't think we wanted to say the words aloud. You see, neither Darrius nor I have attended the creation ball since it's a reminder A reminder of a night we can never forget. It's the night that changed our lives forever," he reveals. I can hear the compassion and the hurt in his voice. A night that changed their lives forever, but what could that be?

"Oh no, what have I done!" I realize what he means, and I lift my head to look at him. He is still holding me, and I place my head down in my cupped hands shaking it back and forth. *How could I have been so stupid?*

"Please Leyla, don't blame yourself. You didn't know, you didn't. You're the one who should be upset. You're the one who has suffered the consequences of someone you've never even met," he tries to soothe me.

"Darrius, he asked me not to make him go. He asked me and then he jumped out of the car. He left me and it's all my fault," I divulge.

"No Leyla, it's not. Have you not been listening? Darrius will be fine. He needs some space. He knows it's not your fault. There is only one person we have to blame for this situation. The Master," he says coldly. "I believe he knows full well what that day means to us, and he is doing this on purpose to get back at us. I have no doubt he still believes we had something to do with the Caster's escape." I look up at him, and he uses his thumb to wipe away my tears. His touch is soft and warm.

"That's so cruel," I reply. "I won't ask you or Darrius to do this. We won't go, okay. I won't go," I tell him.

"I'm afraid that's not an option any longer. It's too late to change your mind now," Drake informs me and hesitantly lets me go. "Besides, I know why you agreed. You did it so the Master wouldn't be angry. Your instincts were right. I know that. Darrius knows that too. If we play this right, we could put this whole thing behind us for good. This is just the Master's final attempt to prove we did something to help the Caster. He's testing us, and without you accepting, we would have failed," he states and moves some of my hair away from my face.

"Drake, what if we go together? Darrius could stay behind. We could think of something to say so he won't have to attend. He doesn't have to go," I tell him, trying to think of the best solution for everyone.

"I would love nothing more, but I'm afraid not realizing I've already promised to take someone else," he looks saddened by this revelation, and I can't say it doesn't hurt me a little. *Who did he promise to take?* "Leyla, if Darrius stays, the Master will just find another way to make him come. The only way Darrius will go is if you ask him. That's why he ran. He knows that if you ask him, he won't be able to say no. So instead he is going to avoid you," he explains, and it somehow makes me feel better, and yet worse all at the same time.

"Drake. I don't think I can ask him, I mean, he would never forgive me. I don't think I could ever forgive myself," I tell him the truth.

"I don't want you to have to ask, but we both know it must be done. Darrius needs to go, as do I, and we need to put this behind us for good." I can't believe he is serious. How can I do that? Drake leans down and gives me a gentle kiss on my forehead. It fills me with a warm and subtle shock of electricity. "Don't worry, I have a feeling he will forgive you," he lifts back up, but I just stand there frozen. I wasn't expecting him to do that, and more so, I wasn't expecting it to feel so nice.

# Chapter 17
## Mixed Feelings

Darrius still attends my morning classes, but he no longer waits for me after my classes are over. He leaves at lunch, and I don't see him again until the next morning. In class he hasn't spoken a word to me or even looked at me. I haven't been able to pluck up the courage to ask him to come to the ball either. After all, shouldn't the guy ask the girl? I've tried several times, but the words will never leave my lips. I still have time, not much but some.

I will have to miss a couple of days of school to arrive at the Order early. I told Kat that I plan to take a trip, and I ask her to take notes in our shared class. She thinks Darrius and I are going for a romantic weekend, and I let her believe it. It wasn't like I could tell her the truth. I left a little early today. My professor was out, so we didn't have class. I'm home now, and decide to watch a movie, one that always puts a smile on my face. "*Singing in the Rain*". Gene Kelly, he could sing, he could dance, and that smile. I love watching old musicals. My mom used to indulge and watched them with me, even though I know she wasn't a big fan. The only one I could ever get Kat to watch was "*Phantom of the Opera*". She just couldn't say no to Gerald Butler. I do love that one, but there is just something about the classics. Their eyes seem to always sparkle, and their voices are always so refined. The music is stupendous, and the dance numbers are always over the top. Speaking of dancing, I just realized I'm going to a ball, and have no idea how to dance. Dancing in my memory was one thing, but that was Alexandra, not me. I wonder, maybe I can kill two birds with one stone? I turn off the movie and head out my door. This was as good as time as any.

I'm standing in front of Drake's door. I've had my hand up to knock for about five minutes now but haven't been able to do it yet. I hold in my breath and give it a small tap. To my surprise, I hear the nob turn and Darrius answers. I can't believe he heard that.

"Hello," he greets me. "I almost thought you were going to turn around and go home," he admits. I guess he knew I was here the whole time, somehow. "Drake isn't here right now. Do you need to talk to him?" he asks.

"No, I'm here for you. May I come in?" I reply.

He moves aside, and I walk past him. His hair looks partly wet, and he smells like men's soap. He must have showered recently. He is wearing jeans and a tightly fitted t-shirt. It must be one of Drake's. I wonder why he doesn't have any on his own shirts here by now. He shuts the door behind me, walks over, and sits down on one of the bar stools avoiding my gaze.

"I came to ask for your help," I explain. "Can you teach me how to dance?" My words come out too fast because I'm nervous. He looks up at me a little taken aback by my question. I can tell that is the last thing he expected me to say.

"Drake will be attending the ball. I'm sure he can teach you when he gets back," he replies. Wow, no holding back on my account. He starts to walk off, but I reach out and gently grab him by the arm.

"Darrius wait. Drake is going with someone else, and anyway, I want you to teach me. Please?" He hesitantly turns back around to face me. I don't give him any time to object. I walk closer to him and wrap his arm around my waist. I see him flinch a little. I grab his other hand and hold it in mine. His skin feels warm against mine as he gently wraps his fingers around my hand. I feel butterflies in my stomach. "I'm not taking no for an answer," I tell him looking down at my feet. I stand still and wait for him to make the next move. I hear him let out a little sigh.

"Follow my lead. Don't think, don't look down, and mimic my movements," he instructs.

I wasn't looking down to watch my feet. I was looking down to avoid his eyes. I look up as he commands, and he seems a bit more relaxed than when I first walked in. He starts to move, and I follow. We dance in a small circle around the living room. I can hear imaginary music playing in my head. He gives me a little twirl outwards and then brings me back into him. As we come together again, he stops, and I'm frozen in his embrace. I feel myself being drawn in, like on New Year's. There is something comforting about his touch. I feel safe in his arms, like nothing can happen to me as long as he holds me. I dare not look directly into his eyes, in case I get another overwhelming urge to kiss him.

"I know what you're trying to do," Darrius whispers. I can hear a subtle hint of pain in his voice.

"Oh, what's that?" I ask innocently.

He lets me go taking a step back. I look up at him, and as I do, he disappears. I reach out my arm instinctively because I feel like he is still standing there, even though I'm now technically alone. I clench my hand and bring it back in towards my chest. Drake is wrong. I'll never be able to convince him to come. I fight back my urge to cry and storm out.

Since our short dance, I haven't seen Darrius. Drake assures me he just needs some more time to think on things and that he will come around. I'm not convinced. I'm currently packing my bag so we can leave for the Order this evening. I don't expect to see or hear from Darrius until after we return. I pack the nicest dress I own and a couple of outfits for the trip there and back. I'm sure I'll have to wear another armor suit the rest of the time. At least this trip will be less stressful, I hope. I ask Bridget if I could see Mei one more time before I left. There are still some things on my mind that have been plaguing me since my last visit. As I walk out the door, I notice Drake walking across the parking lot coming to meet me.

"Leyla, I'm glad I caught you. Would it be alright if I came with you to your meeting with Mei?" he requests with one of his charming smiles.

"Sure, I'm already packed, so we can just leave after that," I reply. We are meeting at the café this time instead of the bar. Also, Bridget tells me Mei is dying to get out of the loft, which I can't say I blame her. As long as she is careful, the last thing we need is for her to be seen and recaptured. Since the Guardians from the Order know we are coming to the ball. Hopefully they aren't watching us today.

"Excellent, I'll grab your bags," he says happily. I follow him to his car and when he puts my bags in the trunk. I notice there are one too many already in there for just him. I shoot him a curious look.

"Darrius will need his armor and weapons," he explains. *Does Drake know something I don't?* "Thank you for letting me tag along. I promise to behave," he tells me. His eyes gleam making them appear more reptile than ever. He's up to something.

"Drake, since you packed a bag for Darrius, does that mean that you've heard from him?" I ask hopeful.

"No, I have not, but I have faith that he will show."

I wish I had as much faith as he did, but I feel like we are both going to wind up disappointed. I hope I'm wrong though. I send Bridget a text that Drake will be joining me. She doesn't respond, but it shows she read it. I wonder if that meant she isn't too thrilled about him coming along?

As we reach the café, I spot Mei and Bridget sitting in one of the booths along the back wall through one of the windows. Drake accompanies me inside as we head straight over to where they are seated. I scoot in the booth opposite of them, and Drake follows. I see Bridget has already ordered me a cappuccino. It's still hot. I can see the steam coming out the top and the beautiful foam rose that is still mostly intact on top of the liquid.

"I didn't know what you liked, so I didn't order you anything," Bridget says to Drake.

"You must be Bridget, it's nice to finally meet you, officially. Thank you for helping us. Your gift is very special," Drake smiles at her. I notice Bridget's face light up at his compliment. I guess she wasn't kidding when she said Caster's are susceptible to flattery. I don't think I've ever seen her look so happy. "It's a pleasure to meet you as well Liling Mei." Drake says and bows his head shortly towards Mei's direction, who in turn bows her head back.

"The pleasure is mine. I see your good looks and snake-like charms proceed you," she replies and brings her cup, of what I'm guessing is green tea, to her red lips. She looks just as lovely as ever. I hope she is taking this seriously. We need her to lay low since all of our freedoms are at risk. "I know that you're not supposed to know where I am, but I wouldn't mind you coming to visit me anytime," she adds, and I don't like her suggestion. *I hope she is joking.*

"I'm sorry, but if I ever do come to visit you, it won't be to stay," he states. "Mei, I came here because I don't feel like you have indulged us in the whole truth. You say that Alexandra is linked with Leyla, but you must have considered the possibility that Leyla would not agree to help you in your endeavors. You wouldn't have tried to capture her or be here still if you didn't think things would turn out the way you want them to. So what is that you're not telling us?" His voice turns harsh and cold.

Mei puts down her cup of tea, and I see her eyes flash white for one brief moment. I don't think she likes being told what to do. I glance over at Bridget who is just as surprised at Drake's sudden change in demeanor.

"Is there something you haven't told me? Drake is right. Just because the spell worked doesn't mean I will help you," I speak up, hoping she will answer me if not him.

She stays silent for a moment making me feel a little nervous. Drake promised to behave, but I don't know how long he will be able to keep that promise. I understand why he is frustrated. He risked his Guardianship to get her out. In his mind, she is just the Caster who attacked the Order and murdered his fellow Guardians. I never got a chance to tell him, or Darrius, Mei's side of the story. I doubt it would have mattered. I suspect they would believe anything coming from her on that subject.

"My mother gave her life to make sure Alexandra would come back," she starts breaking the silence. "I'm here to make sure that her last wishes weren't for nothing. I want Leyla's help to bring change. The change both Alexandra and my mother were trying so hard to accomplish before their deaths," she reaffirms. This is the same thing she's already told me. What is it that she is leaving out? What makes her so sure I will help her?

"Leyla isn't going to be a part of your schemes. I won't let her die trying to help you. She's not even a Guardian. I won't let her and Alexandra share the same fate," Drake objects, sounding so sure of himself.

"You were right. I wouldn't have come unless I knew how this would play out," she pauses and looks directly at me. She smiles at me making me feel uncomfortable. "Leyla is going to help me whether she wants to or not. She doesn't have a choice, I'm afraid." Mei takes another sip of her tea, and all eyes are on her.

"I didn't volunteer to get you out just so you could put Ley in danger," Bridget speaks up on my behalf. "She's a good person who doesn't have a choice about what's happening to her. It's not okay for you to just expect her to sacrifice herself for a cause she knows nothing about. She saved you. If it weren't for her, you would still be in that cell starving to death!" I didn't realize how much Bridget cared for me. I don't deserve a friend like her.

"I do appreciate everything you've done for me, more than you'll ever know. I don't want anything bad to happen to you either. I'm sure by now you've been seeing Alexandra's memories and maybe even sharing in some of her abilities. As soon as the Order finds out what is really going on, do you really think you'll be able to keep your normal life here? You will no longer be able to pass as a true mortal, not with such a powerful spell running through your veins. A spell, by the way, that cannot be reversed. I want you on my side so I can protect you. I explained how the spell works, and I told you that sometimes the old self could overwhelm their future self. If Alexandra's spirit is stronger than yours, which I'm guessing it might be, it could consume yours and leave you a prisoner trapped in your own mind." Her words shook me to my core. How could she say such a cruel thing?

"You're telling me that if I refuse to help you that Alexandra will take over my body and make choices for me?" I can barely believe the words coming out of my mouth.

"Yes, that's exactly what I'm saying. If Alexandra wants to, she has the power to do so. However, I'm telling you this as a courtesy for saving me. I like you, and I owe you. Make the right choice. I'm giving you a chance not to let that happen, a chance for you to still be in control. You're smart, cunning, and I think you can help me just as much or more as Alexandra could."

I look at Mei with nothing less than disgust. It hits me like a ton bricks. I finally understand why she wanted to kidnap me. She was going to hold me until I either agreed to help her or until Alexandra decided to take me over. She was going to let Alexandra have free reign over my body and mind. The thought of it makes me sick.

"Please don't look at me like that. You don't fully understand the history between the Guardians and the magicalkinds. Let me fill you in. They betrayed and murdered Alexandra and my mother in the process. She was the only person I had left in this world that I loved. Despite this, I'm not asking you to help me with revenge. No, I only ask to carry out what they tried to do so long ago. Equality for those magicalkinds still mortal at heart and who had no choice in their magical abilities. Those born or cursed with it. We all die, just as you do. We should be given a second chance at life or given peace in our suffering at our deaths. Not to mention we are being hunted down to the point of non-existence, without justifiable cause. Why should the Order get to decide if we are worthy or not? They all were given a chance to choose their gifts. We had no choice. That's all I want, Leyla, and all I'm asking. Hate me if you wish, but I will never give up on my dream. Alexandra chose to bond with you, which means she believes you would take her side," she finishes, and my jaw drops. I feel Drake grab my hand making me look over at him. He is tense, and I can only imagine what he is thinking right now.

"Leyla, we need to leave now, before I do something rash," he lets go of my hand. "I will pull the car around. I won't stay here and listen to one more lie!" Drake announces and gets up abruptly. He storms off, and I turn back to see Bridget who looks horrified. She looks exactly how I feel right now. I get up and start to follow after Drake.

Mei grabs my arm from across the table making me I stop. "Believe me or not, it makes no difference to me. Your fate has come for you, Leyla Gray, and you will have to make a choice. I just hope you make the right one." She lets go of my hand, and I leave her without a response. I can't stomach any more of this.

As I reach the exit, the cold air hits me. I feel a little better. It had gotten so hot inside of the café, probably from my rage boiling my blood. Drake drives around and picks me up. He starts to speed off. Mei just accused the Order of not only killing her mother but Alexandra as well. He must be so angry, and I can't imagine what Darrius' reaction would have been if he had been here. Darrius, I wish he hadn't left us. I think we all need to be together right now. I think we all need each other. While I was at the Order, I learned that the Guard, the Sword, and the Light can communicate through thought if they are in the same group. I didn't know if that was true, I never really stopped any Guardians to ask, but I feel something telling me to try it. I close my eyes and try to clear my mind.

*Darrius hear me. I don't want to ask you to come, but I need you to. We need you by our sides. If your friendship with Drake means anything to you. If I mean anything to you, please come to the Order. I'm sorry, I'm so sorry I have to ask this of you, but please, please come.*

Drake has remained silent almost the entire way. I know he is still angry. I decide it was best to let him hold onto it for a while. I couldn't say anything to help him anyway. I'm the one who let my better judgement get the better of me. I'm the one who disregarded the rules to get Mei out for my personal gain. How could I comfort him, when I'm ultimately the reason he's in such pain right now? When we finally arrive, instead of parking on the street this time, Drake pulls into a private entrance. It appears to be an underground garage. As soon as he pulls the car in, I can see Helen and some other Guardians waiting for us by the elevator. I didn't know the Order had an elevator. We get out, and she walks over to us. I notice Xander now as well. He smiles when he sees us, unlike Helen. She has a look of impatience on her face.

"You've finally arrived. Xander, will you please take their bags to their rooms," Helen instructs. Xander's smile turns to a frown, but he obeys. "Where is Darrius?"

"He will be arriving soon. He had somethings to take care of first." Drake covers for him, and she seems to buy it. I guess he believes it too, or he wouldn't have been able to say it.

We all take the elevator up, and I feel like I can't breathe. I'm not as nervous as I was the first time I came here, but I still wasn't sure what to expect this time either. We reach the main floor and more Guardians are there to greet us. The Master seems to be taking a lot of extra precautions. As we move into the large entry, I notice that the round table has been removed. The chandelier is now raised higher than before, and it's completely lit. There are chairs along the window to my left. I notice the large curtains are pulled back from the floor-to-ceiling glass window. There are music stands as well, it looks like they are for an orchestra. There are red and gold banners hanging every few feet from the vaulted ceiling with the Guardian symbol on each one. The stairway leading up is laid with a red carpet, Tall vases with fresh flowers are spread out all over the room. Each arrangement is subtly different, and there are several varieties of flowers in each vase. This must be the room they will have the ball in. It makes sense. It's more than big enough to hold a large crowd. We head up the stairs to our rooms from before. It's a familiar walk.

"Please get some rest. Xander and I will be here in the morning to accompany you to breakfast. Goodnight," Helen says before departing.

I look over at Drake, and he glances at me for only a moment before heading into his room. The brief moment I caught his eye he looks part worried and part tired. He did just drive us here and I bet he is concerned about Darrius. I am too, if I'm being honest. I follow his lead and walk straight into my bedroom and close the door behind me. It almost feels like I never left. I wonder if sleeping here will have the same effect on me as the last time. It would be nice not to have my nightmare play through my mind all night. I lay down on the bed and sink in. I'm more tired than I realize. I don't even bother getting fully undressed. I just slip off my jeans and snuggle up in the covers. I fall asleep almost instantly.

I'm awoken by a loud knock on my door. I reach for my phone and realize I've slept till almost eight. It's my fault, I forgot to set my alarm before I went to sleep. I hear the knock again and realize it's not just a dream someone is really at my door. I raise up out of the bed and pull back on my pants from the night before. I walk up to the door and quickly open it. Xander is standing on the other side.

"Sorry to wake you, I'm here with your armor. They forgot to place it on your bed last night," he informs me. He avoids looking directly at me and reaches out his hand towards me holding the armor. I take it from him.

"I thought maybe it wasn't here on purpose and I would be able to wear normal clothes," I reply.

He ignores my snarky comment and takes off. I better hurry and get ready before Helen arrives. I don't want to get a lecture from her about being on time. Last night I did sleep deeply, but I was plagued by my nightmare. Not only that but it was much more vivid and intensified than usual. If felt more real last night than it ever had before. I take the quickest shower I can and I'm barely dry as I pull on my armor. I wrap a towel around my head temporally and brush my teeth as quickly as I can. I hear another knock on my door and I'm sure it's probably Helen about to rush me. I walk over to answer it and when I see who is on the other side I suck in some air.

"Darrius! You came," I murmur in shock. I feel my towel slowly fall off my head, and my wet hair is suddenly touching my skin. Darrius catches it right before it hits the ground and hands it to me. I peek out behind him and I don't see anyone watching us. I grab his arm and pull him into my room much to his surprise.

He avoids my gaze for a moment. "I suppose the saying time heals all wounds, doesn't apply to me," he confesses.

"I'm sorry you had to come," I tell him. He walks over towards me and takes my hand. I'm taken a little off guard.

"No, don't be sorry. I shouldn't have left you. You have my word that from now on, I will never leave your side," Darrius promises and gently squeezes my hand.

He brings my hand up to his heart and I can feel it beating from beneath his armor. It's almost racing faster than mine. He is being so open with me all of a sudden. I feel my skin getting warm and the hair on my arms and neck start to stand straight up. He is looking deeply into my eyes and they are pulling me in like normal. I'm willing to drown in them as long as we can keep staying in this moment. He takes a step closer to me and leans his head down. His nose is nearly touching mine. I can feel his air against my cheeks as he breathes. Why does he go from being shut off from me to these outbursts of intensity? Why can't he just stay in the middle somewhere. I'm starting to ache for him, for his lips. I want to kiss him again. Or is it Alexandra who wants me to? I don't know who is in control, me or her. To my dismay he lets go of my hand and takes a few steps back from me. The warmth I feel still lingers all along my skin, and I know I must be blushing.

"Something happened while I was away, didn't it? I heard you cry out to me," he reveals, "there must have been something that prompted that." I'm hesitant to reply. He just arrived and if I tell him what Mei said, he could act rashly and leave again. "It's okay, you can tell me," he assures me.

"Are you serious about staying, because what I have to tell you may make you want to leave again," I declare. He looks at me a little confused. "Drake and I met with Mei and Bridget before we left for the Order. Mei told us her mother cast the spirit link spell on Alexandra because she hoped that their dream of saving the magicalkinds would live on. Alexandra thought that some of them were worth saving, which is why she joined with Liling Lien. Mei came here because she wants me to do the same," I pause and with every word I see him getting more and more infuriated. "Darrius, Mei said that if I don't decide to help her, Alexandra would chose for me and..." I stop unable to repeat her words.

"What are you talking about?" he questions, his voice rough.

"Alexandra could trap me in my mind, and I would no longer be in control of myself," I reply. I watch him clench his fist. I know I should probably stop here but I have to finish. "Mei also told us that the Order had something to do with Alexandra's death." I hold my breath and watch for his reaction.

All the color drains from his face and his eyes look soulless. I stand still and silent waiting for him to process. I didn't think it was possible, but he seems even more outraged than earlier. Something takes over, I can't stand to see him like this. I walk over to him and wrap my arms around him hoping it will calm him down. I don't want him to leave again. If he does, he might try and find Mei, and he might do something reckless. I hold him tightly and to my surprise I feel both of his arms tighten around my waist in return. I feel his body loosen and he falls into mine resting his head on my shoulder. I lift my head from his chest and he moves his head level to mine. Our eyes lock once more, and I'm overcome with the desire for his lips on mine. He starts to lean in, and I think I'm about to get my wish. I close my eyes and I'm ready to taste him once again. However, I feel him start to move away from me and he slowly lets me go. I open my eyes and I can see the longing in his. Why did he back away if he wants the same thing as I do?

"I should go and let you finish getting ready. I will see you down at breakfast," Darrius changes subjects. He heads for the door and opens it. "Thank you for telling me," he states turning his head to me briefly and then walks out. My heart is still racing, and my body is still hot. I didn't want him to leave, but I think it was for the best. I wish I had better control over myself when he acts like that, but I don't. When he opens himself up around me, I can't help but to sink.

I thought the idea of arriving early was a little unnecessary. However, I realize now that it wasn't. The Order has gotten so crowded from groups of Guardians arriving daily from different states. I would have never guessed this place could seem cramped but walking through the halls reminds me of campus when classes let out. Everyone is trying to avoid bumping into each other almost everywhere you go. There are always groups huddled together here and there. The ball is tomorrow and with so many people here now they have two breakfasts, two lunches, and two dinner times to feed everyone. I can't even go for a walk in the garden outside without seeing several people walking around. I've been staying mostly in my room or the library. No one seems to be interested in reading at a time like this. I'm not alone though, Oscar has been following me around like a puppy.

The Master brought him to breakfast the morning after we arrived, and after greeting me cordially he left Oscar to guard me as before. I can't say I know what Darrius and Drake have been up to. The Master has several guards escorting them everywhere they go. His goal appears to be keeping them away from me as much as possible. I'm not sure why the Master wants to keep us separated. I know that Darrius and Drake make daily visits to his office for constant questioning. I think he is trying to catch them in a lie, but so far so good it would seem. They aren't in the dungeon so they must be keeping up the innocent act convincingly. I'm currently in the library sifting through books trying to find one that interests me. Oscar is lying in one of the chairs napping quietly.

"Leyla, there you are," I hear Drake's voice, and I turn around to see him entering the room. He walks over quickly to me looking over his shoulder. "I don't have long, but I wanted to check on you. Are you doing okay?" he asks and smiles revealing his sparkling white teeth.

"I'm fine. Are you and Darrius alright? I know you've seen the Master every day," I reply.

"Yes, we are fine, no need to worry about us. I'm sorry the Master has been keeping us apart, but I'm also glad," he informs me, and I look at him curiously. "That must mean the Master doesn't believe you had anything to do with what he thinks we did," he explains, and I understand. The Master doesn't believe I'm involved. If he did, he would be questioning me too. "Look, there is another reason I'm here." He raises his arm and uses his hand to push some of his hair back away from his face. It's gelled down, but it looks like some strands are still trying to sick up. He walks closer to me and he takes one of my hands in his. "I wanted to tell you myself before the ball. The reason I couldn't take you is because last time we were here someone asked me to accompany her, and I said yes, not realizing I would be coming," he reveals.

"It's alright, I understand. If you came to apologize, it's really not necessary," I assure him. "Who are you taking?"

"Helen," he answers. *Her?* Really out of everyone, he's taking her. He squeezes my hand, no doubt seeing the look of shock and disapproval on my face. "Somehow, I knew you wouldn't approve," he comments almost laughing. I didn't find it that funny. "Leyla, I want you to know I would much rather have escorted you. When you asked me the other night, it was all I could do to resist." Letting go of my hands, he smiles at me making it hard for me to be mad at him. He smells good, even though he is wearing his cologne a bit strong today. I didn't mind though, part of me wanted to bury my face in his armor and soak it in. *What is wrong with me?*

"Oh," I say not being able to think of anything else. Drake looks down on me intently. I can't help but notice how handsome he is. I feel like the first time I met him, speechless. You would think the closer we get and longer we're around each other, it would be easier for me to feel relaxed around him, but it's not. I wonder if this is how Alexandra felt around him? After all, she confessed that had things been different, it could have very well been him Alexandra chose.

"I've got to get back before they notice I've escaped," he jokes. He walks off just as quickly as he arrived. *Leyla, why are you so disappointed all of a sudden?*

# Chapter 18

## Let's Have a Ball

My body is on an emotional rollercoaster ride. My heart and mind are both confused. Up and down I go, back and forth between Darrius and Drake. If I were smart, I would push them both away. I'm not sure if what I'm feeling is even real. Could it just be emotions coming through from Alexandra? How can I trust what I feel when I know she's a part of me? I need to get a better grip on my feelings. I need to keep my guard up around them.

I barely slept last night between my nightmare and thinking about them. The ball is only a few hours away, and all I've managed today so far is to take a shower. I've been stuck in this room all day. No one has come to check up on me, surprisingly, but I'm sure they are all busy getting ready. I almost don't want to go at this point. The thought of me dancing so closely with Darrius, isn't going to help any feelings I may or may not have about him.

"Leyla, are you in there? May I come in?" Helen knocks on my door, I guess someone finally noticed I wasn't around.

"Come in," I reply sitting up from the bed. I can tell she is surprised to see me still in my pajamas. "I didn't feel well this morning, so I overslept," I explain. She lets out a little laugh making her whole face brightens up. What's gotten into her?

"I'm sorry," she says in between her laughs, "it's just I forgot that happens. I can't remember the last time anyone around here slept in," she elaborates. For a second she almost seems like a normal girl. I guess being second in command doesn't come with a lot of downtime. I sometimes forget how dedicated the Guardians are to their duties. "Are you feeling better now, or do you need to see a healer?" she asks, and she sounds concerned.

"No that's okay. Umm, I hate to be rude but is there a reason you came up here?" I ask in return.

She nods. "It's time to get ready; we have to arrive promptly before everyone else. We can't be late since we are hosting. Even you since you're our guest," she answers. "Please slip into something more appropriate and follow me," she commands. She's completely back to her old self now, barking orders.

She waits for me outside my door as I slip into my armor. I follow Helen down the hall, but instead of going down the stairs, we continue to a matching corridor on the other side of this floor. We walk about halfway down the hall then she stops to open a door to the right.

"We're here," she informs me and walks into a large open room. I follow her in, and my feet stop a couple of feet past the doorway. The room is nothing but rows full of dresses hanging on either side of the wall. At the back is a large pedestal surrounded by mirrors on three sides. "We have many dresses in here from different eras. You may choose one to wear tonight. There are shoes in the drawers down below, and at the back wall are cabinets with jewelry you may borrow." She has to be joking. It's like I walked into an upscale department store for famous people. This is astounding. "Only the Order leaders can pick from these dresses, so there should be plenty to choose from," she informs me.

"I can't believe this room was just on the other side of the hallway this whole time," I reply still in awe. I guess there was no need for me to pack a dress. I feel like somehow I should have anticipated that. "I'm not sure if I will be able to decide," I admit aloud.

I know one person that would love this room more than anyone. Kat, boy, I could see her murdering someone to get in here. I wish she was here with me instead of, well. I turn around to see Helen has already picked out a dress. How did she decide so quickly? I don't get her. I comb through them all trying to choose just one. I look back over at Helen who has already changed into her pick. She looks gorgeous, and her choice suits her. Her dress is a soft pink and has sheer petal sleeves. It's fitted around her figure and hangs straight down to her ankles. It had a silk layer underneath with a sheer tool layer on top. It's embroidered with real-looking pink roses strung around her waist like a belt hugging her hips. She digs through the drawers until she finds some small pumps to match. She looks up at me and catches me staring at her. She gives me a frown.

"Don't stare at me like that. Shouldn't you be looking for a dress," Helen hisses at me.

I can't believe Drake agreed to take her to the ball. Although, now that I think about it, she does seem to like him. He is the only one she seems to act human around. Seeing her in that dress doesn't do anything for my confidence. She looks gorgeous, like an angel. She lets her hair flow wavily down her back, and her bangs are pushed to each side showing her full face. I can't help but wonder how Drake will feel when he sees her tonight. Not that it matters.

"Seriously, what are you staring at?"

"Sorry, it's just you look really beautiful," I reply honestly.

I see her cheeks turn a little pink, and she turns herself around. I guess my comment took her by surprise. Maybe there is a normal girl under there somewhere? I turn my attention back to the gowns, and I see one closer to the end of the racks that catches my eyes. I quickly change into it and then walk up to the pedestal to see how it looks on me.

"Woah," I say aloud. This dress is amazing, and it makes me look slim but yet still shows my curves. The color complements my skin tone. It doesn't wash me out or make me appear orangey. I didn't expect it to look this good.

"I like it. Do you need help zipping it up?" Helen asks behind me.

Her way of complementing me back, I'm guessing. I nod remembering that zippers on dresses are apparently my Achilles' heel. The dress has long sleeves and a short V-neck top. I run my hand down the dark blue satin bottom. The top is fitted like a corset. It's blue as well, but it has sparkles covering every inch. The bottom half flowed out starting low on my waist. The front of the dress stops at the tops of my knees while the back touched my ankles. She quickly zips me up. "I'll get you some shoes," she says and starts to hunt through the drawers again. She pulls out some dark blue high heels with lace string ties. I wasn't sure about dancing in them, but they did compliment my dress rather well.

"What are you going to do for your hair?" she asks handing me the shoes.

"I wasn't planning on changing it. Why do I need to?" I reply. I see Helen roll her cool-blue eyes in the mirror from behind me. She twists up my black wavy hair and holds it up high so I can see what it would look like. "That does look pretty good, but I would never be able to get it to stay," I confess.

She shrugs my comment off and walks over beside the mirror to one of the dressers. She pulls out a large decretive hair comb with a sliver lace pattern.

She walks back over and puts my hair up using the comb. She tucks in each strand then she takes a step back. I admire her handy work in the mirror. *That was nice of her.*

"We should head back to your room. You need to put on some makeup if you want to blend in with the rest of us," Helen comments. Perhaps I spoke too soon.

We head back to my room where Helen sits down on my bed as I put on my makeup in the connecting bathroom.

"You do know what you're doing, right?" she asks sarcastically. I just ignore her and continue putting on my base.

"Helen, you seem anxious," I say glancing over at her. I notice one of her legs hopping up and down repeatedly.

"More like impatient," she replies, crossing her arms. She lets out a sigh. "Actually, this is my first time to attend the creation ball," she admits.

"Really? Why haven't you gone before?" I ask in shock.

"The ball is only held once every hundred years," she informs me. "I wasn't exactly around for the previous one," she goes on. "I've only been a Guardian for about twenty years now. After I went through the tests and the training, I was chosen to become a Sword. However, the Master decided a few years ago that I was to become his second. Since I haven't been here as long as most of the other Guardians, I have to prove myself daily that I deserve the position." I stop in the middle of applying my mascara and walk over towards her.

"I had no idea. You must be under so much pressure. It didn't even dawn on me that you are newer to this. I assumed you'd been a Guardian just as long or longer than Darrius or Drake," I say. I didn't realize. I guess there is a lot I don't know about her. She looks up at me with a sad look, which is a new look for her. "Helen, how did you become a Guardian?" The words slip out of my mouth before I realize it. I didn't mean to say that out loud. "I'm sorry," I start to waive my hands at her, "you don't have to answer. Forget I asked," I implore her. She looks at me and softly smiles.

"It's okay. We normally don't share how old we are or how we died with each other. It's an unspoken rule, but if you really want to know," she offers. I'm a little surprised she agreed. I nod my head yes. "Okay, but you have to promise not to tell anyone I told you." I shake my head yes again. I sit down next to her on the bed. "I had just graduated high school. Some friends and I took a road trip to check out a college we were all interested in enrolling. We had a fun weekend planned, but while we took our tour, some boys were handing out flyers to a party they were throwing that night. I didn't want to go, but my friends did, and I couldn't think of a good enough reason not to, so I went. We arrived a little late, but the party was still raging. There was alcohol there, of course, but I volunteered to be the designated driver. I didn't care much for beer, so it was no loss to me. I was just happy to dance and watch my friends have fun," she pauses, and I can see it in her face. She looks terrified all of a sudden.

"If you need to stop, it's okay. I don't want to push you to tell me," I insist. She's about to tell me how she died. I can't imagine this is something easy for her to think about, let alone say aloud.

"It's fine. It's just I realize this is the first time I've ever said what happen to me out loud to anyone," she replies somberly. "As it got late, I began going around trying to round all my friends up to head out. I couldn't find one of them, so I started going room to room looking for her. One of the boys who lived at this house saw me looking and offered to help. He told me that he thought he saw my friend go into a room upstairs. I followed him naively. He took me to his room, and when I got in, my friend wasn't there. Thinking I must have been drunk like him, he locks the door behind us, and he starts to walk closer to me. I ask him to back off and unlock the door, but he doesn't listen. He's completely wasted, and he grabs me. I start to panic and try to get free, but he was too strong. He puts one hand over my mouth and throws me on the ground. I keep screaming, but the music downstairs is playing so loud that no one can hear me. I struggle trying to free myself the whole time, but I wasn't strong enough," she pauses again, and I can feel wet tears start to roll down my face. She can't look me in the eyes, and I don't think I wanted to see the pain in them anyway.

"I finally manage to push him off me after it was too late. I start to head for the door to unlock it. He gets up and pulls my hair. I fall back to the ground. I scramble to my feet, but he is now at the door blocking me. I didn't know if he was scared to let me leave because of what I might say, or if he wasn't done with me. I start to back away from him. I'm scarred, worn out from fighting, and terrified that I wasn't getting out. The house was currently being remodeled. In his room they were putting in a new window. They had already taken the old one out and in its place was only a sheet of thick plastic to block the opening. I kept backing away, not realizing it was even there. I must have pressed too hard up against the plastic because it started to tear. Whoever put it up didn't make sure it was secured all the way. I don't remember falling, but I fell, and then I died," she finally looks up at me. I see a single tear roll down her cheek. "The only thing I remember is the look on that guy's face right before I fell. His eyes were devoid of any remorse. He didn't even reach out his hand to try and catch me," she says, remembering it as another tear rolls down her other cheek. I wrap my arms around her and pull her in tightly.

"Helen, I'm so sorry," I don't know what else to say. I can feel tears running down my cheeks. She's acting so strong. I'm more of a mess, and it didn't even happen to me.

"Guardians save or help those who die tragic deaths. However, Guardians are also chosen out of those people as well, if the angel thinks you're worthy," she informs me, and I release her. I believe Darrius tried to explain that to me already, but I didn't realize what that fully meant until now.

"I'm sorry," I say again, "but I'm glad you were chosen. If anyone deserves a second chance, it's you," I assure her. She looks at me with pity, and I feel like I'm missing something.

"I'm grateful I was chosen. However, we Guardians don't realize what this responsibility really means. Most of us want to live and are honored that the angel chose us to help others like us. However, we live every day knowing that our friends, family are out there right now living. They are living their lives while we are stuck in our Orders, never able to see them again," she tells me, and I feel sad all over again. "Or worse, they die, and we never get to say goodbye." If I had got to live knowing that I'm alive, but everyone I loved thought I was dead or would die thinking I was dead. That would kill me every day. "Leyla, I know we haven't exactly been close. It's not that I have anything against you, but it's hard having you around. I'm just jealous. I'm jealous that you can leave tomorrow after the ball and go to school. You can see your friends, go shopping, or see a movie. You get to have a normal life. You're a reminder of a life us Guardians can no longer have," she discloses, and my heart feels suddenly very heavy in my chest.

"I see, I didn't realize," I say honestly.

"It's alright," she says and stands up. "Thank you, Leyla. Thank you for listening to me," she smiles. Her face looks happy, but there is nothing but sorrow and pain in her eyes. They are as cold and distant as their icy color.

She's putting up a wall to protect herself. I see that now. I was wrong about Helen. I was wrong about a lot of things. There is so much more I don't know or understand about the Order or the Guardians. "We better be going soon. You might want to fix your mascara, it's running all down your face," she informs me almost laughing. "Also, remember once we leave this room, you're Alexandra," she reminds me on a more serious note.

"Yes, I understand. I won't do anything to draw attention to you or the Master. I promise," I assure her, it's the least I can do.

As we head down the red-carpeted stairs, I notice the pillars are now wrapped with red material. The musicians now sit in their chairs reading their music and tightening their instruments. There are long tables set against the wall to my left. They have cakes and different colored liquids in several punch bowls. Each female Guardian looks as if they could be on the cover of Vogue, each one more beautiful in her dress than the next. All the male Guardians are wearing black fitted suits. I also notice everyone is wearing black masks. As Helen and I reach the end of the stairway Darrius and Drake meet us. I recognize Drake's green eyes and charming smile, and Darrius' blue eyes piercing my own as he bows his head ever so slightly in my direction. Both their suits are fitted so tightly I didn't see how they could breathe, let alone move. They look irresistible and dashing. I'm suddenly nervous. I'm about to dance, and I never really got to practice. I hope I don't make a fool of myself.

"Both of you are the most stunning women I've ever seen," Drake announces. He gives us a half bow. Helen and I do the same in return. "Helen, this is for you," Drake says holding out a feminine black lace mask.

She turns, now facing away from him. Taking the mask by the black silk strings, Drake ties it delicately behind her hair. She is facing me, and I see her blush a little as he does so. She turns back around, and he takes her hand as they walk off. I look over to Darrius, whose eyes I don't believe have left me since I've been standing here. He is holding a similar mask in his hand as well.

"May I?" I nod yes and turn around to let him tie it around my head. Once it's on, I turn back to see he is still intently staring at me, and I can't help but turn away from his gaze.

"I'm sorry again that you had to come," I start to apologize, but he stops me. He takes his hand and presses it gently onto my lips. He then moves his hand to my chin and pulls up my face up to make me look into his eyes.

"Seeing you like this is worth it a thousand times over," he admits in a passionate tone. My heart flutters, and I instinctively move my eyes away from his. His words took me by complete surprise. "Shall we," he states and removes his hand from my face. He holds out his hand palm up and I take it. I shyly follow him onto the dance floor, still looking down.

I notice everyone starting to settle down to look up towards the top of the stairs. I follow along to see what they are all staring at. At the top, in all his glory, stands the Master. How wonderous he looks, and he wasn't the only Master there either. There are several. All of them are distinguished by their white hair. Not only do they have white hair, but all the men are wearing white suits with gold embroidery, and their masks are also white. They cover the top part of their faces stopping right before their lips. The women all have on white dresses fitted and decorated differently with gold accents. Their masks are all white with lace designs, and like mine, they only cover their eyes. They all command such presence.

"We have gathered this night to remember and honor the day the first Guardian was created," the Master of St. Louis starts to speak, and I recognize his robust voice. His eyes find mine and I stare back. "Tonight we celebrate together as one. The Guards," he pauses, and I assume all the Guards cry out harmoniously. "The Swords," he continues, and all the Swords cry out louder. "The Lights," he finishes and the biggest shouts of all erupt. Then everyone in unison begins to chant. "I can never lie. I can never die. I come for you with vengeance. I come for you with justice. I am balance. I am death." The Master smiles satisfyingly. "Let the ball begin," he announces and there is another all-around cheer. He nods his head to the musicians, pulling his gaze away from me, and they begin to play. I pull my focus away from him as well. Drake and Helen take the lead on the dance floor, and Darrius and I follow. Even Xander has a partner.

"Hold me tightly and follow my lead. You'll be perfect," Darrius whispers to me, and we start to take off around the room. I feel butterflies in my stomach like the last time we danced.

We move slowly at first but pick up the pace as the tempo does. We move in a large circle around the room keeping a short distance between each couple near us. I manage to keep pace with Darrius thus far. The beat isn't too fast, which helps. He lets go of my waist suddenly and uses his other arm to twirl me around. I start to anticipate his movements as if I know what I'm doing.

Perhaps Alexandra is taking over for me? We sway back and forth and move around and around. The music reaches a peak and Darrius' hands lift me effortlessly off the ground and swing me all the way around in the air. His hands hold me firmly at the waist, and I can't help but be sensitive to his hold on me. I look down into his eyes as he twirls me, and he appears happy. His eyes are shining up at me like sunlight dancing on top of the water. As he sets me back down and the music starts to slow. We are left standing closely together staring into each other's eyes. His hand is still around my waist and I feel him tighten his grip on me. He moves one of his hands up my back sending shivers down my spine. He reaches my neck and gently bends me backward. His other arm is curled around my waist supporting me. The music ends, but we are stuck in our moment. My heart is pounding in my chest. His blonde hair shines from the light of the chandelier above, and I watch one strand fall onto his forehead as he lifts me back upright. I reach for his face and move it away. I leave my hand on his fair skin for a moment and then bring it back down to my side.

Everyone starts clapping around us breaking my attention from him. We both begin to do the same. If this is just the first dance of the night, I don't know how much more I can handle. He takes my hand and leads me off the dance floor.

"Leyla, there is something I need to tell you," Darrius bends down and whispers in my ear as the music starts to play again. "We told the Master the identity of the Caster," he reveals, and it takes me a moment to comprehend.

"Darrius, why would you do that?" I ask in disbelief.

"Excuse me, may I have this dance?" I freeze in place at the sound of the voice. I turn to see the Master. He has his hand out towards me awaiting my hand in return. He's even more striking standing right in front of me than atop the stairs. He doesn't take his eyes off me, and I can't help but want to look over at Darrius, but I fight the urge.

"Of course," I answer and take his hand. He smiles sweetly at me, and I wasn't sure how I should feel about it.

We wait for a break in the couples and join in. The Master moves his free hand to my waist, and his grip is less tight than Darrius' was moments ago. I want nothing more than to run back to Darrius and ask him what he was thinking telling the Master about Mie, but I couldn't. We move in rhythm to the others around us. I can't take my eyes off his and I hope I don't step on his feet. Although, he seems to me almost carrying me around the dance floor. His eyes are sparking like fire, but not in a furious way, it's more gently. He moves his hand from the side of my waist to the center of my back and pulls me in a little closer. I suck in some air, and I feel my face start to get warm. I was confused, worried, and shy all at once. I didn't know what to think about this, should we be dancing? The Master of the Order dancing with a mortal, I'm pretty sure that's a hard line that shouldn't be crossed. The melody picks up and he releases me only a moment to twirl me around. When he brings me back, I feel his finger slip through mine.

"Leyla, are you sure you're not a Guardian?" he whispers taking me by surprise. *Does he know? How could he?* I feel my heartbeat start to pick up. I shake my head yes. "Well, you dance like one. Also, you look absolutely elegant in this dress," he declares with a brief smile.

"Thank you," I manage to get out.

The music slows and then stops. We both clap and give each other a little bow, before I turn and leave the dance floor. I head straight for Darrius, and I see him standing frozen in the same spot I left him in. I couldn't read his face, not because it was blank, but because I've never seen him with such an expression before. He must have been watching the Master and I the whole time.

"I believe you owe me an explanation," I whisper reminding him of our earlier conversation. He nods.

"We had to give him something so he would be satisfied to leave us be. We told him that a Caster contact of ours told us her name, and that was all. I told him I was late getting here because I was trying to find out if she was nearby, which was partly true. I figured out that you were meeting her in the loft above the bar. Imagine my surprise when she was no longer there. She has moved out and I don't know where," he reveals. Does he mean that he was planning on coming to the ball this whole time?

"She may not be in the loft, but she isn't going to go far. She's not leaving until she gets what she wants, which is me," I assure him.

"True, but I don't like the idea of her roaming around as she pleases. She is out by our graces. I have no problem ending her, especially since we now know what she has planned for you," he states harshly. I was about to retort, but I suddenly feel warm all over. My stomach turns in knots, and my skin feels hot. I don't feel so well. My head starts to ache with intense pain. Was I about to have visions again? I thought I was past that. I back away against the wall and crouch down rubbing my head. "Leyla, what's wrong?" Darrius bends down and whispers with concern. I look past him, and I watch in confusion as the dance floor shifts into a road. Lamp polls pop up and I see houses. Something wet hits my cheek. I go to wipe it, but there is nothing there. I look up and instead of the tall ceiling, all I see are dark storm clouds. What's happening to me? Why am I seeing my nightmare? I'm not asleep. "Leyla?" I realize Darrius is still crouching in front of me and I make myself stand as he does the same.

"Something is wrong," I finally answer him.

My skin heats up again and my headache is back. It hurts. It hurts so bad I can't stand it. I rush out of the room and I think I hear Darrius behind me. This dress starts to feel too tight, and I can't breathe. I need some fresh air. All of a sudden, I hear a familiar shrill scream. I run even faster. I make my way out to the garden and the night air feels good against my skin. I take in a few deep breaths, but I still feel hot and my head still hurts. I hear the scream again. I look around, but there is no one out here.

*Why is this happening?* "Stop!" I shout out. "Stop it!" I cry.

My eyes are clouded, and I notice a familiar tree appear that shouldn't be here. Even though a part of me knows it's not real, I walk closer to it and there is a body, just like my nightmare. As I start to walk towards it, heat starts coming from my hands. I look down in shock. My hands, they are starting to light up. Soon I'm engulfed in a bright white light spreading like flames over my whole body. It's hot and blinding. The light keeps getting brighter and brighter, and soon it's all I can see. The light feels like never-ending energy pulsing through my veins. Before I know it, I'm several feet in the air. I'm somehow lifting myself off the ground. I can't stop it. Whatever this is, I can't stop it!

"Leyla!" I hear Darrius' voice call out my name. I can hear him, but I can't see him.

"Leyla!" Is that Drake? I still can't see anything but light? Just as quickly as it began, I feel the light and energy fade from my body and feel heavy. I begin to descend, and someone catches me.

"Leyla!" Darrius. "Leyla open your eyes, look at me," he shouts. "Leyla look at me," he demands. *Darrius, I can't…*

## Darrius Stone

Her lifeless body is lying in my arms, and this night has proven that it is nothing more than a curse for me. First Alexandra, and now Leyla.

"Darrius is she…" Drake, I hear his voice behind me. I didn't realize he was here. I look over at him and Helen is at his side. They both have a look of terror on their faces.

"I can hear her heartbeat, but it's slowing," I tell him with fear. *What do I do?* I have no doubt this display was Alexandra's power coming through. Leyla is mortal and her body isn't handling this well. The only one who knows about this damn spell is Mei, and she's the last person I can go to right now. If we leave suddenly and follow her, it will be the end of all of us.

"I thought, I thought she wasn't a Guardian?" Helen's voice trembles in shock. I glance back at her to see her skin turn pale as she looks over Leyla's limp body, like she is going to be sick.

"She is mortal, it's hard to explain, but she is," I reply.

"If that's true, then the fact that she is still breathing is a miracle. Her body just released tons of magical energy," she observers. Her words echo through me overcoming me with pain and anger. *Alexandra, how could you let this happen? Why are you doing this? Why would you let this spell be cast on you? Can't you see it's just bringing me more pain?* I clench Leyla tighter in towards my chest.

"I won't give up on her," I state boldly. "We have to help her, Helen, what do we do? We need a healer, but we don't want what just happened to get out. Can you agree to this?" I plead with her.

"Please Helen, give Darrius and I a chance to explain before you reveal anything to anyone. She needs a healer now," Drake speaks up. She seems to listen to him, maybe his words will get through to her.

"Follow me," she finally answers and speeds off. We both follow. When we arrive at the medical ward, I lay Leyla down on one of the beds. "Everyone is at the ball; I will go and get someone I trust to examine her. You two should get back before the Master notices you're gone. I will handle this for now," she commands. Drake and I leave hesitantly. As we reach the ballroom, I notice his face is full of worry and sorrow. I know exactly how he is feeling right now. If anything happens to Leyla, I don't know what I will do.

"Darrius, what happened?" Drake asks. I'm not sure how much he saw, so I will just start from the beginning. It's playing through my mind right now anyway.

"I was explaining to her that we told the Master about Mei. I didn't want to keep it from her in case he said something to her about it. She started acting strange, she backed up against the wall, and she was holding her head. I ask if she was alright, and when she looked up at me, she didn't even see me. She looked past me as if I wasn't even there. She ran out and I followed. She got to the garden and started to yell, but I don't know at what or to who. Then," I pause remembering the startling sight, "she started to ignite like a flame. I was in such a shock that when she fell, I almost didn't catch her." I look over Drake and he is shaking his head in disbelieve. "She shone brighter than a star. I've never seen anything like it. This has something to do with that spell," I conclude. "If Alexandra is trying to take over Leyla's body, I need to know. We need to find Mei. We need to know the truth about this spell and the full effects it has," I state angrily. "I looked for her before I arrived, but I'm not sure where she is now," I admit frustrated.

"I doubt she's gone far. It won't take us long to track her down. Darrius," he starts in a more serious tone than I'm used to from him, "do you really think Alexandra is trying to hurt Leyla?"

"I don't know," I reply. "Right now, I don't want to think about it. I just hope Leyla can recover from this." *I swear if anything happens to Leyla, I'm going to kill that witch.*

# Chapter 19

## Set in Stone

**Leyla Gray**

*"Leyla," someone calls out my name from far in the distance. "Leyla," it calls again.*

*"Hello," I call out. Why do I feel so weak? Where am I? I look around to nothing but white. I feel something warm touch my hand. It grabs hold of me as it's leading me forward. I can't see what's got me, but I follow. The emptiness around me starts to fade.*

*"Leyla," that voice repeats, and I finally recognize it.*

*"Alexandra? Is that you?" I guess.*

*"It's not a dream…" she whispers, and I start to see a road with houses and cars, and even street signs. "Look, Leyla, look," she instructs, and I obey.*

*I look around, and it looks like my nightmare for the most part. I read one of the street signs and recognize the street name. I know where this is, this road is by the campus. I look around at all the homes again. I recognize this road. I know where this is. It's like I'm seeing it for the first time. It's all so clear now. She pulls my hand and we start to move again. "It's not a dream," she tells me again. It's not, then what is this? What is she trying to make me see? She leads me to the body, and we are standing inches from it. The last time I tried to reach for it, I sunk below into darkness. She squeezes my hand like she is telling me it's okay. I turn the body over. I can't make out the person's face, but it's definitely a woman's. Why can't I see the face? I hear thunder and it starts to rain. I feel drops of water on my face, but it's not from the clouds. I use my free hand to wipe away a tear. Why am I crying? I look back at the body. Do I know who this is? Does my brain know who's in front of me, but my eyes just can't see it? Alexandra squeezes my hand again. I guess that means I'm right.*

*"It's not a dream," she says again, and then I feel her let go of my hand.*

*"Wait, don't leave me, tell me what is going on, tell me who I'm looking at?"* I cry out. *Think Leyla, what is she trying to tell you? If I know this place, and I know the person, what is this? A vision? Am I meant to stop this? Is someone I know going to die? I don't know for sure, but I think I'm right. This nightmare hasn't been a dream at all. It's a warning, or precognition, of what's to come. Someone I know, someone I might even love, is going to die!*

"Leyla," I hear my name again, it's spoken by a woman, but it's not Alexandra. I slowly start to open my eyes to a dimly lit room. I'm lying down and my whole body aches. "You're awake," the voice speaks again, and whomever she is, she sounds relieved. I try to move my head, but it's too heavy. Someone leans over me and I see them clearly now.

"Helen?" I see her nod. My voice is coarse, and my mouth feels dryer than a desert.

"Let me help you sit up," she offers.

Moving her hand to behind my back, she pushes me up and then leans me forward. It takes all my strength to sit upright. She grabs some more pillows and positions them behind me to help me steady myself. I look around seeing a bedroom. It's similar to the one I stayed in, but this one is bigger. It has a larger sitting area and a closet. Is this Helen's room?

"How are you feeling? Do you need anything?" her voice is calm, but her eyes are looking me over worriedly.

"I'm parched and sore," I answer honestly. My stomach growls, apparently I'm hungry too. Helen nods and gets up to walk towards her door.

"Don't move and keep quiet. I'll be right back," she instructs, and I see a blur of her as she races off. *Keep quiet.* I repeat her words in my head. I wonder what made her say that.

Only, a few minutes pass before she instantly appears next to me like she was never gone. She has a tall glass of water and a bowl of soup in her hands. She holds the glass rim up to my lips as I swallow down each drop. It tastes so refreshing.

"Here, I'll feed you, take it slow," she insists and starts feeding me a small spoon full at a time. I almost object to her help, but I realize I'm too weak to. I don't know why I'm so out of it. Helen looks at me seriously making me worry a little. "Leyla, do you remember what happened?" she asks somewhat hesitantly.

"Not really," I reply. I start to think about it for a moment. I don't know how I got here. I remember my dream and Alexandra talking to me, but what was I doing before that? "The ball," it comes to me, "I was dancing. That's the last thing I can remember."

"I see," is all I get as a response. She feeds me the last of the soup and my hunger is starting to dissolve. "Would you like more?" she offers.

"No, thank you. Actually, I need to get up," I tell her, and she looks at me with surprise.

"Leyla, I don't think you're ready for walking," she objects.

"Just stand me up, please," I insist. She still doesn't look too sure, but she obliges me. My legs feel wobbly as she helps me off the bed. I'm only able to stand for maybe a minute before I have to sit back down. "Helen, what happened? Why am I in your room, and why can't I seem to stand?" She looks at me again with that worried look. She takes a moment to respond as if she is debating whether or not to tell me.

"Something happened to you at the ball. You ran out into the gardens where you were consumed by the abilities of a Light," she explains, and my heart skips a beat. I displayed abilities, and in front of her? How do I not remember that? "Leyla, the power consumed you, and I believe through some of Alexandra's healing abilities and your own will, your body recovered," she finishes.

"What did you just say?" How does she know that Alexandra and I are connected?

"Darrius and Drake, they filled me in on what is happening to you," she explains. I stay silent. How much did they tell her? What should I, and should I not say? Does she know they helped me with the escape of Mei? I don't know what to do. "It's okay. You don't need to worry. I'm not going to turn you to the Master," she says no doubt seeing the panic in my eyes. "Leyla, you've been in a comatose state now for six days," she reveals.

"What!" I exclaim in shock. Six days, that's crazy. Everyone must be so worried. "Oh no! Kat, Bridget, Drake, and Darrius. They must be, well they must be freaking out," I think aloud my voice shaking a little.

"I'm not sure about Kat or Bridget, but Drake and Darrius know you're okay. They aren't far from here. They have been waiting anxiously for your recovery," she divulges. "They weren't able to stay here much longer after the ball. I've been hiding you in my room these past four nights. No one else knows you're still here," she assures me. I'm still unsure what I can talk to her about, but I know she helped me. For that I'm grateful. She kept me hidden, and therefore kept me, Darrius, and Drake safe.

"Thank you, Helen, for helping me. I'm sorry that you've had to watch over me. I know this couldn't be an easy choice," I tell her. She looks away from me so I'm not able to read her expression.

"Don't mention it. I just feel bad for your situation, is all, we aren't best friends now or anything. Don't get the wrong idea," she advises. There she goes again putting up her wall. She won't tear it down for anyone, it would seem. I smile, but she doesn't see it.

"I don't want to go back to sleep. I need to get up and move around. I need to get back to Darrius and Drake. Can you take me to them?" I ask hopeful.

"You want to leave now? You just woke up. You're not strong enough to move around," she replies harshly, crossing her arms still looking away from me.

"Maybe, but I need to go. You've kept me hidden this long, but now that I'm awake, I shouldn't be here. It looks dark outside," I mention seeing no light coming through the curtains. "If it's late, wouldn't it be best to leave now?" I suggest. She finally looks back at me annoyed.

"Very well. I'll carry you and faze you out of here. You're not strong enough to walk very far on your own," Helen agrees, but I can tell she isn't happy about it. "However, before you leave, you need a bath and a change of clothes. I'll go run the water. A hot bath should help relax your muscles, and I don't know if you noticed, but you smell," she jabs. I wasn't mad, I know she's just putting up her wall again, but it won't push me away.

After the bath, I feel not only clean but also less weak. Helen gives me one of her normal outfits, and it's much appreciated. She follows through on her word and she picks me up to faze us into the mirror world. She runs us out of the Order within a blink of an eye. We don't travel far, just a couple blocks away to a tall building. We speed through the entrance, but she doesn't un-faze us until we reach the elevator. She sets me down and I see her hit the button for the tenth floor.

"Where are we?"

"This is a hotel. Drake and Darrius have a room here," she answers. Her mood seems somber, and I wonder what thoughts are going through her head right now.

"Helen, why did you agree to help me?" I ask bluntly.

She ignores me and stays silent all the way to the top floor. I didn't think she would respond, but I had to ask regardless. The elevator stops and she walks out into the short hallway. I follow as the doors to the elevator close behind us. There are only two doors on this level, and one of them leads to Darrius and Drake.

"I saw something impossible happen to you," Helen starts to answer my question and I'm taken aback. She turns and faces me, and her artic eyes pierce deeply into mine making me feel nervous suddenly. "My curiosity won me over that night. I agreed to give Darrius and Drake a chance to explain things to me. I should have turned you in, all of you, to the Master," she admits her gaze becoming more intense, and her tone is firm.

"You still can," I point out, "if you wanted to." I rock back and forth on my heels and try to keep from looking away from her.

"Yes, that is true," she whispers. She walks over and knocks on the door to our right. She comes back over and hits the button for the elevator, and she steps in as the doors open. We are now facing each other, and her eyes meet mine once again. "I don't want to be the one responsible for taking you away from your normal life," she reveals. "Don't make me regret my decision," she adds ominously. The doors to the elevator start to shut. "Goodbye, Leyla. I truly wish you a happy life, don't waste it."

The doors close after her advice to me. *Goodbye*? The word echoes in my mind. I just realize I will probably never see her again after tonight. If I were the same me a week ago, I probably would have been glad, but I'm not. I'm suddenly filled with sadness at the thought.

"Leyla!" I turn myself around to see Drake inside the open doorway leading into the suite behind him. His face is drained of its normal lite and carefree manner. "Leyla, I can't believe it. You're finally awake." He sounds unsure of his words.

He comes over to me and holds my face in both his hands, as if to make sure I'm standing here. Feeling my skin, he smiles, and his expression turns from worry and shock to relief. He smiles and removes his hands from my face. He wraps them instead around my back and pulls me close into his embrace. I do not object, in fact, I'm just as happy to see him as he is to see me. He lets me go and takes one of my hands and leads me into the room. I see a wall of glass windows and a doorway leading out onto a balcony at the back of the room. Directly in front of me is a seating area with a large wooden coffee table with two couches and two chairs surrounding it like a square. To my right are two doors and to my left is a small kitchen area.

One of the two doors opens, and Darrius walks out. He stops instantly when he sees me, and his face looks more relieved than Drake's had. Once again, I get a feeling of happiness as I see his face. He speeds over, almost knocking me backward, as he pulls me into him. He holds me so tight that I almost can't breathe, but I don't mind. I feel Drake let go of my hand, and I wrap both my arms around Darrius briefly in response.

"Leyla, I knew you would come back. I knew it," Darrius states softly in my ear. His voice is trembling, and it almost sounds as if he is about to cry. He lets me go and smiles with relief as Drake did. My legs start to give way a little and I fall forward slightly into Darrius. He catches me and sits me down in one of the seats. "Take it easy," he instructs in a gentle tone.

"Sorry, I'm fine. I just need more practice standing, apparently," I joke. He sits down on the middle of the couch to my right, and Drake sits on one of the armrest. They are both looking me over intently both still worried about me.

"Leyla, how did you get here? Did Helen bring you?" Drake guesses, and I nod yes.

"Do you need anything to eat or drink?" Darrius asks.

"No, I've already eaten," I answer. They both continue to study me. "I'm sorry to have made you worry. Helen told me how long I've been out of it. I bet I'm so behind at school," I add trying to lighten the mood.

"Don't worry about school. We covered for you. We emailed your teachers that you have been ill. Kat thinks you're sick too, but Bridget knows the truth," Drake tells me. "We're in your classes remember, so we just turned in your work for you. You're not behind," he smiles, and I'm glad to hear they have taken care of things for me.

"Leyla, I hate to ask but did Helen explain what happen to you? Do you remember?" Darrius inquires.

"Helen said I used some of Alexandra's abilities, but I don't remember doing it. Nor do I know how I did it," I reply.

"Was it Alexandra? Did she panic when I told you the Master knows Mei's name? Did, did she do this to you?" Darrius asks, and his voice sounds upset.

"No, that's not it at all. I don't think Alexandra is making me do anything. I think it's just the spell. I can tap into her abilities when I'm stressed. I didn't panic because you told me about Mei. I was in pain because of my nightmare," I answer, and they both look at me curiously. "This isn't the first time I've used a Guardian ability. When those two men attacked me that night, one of them grabbed me and I somehow moved out of the way. I thought time had just stopped somehow, but I realize now I just moved that quickly. Alexandra isn't trying to hurt me. She is trying to protect me. I really believe that. When I was unconscious, she spoke to me. She's trying to help me," I reveal.

"What are you saying, Leyla? What nightmare?" Drake asks in alarm.

"The first time I had my nightmare was the night at Kat's when we went home for the winter break. I thought nothing about it at first, but it was persistent. Besides dreams of Alexandra's memories, I've had the same dream almost every night since then. However, I know now that it's not a dream but a vision. Alexandra helped me realize that. I've been seeing someone die over and over in my mind. I can see the scene so clearly now, and I know it will happen on a stormy day somewhere close to the campus. I know that the person who dies is a girl, but I can never make out her face. Every fiber of my being is on fire to save them, and I feel like nothing else in the world is more important than doing so. I can never do it though. I can never save them," I finish. I feel a heavy weight lift off of me. It's such a relief to tell someone about this and not have to keep bottling it all up inside anymore.

"We had no idea. Why didn't you tell us about this?" Drake questions me.

"Honestly, I thought I was going crazy, and there was always something else going on. I'm sorry I didn't tell you guys until now," I apologize. It's not that I meant to hide it from them. I just didn't know it was important.

"Leyla," Darrius says my name, and his tone worries me. "This vision that you've been seeing, it is another Guardian ability. You know there are three positions that we Guardians can have?"

"Yes, the Guard, the Sword, and the Light," I reply.

"Correct. The Light has a vision of who their charge will be. The Guard's responsibility is to find that person and learn as much about them as possible. We follow them in the shadows to figure out when and where the tragedy will take place. While the Guard acts in the background, the Sword protects the charge in plain sight," he pauses, and Drake takes over.

"The Sword can be that stranger you meet, the friend you have for a short time, or a neighbor. We blend in and try to make sure we are by the charge's side when the event occurs, if at all possible. Also, if there is magical influence involved, it's our responsibility to intervene and take care of it. If we do intervene, we must erase any proof that might be left behind," he says. I think back to my encounter with him that day in the snow. He used his gift to burn those men's bodies as if they weren't even there. I guess that's what he meant.

"Once the event happens, the Guard can either step in behind the scenes and keep our charge safe or the Light steps in," Darrius continues. "The Light's gift is, well, their light. It's warm, comforting, and it takes any pain away. If the charge dies, the Light carries their soul to what we call the In-Between. Then, as far as we know, they are taken up further by the Angel of Death to be judged. You've no doubt heard the saying that when you die, you see the light. Well, it's not just a saying. It's true," he finishes, and I try to process.

"Wow," I murmur in awe. I had no idea so much went into it. "So are you saying that I'm right about my dream being a vision? Someone I love is going to die?" I ask, finally putting everything together.

"Yes, and no," Drake answers. "You are having a vision of someone who is going to die. It is strange that you can't see who, but it doesn't exactly mean it's someone you love or even know. Unless you can see them, you won't know for sure. If you were a true Light, you would be trained how to see your visions at the Order properly," he elaborates.

"I see. Well, I can't explain it, but I know it's someone close to me. I just do, and I have to save them," I add, not meaning to argue, but I know I'm right.

"Absolutely not. That is out of the question," Darrius replies sternly. I look at him with confusion. I turn to Drake, and his look tells me they are both in agreeance on this. *Why are they acting like this?* "You're mortal, Leyla, and what you just went through proves you can barely handle using Guardian abilities. If you save this person, you could open the door to more visions, more abilities. It will never end. You're not a Guardian, and if the Order ever found out what you did, everything me and Drake have done will be for nothing. We've just escaped suspicion, and luckily no one found out about what happened to you at the ball either. However, if you do this, they will find out, and they will take you away from us," he responds harshly.

"Leyla, Darrius is right," Drake agrees. "We just got you back. We won't allow you to put yourself in danger. Don't you see this is just what Mei meant when she said Alexandra would take over? The more you use her gifts, the more you let her in," he stands up from the armrest and looms over me. "I know you said Alexandra helped you, and we both want to believe she won't do anything to hurt you. However, the fact is we don't know her as well as we thought," he admits, and his voice raises in anger. He glares down at me with hurt in his eyes.

He turns away from me and storms off into his room shutting the door loudly behind him. I've only ever seen him that angry one other time, and that was when Mei told him that someone at the Order murdered her. I look back over at Darrius, and his expression isn't exactly any friendlier.

"I'm sorry, I don't mean to hurt either of you. I know what you've said makes sense, and I understand that you're angry about what the possible outcome could be if I save this person," I pause and turn from his gaze and look out instead to the night sky and the lights of the city.

"But you want to save this person anyway," Darrius finishes my sentence for me. I can't look at him to tell him otherwise. I hear him sigh. "You should rest now; we will leave in the morning. Please take my bed. I will stay out here tonight," he insists. I push myself up from my seat. I don't feel like sleeping, but I'm in no position to argue. I start to walk, but I don't get very far. I begin to drift back, and Darrius is behind me instantly. He picks me up and carries me into his room lying me down on the bed. He leaves me on the bed and walks over to the wall, and flips off the light. He walks over to the door leading back into the seating area. "Goodnight Leyla, sweet dreams," he whispers.

"Goodnight, Darrius," I reply. He starts to shut the door but stops.

"Leyla, listen. Just as you feel you need to save this person, know that we feel the same way about stopping you. We won't back down from this. We will stop you, no matter what," he warns then closes the door.

We leave in the morning, just as Darrius said. They both seem to be giving me the silent treatment. We pull into my apartment, and I'm so glad to be back home. Not as badly as the first time we left the Order, but still. Drake unloads my things and takes them into my apartment for me. Both of them leave me for now, but I know they will just be across the way watching me. I'm starving, and before I start to unpack, I need food. I walk to my fridge and all I have is breakfast foods to cook. I heat a pan and pull out eggs and a package of bacon. I probably should have had more than a slice of toast before we left, but I felt like the guys were in a hurry to leave, so I didn't order a lot. As I'm beating the eggs, I hear a knock on my door. I put the bowl down and walk over to answer it. As I open the door, I see Bridget standing on the other side. I'm surprised to see her here. How did she know I was back?

"Leyla!" Bridget shouts my name and throws herself on me. She hugs me for a brief moment and then lets herself in. "I'm so glad you're alright," she states happily. I close the door behind her, and she sits down at my table. "Are you about to make some food?" she asks, pointing to my stovetop and the carton of eggs.

"Yes, are you hungry? I've just got eggs and bacon," I reply.

"That sounds great actually. I skipped breakfast this morning," she informs with a smile. I go back over to finish beating the eggs and pour them into the pan.

"How did you know I was back?" I ask her curiously.

"Drake texted me. I've been waiting all morning for you to get back," she answers, and I turn back to look at her.

"Texted you?" What is she talking about; neither Darrius nor Drake have phones. She's got to be joking.

"Ya, why are you looking at me like that? Didn't they tell you I made them get cell phones?" I shake my head no. "Ugh, those guys. When they came to school without you, I knew something was up. We may not have the same classes together, but I noticed. That and I remembered you told me when you would be back, and when I didn't hear from you, I got worried. I told them it was time for them to join the modern world of communication," she explains, and I'm astounded that they listened to her. I finish cooking and bring the food over, and she starts to scarf it down. I guess I wasn't the only one starving.

"Bridget, did they explain to you what happened to me?" I wonder.

"For the most part, they said you tapped into Alexandra's abilities, and your body couldn't handle it," she states in between her bites. "Oh, and apparently, you've been hallucinating too. They texted me about it last night," she adds.

"They're visions," I correct her.

"Humm, ya that might have been the word they used, now that I think about it," she corrects herself. "What exactly did you have a vision of?" she asks as if it was nothing to be alarmed over.

"Well, apparently as a Light, Alexandra has the ability to see her charge die. I've been having one of these visions. I can see where the body is and where it's going to happen. However, what causes it and who it is, alludes me," I explain and let out an agitated huff. "I know it's a girl. More importantly, I feel like it's a girl I know, someone I care about," I go on. Bridget stops eating and looks up at me. I can see in her eyes that she is putting the pieces together.

"Oh my God! Could it be me?" she asks looking horrified.

"I don't know. That's what I need to find out. The day it happens there is a storm. We are coming up to our rainy months, so I don't think I have much time to figure it out. I'm worried. Darrius and Drake refuse to help me. They want to stop me, in fact," I reveal frustrated. I cross my arms and lean back in my chair.

"How would they be able to help you if they wanted to, that is?" She seems interested.

"They said that at the Order they could teach the Light's how to make out their visions. The only time I was able to figure out anything was when I was unconscious. Alexandra helped me. She opened my mind to see things around me more clearly," I answer. "I'm worried, though. I didn't have the nightmare last night. If I can't see it anymore, how am I supposed to figure out who the person is?" I ask more to myself than her.

"I hate to say this, but it sounds like there is only one person that could or would, help you," she suggests.

"Who?" I ask cautiously. She stares at me until it finally hits me. "You mean Mei?" She nods yes. "I don't like it," I comment disheartened. "Besides, she's not even here anymore. Darrius said she left the loft and we don't know where she is."

"She's not far. We've kept in touch. Just one word, and I can ask her," she states.

I let out a defeated sigh. "Fine." Bridget grins and pulls out her phone. I watch her fingers start to fly over the keys. Just moments after she hits send, her phone lights up with a reply.

"That was faster than I expected," she admits, and I was thinking the same. "Mei says she can help. She says she is here for you whatever you need." Bridget reads the response and looks up at me for a reply.

"I don't trust her, but I need her. Tell her I accept her help, and I want to meet," I decide.

"Alright, when?"

"As soon as possible," I reply, and Bridget looks at me unsure. "I told you, I don't have time to waste," I repeat seriously. I won't sit back and do nothing.

Someone is going to die, that I know for sure, and when I figure out who it is, I will save them.

# Chapter 20

## What They Don't Know Won't Kill Them

Mei agreed to meet the very next day. Bridget and I leave school together, and I told Darrius and Drake that we are just planning on catching up and spending some time together. We purposely left out the part about me meeting up with Mei for obvious reasons. I'm not sure what to expect from Mei, but I have faith that she will help. What other choice do I have but to trust her? Bridget drives us to the Beverly Meadows suites. It looks like a resort. I didn't exactly see how hiding here was such a great idea. It wasn't exactly low-key. We walk in and make our way to the reception desk. Bridget gives the young woman behind the counter a fake name. I guess Mei is at least smart enough not to use her real one. The woman smiles and waives one of the bellhops comes over.

"We've been expecting you. Your friend is staying in our presidential suite. Greg, please escort these two ladies up to the suite," she instructs. Greg nods and takes off. Bridget and I follow without hesitation. This place it reminds me somewhat of the Order. The floors are sold royal-blue marble, with off-white crown molding, decretive oil paintings, and at least fifty-foot vaulted ceiling. Greg takes us to one of four elevators. He takes us to the top floor, leaving us in the hallway. This level only has one door. Bridget knocks and we wait silently for someone to answer. To both of our surprise, a man opens the door.

"Hello, you must be Bridget and Leyla. Please come in. My lady is expecting you," the man announces and moves over to let us pass by. He is dressed in a nice grey suit and has long black hair covering most of his face. His skin is pale. He is about my height, and his body is slender. "Please have a seat in here," he invites us timidly into a room with a few chairs and a small table. "Help yourself to some tea and cakes. I will inform my lady you've arrived. She will be joining you shortly," he informs us as he leaves the room. We both take a seat, and I help myself to a cup of tea. It's still warm.

"You came. I was afraid you might change your mind," I hear Mei's voice and look over to see her come in.

She is wearing a sophisticated green dress. The top is made out of thick lace, and it's fitted around her petite figure. The bottom is smooth, and it seems to be made out of real silk. It reaches down to her ankles, and I notice she has on matching green heels. The sleeves are long, and they ruffle at the end of her wrists. She has her long hair pulled up behind her head. She's breathtaking, as usual. Her makeup is natural, except for her lips that are the color of scarlet.

"I'm glad to see you, even though I know it's not a social visit. I almost believed after our last meeting, I wouldn't be seeing you again anytime soon," she admits, sounding upset about the thought. Mei sits down and pours herself a cup of tea. The scene is so familiar to me. I almost thought we were back in the loft for a moment.

"Mei, I'm grateful for your help," I remark.

"Don't mention it. I owe you. Whatever you need, I will help," she promises and then takes a sip of her tea. "Please tell me, what is it that you need from me?" she asks, her tone sweet as sugar.

"Before I do, I can't help but to ask. What are you doing here? I mean, don't you think that it would be easy for someone to find you here," I clarify. She looks up at me and smiles.

"No, not at all. I'm very comfortable here. As you know, I'm not staying here under my real name. Soto, the man you met earlier, is my assistant. If I need something I can't get here, he goes out for me. He also tends to the day-to-day and greets everyone for me. No one has seen me. They only know what he looks like. Not to mention this is the last place the Guardians would think to look. I'm sure they think I'm bunkered down hiding out in a cave somewhere, so they won't find me here. Don't worry about me. I know what I'm doing," she answers sounding sure of herself. I guess she has a point, she's pretty secluded up here, and I doubt they would think she is living in luxury at a time like this. I certainly didn't expect it. "Now, back to my question. Won't you tell me why you've come?"

"I've previously been having visions of someone who is going to die. I know it's someone close to me, but I can never see their face or make out any defining features. I hoped you could help. I'm worried. The past two nights I've seen nothing of my vision. I don't think it's going to come back. Without seeing it again, I don't know how I'll be able to figure it out in time. I'm here because I am willing to do anything I can to save whoever it is I've been seeing," I explain as she requests.

"So, do you know of a way she can get her vision's back?" Bridget asks more straightforward.

"I may not know everything about the Guardians, but I know magic. If your vision is gone, I doubt it will return. However, if you've had this vision as much as you say, I think I know a way for you to see it again," she answers, contradicting herself. "I can't promise you will see this person, but it's worth a try." She puts her cup down and lets out a little chuckle. Bridget and I look over at each other, both of us thinking the same thing. "I'm sorry, I don't mean to laugh, but it's just you already had the answer. You really didn't even need to come," she says with a grin. "The answer to your problem is sitting right here," she states looking over at Bridget.

"The answer is me?" Bridget guesses pointing a finger at herself, and Mei nods yes.

"Well, you're magic. I believe your gift will help Leyla see her vision as if it was right in front of her," she hints, and this time when she smiles, it's more out of satisfaction than amusement.

"Bridget, can you use your magic to recreate my vision?" I ask, finally realizing what Mei means.

Bridget thinks for a moment. "I guess, as long as you describe it to me, I don't see why not. I wouldn't be able to do it for long. It will take a lot of my energy, but it's possible," she answers, and she sounds pretty sure of her ability.

"You're welcome to use my place to reenact your vision," Mei interjects. "Please make yourself at home. No one will bother you here." She gets up from the table and takes her leave.

I'm a little stunned she didn't want to stay and watch. It's a generous offer to let us stay here. If I'm being honest, there isn't any other place we could go without the guys finding out.

"I think we should just meet here after school until your vision becomes complete," Bridget suggests, and I turn my attention back to her. "We'll come back tomorrow and start," she says and smiles at me. She picks up one of the cakes sitting on the table and shoves the whole small square into her mouth.

"Thank you, Bridget, you can say no," I state feeling a bit guilty. I've been asking a lot of her lately.

"No way, I'm helping you. Besides, you're not the only one who wants to find out who it is you're seeing," she implies referring to herself.

"Pardon me, but if you're both ready to leave, I will escort you out." Soto appears in the hall behind us, and he is waiting patiently for our reply. We both get up and follow him out the way we came. "Thank you for coming. We will await your next visit," he assures us politely, bowing his head at us ever so slightly. We turn to walk away, and I hear him shut the door behind us. Bridget walks over and hits the down arrow for the elevator. The doors open right away and we both step in.

"Am I wrong, or did I feel a little hostility between you two," I guess looking over at Bridget as the elevator starts to take us down.

"You caught that, huh? I'm not scared of Mei. Her family might be from a long line of Casters but so are mine. Not to mention she isn't in her territory. She doesn't have as many friends over here as I do. I know I told you we keep to ourselves, but if I needed it, others would come to my aid if she tries to start anything. I'm not happy about why she is here. If anything happens to you because of her doing, she will regret it. Not to mention she has caused unwanted attention to the Casters anywhere near St. Louis. The Guardians can sometimes group us all as one," she explains in a tone more serious than her norm.

"But Bridget, didn't you say that the older the Caster the more powerful they are? If she is Liling Lien's daughter, she's got to be hundreds of years old," I mention.

"You were listening to me. I don't recommend that," she jokes, but I can tell she is deflecting my question because I'm not wrong. As we reach the ground floor, my phone starts to go off in my purse. I recognize the ring tone and dig around for it.

"Kat, hey, what's up?" I ask answering her call. "Oh, okay, that's great," I reply to her news. "I'm with Bridget. Yes I know I miss you too," I tell her. "Ya, sure, I'll let her know. Okay, I'll see you tomorrow in class. Bye." I hang up.

"What was that about?" Bridget inquires.

"Kat told me that she and Kent have decided to move the wedding up to this summer. She says she will be out of town the next few weekends to go home and plan, but she wants to get together soon. She invited you too," I reply. Bridget nods and smiles towards me, thankful for the invite.

We've been meeting at Mei's every day after school. I feel bad for taking up so much of Bridget's time. After helping me, she has to go to work most nights. We've been at this for over a month now, and though my surroundings become more and more recognizable, the girl's face still eludes me. I'm at the point now where I feel like giving up. Darrius and Drake don't seem to mind all the time I've been spending with Bridget, mostly because they don't know what is going on. It breaks my heart not telling them the truth, but I know they would stop me. I know they just want to protect me, but I won't let someone I love die. Not if there is something I can do about it. Now that spring is finally here, we've had a nice reprieve from the colder weather.

Every time it rains though, I panic. April showers might bring May flowers, but it brings me only anxiety. I'm happy that during school my life is somewhat back to normal. Once I can put this behind me, I'm not sure what I'll do. I've been thinking about it recently, and I'm worried. Putting my vision aside, I'm curious how long Mei will stay around to wait for something that may or may not happen. I'm convinced she is wrong about Alexandra, and I honestly believe she won't take over my body. I think she wants me to make a choice for myself. My biggest concern, however, is Darrius and Drake. How long is the Order going to let them stay around me, a mortal? Won't they be called back in to perform their duties? I know they act as they would never let me go, but I'm not sure how much freedom of choice they really have on the matter. What if their Order leader demands they return? Won't they have to go?

"Leyla, hello? Earth to Leyla." I snap out of my thoughts and look over to Kat. She is staring at me from her seat next to me in our history class.

"What? Sorry, did you ask me something?" I reply.

"Yes, I was asking if you and Bridget want to hang out this Friday? I don't have to go home this weekend, so I figured it would be nice to get together," she asks again, though this is the first time I heard it.

"Oh, that sounds great. I'll ask Bridget and let you know," I respond.

"Perfect, well class is over now, so I'll see you tomorrow," she informs me as she gets up from her seat. She walks out of the class, and I start to pick up my things.

"You seem distracted today. Is everything alright?" Darrius asks walking over to me? He hands me one of my books that I hadn't noticed fell on the floor.

"I guess I'm a little out of it today. I probably just need some caffeine to help wake me up," I deflect, not wanting to go into the real reason. Although, now that I think about it, caffeine doesn't sound too bad. "I think I will walk over to Prairie Rose on lunch and get a cappuccino before my next set of classes," I tell him.

"We can go now if you want," he offers.

"No, that's okay. I can wait one more class. Thank you though," I state grateful at his offer. "Oh, Darrius, by the way. I was thinking, I know this semester is almost over, but I don't see a reason why you should have to keep sitting away from Kat and I. Would you like to sit with us tomorrow, if you want, I don't mind?"

"If you want me to sit with you, I won't object," he agrees.

"Also, that goes for all our classes. If you want?" I add a little shyly. I think I see him smile for a moment. I wasn't sure though, because he turned away from me so quickly after I asked.

"I want to," he replies softly, his head still turned away from me. His response made me happier on the inside than I know it should have. "Shall we go to your next class?"

Darrius offers to come with me one more time, but I tell him no. Seeing him having to wait in a long line just for me to buy coffee wasn't something I expect him to do. I've used up almost my entire lunch period waiting to get this cup, but it was worth it. As I walk back to the campus, I notice they are starting to block off one of the streets for road repair. I decide to turn down the next street over to avoid it. It will take me a little longer, but it will still get me there. I'll probably be a bit late to Spanish, but it will be alright. I'm sure I can get anything I missed from Drake. As I get to the end of the street, something I see makes me halt. I'm standing at a four-way stop about to turn left down the road towards the campus. However, instead of turning left, I turn right. I run over to the opposite side of the street and stand on the sidewalk. I pause in front of a large lonely tree just a few feet away from me on the grass. *This tree looks like…*

I suddenly drop my coffee, and though my eyes are open, I feel like they are shut. I see my nightmare! My vision is back, and in daylight. I can see it in front of me like I did that night at the ball. The images flash by so quickly. My brain fasts forwards to where I'm standing by the body. It's the same place I'm standing right now, only it's pouring down rain. I feel drenched even though,

I know I'm not. I look down to see a petite short figure laying unnaturally on the ground. *I see her! I see her!* Her broken body and her twisted limbs, I see her blood being washed away.

"No!" I shout. "No!" My vision clears, and my eyes feel open again.

I see the leaves from the tree swaying in the wind, and I feel tears start to fall down my cheeks. My body goes numb, and I hit the ground hard. I fall forward catching myself with both my hands leaning my head towards the ground. *Why?* Why does it have to be her? My hands form fists as I hit the ground in anger. I start to cry harder; this can't be right.

"Leyla!" I look up to see Drake running towards me from up the street. "What's wrong?" he asks frantically, no doubt seeing the tears rolling down my eyes. He reaches for me and holds out both hands. As I take them, he pulls me up. "What's wrong Leyla, what happened?" he asks again more panicked.

"This place," I'm crying so much it's hard to talk, "this place is where she dies," I manage to get out.

"This place," he pauses and looks around. "You've seen who it is?" he inquires realizing what I mean. I look up at him and nod yes. "Who is it," he implores me? I stare up at him and try to calm myself down. His voice is anxious, but his face appears calm. His hair moves around his forehead in the wind. It looks almost black in this shade than its normal brown. His eyes are holding my gaze. They are like a serpents enticing me not to look away or even blink. They're dark in the middle, but around that they are bright green like the leaves around us.

"How did you find me?" I ask deflecting his question. He raises one of his thick eyebrows at me, putting him off.

"You weren't in class. I found Darrius who told me you went to get coffee over an hour ago. I've been speeding through the streets around here looking for you. Seems I found you just in time," he replies. "I would like an answer, Leyla. Who did you see?" he asks, getting back to his question. He's reading me with those eyes trying to pry it out of me, but I'm not ready to say it out loud yet. "Tell me, won't you," he pleads his tone gentle, and I can no longer refuse his request.

"It's Kat," I reply. "Drake, my best friend is going to die." I feel my tears start to multiply again. He pulls me in tighter.

"I'm sorry, Leyla, I'm so sorry," he whispers. His words comfort me, but it doesn't take away the fact that I saw her broken and bloodied moments ago breathing her last breaths. "I know what you're thinking right now, and I don't blame you," he speaks up. I feel one of his hands leave my back and move up to my head. I lean my head into his chest as he starts to stroke my hair. I can hear his heart racing.

"I don't want her to die. How can I not do something?" I confess. He pulls me in again even tighter.

"Listen to me, Leyla. If you do save her and you happen to trigger the light, there will be no hiding you. You cannot change her fate, and as much as Darrius and I would like to, we can't either. Taking matters into our own hands would bring grave consequences. I won't be taken away from you, nor will I let you be taken away from me." He clenches me tighter, and I can barely breathe at this point. I look up at him. His eyes are looking down at me in agony. The thought of losing me is tearing him apart. I don't want to cause him this pain, but I won't let Kat die. "Please, I beg you, don't do anything, Leyla. Not only for me but for Darrius as well," he pleads.

He brings his hands up to my face, and he uses his fingers to wipe away my tears. I can see this is killing him to ask. He moves his face lower and closer to mine. Knowing what he is about to do, I should stop him, but I don't listen to myself. I close my eyes as he gently presses his lips on my forehead. I feel electricity course through my whole body for a brief moment once again. His lips linger for only moments before I feel him start to pull away. He pulls me in again more tenderly this time. He leans his head down on top of mine as he continues to console me. It was only for a moment, but that kiss made everything go away for just a little bit.

# Chapter 21
## Living Nightmare

I ask Drake to go back to my classes and take notes for me. I didn't want to miss them, but I don't feel like going back either. He seemed to understand, and he told me he would check on me later. I'm almost to my apartment now. There is no longer any reason for me to visit Mei. I send Bridget a message that I won't be meeting her tonight. She doesn't respond, but it shows she read it. I park and walk up to my door and let myself in. I crash down on my couch and sink in as low as I can. *What am I going to do?* I don't want to hurt Darrius or Drake, but how can they ask me to do nothing. Why can't they just have faith in me that everything will work out?

I laid down for too long and dozed off. I'm woken up by a loud knock on my door. It must be Drake coming to check on me. I wonder how long I was out. I raise from my couch and go over to answer the door. When I open it, I see the last person I expect to.

"Mei?" I'm confused to see her here.

"Hello Leyla, you and Bridget didn't come to see me tonight," she explains the reason for her visit somewhat. I'm not surprised she knows where I live. I can't say I'm thrilled to see her out and about. So much for her not leaving her suite. "I got worried, so I had to come," she adds as if she read my mind. I step outside instead of letting her in. I see the sun starting to set behind her so it must be six or so.

"I'm fine. I just didn't feel like coming over," I tell her. "Actually, I won't be needing to come over again any time soon," I add, my tone short.

"Oh, really," she says and looks annoyed. "Then can I assume you've seen who it is then? You know who is going to die?" She lets out a huff of air. "Who did you see?"

"My best friend," I reply. She pauses for a moment. She has a look on her face as if she disappointed in my answer.

"If it would have been Bridget, would you still want to save her?"

"Of course," I reply without hesitation. Mei smiles at me and her demeanor changes.

"If it would have been her lying there dying in agony, she would have been left to it. She would suffer until the very end. There would be no light guiding her beyond, no shot at a second chance. Forgotten, abandoned, and discarded. She isn't worthy, just because she is a Caster," she declares vehemently. Her face goes from hard to soft. "I know you would save her without a second thought. That's why I know Alexandra chose the right person. You have a kind heart just as she did, and you see things more fairly than most. I know you don't understand yet why you're so important, but I know you will soon," she pauses. "Which is why I can't let anything happen to you. If Darrius and Drake don't stop you, I will," she warns. "You cannot save Kat. You will expose yourself, and the Order will take you." My anger builds.

She has no right, no right to tell me what to do. I start to turn around to walk back into my apartment. However, I stop in place and I feel something around me constricting me. I can't move. I'm frozen. My limbs tense up as if there is an invisible rope tied tightly around them. Mei walks around me, and both her eyes are glowing white. She is holding one of her hands up, holding me in place. *She just cast a spell on me!*

"Don't make this difficult. You didn't let me finish," she hisses, and her eyes stop glowing. She releases me from her spell, but now she is standing in front of my door.

"I have nothing to say to you, and I no longer care to listen to anything you have to say," I reply defiantly.

"I very much doubt that," she smiles devilishly. "I can save Kat for you, but I will need something from you in return."

A light turns on in my head. She knew once I realized who was going to die, I would try and save them. She's been waiting for this moment this whole time. She wants to swoop in and do me this favor so I can promise to be her tool in return.

"You want me to agree to join you?"

"I would like you to help me," she clarifies.

"Why do you want my help. I'm not a real Guardian, and even if I was, what is it you think I can do?" I demand to know.

"There are only a few people that know you're not, and with practice, you can master the Guardian abilities. We can go to the Orders one by one and convince them that killing the magicalkinds isn't the answer. With a Guardian on our side, others will start to follow," she answers, and I'm appalled at her solution.

"You want to go to each Order and make them change their minds," I correct her. "If you start invading, it will just confirm what all the Guardians think about you and all the other magicalkinds. You will accomplish nothing," I tell her off. "If this is how your mother and Alexandra did it, no wonder they aren't here right now," I say cruelly, and I immediately regret it. I see her eyes flash white again for a moment. "I'm sorry, I didn't mean that. I just don't think forcing your ideas on people is going to make them change their minds. Shouldn't you want them to come to your side on their own?" I suggest.

"My mother. Alexandra. They tried to do it the peaceful way. Alexandra knew deep down that hunting down and killing us without real cause was wrong. She tried to reason with the Masters. Asking them to try and create some kind of peace. She started to ask for more proper and thorough investigations to prevent meaningless deaths. It seemed to work for a while. Most of the Masters were not opposed to meeting her halfway. However, Alexandra eventually pushed her luck, and those that didn't feel the same way started to plot against her. The Order lured her and my mother into a trap, and they killed Alexandra. My mother gave her life to cast the Spirit Link spell on her," she pauses and touches her bracelet. "Don't you understand, going about this peacefully and reasonably is what got them killed. I'm tired of watching my kind die in agony for no reason. All of them good, kind, and intelligent people. The Guardians will listen to what I have to say, one way or another," she demands in a rage.

"I'm sorry to disappoint you, but I won't hurt any Guardians, Casters, or any other magicalkinds for that matter. I cannot accept your offer," I insist. I feel for her, I do, even though she is currently my least favorite person in the world right now. However, I won't be a part of something like that. There is a moment of silence between us, and I'm wondering what she will do next.

"I told you, I won't let you get hurt. If you don't want to help me, that's your choice," she states, defeated. I feel her release her magical hold on me.

"Are you saying that you will help save Kat?" I question in disbelief.

"No, I'm afraid that's my only leverage. If you change your mind, you know where to find me," she states. I'm afraid she will be waiting for a while. I will never come to her. I will save Kat on my own.

"Mei, I don't know what you think you're doing here, but leave now!" I feel a soft touch on my shoulder. I turn just my head, and I realize the angry voice I hear belongs to Darrius. He is scowling at Mei. "Leyla, I came to check on you. Is everything alright?" he asks, still glaring at her.

"You must be Darrius. Don't worry, I was just leaving," Mei announces smiling towards him. She walks past us, and we both turn to face her. She glances from me to him. "I was just telling Leyla that I won't let her get hurt. She knows now who it is that's going to die, and I know she is planning on doing something stupid." Darrius looks down at me disapprovingly. I look back at Mei, and if my look could kill, she would be up in flames right now. It wasn't her place to tell him. "Goodbye, for now." Her eyes turn white and she vanishes into thin air. I guess there was no question about it now. Mei can faze.

"Leyla is it true what she said? Do you know who is going to die?" he asks and I'm surprised Drake hasn't already told him.

"Yes, it's true. I've been visiting Mei, and Bridget has been helping me see my vision through her magic. Today I was walking back to the campus after I left you. I happened to stumble onto the place I've seen in my vision. It came to me all of a sudden, and I did finally see who it is," I pause. "I'm sorry I didn't tell you and Drake I was going to Mei's with Bridget," I apologize, and I turn to face him.

"It's alright. I understand why you did so," he replies, and he doesn't seem mad. "Who is it?" he asks again his tone soft.

"It's Kat," I reply with sadness in my voice.

"I'm sorry, Leyla. I know this must be hard for you." He starts to put his hand back on my shoulder, but I brush him off.

"Stop, please I already know what you are going to say," I state holding up my hand. I know I'm being harsh, but I don't need a third person in a row today trying to talk to me about this. "I'm sorry, it's just I need to be alone right now," I inform him more calmly putting down my hand.

"I will leave you then if that is what you really want?" he asks me as if he hopes I will ask him to stay.

"It is," I whisper, and I walk back into my apartment.

I wasn't mad at him, but Mei put me in a bad mood, and I really do want to be alone. I hope he knows that. I hear my phone go off, and I see Kat has texted me. She wants to know if I talked to Bridget and if we will be hanging out this Friday. I completely forgot about it. I send a text to Bridget and see if she wants to join us. She replies right away. She says yes, but she won't be off until ten, so she'll have to come over later. I let Kat know and she sends me back a happy face emoji. I won't waste any time with her I can get. I'm glad we are going to be able to spend some time together. So many things have happened that I wish I could tell her.

The week fly's by, and both Darrius and Drake have been nice enough to give me some space. If we talk, they don't bring up my vision or Kat, and I'm thankful. I know it must be hard for them not to talk about it. I know they want to stop me from doing anything, but I'm afraid it's not their choice. Kat asks me to meet her at the Golden Cow after school for dinner. I'm stopping by my apartment first to grab my overnight bag I left this morning. I plan on spending the night at Kat's and possibly even Saturday night as well. I leave my Jeep running and hurry into my apartment to grab my bag from off my counter. As I walk back out, I see Darrius standing beside my Jeep waiting for me.

"Leyla," he calls my name out with suspicion.

"Darrius," I say back mimicking his tone.

"Where are you headed?" he asks.

"I'm spending the night with Kat. She, Bridget, and I will be hanging out this weekend. It's girls only, so I'm afraid you're not invited," I add jokingly. He looks at me unconvinced. "I know I lied about Mei, but I'm telling the truth. We are just hanging out," I assure him.

"Fine, but after Mei showing up here, we have decided to keep a better eye on you," he informs me.

"We?" I question.

"Yes, we." Drake walks over, and they both look at me sternly. "Darrius told me Mei came by, and we don't like her getting involved," he backs Darrius up.

"I appreciate your concern, but she expects me to come to her. I don't think she will show up here again," I voice my opinion.

"Perhaps, but as important as we think you are to her, we doubt it. She may not come herself, but we all know she's not passed using other people to do her bidding," Darrius points out, and I couldn't argue his point. I look at both of them, and it seems I won't be able to change their minds about this.

"Well, I'm not inviting you to come. I want to spend time with Kat, and that goes without an explanation. If you're going to insist on tagging along, you've better keep your distance. I don't want to see you, so faze if you have to. Are we clear?" I may not be able to stop them, but at least I can set some boundaries. Drake nods nudging Darrius.

"We will keep our distance," Darrius promises.

"Thank you," I reply and climb up into my Jeep. I watch them both disappear from view in my rearview mirror as I drive away. I may not see them anymore, but I know they aren't far behind me.

I reach the Golden Cow, and even though I went home first, I still manage to beat Kat here. The waiter seats me at a booth, and I decide to wait for Kat before eating. She walks in shortly after I'm seated, and I spot her right away. She has changed her clothes from earlier today. She is wearing dark skinny jeans and a white top. My best friend has her hair in a bun on top of her head, and she is wearing white flats to match her blouse.

"Have you been waiting long?" she asks as she comes over and sits down opposite me.

"No, not at all, though I'm surprised I beat you here," I confess.

"So, I have to admit I have another reason for asking you out tonight," she admits.

"Oh, really," I say interested.

"How would you like to come with me to pick out my wedding dress?" she offers, and I almost choke on my noodles.

"Wow, honestly? I'd love to. Are you sure your mom won't mind?"

"Probably, but we've done everything else together. I thought it was time I do something with my maid of honor. Besides, with her there, I probably would wind up picking out the one that she likes just to make her happy instead of getting the one I really want," she suggests, and I agree with her logic. She pulls out her phone. "I made a reservation for six-thirty. We should be able to make it if we leave in about ten minutes. Are you almost done?" I nod yes. I was planning on getting seconds, but I think I'll pass so we can go. When Kat says ten minutes, she really means we should have left thirty minutes ago. Her perception of time is horrible.

We quickly pay, and take her car, leaving mine to pick up on the way back. The shop we are going to is appropriately named Dreams Come True. I've never been into a bridal shop before, and when we walk in it's a little overwhelming. There are so many dresses they all start to blend in together. The lady at the front takes Kat and I into a private room with a dressing area. The back wall has a full-length mirror. She even offers us champagne while we wait for an associate to dress Kat. Another woman arrives, and after speaking with Kat briefly, she brings in several dresses. Kat tries them all on and she looks stunning in all of them.

"I don't know which one I like more. Any ideas?" Kat asks looking at herself in the mirror.

"I'm not sure. What don't you want? Maybe we should start there," I suggest.

"Well, let's see. It's going to be in June, so nothing long-sleeved or thickly layered. I don't want a long train either, since there will be dancing. I like lace, but I'm not opposed to something else if it looks good," she lists.

"One second, I'm going to go look and see if I can't find anything. Just keep trying some on while I'm gone," I tell Kat and get up and let myself out of the room. I comb through the racks, and finally, I spot one that I think she will love. I take it down and rush back into our room. "Here, try this on," I relay handing her my pick. She slips off the dress she is in now and slides into the new one. It's fitted and sleeveless. The top part has a detailed lace design, and it spills over to the bottom. There are only two layers. The top is sheer, and the bottom has a layer off-white silk. It's falls between her ankles and her knees, which will be good for dancing and moving around in. It looks gorgeous on her.

"It's perfect!" she exclaims. It makes me feel happy to know she is.

Kat leaves her dress there to be altered, and she drives me back to my car. I follow her back to her house, and I notice Kent's truck is gone when I pull in behind her. "What's Kent up to?" I ask her as we walk inside.

"He is staying with one of his teammates tonight. I'm not hanging around to get stuck watching a bunch of chick flicks, I believe are the words he used," she replies, and we both laugh. "Hey Leyla, I couldn't help but think back to when we were kids on the way home. Remember when we used to steal our mothers' wedding dresses and play pretend. We would ask my dad to stack up the hay in rows, and we would both walk down the aisle together to marry our imaginary princes," she reminds me.

"Ya, you're right, I had forgotten about that. Your mom was furious when she found her wedding dress with grass stains," I reply.

"So Leyla, how are things with you and Darrius going. I don't mean to pry, but you two seem like an odd couple. I mean, I never see you hold hands or talk sweet to each other. Also, I could be crazy, but I could have sworn I saw you with Drake the other day coming out of a class together," she observes, and I feel my stomach do a flip.

"Well, actually, Darrius and I aren't really dating. We're just friends. I mean we did have that weekend on Valentine's day, but nothing physical is going on," I cover remembering I used that as an excuse to miss school.

"Nothing physical? I'm pretty sure I saw you and him making out on New Year's," she disagrees, and I blush.

"We weren't making out, and that was different. Everyone was kissing someone," I deflect. "Anyway, back to your other question. You're not going crazy. I do have some classes with Drake. Not only that, but they both know each other," I pause, and she looks surprised at my revelation. "They're actually friends, and to top it all off, they live in the same apartments as I do," I go on.

"No way!" she exclaims excitedly. "That is so much more interesting than I could have come up with. So what's the problem? Are you not wanting to commit to Darrius because you have feelings for Drake?" she guesses.

"Umm, no it's not like that. I don't trust my feelings for either one of them. I mean, I think they are still stuck on someone they loved. You see she died, and I think they may only like me because I remind them of her," I answer honestly. "They aren't making it easy though. I've given in to my better judgement a few times. It's getting harder and harder for me to push my feelings aside. I just don't want to hurt either one of them or myself," I admit.

"Leyla Gray, you have to be honest with yourself and both of them. It's not okay to just string them along and not pick either one," she scolds me, and I wasn't expecting that. "If you really want to get closer to one, then the other will understand if they feel about you the way you think. Or if you don't want to hurt either of them, then you need to tell them both to back off and not give in to your temptation," she instructs. "If you truly have to pick, think of the one you can't live a moment without. Think about who takes your breath away whenever you see them. Most importantly, which one can you truly be yourself around. Pick the one who loves you for you," she finishes sincerely.

"Wow, Kat, where did that come from?" I ask impressed.

"From someone smart like you, your mother. She told me that one day while I was waiting for you to get ready for something. I don't remember that part now, but I will never forget what she said. Also, that's how I feel about Kent, which is how I know he's the one," she replies. Her face changes from serious to enlightened. I wonder what thought just went through her head. "Hey, maybe you could decide soon, and we could have a double wedding!" she proposes excitedly.

"Oh, Kat, you always know how to make me laugh," I say smiling.

"I really am glad though," she changes her tone back to a serious one, "that you found someone. I hope whomever you chose will make you happy," she states. I look at her and fight back my tears. If I start crying now, she will want to know why. I don't want to lose her. Between her and aunt Alice, they are the only people I have left from my childhood. Darrius and Drake just don't understand. How could they ask me not to save her? It's not fair. If I choose to save Kat, I could lose them, but if I decide not to, I lose Kat. Either way, I lose.

# Chapter 22

## Eternal Choices

Just as Kent had guessed, Kat and I watch chick flicks on Netflix waiting for Bridget to get off work. It's nice getting to spend this time with her. It felt like old times before I met Darrius or Drake.

"Hey, Leyla. I've got an idea," Kat announces from the kitchen. I look back over my shoulder to look at her. "Why don't we go meet Bridget at NightSky? It's only a few blocks down the street, and I'm kind of hungry again," she informs me. I look at the time on my phone and it's just now ten.

"Okay, I'll let her know not to leave," I reply. I send Bridget a text that we are coming to meet her. "She texted back. She said that works out because she really could use a drink after the night she just had," I read Bridget's reply aloud.

"Perfect," Kat smiles happily. I get up and walk over to grab my bag to leave. "Where are you going?" Kat looks at me perplexed.

"What do you mean, we're leaving aren't we?" I answer confused.

"You can leave yet, not dressed like that. Just because we are taken does not mean we can't still look our best in public," she enlightens me, and I just roll my eyes. "Come on, I'm sure I have something cuter for you to wear," she insists, and I follow her back to her room. She digs through her closet and pulls out a cream-colored dress with a black bow stitched in around the waist. I change into it, and it comes to about my knees. It's tightly fitted, and I feel like it's probably one size too small on me. "Here, wear these black flats, since we are walking," she calls out throwing her shoes at me. I put them on and let out a little sigh.

"Alright, are you satisfied? Now can we go?"

"Sure, right after I do your makeup," she winks, and I can't help but give her a smirk. Kat changes into a dark blue sequence dress. It shines every time she turns as the light catches it. She does my makeup as promised and then, satisfied with her work, we finally walk out together.

We arrive at the bar in no time, and I can hear the music blaring before we reach the door. We both flash our IDs to the bouncer, and he lets us in right away. It seems to be a little crowded, not as bad as New Year's, but it's busy. I spot Bridget at the bar. I grab Kat's hand walking over towards her. She already has two seats open for us next to her.

"Hey Leyla, how are you? It's been a while." As I sit down, Nick comes over to greet me. He looks happy to see me, or maybe he's just in a good mood.

"Hey Nick, I'm good. How are you?" I ask back. I'm surprised he remembers my name since we've only met a few times.

"Better now that you're here," he replies, and I'm not sure how to respond. I hear Bridget next to me clear her throat and Nick turns to her.

"What can I get you ladies to drink this evening?" he asks, taking the hint.

"Double whisky sour, for me," Bridget replies.

"I'll have a light beer," Kat answers. "Please," she adds.

"I think I would like a margarita on the rocks, with salt," I decide.

"Coming right up," he says and smiles. He walks off towards the other end of the bar, and I look over at Bridget and Kat who are both starting at me.

"What, why are you guys looking at me like that?" I ask curious.

"Oh, please he's totally got a crush on you," Bridget states boldly leaning over in my directions to give me a pat on the back.

"What! No, he doesn't," I reply embarrassed.

"He totally does," Kat chimes in. "Of course, that's the last thing she needs right now. She already can't make up her mind. Let's not throw a third guy in the mix." She starts to laugh. I didn't find it amusing in the slightest.

"I'm guessing you mean Darrius and Drake," Bridget suggests and Kat nods, still chuckling under her breath. "Those two are trouble, but if I had to choose, I think it would be Darrius. He is fun to argue with, and I like the tall brooding type," she admits. I'm so less than thrilled this conversation is happening right now.

"Not me. I would definitely go for Drake. I like them confident and strong, plus he's so hot," Kat disagrees dreamily. "I mean, I'm already taken, but I'm just saying," she adds covering for herself. Nick walks over with our drinks just in time. I grab mine and start to swallow until it's gone. Bridget and Kat start laughing at me and when I empty the glass, Nick looks dumbfounded.

"That was delicious. May I have one more please?" His face changes from shock to impressed. He smiles and takes my glass and heads back down the bar to make me another one. I feel suddenly sick, but it's not because of the drink. I just remembered Darrius and Drake are out there somewhere watching me. The thought of them hearing this conversation right now makes me want to throw up. Hopefully, they are fazed, and they didn't hear a word of it.

Thankfully, as the night went on, so did the conversation. It's almost time for the bar to close and Kat, Bridget, Nick, and I are the last ones left. We all close out our tabs making sure to leave Nick a big tip. He waited on us all night attentively, even though he was working the whole bar area to himself. I watch as he wipes down the bar in front of us. I feel a little bad. He probably could have closed early if we hadn't stayed till the last minute.

"I'm going to grab my stuff from the back, and then we can go. I'll just walk back with you guys and come get my car tomorrow," Bridget announces and hops down from her bar stool.

"Do you ladies need a ride home? I wouldn't mind dropping you all off," Nick offers and stops cleaning. He asks in general, but he is starting at me for a response.

"Thank you, but I only live a few blocks away." Kat answers for me.

"Alright, if you're sure," he looks over at me for confirmation.

"There is no changing her mind I'm afraid. We'll be fine. We are all walking together," I assure Nick. "Thanks for asking. That was nice of you," I tell him. Bridget comes back with her school bags and what looks like an extra set of clothes. We all say goodbye to Nick and walk out of the bar. The night air is crisp and it's slightly cool. The sky is clear, and I can see many stars as well as the crescent-size moon.

"That was fun," Kat declares. "I'm glad we came to see you," she adds looking over at Bridget.

"Me too. I had a long day. Now I'm ready for bed," Bridget yawns. I'm glad we came out as well, but I wasn't ready for the night to end. As we reach Kat's house, I turn to look back down the street. I wonder if Darrius and Drake can see me right now? I'm sure they're close. I've been thinking about Kat's advice to me all night. She was right earlier when she said I needed to let them how I feel. I plan to, as soon as I can figure it out myself. Until Kat is safe, my decision will have to wait. She's more important right now.

"Leyla, why are you just standing out there? Come inside," Kat yells to me from her doorway.

"Coming," I reply, and I smile before I turn around. Going out tonight was just what I needed When I walk in, I see Bridget is already passed out on Kat's couch. I was going to offer to share the bed in the spare room with her, oh well. She looks pretty comfortable as is.

"I'm going to bed. I'll see you in the morning," Kat waives goodnight and heads for her room. I do the same and change out of her dress and back into my shorts and t-shirt from earlier. I wash the makeup off my face and pull my hair back into a ponytail. I don't feel tired, but I know I probably am. I lay out on the bed and close my eyes.

I hear a buzzing noise, and before I open my eyes, I grab for my phone to turn it off. I hit the button, but the noise doesn't subside. I force myself to wake up and look at my phone, but no one is calling me. I hear movement from next door, and I realize it was Kat's phone that went off. I hear her mumbled voice on the other side of the wall. I hear the opening and shutting of her doors. I wonder what she's up to at six am. Kat darts past my room, and I hear the front door close shortly afterward.

Since I have my phone in my hand, I go ahead and text her to see what's going on. I get an immediate response. Apparently, Kent's friend was temporarily keeping his sister's cat, and Kent is very allergic. She said he is fine and that they got him to the hospital close by for a shot. She only left to bring him a fresh set of clothes with no cat hair on them. I'm glad it was nothing too serious.

I roll over and close my eyes. I'm tired, but something tells me I won't fall back to sleep right now. I get out of bed and walk past Bridget, still passed out on the couch, into the kitchen. I grab some juice out of the fridge and pour myself a glass. I look outside and it seems dark. I know it's still early, but there should be some light coming up from the horizon by now. I gulp down the cool liquid, as I swallow, I see a flash of light outside the window above the sink. *Was that lightning?* I'm hoping it's my imagination, but then I see another one moments after, followed by a loud boom of thunder. A storm? According to the recent forecast, it's not supposed to rain for at least another week. I watch the droplets of rain splatter on the pane one after the other.

"Kat!" I gasp. I run back into the room and lace up my shoes. I grab my phone and my keys and rush out the door. I start calling her repeatedly, but she won't pick up. "Come on Kat, pick up," I say aloud frustrated.

The lightning gets closer and the rain starts to pick up. I'm standing by my Jeep, debating whether or not I should start heading off after her. What do I do, what do I do? Could I be freaking out for nothing? I stop calling her and call Kent, but he doesn't answer either. I'm just going to go. I start to unlock my door, but my keys are suddenly stolen from my hand. I stumble back from my Jeep in shock, trying to figure out what just happened.

"Leyla," a familiar voice calls my name. I turn to see Darrius appear into view a few feet away. My keys are being held tightly in his hand.

"What are you doing? Give those back!" I demand. This was no time for him to play around.

"No, I can't do that. I know what you're about to do. I saw Kat leave a little bit ago. I won't let you leave," he replies. My heart starts to race, and I can feel my temperature rising.

"Darrius, this isn't funny. Give me back my keys. I have to leave!" I insist. We stare back and forth at each other, and he doesn't seem to be changing his mind. "Fine, I'll go on foot," I announce, and I start to run past him. He looks surprised at first, but I only make it about a foot past him before he grabs me. "Let me go Darrius." I struggle to get out of his grip with all my strength. "Let me go!" I shout.

"Don't do this, Leyla. You can't save her, you can't," he begs me, and I hear his voice shaking.

"Yes, I can. You have to let me try. You have to let go," I plead back. I hear thunder crack loudly in the sky. It's so close my ears ring. The rain starts to pour down so heavily I can barely keep my eyes open. I'm instantly soaked, and so is Darrius, whose grip just keeps tightening on me. "Darrius, you have to let me go. It's my choice, please," I say in desperation, but he keeps ignoring me. I'm so angry, and my anger turns to tears. I start to cry. "Please!" I scream. Suddenly I feel Darrius' hands release me, and I hear him fall to the ground. I turn quickly and I couldn't believe my eyes.

"Go, Leyla," Drake commands. He has Darrius on the ground holding him down. Darrius is scowling up at him, and I can tell Drake is trying with all his might to keep him there. "Hurry, I can't hold him like this forever," he shouts.

"Drake, if you let her go, I will never forgive you," Darrius spouts angrily at Drake. His voice is harsh and serious.

"Leyla, go!" Drake demands again, and I turn around and start to run.

This may all be for nothing, I could be wrong about this, but I have a feeling. I start to head for the intersection, where my vision came to light. I'm running faster than I ever have in my life. I hope Drake can hold Darrius down a little longer. I just need to get there, and I'll know for sure.

I reach the tree and stop. I lean over to catch my breath. It's still pouring, but the branches and leaves are giving me a little break. I linger looking down all the streets leading up the four-way stop. So far I don't see anything. I can't help but feel a moment of relief. I let out a sigh and fall to the ground. She's going to be fine. You're just overreacting. Lightning strikes feet away from me, and I jump back to my feet. It scared me to death, but it forces me to look up. I see a white car approaching too fast on my right. Thunder sounds again overhead. Kat, I see her car coming down the road. I realize what's about to happen. I don't have time to waste. The white car is coming too fast, I don't have time to think this through like I would like. I can't use any abilities. I can only save Kat as a mortal would.

With no time to waste, I rush out onto the road towards the white car. I feel the water wash over my ankles as I step onto the street. I can barely see anything in this rain, and it's falling so hard it stings my skin everywhere it hits. I try to get as close to the white car as possible, hoping the driver will see me and start to stop. I look over to see Kat is getting closer. I hear a horn and brakes squealing. The driver of the white car finally sees me. I turn to move out of the way, but it's too late for that now. The front of their bumper clips me. The impact throws me, and I fly forward. My head hits the sidewalk with a loud cracking sound. I feel immense pain throughout my entire body and then nothing. My limbs go numb and my vision starts to blur. The rain washes over my body, and I can see my blood being carried away by the small current. *Did I save her, did I save Kat?* My breathing slows, my eyes close, and I fade into darkness.

I slowly open my eyes and I'm standing all alone. I look around, but all I see is a sky full of large clouds. I look down and I'm standing on stone. I turn in a circle noticing I'm on a rooftop of an ancient looking building. I'm too scared to walk to the edge. In the sky around me the sun is hiding behind the massive multitude of clouds. I can't remember anything before now, and I feel like I'm in a dreamlike state. *Where am I?*

"Hello?" I call out, and my voice echoes around me. "Is anyone here?" I start to worry a little. Am I really alone? I look around again, but I don't remember how I got here.

I see the clouds start to part on the other side of the building. Something is coming through with great speed. It brings with it a blinding light. It lands on the ground in front of me shaking the entire building. I cower away from the being, and I have no choice but to bring my hands up to cover my eyes from the light. If I didn't know better, I would say I'm looking directly at the light from the sun. I feel the warmth from this new presence as well, not unlike the heat from sunlight.

"Do not be afraid, daughter of the father," a booming, strong male voice bellows around me. The voice commands me to do the one thing I cannot.

I'm now more terrified than I was previously. I try to remove my hands to get a better view of the person the voice belongs to, but it's no good. The light is blinding. The only thing I can make out is the aura emanating off. I suddenly hear beats of wind, and strong gusts start to hit me. Each one is stronger than the first. I fight to keep myself steadily on the ground. I open my eyes again to I see him jolt off the roof and fly up into the clouds, taking the warmth and light with it as it goes. *Wings?* I saw wings.

"The child with two souls, I have brought you here to offer you a choice," he speaks again, and it sounds like someone keeps turning up the volume with each word. I move my hands from my eyes to cover my ears.

"Are you, could you be an angel?" I whisper timidly, but I doubt he heard me. I search the sky to try and catch another glimpse, but he is flying too fast around me. His speed is incredible. I can't keep up. All I see is his light shining in and out of the clouds. I don't think he wants me to look upon him fully.

"I am Maveth, the Angel of Death," he finally answers, making me more frightened than before.

*The Angel of Death, am I dead?* I try and process. I'm not sure how to feel or what to do.

"I've brought you here to offer you a choice," he repeats from somewhere above me, keeping his distance.

"Where is here?" I ask looking around, still confused.

"You are *Nowhere*. This place is in-between Heaven and Earth," he answers. The place In-Between. I do remember Darrius mentioning this place. This is where the Light guides people's souls. "I can take you back to your body. I can bestow upon you the same gifts as the soul you share. You could become a Guardian," his offer sends shivers down my spine. *Me, a Guardian?* I would be able to go back. I would be able to see Darrius and Drake again. "Before you answer, my offer comes with a request in return," he warns. A request, what could I do for an angel? "There is disorder within my Guardians," his voice sounds angry, and I cringe. I hear the beat of his wings getting louder. I look up to see the clouds part again. He lands like a bullet just feet away. It knocks me to the ground again instantly. "There are those who abuse the power they have been given, and they have forgotten that they are to help their fellow man and not rise above them." His voice is so angry, and I stay on the ground, frozen in place by fear. I keep my head turned away from him. "I request that you help me expose those who have forgotten their place," he states. His words make me think of a certain Caster. Perhaps she wasn't so wrong about the Guardians after all.

"What is my other choice?" I ask nervously.

"I will take you home, Leyla Gray," his voice softens, and I need no further explanation. I don't even need to think about it. I know what my heart wants.

"I accept your offer. I will become a Guardian." Maveth takes off again, moving away from me once more. He now hovers above me.

"Do not be so quick to answer, daughter of the father. The task I ask of you won't be an easy one. Consider that your life will be in danger. I cannot promise you protection, and you will no doubt be met with resistance. I can only ask to bring your spirit back once," he cautions me. His tone is serious.

I understand what he is asking me to do. I could be going back only to fail and end up right back here. However, I have to try. I turn away from Maveth and look up at the clouds towards the Heavens above. I'm sorry mom. I'm not ready to die yet. I hope, no, I promise to make you proud of me.

"I still accept. Where do I start?" I reply and turn back to see Maveth move up higher away from me. His golden light is still bright, and I still can't look directly at him for very long, even with him so far above me.

"Start with the death of the soul you share. Those responsible are the Guardians I speak of." I can't help but to gasp. The Order is responsible for Alexandra's death. "Expose those who have become unworthy. As you share another Guardian's soul, once I bestow upon you the gifts, you will become different. You will be faster, stronger, and more powerful than those around you. I can only offer you this as protection, since I am unable to intervene myself. You will have no other Master but me. Bring the judgment I cannot and fulfill my request. If you do, you will have my favor."

He takes off higher and higher, the beats of his wings making the clouds disappear around him. His light is getting brighter by the second, taking up the whole of Nowhere. I feel the warmth from it as if he is right beside me.

"Father, bless your daughter with the blessings of a Guardian," Maveth's voice becomes deafening. I hear a boom like thunder, and I am suddenly paralyzed. My back stiffens, and my limbs straighten. I am being lifted off the ground slowly in a beam of soft light. *What's happening?* "May you never lie. May you never die. May you bring justice and vengeance. You will be balance. You will be death." As he speaks, I start to feel warm all over, and my body is on fire. I feel weightless and refreshed. I feel better than I ever have in my life. A burst of adrenaline rushes through me, coursing through my every nerve and blood vessels. My body is changing, and it's amazing. The light encompassing me fades, and I begin to fall. Maveth catches me. His light it's no longer blinding, but it's still bright. We begin to descend. I watch the ancient building and the sky above fade further from view. I feel like we are moving faster than a jet.

I make contact with my body. I pull myself off the ground, and I watch as everything around me happens in slow motion. I've gone back in time like I never left to begin with. The white car is still halting to a stop. Kat has swerved, and both vehicles have narrowly missed each other. I did it. I saved her. As things start to move more normally, I take off before either driver sees me. I take off for Kat's house, where I had left Darrius and Drake. When I get there, they are gone. *Did they see?* Did Darrius get free in time to watch me die? I wasn't sure, but I race off to their apartment. My feet carry me with such quickness, I feel as if I could take off any moment and start flying. Everything around me should be a blur, but I can see with complete clarity. I get to Goldfinch within seconds and stop in front of Drake's door and knock. No one answers, so I let myself in.

"Darrius, Drake, are you here?" I call out for them. Drake's bedroom door slowly opens, and he walks out and stares at me.

"Leyla?" he whispers in awe. Before I can respond, he rushes me and begins to brush the hair back from my face. He wraps both his arms around me and begins to twirl me around letting out a relieved laugh. He sets me back down and smiles at me, a warm, boyish smile. "I'm so glad I haven't lost you," he confesses in happiness. His eyes look red like he has been crying.

"You haven't lost me. I couldn't let either of you go," I tell him. I look around the room. Someone is missing. "Where is Darrius?" His face changes as if he realizes the same.

"He finally fought me off, and we both headed off after you. We reached you in time to see you," he pauses looking away from me, "laying on the pavement," he finishes. "I thought he came back here, but he's gone," he explains somberly. I see him close his eyes to concentrate on something. I stand silent. "I see him," he states, eyes still closed. Of course, we are all connected. How could I have forgotten? "He's made it pretty far. I think he is headed for the Order," he sounds panicked and opens his eyes.

"Drake, why would he be going there?" I ask confused. That would be the last place I expect him to go. He looks over at me with worry.

"Leyla, you need to go to him," he commands, and his tone scares me. "You need to go to him now," he repeats urgently.

I nod and leave as quickly as I came. I close my eyes and try to concentrate. It's a little blurry, but I can see him. Trying to manage all these new gifts isn't easy. The look Drake gave me before I left tells me that Darrius is about to do something stupid or dangerous. Thank god I'm faster, if I wasn't, I don't think I could catch up with him in time.

The gap between us begins to close, and I think I'm finally catching up. I've been running for at least an hour now, at least I think I have. I'm not tired or sore at all. I can see the skyline of St. Louis miles away. I close my eyes briefly, and I can see Darrius is not too far ahead. I recognize the surroundings based on the couple of trips we've taken. He's further than I would have liked, but he hasn't gotten there yet. I'm going to catch him just in time. I've been calling out to him through my mind, but it's like he is blocking everything out. I think that's why my vision of him is blurred. Darrius thinks I'm dead, and it's all my fault. *Come on, run faster Leyla!* I feel my momentum quicken. I'm almost there. I'm so close.

"Darrius!" I call out, finally catching up. "Darrius," I call out again. Why isn't he stopping? He must be able to hear me? "Darrius!" I shout out louder. Still, he ignores me.

I try and get closer, and I realize I'm going too fast. I won't be able to stop myself in time. *Oh, no!* I try and slow down as much as I can, but I crash into the back of Darrius. We are both thrown forward, and then we start to roll as we hit the ground. It doesn't hurt, thankfully, but it definitely wasn't the way I had intended to stop him. When we are no longer moving I wind up on top of him. He turns his face away from mine. I scramble to get off of him, and he looks over at me, and his eyes are empty. I see nothing as he looks right past me as if I'm not even here.

"Darrius, it's me," I whisper. His skin is snow-white, and he looks ill.

"Why do you haunt me? Is this some cruel joke, is the heavens laughing at me?" he snaps cruelly.

"Darrius, it's me. I'm okay. I'm here, I'm here," I try to convince him. He studies me and his face relaxes, but his eyes are still empty. They are dark like the bottomless depths of the ocean.

"Just leave me alone. Get away from me, whatever you are! I saw Leyla, she is dead, she is dead," he announces and puts his hands over his face and starts to shake his head vigorously. I walk over to him and throw myself onto him. I feel him shake as I hold him. I look up as he moves his hands away from his face. I see tear after tear start to slowly roll down his cheeks.

"Oh, Darrius," I sigh softly. I wrap my arms tightly around his chest, and I pull myself as closely as I can into him. "I'm not going anywhere," I promise. "I'm sorry, I'm sorry I did this to you," I apologize. I start to wipe away his tears. My statue of stone is crumbling to pieces in my arms, and I've come just in time to keep him from falling completely apart. He stops my hand and takes it into his, and he squeezes it.

"Leyla," he asks like I may be real after all. "Are you truly here?" I take his hand and put it onto my chest. His hand feels cold against my skin, but I let him feel my heartbeat. His eyes widen in shock. He takes both his arms and grabs me bringing me back into him. "I don't understand how you are here, and right now, I'm not going to ask," he stammers and pulls me in tighter. "Leyla, I will never part with you again," he vows, and my heart starts to race. I can feel my skin begin to warm. His words are unexpected, and his tone is serious yet gentle. I don't know how to respond, so I just let him hold me. I wonder if he realizes that it's him, Drake, Kat, Kent, and Bridget I came back for. I wasn't ready to leave any of them.

Our reunion is brief, and we run back to Drake's apartment. Drake is pacing the floor when we both arrive. He looks at both of us with relief as we walk in. "I knew you would catch him," he affirms. I hang my head down and look at the ground. I start to shift my body back and forth in place. I didn't know if they were ready to hear what I had to say, but it couldn't wait.

"I did die, I died, and I was brought back. I'm a Guardian now," I finish and bravely look up at both their faces. They don't look upset.

"I think we've figured that out," Drake smiles. "However, what I haven't figured out is how you have come back without an assigned Order," he replies. I shoot him a confused look. "When Guardians have been chosen, they wake up in an Order. Someone explains to them what they are and how they got there. We remember our deaths and our lives thus far, but we can't remember the angel," he explains.

"But I do remember what happened to me. Maveth saved me, and in return I promised him something," I reveal.

"Leyla, are you saying you know what the Angel looks like? You remember talking to him?" Darrius speaks up in complete awe.

"Yes, well, I never really got a good look at him, but I remember everything," I answer.

"What did you promise?" Drake inquires, and he looks just as shocked as he sounds.

"There are those in the Order than have become above their fellow man, that's what he said. He wants me to seek them out and deliver the justice he cannot," I reply.

"And just how are you supposed to do that?" Darrius snaps with skepticism in his voice.

"He told me to start with the death of the soul I share." I grab both of their attention immediately, and they both look at me like I expected. I watch the horror in their eyes as they comprehend what I'm telling them. This is the moment I've been dreading. "I can't just go to the Order to become a regular Guardian. I must work behind the scenes and uncover what happened to Alexandra. Only then will I know what to do next. I don't know how long it's going to take or where to start. All I know is that I'm going to need both of you. I don't want to ask, but I don't know anyone who would want justice for

Alexandra more than you two. Will you help me?" I request, and my throat is tight. I hold in my air in anticipation of their answers.

"If this is what the angel has asked of you, and if it means getting justice for Alexandra, then I will help you until my last breath," Drake answers and we both turn to face Darrius.

"I won't lose you again, and if this is what I have to do to keep you safe, then I'll be there every step of the way," Darrius agrees. My heart flutters and I let out my air. I know I don't deserve their help, and I don't deserve them. I'm more relieved than they will ever know. "You still need training. You need to become a full Guardian before you make any moves. It will be harder to gain trust if you don't go through all the same trials that everyone else has," he advises.

"He's right. You need to pick an Order and make it appear as if that's where you wound up after being saved. We need to be smart about this," Drake agrees. "Alexandra didn't die here. She died in Europe. That's where our original Order is, where we all met. However, a lot of the seconds came over to the states and became Masters. There have to be several of them who remember Alexandra and us. They may even know what happened," Drake reveals.

"The Master told me that he had done some digging and made a comment that I was a stunning replica of Alexandra. I think he knows plenty about all of you. I think we should start there," I declare. They both look at me unconvinced.

"Are you sure that's where you want to start?" Drake questions my decision.

I nod yes. "Also, I know you don't want to hear this, but there is someone who we can ally with for help, someone who knew what happened to Alexandra before we did," I hint. I hate that these words are about to come out of my mouth, "I think we need to go have a chat with Mei," I suggest. Darrius crosses his arms.

"Anything we want from her, she will just want something back that I'm not willing to give. I won't let you help her Leyla. She might have been right about Alexandra, but she is bad news," Drake objects.

"Agreed. I don't trust Mei either. With every truth she gives us, there is always a part that she keeps hidden from us. We all know she wants you, Leyla, and I'm not willing to give you to her either," Darrius states. Boy, are they both stubborn sometimes. I guess they do have a point. Going to Mei would be like walking into the lion's den, but I don't see any other way.

"Have some faith. We need to talk to her. I won't promise her anything I can't keep. Alexandra worked with Liling Lien. Maybe I can find a way to work with Mei. I know it's not the ideal choice. However, we need to talk to her. I've made up my mind," I add sternly. They both nod their heads, though neither of them is thrilled about it by the looks on their faces. "Oh, one more thing. I know you want me to head for an Order right away, but I can't, not yet. I want to go to Kat's wedding. I know it's a detour from my plan, but I have to do this. If I'm going to have any peace about leaving her and Kent behind, I need to go. They will have each other, and I can be happy about that. They can start their life together, and I can have one last memory of them before I have to leave them behind forever. I know it's unfair of me to ask this. I know no other Guardian had this chance. However, I also know in my heart that if they did have any chance to get closure, they would have," I plea.

"You're being selfish, but if all of us Guardians had one more chance to say goodbye, I think we would all take it," Drake doesn't argue.

"As soon as the wedding is over, we leave. You will have to leave this part of your life behind," Darrius adds, and I hear a sad undertone in his voice.

"I know. Thank you both for understanding," I reply. All I want is a chance to say goodbye.

As I walk over to my apartment I feel heavy with sorrow. This place is no longer my home. I walk over to my window and push open the pane. There is a nice cool breeze that blows in, and it carries the smell of fresh laundry from next door. I see the fields in the distance with tiny green sprouts popping up from the dirt. Just two more months, and I'll be leaving this place behind, possibly never to return. *Can I do this?* Can I be the Guardian, the angel Darrius and Drake need me to be? I watch the sun slowly sink into the horizon. I will burn this picture in my memory and hold on to it tightly. Every time I see it again in my mind, I will think of Kat, Kent, Bridget, and my aunt Alice. I have to leave them behind and say goodbye, but I don't have to forget them. They will always be with me in my heart as I dive in headfirst to whatever my fate holds for me. There is no turning back.

CPSIA information can be obtained
at www.ICGtesting.com
Printed in the USA
BVHW051542310522
638503BV00007B/144